A MOTHER'S LOVE

A MOTHER'S LOVE

A NOVEL

SARA BLAEDEL

Translated by Tara Chace

DUTTON

DUTTON

An imprint of Penguin Random House LLC
1745 Broadway, New York, NY 10019
penguinrandomhouse.com

LIBRARY OF CONGRESS CATALOGING-IN-PUBLICATION DATA

Names: Blædel, Sara, author. | Chace, Tara, translator.
Title: A mother's love: a novel / Sara Blaedel ; translated by Tara Chace.
Other titles: Tavse enke. English
Description: [New York] : Dutton, 2025.
Identifiers: LCCN 2024036574 (print) | LCCN 2024036575 (ebook) |
ISBN 9780593850541 (trade paperback) | ISBN 9780593850558 (ebook)
Subjects: LCGFT: Detective and mystery fiction. | Novels.
Classification: LCC PT8177.12.L33 T3813 2025 (print) |
LCC PT8177.12.L33 (ebook) | DDC 839.813/8—dc23/eng/20240923
LC record available at https://lccn.loc.gov/2024036574
LC ebook record available at https://lccn.loc.gov/2024036575

Printed in the United States of America

1st Printing

The authorized representative in the EU for product safety and compliance is
Penguin Random House Ireland, Morrison Chambers, 32 Nassau Street,
Dublin D02 YH68, Ireland. https://eu-contact.penguin.ie

For Lars and Andreas

♥

A MOTHER'S LOVE

PROLOGUE

I stepped back in shock, silently trying to comprehend what had just happened. Paralyzed, I saw the blood flowing in slow motion across the floor and down into the cracks between the worn floorboards. The silence hummed in my ears as I watched the motes of dust shimmering sluggishly in the light from the windows.

My morning had started early, the sun low in the sky as I sat over my coffee and thought through the day's obligations. There were good days and there were bad days. This one, I had sensed, would be good.

But here we were.

Adrenaline pumped through me. After the first few blows, I already knew that she was no longer conscious. The muscles in my arms trembled—even so, I struck again.

A sound from behind brought me back. I quickly collected the heavy cutting board from the floor, surprised that so much blood was pouring out of the copper-colored hair. The gash on the back of the head didn't look like much.

I heard a car drive by outside, normal, everyday sounds slowly returning, and I realized that I had to get away, fast. I didn't worry about covering my tracks. In a way I didn't care. Tucking the cutting board under my arm, I simply walked out of the restaurant.

Well, I thought, *I'm done with that.*

Now I could finally find some peace.

CHAPTER 1

"I don't recognize a single one of the names on this list," Louise Rick fumed, tossing the piece of paper across the desk at Søren Velin. "We've been discussing this new travel unit for a month and a half. We've been planning for ages. We've agreed. But what the hell was the point of all those preparations if you're just going to scrape together a few of the dregs from different police districts and call them my new team?"

She was so angry that she wanted to storm out, but she pulled herself together and forced herself to explain. Slowly.

"None of us know each other. We haven't worked together before. We have no basis for being able to leverage each other's strengths. These are all the things we agreed couldn't happen."

Her very first partner from the Homicide Department shrugged. Søren Velin had been a bigwig in the Danish National Police for years now, and one of the many projects he'd been put in charge of was establishing a new travel unit to replace the old Mobile Task Force. After a failed investigation into the murder of a young teenager in

Korsør—a case that had landed squarely on Velin's shoulders—he received permission to set up a special travel unit, an investigative group that could be ready to help the country's twelve police districts solve violent crime cases on an as-needed basis. That travel unit had come to be known as Police District 13, or simply P13, and Louise had been selected to lead it.

"You know as well as I do that the government has cut the National Police force in half," Velin said. "Things have changed."

"Up yours!" Louise snapped. "I gave up my position as head of Homicide to lead P13, and now that we're at the starting line, you do an about-face and take back everything you promised?"

"Okay, stop," he said, holding his hands out to her pleadingly.

"Find someone else," Louise replied, heading for the door.

"They're waiting for you in Odense."

"Let me tell you something!" She spun on her heel and was right up in his face in a couple of quick steps. "I didn't take this position to fail, or to have an excuse to not be home with my son and the other people I care about. I took this job because I believe I can help make a difference and contribute to increasing the clearance rate. That I can help police districts when they get bogged down in their investigations. But it's not something I can do on my own. That's been the agreement the whole time, that we would put together a small team of the *very best*. The Mobile Task Force was ten times as big as what you've promised me, with a budget to match. Yes, I agreed to use local crime scene technicians and forensic pathologists and I get that it's still too early to attach a permanent police prosecutor to our unit, but I want the top candidates—the very best investigators—not the sloppy seconds that police districts around the country can't wait to get rid of."

"You're meeting Grube in Odense," Velin said calmly. "I'm sure he'll fill you in on folks' strengths and weaknesses."

Louise shook her head as she stared at him.

"We have been talking about this for a month and a half," she repeated quietly. "We've carefully planned how we can make this work so that P13 can become permanent, so that we create a National Investigation Department we can be proud of. And then you drop the ball when we're *this* close to the goal."

This time, Louise left his office before Velin could protest.

Logically she knew it wasn't wholly Velin's fault: No one had predicted that the National Police would be hit by a political austerity knife right as they were laying the foundations for the new travel force. When it came to the funding allocations, that was entirely dependent on which way the wind was blowing.

But the fact remained that the travel force hadn't been nixed entirely. And Louise was still in charge, so she went straight from Velin's office down to the police garage to pick up the unmarked police car that had been allocated to her new investigative unit.

Louise was sitting in Velin's office later that morning when the call came in. The victim was a thirty-eight-year-old innkeeper from Tåsinge who had been found murdered on the floor of the inn's restaurant twenty-four hours earlier. A local resident had called emergency services at 10:48 a.m.

Louise didn't know much more than that. No witnesses had come forward, and the Funen Police in Odense and Svendborg were working on the assumption that it could be a robbery-murder, though there wasn't yet a report on what, if anything, had been taken from the restaurant.

"Are you home?" Louise asked when Jonas answered his cell phone.

"Not yet," her foster son replied. "But I've arranged with Eik to stay with him while you're gone."

Louise had texted Jonas as soon as she found out that she was going to Tåsinge.

"No," she said simply. "You can't. You're staying in the apartment and taking care of Dina."

She knew how harsh she sounded. Their deaf Labrador was perfectly content to have Melvin look after her, but their downstairs neighbor had his hands full now that his girlfriend, Grete Milling, was in bed with a bad case of pneumonia. The elderly couple had both been seriously impacted by Grete's illness. Her infection numbers were far too high, and she had even been hospitalized for a few days, then sent home again even though it was clear to everyone that she was still extremely sick. Caring for her was taking a toll on Louise's seventy-nine-year-old downstairs neighbor, even though he tried not to let it show.

"Fine, I'll just bring Dina out to Eik's place with me. I've done it before," Jonas protested. "She and Charlie get along great."

Yes, Louise could just imagine. No doubt about it, it would be cozy with Eik's big German shepherd, a retired police dog of a substantial size; Dina and Jonas; Eik's daughter, Steph; and Eik himself in his little studio apartment in Copenhagen's South Harbor neighborhood. A tight reluctance coalesced in Louise's chest. She still hadn't seen Eik since he'd gotten home from his trip.

The six-month-long leave of absence they had set out on together.

The dream trip with their two teenage children that was supposed to bring the small blended family together but had instead broken Louise's heart. She could still feel the sorrow and rage that had struck when Eik told her that he wasn't ready to get married after all, even though he was the one who had proposed to her.

"You're staying home," Louise decided. "Melvin needs your help. He doesn't have the strength to take care of Grete while she's bedridden."

Silence on the line.

"Enjoy the hygge," Louise continued, trying to win him over. "You can do puzzles and read history books. You always have a good time together."

"Mom," he interrupted, "I'm seventeen!"

"Well then you can make some of that music you're so into," she suggested instead. It still melted her heart when he called her Mom. Jonas had been living with her since he was twelve, and they had become a unit. A family. Melvin was also a part of that unit, and she knew that Jonas thought of him as a grandfather, which made her feel slightly less guilty about pressuring Jonas to stay home on the grounds of helping Melvin and Grete.

"I stopped making music a long time ago," he replied quietly.

There was a tense pause, but Louise didn't back down. She couldn't bear that he'd rather go to Eik's place.

"You'll find something to do," she said. "Just spend time with Melvin. He missed you a lot when you were traveling."

"Okay," he finally said. "Maybe I can order food and we can watch a movie or something."

"Exactly," Louise replied, feeling like she had prevailed in some sort of one-sided battle against Eik. "I'm just on my way home to pack some clothes, but I won't have time to take Dina for a walk.

They're expecting me in Odense and I'll be stuck in the afternoon traffic, so I have to rush."

"I'll walk her," Jonas said without hesitation. That was one fight they had never needed to have. Back when the yellow Lab came into their lives, Jonas promised that he would take care of her. He always lived up to that promise.

Louise arrived at the police station in Odense to find that she was the only member of Søren Velin's travel unit who had bothered to show up. Her annoyance made her pull her chair to the desk of Deputy Chief Superintendent Grube with unnecessary roughness.

"You'll get a communications officer from my department," Grube said as Louise took her seat across from him in his utterly nondescript office on Hans Mules Gade. This was the first time Louise had met the man, and her first impression was that he didn't seem particularly impressive. He made it sound like the Funen Police were about to hand P13 a priceless gift in the form of one thirty-one-year-old investigator.

Her first team member was to be a young Swedish woman who would be responsible for all digital information, telecommunications, and surveillance—provided there was even a single camera in Tåsinge. Grube wasn't quite able to confirm or deny that for her.

"How much experience does she have?" Louise asked, looking at his graying temples and tired eyes and attempting to sound neutral.

"Lisa Lindén is one of the best. She comes from the Central Jutland Police. I managed to snag her a year and a half ago. It's not exactly a secret that we're having some gang and drug problems here in the city."

No, no secret about that, Louise thought. This was one of the things Odense was notorious for in police circles.

"Does she speak Danish or only Swedish?" Louise asked, already fearing what might get lost if Lindén was responsible for bugs or wiretaps.

Grube leveled a stare at her before nodding.

"Of course she speaks Danish. She's from Holstebro. She grew up in Herning but was living in Holstebro when I convinced her to move to Odense. She lives in Ringe now with her boyfriend, who's also thoroughly Danish, in case that's important to you."

Touché, Louise thought. They had really gotten off on the wrong foot and it was mostly her fault. She needed to pull herself together, but her disappointment that the team she had been promised amounted to a poorly-cobbled-together group of people she'd need to hand-hold to success was overshadowing her excitement over the travel unit being called out to assist on its first case. She knew herself well enough to recognize that her disappointment was primarily due to one thing: She was scared shitless of failing, of not being enough, and of not solving her first case. Performance anxiety.

She was deeply engrossed in this negative conversation with herself when she finally realized that Grube was speaking to her.

"Lange," he repeated patiently. "He's coming down from Hjørring. He called just before you arrived and asked if you were meeting here or if he should catch up with you in Tåsinge."

"And what's Lange's profile?" Louise asked, leaning forward in the chair, determined to put her bad attitude behind her.

Grube interlaced his fingers and stared down at the papers lying in front of him for a moment. Louise didn't get the sense that he needed to read from them, but rather that he wanted to make sure he correctly phrased whatever he said next.

"He's good with details. He sees everything and he understands what the forensic techs find. Plus, he remembers what people tell him."

Louise nodded. That was worth its weight in gold, she had to give him that much.

"So, you and Velin think that he'll take care of questioning and interrogations and the crime scene," she concluded. "Who will handle the family?"

The one time she'd been loaned to the old Mobile Task Force she'd gotten to see the many moving parts of a team like this. There had been a communications officer, a clerk who kept track of every report and had a clear overview of the case as a whole, an investigator responsible for questioning and interrogation, another who solely questioned family members, a team of technicians, and someone focused specifically on the crime scene.

"You will," Grube replied in a way that made it sound as if that was obvious. "And you'll bring in the forensic techs from Fredericia."

They sat in silence for a moment while Louise waited for him to continue, but he didn't say anything else.

"And of course we'll handle anyone who calls in," he said, once again making it sound like he'd given her a gift.

Louise nodded. It was essential to have someone to answer the calls that came in about a case, one person who had a comprehensive view of the investigation and was able to assess which tips should be taken seriously and acted on.

"Does this mean there won't be a clerk appointed to the unit? You'll handle all the reports from here?" she asked, eyeing him.

He nodded. "That'll be easiest for everyone."

"And that person will then report to me on a daily basis? Or how do you envision this being coordinated so that we don't lose information?"

"It will be reported directly to me," Grube replied, "and then I will sort through the information and pass anything relevant on to you."

She opened her mouth to protest, then restrained herself.

"Who else is on the team?" she asked instead. "Are the rest of the investigators from here or are they being brought in from other police districts?"

Louise knew that the Funen Police were hopelessly behind when it came to staffing and were often forced to hand off work to other police districts. She also knew that Grube was notorious for saying one thing and doing another, and that he didn't step in proactively to support his officers. So, she had decided that she would have as little to do with Grube as possible as soon as she'd found out she'd be assisting the Funen Police.

"There won't be anyone else from here, but you'll get two of the investigators from Svendborg who were at the discovery site yesterday. They've already interviewed the guests who spent the night before the killing at the inn."

Louise started doing the math. So other than herself, the new travel unit consisted of a young woman with a Swedish-sounding name, someone named Lange from Hjørring, technical assistance from Fredericia, plus two locals from Svendborg.

"You'll have an office here in the building, and it'll probably be easiest for everyone if I handle contact with the media."

Louise leaned over the desk.

"That's not going to happen," she said firmly. "My people and I will get an office at the Svendborg station. We're not going to waste our time driving back and forth when there's a police station down there. If you have a problem with that, then you shouldn't have asked for our assistance."

She stared straight into his eyes until, finally, he nodded.

Louise leaned back again.

"Can you get ahold of Lindén so we can get started with a briefing?" she asked. "I assume you'll update us before we drive to Tåsinge."

"Lindén won't be joining us until tomorrow," he said apologetically. "Her kid is out sick for the first time, but she said she'd be fine to come in tomorrow."

Louise stared at him, speechless.

"Then I assume you'll find someone else? Someone who can start today. We're already twenty-four hours behind." She didn't even bother rattling off the line about how the first twenty-four hours of a murder investigation were the most important, because surely he darned well knew that already, she thought irritably.

"I don't have anyone else," he said, looking over at the door as if someone was coming. No one was.

So, Lisa Lindén hadn't been his first choice. She was just the one he could do without, because you couldn't really rely on the mother of a young child.

"And the briefing?" Louise repeated. "Who's going to tell me what we have so far? Or would you prefer that we hold off on starting the investigation until your people are ready to work?"

"It's best that you talk to the officers in Svendborg," he said. "All I know is that it concerns the woman who has been running the

inn since her husband's death last year. She lived alone in an apartment above the inn. She died from bleeding following one or more
powerful blows to the head, probably with a heavy object with a
sharp edge. She had a four-inch-long curved gash on the back of
the head, which went into the cranial bone. In the postmortem, it
appeared that about fifteen minutes elapsed before the victim bled
out. The deceased was taking blood thinners for a blood clot in her
leg that occurred following a flight home from Thailand two years
ago. The technicians are still working at the inn but haven't briefed
me yet on their findings."

Louise caught herself shaking her head. What the heck was
the point of knowing how long it took the woman to die when he
couldn't tell her *when* she died?

"Names?" she inquired.

"Dorthe Hyllested—"

"Of your investigators," she interrupted him, "the ones I need
to talk to. Where will I find them, at the police station or in Tåsinge? Where am I staying? Has anyone here arranged accommodations? I don't think Lange's going to be driving back to Hjørring
for the night, either."

"You'll be staying at the hotel in Troense," he said. "Rooms
have been reserved. Lindén is staying at her own place."

"You need to arrange an office for us in Svendborg," she said.
"And then you need to convene the officers I'll be working with so
we can hold a joint briefing."

"You should prepare yourself for the fact that they're under a lot
of pressure in Svendborg," he replied. "Svendborg may sound idyl-
lic, but there's trouble in that town. We're talking fights, violence,
drugs. The drug trade's ravaging Svendborg, and there aren't

enough police to fight it. That's what we're up against. People are scared, and they're complaining that we're not visible enough, that we're not increasing the police presence on the street. So, to be completely honest, I asked for your assistance because, frankly, I don't have enough personnel to carry out a homicide investigation."

Louise stared at him in disbelief. So, this wasn't even about drawing on her specific investigative skills. He was just trying to scrape together extra bodies so he didn't need to devote a team to the investigation, which would further strain his district's ability to carry out their routine workload.

"I don't think this will take very long," Grube continued, undaunted. "It's probably a property crime, and if anything is missing from the inn, eventually it'll turn up on the local classified ad forum, the Blue Pages. If not, it probably makes sense to look into the victim's relationships. Maybe something as simple as jealousy. The woman lived at the inn for the last eight years, since she and her husband took over the place, so all of her acquaintances should still be in the area."

He was probably right. The vast majority of murders were categorized as acquaintance killings, where the victim and the killer knew each other.

Louise stood up wearily. "Do you have an address for the inn?" she asked, realizing that she couldn't expect much more help from the man. The only thing she knew for sure was that the critical first twenty-four hours of the investigation had been lost entirely.

"When you get to Bregninge, head toward Vornæs, and then take the exit at Strammelse. The inn isn't that far off the main road. You can't miss it."

She wondered briefly if GPS hadn't made it to the Funen Police yet, then figured he probably just didn't want to go to the trouble of looking up the exact address.

"And I'll meet your people out there?" Louise asked. It was three in the afternoon, so Lange wouldn't be down from Hjørring for another couple of hours.

For the first time, Grube gave her a slightly apologetic look.

"I'm not sure there's still anyone out there right now. If the technicians are done at the site, they'll probably have left."

"But what about the investigators?" she asked. "Do they have people at the station for questioning or are they still knocking on doors, canvassing the neighborhood?"

"I'll ask Niklas and Lene to meet you out there. They can update you. Maybe you'd prefer to check in and get settled in Troense before you head to the crime scene? I'm sure that would work for Lange. Then you can do a joint briefing."

Louise picked up her duffel bag off the floor and shook her head.

"No," she said. "I wouldn't prefer to check in first. What I would prefer is to get out on the crime scene to see what happened, inspect the location, and get a list of the people your officers have spoken with. Please have them meet me there. I'll take over the investigation from here."

She stared him in the eye, unblinking, until finally, he nodded his agreement.

CHAPTER 2

Strammelse Inn was a two-story whitewashed main building with a red tile roof and a single-story addition that seemed to contain a row of rooms. A short gravel road led to the parking lot, which sat at the edge of a large wooded area. In front of the inn, vast fields spread out in a countryside idyll. Louise let herself enjoy the view for a breath, then she locked her car and headed over to the inn.

It was deserted.

She determined as much after circling the building. No signs of the technicians' work. No crime scene tape across the door, or around the parking lot for that matter.

"Amateur assholes," she muttered, tempted to call Velin and break the news that Deputy Chief Superintendent Grube had screwed them over and was using P13 to scrounge up extra manpower.

A police car parked alongside her and discharged a man in his mid-thirties and a woman who looked slightly older than Louise.

"Louise Rick!" the woman said energetically, holding out her hand. "I'm Lene Borre, and this is my colleague Niklas Sindal. We're so glad to have been granted the assistance, but we'd expected it to take a few days to go through."

Right, now you can get back to your desks, Louise thought as she shook the woman's hand. She was completely unprepared for the thump on the back she received from Sindal, who had locked the car and come over to join them.

"I know Mik Rasmussen, deputy detective in Holbæk," he said. "We took a training course together on cognitive interviewing. So I've already heard all about you."

Louise stared at him, attempting to keep her expression neutral. It was one thing that he *knew* her ex-boyfriend, but she was definitely not a fan of the fact that they had specifically discussed her.

"You failed to cordon off the scene," she noted, choosing to ignore Sindal's outburst of familiarity.

Borre and Sindal exchanged a quick look, then silently set off across the parking lot toward the back door of the inn.

"We've been out here all day," Borre said, her tone now noticeably darker, less welcoming. "The technicians were still here when I went to pick up Niklas half an hour ago. The forensic technicians didn't tape off the area because I told them I was coming back, once we heard you were on your way."

"Sorry, that's not how I meant it," Louise said, even though that was precisely how she had meant it. Sloppy work, but the way Borre defended it made her think that the explanation was sincere.

"I'd hoped we could start with a briefing, but Lange's coming from Hjørring and won't be here for another hour. So maybe you could show me around in the meantime. Are the technicians completely finished, or do we need to suit up to go inside?"

"They're done," Sindal replied, unlocking the door.

They entered a wide back hallway with doors on both sides, one leading to the inn's kitchen, the other to a large linen room with tablecloths, napkins, and candles arranged on the shelves. Farther back there were stacks of high chairs and dried table decorations. Louise turned to follow the two officers into the kitchen.

Sindal had a black briefcase under his arm and was already on his way over to a swinging door that led into the inn's dining room when Louise stopped him, surveying the space. The windows looked out on the parking lot and the edge of the woods. The room was clean, and the large industrial dishwasher was closed. There was a crumpled pile of tea towels on the shiny stainless-steel counter by two large refrigerators, and Louise noticed that the trash hadn't been emptied. Despite the clean surfaces, it was obvious that forensics had been at work. There were still marks on the floors where shoeprints had been collected, and it was clear that they had also searched for fingerprints, especially on the swinging doors.

"Could you tell me what we know so far?" Louise asked. "Just a quick rundown. Then we can go through the more detailed version once Lange arrives."

"She was lying in there," he said, pointing toward the dining room.

"Who found her?" Louise asked, walking over to the door. They proceeded into the dark restaurant with exposed beams on the ceiling and framed watercolors on the walls. Little lanterns on the tables held tealights and vases of dried flowers. Feminine, Louise thought.

"Jack Skovby, age thirty-nine. He lives in Nørre Vornæs but he was born here in Tåsinge. When we brought him in, he said he has a company called Skovby Enterprises. He comes here twice a week to mow the lawn, and since Dorthe's husband, Nils, died, Jack's helped her out with odd jobs. When he came yesterday, it was to mow the lawn and take care of something in the yard, but he poked his head in before he started to find out if there was anything else he should work on."

"And he found Dorthe Hyllested on the floor," Louise concluded.

Sindal nodded.

"We checked his alibi. He came straight here from a farm in Bjernemark, where he's repairing a greenhouse. That was confirmed by the farm's owner, Helene Funch. She said he left at around ten-forty."

Louise nodded.

"That doesn't rule him out, does it?" she asked, eyeing them questioningly.

Borre shook her head.

"I guess it doesn't, but I have to say that he didn't seem like someone who had bashed in a woman's head when we got out here. He seemed genuinely shocked. Plus, the blood had already started to dry, so we assumed that Dorthe must have been dead for about half an hour when he found her. It took another twenty minutes from when we arrived until the postmortem examination began. And the doctor's assessment was also that she'd been dead for at least an hour at that point."

"What do we know about Jack Skovby?" Louise asked, peering through another doorway that led to a small area with the front desk and a counter.

"It seems like everyone knows Jack. He and Nils were good friends, and like I said, he helped Dorthe maintain the inn after her husband's death."

"And what do we know about her?" Louise sat down with the two officers at one of the window tables. The little country road that ran by the inn seemed deserted.

"Dorthe Hyllested is originally from Thisted," Borre began. "She owned and operated this inn with her husband, Nils, until he died after an accidental fall earlier this year."

She looked over at Sindal.

"Her husband was whitewashing the chimney here on the main building," he added, pointing up at the ceiling above them. "He lost his balance on the ladder and fell down."

"Since her husband's death," Borre continued, "Dorthe has been running the inn on her own. We're not aware of any problems out here. Most of the guests are tourists. We're heading into the down season now, but it's usually quite busy here until the fall holidays."

"Have you managed to talk to all the guests who stayed at the inn Monday night?" Louise asked.

They both nodded.

"Do you want to see the upstairs rooms?" Borre asked.

Louise motioned for Borre to lead on, and the three of them walked to a staircase opposite the front desk.

"We located and spoke to all of them," Borre explained as they climbed. The carpeted staircase was flanked by more watercolors interspersed with dried lavender bouquets that had long ago lost any scent they might have held.

Louise paused when they reached the top of the stairs, looking around. The walls were painted a dusty green, covered in more paintings, and a small table held a tall vase full of cattails.

"Eight of the rooms were occupied the night before the killing,"

Borre said as they proceeded down the hall. "I have to say, that's pretty good for the first day of the week in the off-season."

The investigator's tone seemed calculated to let Louise know that, despite the décor, the inn certainly wasn't failing—or at least it hadn't been before the death of its remaining owner.

Louise peeked into one of the rooms. It was cozy in a way that had been stylish in the nineties, but somehow still worked here, from the floral bedspread with its orange throw pillows to the big, decorative fan hanging over the headboard.

Several of the guest-room doors were open. The wall colors varied, but the style was the same. Not entirely dated, but not contemporary by a long stretch. Louise couldn't help but wonder if it was a reflection of the inn's owners' personalities, as they'd likely renovated the place themselves after taking it over. She was drawn to something in the place, to that little bit of homey atmosphere in the rooms that was so at odds with stylish hotels that ended up cold and bland.

"Two of the guest rooms were reserved by a master mason from Svendborg," Borre said as they continued down the hall. "His people are in the middle of an extensive renovation on a large farm over by Valdemar's Castle."

Louise paused.

"Wouldn't it be just as fast to drive from Svendborg to Valdemar's Castle as to do the trip from here?" she asked.

Sindal nodded his agreement.

"But it's cheaper for him to have them stay here than at a hotel in Svendborg," he replied.

"So what you're saying is that he's using foreign labor rather than local tradesmen, and he needs to put them up in a hotel as a result?"

Both officers nodded, and they continued their survey of the empty inn.

A couple of the rooms at the back were single rooms, narrow, a bit cramped, and with less attention to aesthetic detail. It occurred to Louise that not every room had its own bathroom, meaning that guests using communal bathrooms would have spent more time out in the hallway and were more likely to have noticed something.

She asked Sindal to take a closer look at the tradesmen's statements and talk to them again in case proper emphasis hadn't been placed on what they might have noticed going to and from the bathrooms.

Directly across from the single rooms was a door leading into a large, old-fashioned bathroom with a walk-in shower, a sink, and a bath mat that matched the cover on the lid of the toilet. There was a towel on the floor, and it was obvious that the room hadn't been cleaned since the guests left the inn.

"The tradesmen left before breakfast was served," Sindal reminded her. "And the night before the murder, they didn't get back to their rooms until late. None of them seem to have had any contact with the other guests."

"Try anyway," she replied simply. "Find out if they knew anyone else at the inn. If they came here regularly, maybe they recognized someone." She figured some of the regular guests might have noticed if there had been problems, either internally or with any of the other guests.

"They knew Dorthe, of course," Sindal replied quickly. "They've been staying here for almost two weeks. But I don't actually know if they knew any of the other guests. I'll find out."

"Were any other guests at the inn when the murder took place?" Louise asked. They had made it back to the staircase and begun to descend.

"No, all the rooms were empty. The tradesmen had already left for the day. Then there were two elderly couples who had reserved rooms until Thursday. They'd come to Tåsinge to do one of the historical walks retracing the footsteps of Elvira Madigan and Sixten Sparre, and left the inn at nine-thirty a.m. They didn't return until late afternoon, at which time they were informed of what had happened."

"So the murder happened between nine-thirty and ten forty-eight a.m., when you received the emergency call?"

Sindal shook his head as the group seated themselves around the table in the dining room once again.

"Room 5 didn't leave the inn until closer to ten a.m.," he said, "and Dorthe was standing at the front desk when they left."

A good forty-five minutes before Jack Skovby called emergency services, Louise noted to herself.

"Do all the guests have an alibi for the time of the murder?" she asked.

Borre nodded.

"We think they do, actually. One of the remaining three rooms was occupied by a younger couple who were going to visit the woman's parents in Langeland. They left one day early for their trip so they could spend a night on the road, to have a little fun and gear themselves up for the visit, as the man put it. His parents-in-law confirmed that they arrived in Langeland around ten-thirty a.m. A businessman with an address in Hørsholm was staying in room 8. He arrived the day before and was only staying for one night. He left the inn around nine-twenty a.m., and his license plate was recorded at the tollbooths on the Great Belt Bridge as he drove through an hour later. The last guests were a married German couple, who were on their way to Odense. We haven't confirmed this yet, but they told us that they arrived at the Hotel Grand at two p.m. They say they stopped at Egeskov Castle on the way and ate lunch in Odense before arriving at the hotel, and we're working on confirming that, too."

Louise nodded. It sounded like they had a handle on the overnight guests.

"How many employees are there here?"

"Two," Borre replied. "Eva Nørgaard is the inn's housekeeper. She looks after the rooms. When Nils died, Dorthe took over the breakfast service herself. Before that, she was only responsible for the front desk and serving in the restaurant. And she has Jon, who's the cook. He doesn't come in until around one p.m., when he starts preparing the menu."

"The restaurant isn't open for lunch, but Dorthe serves coffee and cake in the afternoon," Sindal added.

"Doesn't it take more than one cook to keep the restaurant going?" Louise asked.

Borre shook her head. "The restaurant is closed on Sundays and Mondays, and Jon manages it on his own the rest of the week. He used to have a restaurant in Svendborg. A few years ago the stress got to be too much, so it suited him nicely out here. I was the one who interviewed him. He was really shaken, and at first wouldn't believe that anything had happened to her. It seems like Dorthe was well liked by the people who worked for her."

"So the restaurant was closed the night before the attack," Louise noted.

Borre nodded. "Apparently Dorthe refers her guests to the hotel in Troense on the restaurant's off days."

Troense, where Louise and Lange would be staying if he ever showed up, she thought, looking at her watch.

"Their restaurant is open seven days a week, lunch and dinner," Sindal added. "I ate there myself a few weeks ago. Great food. The hotel is right next to the marina. You'll like it."

Louise ignored that last comment. "Were the employees here when the murder took place?"

"No," Borre replied. "Eva doesn't come in until the morning, and when it's not busy she can decide when she gets here as long as the rooms are ready by two p.m. Naturally she took it quite hard when she heard what had happened."

"Does Eva come every day?"

"She has two days off a week, but they're usually set depending on how busy it is here," Borre replied. "Over the summer they hired an extra housekeeper, but the woman quit in mid-August."

"And who deals with the rooms when Eva's off?" Louise asked.

"Dorthe does it herself," Borre replied.

"Can this be right, that I don't smell any coffee?" someone suddenly called from the kitchen. Then a tall, gray-haired man entered energetically through the swinging door.

Louise hadn't heard the car pull up or the back door open, but the man came over to their table with an outstretched hand and an inquisitive look as he eyed each of them.

"Lange," he said, nodding once they had all introduced themselves.

The first thing Louise noticed was that he didn't seem to be the sort who tried to put on airs. And there was no difference in his attitude when he greeted Sindal versus the two women. So far, so good.

"There's a coffee maker in the little cubicle with the dishes," Borre informed them. "I'll take a cup as well."

"The fact is," Sindal resumed once all four of them were seated again, each with a cup of coffee, "it doesn't seem like we have anything whatsoever to go on. We have no witnesses, no one in or around the inn when the murder took place other than Jack Skovby, who found the victim."

He held up his hands apologetically, as if he had personally failed.

"We still haven't been able to determine if anything was taken from the inn. According to the people we've spoken to so far, there's no obvious motive for the killing. The technicians are working on the prints they collected, primarily interested in the presence of blood from anyone other than the victim, or any unknown DNA in Dorthe's blood. No murder weapon has been found yet. That's where we stand, in a nutshell."

Sindal opened his briefcase and pulled out a laptop. All four of them leaned over the table as the forensic team's pictures of the crime scene appeared on the screen.

Dorthe Hyllested lay on her stomach, both arms stretched away from her body, as if she had been tossed around and had tried to regain her balance with her arms. Her face was turned toward the rear wall of the inn. In the close-ups, Louise saw that the woman's hair was covering her eyes and stuck to her scalp. In the next picture, one of the forensic techs was raising her upper lip with a latex-gloved finger to reveal a row of broken teeth.

"Dorthe Hyllested, age thirty-eight. Slender build, hair a copper-red, dyed, a small heart tattoo on her left wrist," Borre began reading aloud. "Otherwise the report says no distinguishing marks."

"The location where the body was found is where the murder took place," she continued, pointing to the enormous pool of blood under Dorthe's head. "We're still waiting for the forensic report, but during the postmortem there seemed to be no doubt that she had bled to death due to the blows to the head, which resulted in a deep laceration wound. Of course, this needs to be confirmed before it can be recorded as the final cause of death."

Louise got up and walked over to the marked spot; a dark, now dried stain showed where the victim's head had been. It didn't say in the report whether Dorthe Hyllested had been coming from the dining room and going toward the lobby or if she'd been on her way from the lobby into the restaurant when she was attacked. It also didn't mention whether there had been a struggle, though it did say that the tables and chairs hadn't been moved or damaged, so at first glance, it didn't seem like Dorthe had fought with her assailant. They had likely caught her off guard.

In addition to the blow or blows to the back of her head, which had presumably knocked her over, there was also the damage to her teeth, either from another blow to the face or from the fall. But until the police pathologist's report came in, the best they could do was guess.

Louise looked down the row of tables covered with olive-green tablecloths. Only the ones in the back were set. The others had been cleared, and a couple of folded tablecloths sat stacked on the table next to where Dorthe had collapsed on the floor.

"She was setting the tables after breakfast," Louise noted before realizing that it was a fairly unnecessary remark. The others had probably figured that out for themselves.

But she was trying to visualize it.

The guests had left; the breakfast things had been cleared from the rectangular table by the wall that must hold the breakfast buffet. The kitchen seemed to have been cleaned. Dorthe had had time to put everything away and had started to get the restaurant ready again.

"What about family?" she asked. "I assume they've all been informed?"

Sindal nodded.

The murder had been the big story in online papers the previous day. As her old boss in the Homicide Department used to say, you could read about a murder before the body was cold. And in this case, that was almost true. The murder case was on the front page today. It didn't have a lurid headline, but it was there. Louise was fine with Grube being the one to brief the press. As far as she was concerned, he could keep himself busy with that while she got properly immersed in the case.

"They didn't have any children," Borre explained. "She has a sister in Thisted and her parents live just outside Holstebro, otherwise no close relatives. Her parents-in-law live in Herning, and so does one brother-in-law. The other one lives somewhere in Copenhagen. We spoke to Dorthe's parents and sister yesterday and were in touch with her in-laws last night."

"Did any of them say whether she'd been seeing anyone new after her husband's death?"

"No," Borre replied. "Seems like she mostly kept in touch with her sister, and the sister hadn't heard anything about a new boyfriend. To be honest, it didn't sound like she thought Dorthe had fully gotten over her husband's death. She'd become more withdrawn, the sister said, and they hadn't seen much of each other. Dorthe had invited the family to the inn for Easter lunch, and had made the trip to Holstebro for their mother's seventy-fifth birthday in July. But her sister hadn't seen her since then. They mostly texted, liked each other's posts, that sort of thing."

Louise made a mental note to have Lisa Lindén comb through Dorthe's social media accounts when she started digging through the deceased's digital life.

"And there wasn't anything found in the inn that could be related to the murder?" Lange asked, bringing Louise back from her thoughts. The reflexive reluctance Louise had felt at being assigned an older man from Northern Jutland had already evaporated. Lange had watched Borre with a focused look in his eye as she led the briefing Louise had set in motion, listening attentively and taking notes on a notepad he had set on the table in front of him. It also struck Louise that he hadn't so much as commented on having been selected to work on this case with the new, untested travel unit; hadn't complained about having to be away from home without knowing how long the case would last, or that it would no doubt mean long workdays without weekends off. He had simply shown up with a positive attitude and gotten down to work.

After they passed around the laptop with the crime scene photos, it sat in the middle of the table, frozen on a picture of the victim, who had been rolled onto her back and was staring straight up into the air. Ugly, brutal.

"Has the whole inn and all of the rooms been searched?" Louise asked, looking to Borre and Sindal.

They both nodded.

"And the neighbors in the area, have they been interviewed?"

Borre nodded. They'd already spoken with what few residents there were in Strammelse. Naturally, everyone knew Dorthe. "And if there is anyone we haven't talked to, we can safely assume that they've been questioned by journalists. They were swarming all afternoon and into the evening yesterday."

"But it's likely they've lost a bit of their gusto now that it's clear that there aren't any bereaved, grieving children or some crime of passion angle they can dig into," Louise responded. "They don't seem to have learned any more than we have: that Dorthe Hyllested was a well-liked woman who ran a successful business."

"To your earlier questions, we've also been focusing on whether it could have been a lovers' spat," Sindal continued, "but there just isn't anything to suggest that. And it doesn't seem like anyone in the area has seen or heard about Dorthe finding someone new after Nils. No one has noticed anything changing at the inn, or anyone from outside of town who started coming here regularly. There's a seniors' club here in town that usually comes to the inn for coffee and cake on the first Sunday of the month. They were here last Sunday and all know Dorthe, but we haven't talked to them yet."

Louise looked around the table.

"What do you all think?" she asked.

"I think that we should bring the whole gang in for a chat," Lange promptly replied. "We need to find out if Dorthe was sleeping with anyone, or if anyone might have had hard feelings. Maybe she owed someone money?"

"And then we should look over the inn's finances," Borre added.

Louise nodded, sensing agreement that the very first order of business was finding the people Dorthe had a relationship with.

"I agree. It's most likely to be someone in her social circle," she conceded, then told them about Lisa Lindén, whom it turned out all three of the others already knew. "Grube got a warrant this morning. Tomorrow, I'll have Lindén pull the information from Dorthe Hyllested's phone to look into her social media accounts and secure access to any private bank accounts. After that she'll need to go through the inn's finances and all email correspondence. If that doesn't result in any leads, we'll need to take out our magnifying glasses and search for a personal motive."

Louise stood up.

"All right, let's call it a day," she said, turning to Sindal. "You send us all the reports, witness statements from the guests, pictures from the forensic techs, the whole shebang, and then the four of us will spend the evening reading up so that when we reconvene tomorrow not one single thing will have escaped our attention. And send it to Lindén, too."

"Aye, aye, boss," Sindal chimed, and Louise stared at him in consternation.

"We'll meet here at eight a.m. tomorrow, and we'll know everything there is to know thus far."

The others nodded. Sindal remained quiet.

Lange finished his coffee, then suggested that Louise ride back to the hotel in Troense with him so they only had to take one car. She was about to protest when she realized that his suggestion actually made the most sense.

"Do you want the inn cordoned off?" Sindal asked as they emerged outside into the parking lot.

Louise nodded, pleased that the media seemed to have lost interest in the case fairly quickly. A nearly forty-year-old innkeeper from Tåsinge didn't exactly sell newspapers.

"Eight o'clock," she repeated and was about to get into the passenger's seat of Lange's Volvo when her cell phone rang and Jonas appeared on her screen.

"Hi," she answered happily.

"Grete's in the hospital again," Jonas said, sounding choked up. "Melvin's really upset, but he says it's better if I go home and feed Dina instead of staying here at the hospital with them while we wait for a doctor to come and see her."

Louise felt a pang and instinctively looked at her watch. She could be at Bispebjerg Hospital in two and a half hours if she made good time. But then she wouldn't have a chance to read up on the case, and definitely wouldn't get any sleep before she had to get her group up and running tomorrow.

"What are they saying at the hospital?" she asked, trying to calm her concern.

"She hasn't even been examined yet. She's just lying in a bed here in the hallway and they can't say how long it'll take. Melvin called the emergency doctor right before I got home from school. We were about to eat dinner when they finally showed up at the apartment. All the doctor said was that Grete's infection numbers seemed to have spiked; they took her away in an ambulance. Melvin and I took a taxi here."

The words flowed out of him, his voice several notches higher than normal. Much as it pained her, Louise knew it wouldn't have made any difference if Jonas had called her earlier in the afternoon. She wouldn't have driven home. And she couldn't now, either.

"I think Melvin's right," she said in a soothing voice. "Go home and take Dina for a walk. We can't do anything right now but wait and find out what the doctors say. She's in good hands, and that's the most important thing. I'll talk to Melvin, too, so we know what's going on. But make sure you have something to eat. I'll put money in your account. And trust that they'll take care of her until she's better. It's pneumonia, but that can be really rough on elderly people."

"Is she going to die?"

"No, of course she won't die," Louise said. "But she'll need to be treated with some serious antibiotics, which may make her tired and maybe a little disoriented. But they'll bring her infection numbers down. So the most important thing right now is that she gets treatment and rests. It's going to be okay, I promise."

It was quiet for a moment.

"Do you think I should buy something for Melvin?" he asked then. "I mean for dinner? He didn't have time to eat anything because everything happened so fast."

"You could ask him if there's anything he wants," she replied, touched by his concern.

She had gotten into Lange's car and hardly noticed that they'd left the inn. But now he swung down past a little marina and then turned up again behind the Hotel Troense, where they would stay. He had left her alone in a way that gave no indication he was listening while she spoke to Jonas. But after she set down her phone and he turned off the engine, he immediately asked if she was okay.

Louise nodded before getting out of the car and reaching for her weekend bag, which Lange pulled out of the back seat before she could do so herself.

"It's my downstairs neighbor," she explained. "We're like family. His girlfriend is in the hospital and that's not easy on him. He's almost eighty."

"You can drive home and spend time with them," he said. "The rest of us know what to do."

Louise shook her head.

"There's nothing I can do for them anyway," she said, following him into the lobby. A small bell over the door rang as they entered, and they were greeted by a whiff of fried onions from the restaurant.

Louise walked over to the door and peered in. Almost all the tables were occupied, and she realized how hungry she was before turning back to the front desk to greet the young woman who had appeared to check them in. Lange did the talking, then handed her a key.

"Don't take this the wrong way," he said, standing with his travel bag in hand, "but if you don't mind, I'm just going to order room service and dive into the case while I eat. It's been a long day."

"Of course," Louise said quickly, giving him another point. The last thing she wanted was to sit across from a stranger and make forced conversation.

He started climbing the stairs next to the racks of tourist brochures, and she followed him. When they reached the hallway and were about to part, he turned to her.

"Are you sure you're okay?" he asked again.

She pulled herself together and smiled.

"Positive," she assured him. With a hamburger and a glass of red wine in her room, she could easily handle a couple more hours.

But first, a phone call.

CHAPTER 3

Camilla Lind was clearing the table when her cell phone rang. She dumped the plates in the sink and closed the door to the living room, where the cigar smoke was starting to spread.

"Hi," she said, pouring the rest of her beer into a glass.

"What do you know about the murder in Tåsinge?" Louise asked without bothering to return Camilla's greeting.

"Nothing," Camilla replied, taking a long drink. "Absolutely nothing."

There was silence on the other end. Louise was clearly surprised.

"Jakob's probably covering that story," she added, turning on the water and starting to rinse the dishes.

"Jakob, as in intern-Jakob?" Louise asked.

Camilla had told her about Jakob before he'd become a permanent employee on the *Morgenavisen*'s crime beat. "Yes," she replied. "I mean, he was the one who had an article in the online edition."

She pinched the phone between her ear and her shoulder when she started in on the dishes.

"But haven't you been following the murder case?" Louise asked, clearly surprised.

"No, not really," Camilla admitted, filling the sink with water and dish soap.

"It's all over the news. The woman was thirty-eight years old and murdered in the inn's restaurant, not even a bar or pub."

Camilla felt a wave of irritation surge through her body.

"Yeah, I'm not stupid. I just haven't been following the story. I don't know anything about it." She scrubbed the dishes, phone still pinched between her shoulder and her tilted head.

There was silence between them.

"Is something wrong?" Louise asked.

"No," Camilla replied quickly. "I just took a few days off."

More silence.

"A few days off?" her friend repeated, clearly surprised. "Did something happen?"

"No," Camilla assured her, drying the clean beer glasses with a kitchen towel.

"Is it Markus? Did he go back to Julia?"

"Hell no!" Camilla exclaimed loudly, nearly dropping the glass she was holding. At the beginning of the summer, her seventeen-year-old son had told her that he was going to be a father, only to break down shortly after when it turned out that his girlfriend Julia had just made that up to see how far he was prepared to go for her. Only once it was clear that Markus was prepared to take responsibility and stick it out with her did she admit that she wasn't pregnant after all.

"Markus is doing fine," Camilla continued more calmly, draining the water from the sink. "I honestly wouldn't even be able to keep track of all his girlfriends if not for the fact that he documents every single one of them on Instagram to make sure Julia sees them."

Camilla loved her son—a lot—but she had given him an earful more than a few times to make sure he was treating the girls who fell in love with him properly.

After a year of Markus hardly being home from boarding school, their reality was now completely different, to put it mildly. Camilla's son brought friends home every single day. On the weekends there were pre-parties and after-parties and friends staying overnight. She was at her wit's end, even though she was trying so hard to be one of those people who thought it was cool and invigorating to be surrounded by youth and noise. Luckily, Frederik was much better at that kind of thing.

"Do you know who intern-Jakob talked to in Tåsinge?" Louise asked, evidently refusing to accept that Camilla was taking the day off. "Is there any gossip over there? Anyone talking about things that haven't come out in the press?"

Camilla put the call on speaker and set her phone on the kitchen counter while she started putting dishes away.

"Honestly, Louise, I know nothing. I haven't talked to anyone in the newsroom. Why do you want to know what I know? You're the one working the case."

She had seen Louise's message earlier that day, the one where she canceled their get-together that weekend because P13 was assisting the Funen Police. But she hadn't bothered to reply.

"What's wrong?" Louise asked, a little more sharply. Camilla sensed equal parts irritation and concern in her friend's voice.

"Nothing," she replied quickly. "I just went away for a couple days."

"Away?" Louise repeated. "Away where?"

"I'm down at my dad's place in Præstø. I came down here on Friday, and I'm planning to stay for the rest of the week. I have no idea what's going on in Tåsinge or in the *Morgenavisen* newsroom."

"Is your dad sick?"

"No, not at all. I just needed to get away for bit."

"Away?" Louise repeated incredulously, as if it were a swearword. "Frederik just moved home from the U.S. and then you moved out?"

"Yes," Camilla replied curtly.

"Are you two fighting?"

"No, we're not," Camilla practically shouted. "I just need a break."

"From him?" Louise asked cautiously.

"No." Camilla pulled out a chair from the table and sat down wearily. "From family life. It's driving me crazy, the way he's always rummaging around and calling the shots. And Markus is driving me nuts with all the noise and the fuss and the friends on constant pilgrimages in and out of the apartment. I kind of got used to it just being me at home. Now it's nonstop people. Last week I barely managed to stop Frederik from building a temperature-controlled wine storage room back behind the kitchen."

"But the last time we talked you wanted to put a walk-in closet back there."

"Yes," Camilla replied, "but that was for all of us, for coats and boots and that sort of thing. Then Frederik pushed through this idea that we need a safe room in the apartment to protect against kidnapping and as a precaution in case of a break-in."

Camilla realized that just talking about it was making her feel annoyed all over again.

"On the off chance we encounter, shall we say, 'uninvited guests,' instead of trying to scare them off, we're just supposed to rush into a vault and hide? I can't do that."

Louise started to laugh, then grew serious again.

"To be honest, it's a reasonable concern," she said. "You *are* on the list of Denmark's richest families."

"Frederik is," Camilla interrupted.

"You'd be smart to take private security measures," Louise continued, unperturbed.

"Oh, come on! We can't sit there and hide in some vault!" Camilla exclaimed so loudly that her father opened the door to ask if something was wrong.

Camilla shook her head quickly and tried to smile at him, mouthing that she would be right there. She was just about to say goodbye when Louise continued.

"Would you do me a favor and use your Infomedia access to compile everything that's been written about the murder in Tåsinge?" Louise asked.

"I'm taking time off," Camilla replied, not having the slightest desire to spend her evening digging through the newspaper's archive database.

"But your log-in still works when you're off, right?"

"Do you not hear what I'm saying?" Camilla snapped. "I haven't been following it. I have no idea what happened, and it's not my problem!"

It was quiet on the line. For a long time.

"Is there something you're not telling me?" Louise's tone had turned serious. "I'm getting the sense that I should be worried about you."

"No," Camilla replied calmly. "There's nothing wrong. I just unplugged to get some peace. The truth is, I've spent the last five days playing Yahtzee with Dad and I have absolutely no idea what's going on in the real world. I'd really like to keep it that way for a little longer."

She realized belatedly that this would only increase Louise's concern.

"Yahtzee?" Louise repeated. "Do you want me to come out there?"

"No, I don't. There's nothing I'm less interested in right now than some murder in Tåsinge."

Her father appeared in the doorway to the living room again. He held his cigar in his hand and watched her as if he were suddenly concerned, too.

Camilla sighed, exhausted by it all, heavy with the burden of everyone's worry. She gave in before she could think better of it, promising Louise to see what she could find. She hung up the phone, pulled a bottle of dark rum out of the kitchen rack, and followed her dad back into the living room.

Louise was sitting still, phone in hand, when someone knocked on her door. She had ordered dinner from the inn's restaurant and said that she would come down and pick it up if they just called her when it was ready. But the server had insisted on bringing the tray up to her directly.

Never before, not in all the years Camilla had worked as a crime reporter, had Louise ever known her friend to not get excited about a murder case. Camilla was usually the one who called Louise to ferret out the details and press for information so that she could be the first to get the news. This passivity—this apathy—was new. And it was worrying. Almost as worrying as the news Melvin had given her earlier that night about Grete, who had been admitted to the Pulmonary Ward and would be kept overnight until she could receive new scans. He'd at least let the doctors talk him into going home and getting some sleep, as Grete would be asleep herself for the next few hours anyway.

Louise opened the door to find a server holding a tray of food. The Salisbury steak she'd ordered was flanked by a mountain of potatoes. A gravy boat was filled to the brim, and even though she'd only asked for a glass of red wine, there was a half carafe on the tray. She wouldn't suffer any privation while she was staying here, that much was clear.

"Thank you," she said.

"There's a little bar down behind the restaurant if you fancy a beer or a drink," the server said, explaining that it would be open until eleven p.m.

"This will do nicely," Louise assured him, closing the door and bringing her dinner straight over to the desk.

By the next morning it was already clear to Louise that they were dealing with a victim who appeared to be a well-liked and capable woman, one who didn't seem to have had a new romantic relationship since her husband's death. Lisa Lindén, like the rest of the team, had been at it since eight o'clock in the morning, and had thoroughly sifted through Dorthe Hyllested's personal life and the inn's finances before the day began for most.

When Louise had first spoken to the young forensic telecommunications expert, she had been pleasantly surprised to learn that Lindén had also spent the previous evening thoroughly reading all the reports that Sindal had sent around. Not one word about sick children. Quite the contrary, actually; Lindén was the first to express her excitement about getting to work with the new travel unit.

From Lindén, Louise also learned that Dorthe Hyllested's personal finances didn't show any signs of large deposits or eyebrow-raising withdrawals. The inn's finances were also in good shape, and it was actually bringing in a decent profit. There were no major indiscretions in Dorthe's social media accounts, no suspicious messages, no pictures that might make someone jealous. Nor was there anything worth pursuing in her phone messages. Her last text was from Jack Skovby, who was replying to a message she had sent him the day before her murder asking him to mow the lawn in front of the inn. He confirmed briefly that he would be there the next day, sometime between ten and eleven.

Lindén suggested that Dorthe's time was mostly taken up by her work at the inn. Not much going on in her personal or digital life, as far as they could tell.

"What you see is what you get," Lindén had said.

In other words: a dead woman with the back of her head smashed in and no hint of a motive for the killing, Louise thought.

"Do we have keys so we can get in everywhere?" she asked

when Lange started talking about lunch. "Or should we call in a locksmith?"

"The inn wasn't locked when we came out on Tuesday," said Borre. She'd been relying on Lindén to find something in Dorthe's online presence that they could go on, and her disappointment made her impatient. They needed to make progress. Too much time had been lost already.

"The door to the deceased's apartment upstairs wasn't locked, either," Borre continued, "but there's no obvious lead to follow. So far we've focused on the guests who were staying at the inn, along with witnesses in general. I'll take the blame there if we've been going in circles—I decided that the most important thing was to find anyone staying at the inn when the murder took place."

Louise quickly stopped her.

"That's great! I would have prioritized it the same way. The most important thing *is* to find witnesses, especially anyone who may have seen people leave the inn or noticed cars in the parking lot."

When Lange had shown up in the lobby at seven-thirty with wet hair and fresh cheeks, he'd thankfully had the good sense not to brag about going out for a run while Louise was still asleep. For her part, she had stayed up until two a.m. reading through everything: reports, forensic results, autopsy report, and the witness statements. She had to hand it to Sindal and Borre, who along with their other colleagues had interviewed the inn's guests and checked the timing of their alibis—they had actually done a really thorough job.

While Lange and Borre had begun a new search of the area for the murder weapon, Sindal had driven to Odense to meet with the

German tourists, who were able to corroborate through pictures on their phones that they actually had been at Egeskov Castle when the murder took place.

Three canine units were working around the inn, and Louise just had time to say hello before they went off to search for a possible murder weapon. Dorthe Hyllested could have been killed with anything that had sharp edges, so the dog handlers were sent out into the terrain with broad search parameters.

While the others were away, Louise spoke to the president of the Strammelse Computer Users' Group. They met in a low-ceilinged, half-timbered workshop, and two cats immediately came over and rubbed against Louise's legs as her host showed her into the living room.

She declined coffee and sat down on the plaid throw blanket that covered the sofa.

"I'm mainly here to see if there's anything the police should know about the inn, its operation, or its owner," she began.

The man had sat down with some difficulty in an armchair across from Louise. He slowly interlaced his fingers, seeming to weigh his words.

"It wouldn't be accurate to say that they kept to themselves," he began. "But it is always hard for people who come from outside. As if they're a bit reserved or guarded, if you know what I mean?"

Louise thought back to her own childhood in Hvalsø, where anyone who had moved there, regardless of how long ago, remained a newcomer. She knew what he meant.

"But there haven't been any complaints. They always support us locals and they're good about getting involved. For years they've organized a Shrovetide party for the kids, and on the first Sunday in Advent they invite everyone to the inn for æbleskiver and mulled wine."

Louise noted how he consistently used the plural, though it was possible he was including the whole inn in his assessment.

"But otherwise we didn't really follow what was going on. They had their own things to do. I get the sense that they have enough guests, because there are always plenty of cars in the parking lot."

Louise watched the man as he spoke, studying the little flick of his mustache over the corners of his mouth and the cleft in his chin. There was no active dislike in his face, but also nothing to indicate that he'd suffered a loss now that the inn was without an owner. As if reading her mind, he addressed that very thing himself before Louise had a chance to steer the conversation.

"To be frank, there will probably be plenty of people who won't exactly be upset if we don't have to deal with all the traffic going to the inn now."

He clearly counted himself among that group.

"Was there trouble between the inn's owners and the locals?" she asked. "Anything that resulted in any conflicts?"

"No, not at all," he quickly replied. "There was no trouble. We're just not used to so much traffic on our small roads."

Dorthe and her husband had run the inn for eight years, so that was probably something they ought to have adjusted to by now, Louise thought. She waited for him to go on, but he remained quiet as he leaned forward, picking one of the cats up off the floor and placing it on his lap to pet.

"They did well over at the inn," he remarked finally. "They worked hard and it was nice that they were able to attract people in the off-season. After all, that's something everyone in the area has benefited from."

Louise nodded and listened as he explained that the local farm shops and the large organic farming operations all slowed down outside of the high season, while it sounded like Strammelse Inn had kept operating year-round, not shutting down at all over the winter months.

"I wonder what will happen to the inn now," the man mused, still petting the cat's back.

"It's too soon to say," Louise replied. She thanked him for his time and told him not to get up. She could find her own way out.

The other members of her team were sitting around the table eating lunch when Louise returned. The canine patrols hadn't found anything yet.

"They've left the inn but are continuing over toward Bregninge," Borre said, offering Louise a slice of rye bread with liverwurst.

She held out her plate and accepted it, asking if anything had come from the few surveillance cameras they had been able to locate. Lange shook his head. All the material would need to be collected and reviewed.

Louise ate another piece of bread while they updated her on what effectively amounted to absolutely nothing.

They sat together in silence for a bit, then she straightened up with a sudden burst of energy.

"I want us to go through the inn together. Meticulously," she said, looking around. "We'll start over, ransack the whole place, find everything there is to find. We need to get into all the cracks and crevices, look underneath and behind everything."

Her cell phone buzzed, and she stood up and excused herself when she saw that it was a text from Jonas.

> Grete is being discharged from the hospital now. She just talked to Melvin. He says she's going over to their family doctor on Gammel Kongsvej, but she can barely walk. Is it OK if I go home from school and help them?

He had added a heart emoji.

Louise contemplated calling but instead sent a thumbs-up and a heart back. She would call Melvin later. It sounded crazy that the elderly woman was being sent home so soon after her infection numbers had been so high, but she comforted herself with the knowledge that they must have gotten the numbers under control if she was being released.

"Let's turn the whole place upside down," Louise repeated decisively as she returned to the table. "I know you've already searched for the murder weapon, but now we're searching for a motive. And we're looking everywhere: linen room, basement, attic, the office. Look for folders, letters, messages. Anything that could result in animosity, debt, blackmail. Jealousy, sex, hatred. Salacious information about the guests."

She paused for a moment before she continued. "And we'll take our time. This is important, and it's easy to overlook something."

The others understood. They nodded briefly and were about to get up when Borre said that Jack Skovby had contacted them to find out if there had been any progress.

"We also have a couple of journalists who are quite persistent, but I passed them off to Grube. Let me know if you'd like to talk to them yourself," Sindal added.

Louise shook her head and said it was fine for the deputy chief superintendent to handle contact with the press for now.

"Lange, could you have another chat with Jack Skovby after we finish searching the inn? He was the one who found her. Let's see if we can find something by starting from the beginning with him."

In Odense, Deputy Chief Superintendent Grube had told her that Lange was the man who remembered what people said, that he was good with details, that he saw everything. Now he had a chance to prove his worth.

Louise sent Sindal and Borre upstairs to search Dorthe Hyllested's private apartment while she started in the lobby, where the restaurant's reservation book was also kept. Lange had disappeared into the linen room and would then do the kitchen and the cook's order books and contact records.

She had just sat down to review the restaurant reservations when Grube called. A colleague from Odense had already contacted the guests who had reservations and informed them that the inn was closed due to a death.

"What do we have for the press today?" the deputy chief superintendent asked.

"Nothing," Louise replied curtly.

"Motive, suspects? I'm considering holding a press conference later today to accommodate the journalists who keep calling and pressuring us for an update."

"We have nothing," Louise repeated. She was about to remind him that she wouldn't actually be reporting to him, but she stopped herself, remembering that if he was handling the press, she wouldn't be disturbed. "We're searching the inn and the deceased's private residence right now. We've reinterviewed witnesses and we'll talk to the man who found her again later today. That's what I've got for you."

"But that's not really news," he pointed out.

"No," she admitted. "But it shows that we're working hard to find a motive."

Just then she heard Borre call for her from upstairs.

"I have to go," she said, hanging up right as Borre appeared on the stairs.

"Come on," Borre said, motioning impatiently for her to move. Louise stuck her cell phone in her pocket and followed.

Borre guided her past the long line of hotel rooms to the door at the end of the hallway that led into the private residence where Dorthe had lived.

"There's something you need to see." Borre sounded eager as she practically pulled Louise into the apartment.

CHAPTER 4

Louise eased around the piles Sindal had stacked on the floor as he searched the contents of a large writing desk. There was no sign of Sindal himself anywhere.

"Follow me," Borre commanded, urging Louise along through the little living room that contained only the writing desk, a sofa set, and a TV.

Louise had time to register a door that led to a bedroom and a small connecting hallway, where there appeared to be a bathroom. But it was the kitchen they were heading for. The whole room was done in white and blue and reminded her of a Mediterranean restaurant. The dining table and chairs were painted sky blue, and posters of lemon and olive trees hung on the walls. A couple of large braids of dried garlic dangled by the window.

She was trying to take it all in when Sindal appeared in the narrow doorway next to the stove. She briefly wondered if it led to a dining room or if there was a staircase down to the ground floor.

"There's something you need to see," Borre said again, and

Louise couldn't help noticing the look the investigator shot Sindal before he stepped aside to let Louise by.

She walked out into a small connecting hallway and froze.

She sensed Sindal behind her, felt his breath on the back of her head as she stood there in the doorway, staring into a cramped room.

It was dark and windowless. Extremely narrow, maybe just five feet wide and about ten feet long, completely hidden away behind the kitchen.

She stood for a second, staring into the room, while her mind attempted to piece the information together. Along the wall stood a ship's cot with drawers underneath. A bedside lamp above it by the headboard was lit. The bedding lay in a messy heap in the middle of the bed, as if someone had just gotten up. On top of a small, low table by the opposite wall there was an enamel bowl and a half-empty glass of milk. A spoon and a tipped-over high chair lay on the floor next to the table.

Louise heard Lange's voice from the living room as she stepped into the room and looked at an array of Donald Duck comics and toys on the floor. The bowl on the table was half-full of soggy corn-flakes and milk, its surface congealed and brown, and the milk glass had clearly been drunk from. Next to the glass lay a small, light blue, threadbare teddy bear wearing a red cap. In addition to the comics on the floor there were blocks, a worn toy airplane, and a small ball that caught her eye. She allowed her gaze to slide up the wall to the posters and a low shelf with stuffed animals and more toys. There was nothing else in the room.

"What is this?" she heard Lange ask from behind her.

Louse took another step in and lifted the comforter. It probably was no more than three feet long, she thought.

"There was a child here," she stated, turning to the others.

"They didn't have any children," replied Sindal, who had made room for Lange, so he could also look in.

Louise could see that they were all thinking the same thing. If no one had mentioned that Dorthe had been looking after a child, did that mean nobody had known?

They stood in silence, looking around the room.

"Who is the child if it isn't hers?" Louise asked. She walked to the desk and turned over the drawings that were lying on the shelf.

"Four or five years old," Borre guessed from her position by the door. Louise nodded. She wasn't very good at estimating children's ages, but that was her guess as well, somewhere around there.

"I suppose the child must have been picked up before the murder took place," Lange concluded, "and Dorthe didn't have time to tidy up in here."

"Would you furnish a whole room for a child you only took care of once in a while?" Louise asked, puzzled.

"Could it be for her sister's child?" Borre suggested.

All three of them nodded hesitantly.

"She didn't say anything about Dorthe watching her kid," said Sindal, who had spoken to Dorthe's sister the day before.

"So maybe it's a friend's," Borre suggested. "But then, wouldn't the parents have contacted us right away? Wouldn't they have been upset and nervous that their toddler had been here when the murder took place?"

Louise agreed with her.

"They would have at least come forward to say that they'd been to the inn to pick up their child," Borre continued.

Louise nodded again without really listening. She stared at the bed and the bowl with the rancid breakfast, trying to visualize the scene.

Dorthe had gotten up early to prepare the inn's breakfast service. Sindal had explained that breakfast was served from seven-thirty to ten a.m., so she would have been downstairs by seven to prepare the buffet. At some point she could have come upstairs to her apartment to give the child a bowl of cornflakes and a glass of milk. And then what?

Louise took a T-shirt off the bed to see if there was anything else, but it was just the top. No pants or dresses, no duffel bag or little suitcase. Nothing. Just this and a basket of toys on the shelf. She pulled open the drawers under the bed. One contained underwear, socks, pajamas, and bedding. The other had more toys, something that looked like a separated train track, and a bunch of plastic animals for a farm that lay with the wings of the building split apart in a cardboard box. The others followed her search attentively from out on the small landing.

On the wall inside the door hung an old wooden beer crate that had been painted yellow and was being used as a bookshelf. There was also a pencil case on the shelf along with a few coloring things, but nothing that revealed who the little child in the hidden room could be.

"Interesting," Louise said, following the others back into Dorthe's kitchen once they'd searched the bedroom. "And no one mentioned anything about a child at the inn?"

"Nope," Borre replied, opening kitchen cabinets one by one and describing their contents: chocolate spread, fig jam, Choco Pops cereal, crackers, little juice boxes.

She listed a few other things while Louise looked in the cabinet with the dishes and found children's plates and cups with comic book characters on them, which she estimated belonged to a child younger than the one who stayed in the bedroom.

"The housekeeper must have known if Dorthe had a child living here," Lange suggested, looking over at the two local officers.

Borre nodded slowly.

"I didn't ask about a child when I talked to Eva Nørgaard," she replied, "but she also didn't mention anything when I asked her to tell me who was staying at the inn before the murder."

"We'll talk to her again," Louise decided. She asked if Lange had found anything of interest downstairs.

He shook his head and said that he hadn't come across anything.

Louise nodded.

"But first we need to find out who the child is, so we can talk to the parents."

As they prepared to head back downstairs, Louise wondered if she ought to bring the plants from the windowsills, but there wasn't anyone down in the restaurant to look after them, either. Instead, she opened the single living room window slightly to let the stuffiness out of Dorthe's living room. She heard Lange bang the kitchen door shut behind her.

"This is probably the entrance to the private residence that she used so she didn't need to go through the inn every time she left," he said as he walked into the living room. "Have we checked if anyone could have come in this way? Or if the door down there was forced open, so someone could slip into the inn unseen?"

"There's no sign of forced entry," Sindal replied quickly, as if he wanted to emphasize that of course they had checked for that. But he didn't sound entirely convincing, Louise thought.

"There's a patio down there. The housekeeper calls it the sun-garden. It's walled in, so you can't see in from the road or the park-ing lot. Really it's just an enclosed yard."

Lange and Louise were already on their way to the kitchen door, and before they started down the back stairs, Lange handed Louise a pair of latex gloves from his pocket.

The lock on the door was a standard latch that made a loud click when he turned it and pushed the door open. He let Louise by be-fore he studied the door, searching for signs of a break-in.

Picnic table, chairs, umbrella stand. The rest of the small enclo-sure was set up as a playground with a swing set, a sandbox, and a kiddie pool, which was folded up over by the wall now. There were toys and a scooter, a bike, and several different-sized balls spread around on the tiles. Louise thought, as she glanced around, that there was enough there to keep a small day care entertained. There was nothing that looked like it might be used for adult relaxation, no sun loungers or rocking chairs, where you might take an after-noon rest. The outside space was very clearly a child's domain.

"Who has the sister's phone number in Thisted?" Louise asked when they rejoined the others in the inn's dining room. It only took a second for Sindal to pull it up on his computer. It wasn't so much the room behind the kitchen that gave her a strange tingling sensa-tion. It was the playground out back that felt all wrong. She took the slip of paper he offered and retreated to the lobby to make her call in peace.

CHAPTER 5

"No!" Dorthe's sister immediately replied when Louise asked if her sister had a child despite being officially listed as childless.

"My sister didn't have any kids. She dreamed of having one for years, but it never worked out for them, and in my opinion, she eventually made peace with that. But Dorthe loved children, so I can easily imagine her looking after a child for a friend, or maybe the neighbors."

Louise nodded at that possibility, but this didn't seem like just babysitting. It seemed more permanent.

"I haven't heard her talk about a child, but I also have to admit that I wasn't exactly in the habit of talking about kids with my sister. I didn't want to hurt her. Maybe that was wrong of me, but it just felt like it would be rubbing salt in the wound. It's been hard for a long time, whenever we're together as a family and my children end up being flaunted in her face. They always attract so much attention. Maybe it was only me who felt that way, because I knew how much she wanted her own."

She choked up and then cleared her throat. Once she had gotten her voice under control, she continued. "Have you found anything?"

"Unfortunately not," Louise replied. "Right now we're trying to understand who the child might be. We suspect the child slept at the inn the night before the murder. And it's possible that the child's parents may have seen something that we don't know about yet. But we're surprised that they haven't come forward on their own. Given that, we're considering the possibility that the child lived with Dorthe permanently."

"But she didn't have a child," the sister objected again. "I've never heard anything about a child living at the inn."

"What about a foster child?" Louise suggested. "That would be an obvious choice for a woman who wanted a child but wasn't able to get pregnant herself."

"She would have said something about that!"

Louise hesitated, wondering if this was a question that should be asked face-to-face and not over the phone, but there really wasn't time.

"I'm just going to ask this bluntly, and I know it may not come out right. But could your sister have had a child out of wedlock?"

"You mean after Nils died?" the sister asked, confused. "That was only six months ago!"

"No, I mean, could your sister have gotten pregnant by someone else while she was married?"

"No, are you crazy? She wouldn't have kept that a secret. At one point I had the sense that things weren't going so well between Dorthe and Nils, but I don't think she ever considered leaving him, if that's what you mean."

"I don't really mean anything," Louise said hurriedly. "But we need to consider all the possibilities."

"Dorthe never had children."

Dorthe's sister began crying, and Louise regretted that she had pushed so hard.

"I'll talk to her staff. I'm sure they'll be able to explain how it all fits together. Please forgive me for bothering you with something that we might be able to resolve here."

"It's totally fine," Dorthe's sister replied, a sob catching in her throat. She took a deep breath before continuing. "I understand that you need to ask. I just feel so bad for her, because she didn't get to do everything she dreamed of. She wasn't done living, not at all. She was just starting to get over Nils."

"It's completely unfair when something like this happens," Louise admitted. She let the other woman talk for a while before gently wrapping up the conversation.

"It's not Dorthe's child," she told the others as she walked back into the inn's restaurant. "We need to get ahold of the cook. It suddenly hit me that it could be his child. If we assume that he's not together with the child's mother, it would make sense for him to bring the child to work with him on days he has custody. It's possible he made some arrangement with Dorthe and they set up a room where the child could be put to bed so they could stick to bedtimes even if the father wasn't done working until late."

She could easily picture the cook carrying his sleeping child out to the car when he got off work.

"Jon doesn't have any kids," Borre said quickly. "I talked to him yesterday. He lives in Svendborg, and I'd be very surprised if it turned out he's ever had any interest in women, if you know what I mean."

Louise looked at her for a moment.

"Why couldn't he have a child? What does that have to do with anything?"

"He's into men," Borre clarified, spelling it out in a way that made Louise think that if the officer had had a whiteboard, she would have used it.

She nodded.

"I understand that, but it's been done before," she replied, then turned to the others. "We need to have a chat with the housekeeper to find out what she knows about the child. I'll handle that conversation myself. Let's finish searching the inn and the apartment upstairs. And in the meantime I hope that Lindén gets something out of the deceased's cell phone and email account."

"That can't be right, that there's just no lead," Sindal blurted out in frustration once they were again seated around the table in the inn's restaurant after completing their search. He leaned toward the computer and summarized that they had not found a single witness who had seen anyone leave the inn around the time of the murder. Nor had they interviewed anyone who could lead them in the direction of a motive. "I have a strong feeling that there's a personal motive behind the murder. I don't believe she was killed in connection with a break-in or property crime. I can't see what they would have taken."

He looked around at the others.

Louise was inclined to agree with him. She didn't think Dorthe had surprised a burglar, either.

"Agreed," she said out loud, to support him for at least offering something. "It's hard to see a connection to the inn's guests or its operations. But that shouldn't stop us from continuing to look."

"We're wasting our time," Sindal mumbled, but he quickly clammed up when Lange turned toward him.

"Being thorough is never a waste of time," the older investigator snapped.

Louise left the two of them to work out their differences and turned to Borre.

"What do we know about the housekeeper?" she asked.

"Eva Nørgaard doesn't live very far from here. About half a mile away, I'd guess. She's worked at the inn since Nils died and is the only full-time employee other than the cook."

Sindal passed a new slip of paper across the table with the housekeeper's address on it.

"Jack Skovby is coming by within the next hour," Louise reminded Lange. "I think you should start from the beginning again with him. Ask him what the vibe at the inn is like, if there are locals who might be at odds with Dorthe, or controversies we're not aware of."

He nodded without so much as a hint of exasperation over her basic instructions. Once again, Louise found herself thinking how liberating it was that she didn't need to weigh her words for fear of offending anyone. It certainly saved a lot of valuable time without the usual pissing contest taking place.

"Is Lindén looking at the order books?" Borre asked, glancing at Louise. "Maybe something can be gleaned from the reservations that were made recently, regulars, people who came here at steady intervals. They would also know the inn's employees. Even if we think the motive will be found in Dorthe's personal relationships, there could be something to gain if we question the people who come here regularly."

"Agreed," Louise said quickly. "Right now Lindén is working on everything digital, and after that I'll ask her to make a list of the guests who could be regulars. Then you talk to them."

Borre nodded.

It seemed that Sindal had resigned himself to the fact that they had to painstakingly retrace their steps, and he already looked a little tired. Even so, he was the first to get up and push in his chair to signal that he was ready.

"I'm going upstairs to continue in the apartment," he announced and disappeared toward the stairs.

Borre stood up and followed, while Lange finished his coffee.

"You talk to Jack Skovby," Louise repeated, and he nodded. "He must have known the couple who ran the inn well if he's been coming here since they took over the place."

"Should we bring the forensics techs out to look at the child's bedroom?" he asked.

"I think we should talk to Skovby and the housekeeper first and see if there isn't some simple explanation, and then we need to get in touch with the child's parents. They must have been close to Dorthe because it looks like the kid spent a fair amount of time here based on the clothes and the toys. Hopefully the parents can give us a little insight into the personal life Dorthe must have had alongside running the inn. Right now we mostly have the sense that she didn't have a personal life at all. It almost sounds like she spent all her time keeping the inn running smoothly. There have to be some friends or acquaintances who can tell us something."

"But no one has come forward," Lange pointed out.

Louise nodded in agreement.

"Let's see what we get once Lindén is done with Dorthe's cell phone. Everyone has a personal life. We just need to find out what Dorthe spent hers on."

"And a love life," Lange added.

"Maybe that, too. It's rare to encounter someone who associates exclusively with people they know from work," Louise replied. Then she happened to think about herself. What relationships did she have beyond Camilla and her family? None, really. She spent most of her time with them or at work.

"Maybe it's not so rare after all, when you're self-employed," she added. "Self-employed people definitely have their hands full trying to keep everything running smoothly."

Lange, mercifully, agreed with her.

"I'll see you later," Louise said, grabbing the slip of paper with the housekeeper's address as she left.

Louise was just about to get in the car when a Land Rover pulled into the parking lot. She stood there expectantly, watching as the driver turned off his engine and got out of the car.

"Are you Jack Skovby?" she asked after he closed his car door.

He nodded. His eyes darted several times to the back door of the inn as he came over to Louise.

"I was the one who found her," he said, holding out his hand. "I can't believe that kind of thing could happen here. And that she's not here anymore."

Louise took his hand and introduced herself.

"Thank you for coming," she said. "We appreciate your taking the time to talk to us."

"It's no problem," Skovby replied, brushing his thick brown hair off his face. The wind quickly blew it back again. Louise read him as being in his mid-thirties. He was muscular and broad-shouldered under his blue Helly Hansen fleece, and there was no doubt that he spent most of his time outdoors. He had sensitive green eyes and a weathered jawline, which instantly reminded Louise of Eik. She quickly looked away when she realized she had been studying him a little too closely.

"My colleague is waiting for you inside," she said, trying to sound blasé. "We're hoping you can tell us about the child who was staying here at the inn."

He stared at her blankly, then slowly shook his head.

"Dorthe and Nils didn't have a child. I know that for sure."

Now he was the one studying her.

"Did Dorthe ever babysit for someone, or could she have had a foster child?"

Skovby was silent, as if he was waiting for her to say more. He shook his head again.

"There were no children living here. What makes you think there was a child here?" His white teeth gleamed in the golden fall light.

"We found a child's bedroom upstairs, and there are toys out in the yard."

"That's not something I've heard about," Skovby said. "I've been coming here for the last seven or eight years and know Dorthe quite well. I've never seen her with a child. Well, apart from the guests'."

"So you've known the couple who ran the inn since they moved to Tåsinge?" Louise said.

He nodded and turned his face away slightly. Louise saw him take a deep breath before turning back toward her again.

"I've been coming here a lot," he merely repeated, as if that covered the years he had known them.

"It would be helpful if you could tell us a bit about who Dorthe was as a person. If there are things in her life we should specifically be aware of, people we ought to talk to."

Louise had just asked Lisa Lindén to look at Dorthe Hyllested's life during the period before she and Nils moved to Tåsinge. For now, all they knew was that Dorthe had met Nils while they were both working at Munkebjerg Hotel, where Nils had been employed since moving away from Herning and Dorthe had been the receptionist.

"I've met her sister a few times when she's visited. And their parents once," Skovby said.

"What about female friends?" Louise searched his green eyes.

He shrugged and looked away again.

"I didn't know her that well," he replied before turning back to Louise. "She was seen with people in the area, of course. She was social, and people came here to the inn, too, but I haven't met any female friends from outside."

They stood facing each other without saying anything for a moment. She noted the faint whiff of sandalwood and fresh air that lingered on his clothes and sensed that he was more upset about the murder than he was letting on.

Then she pointed toward the kitchen.

"Lange is in the restaurant. You can go on in."

CHAPTER 6

The half-timbered house was whitewashed, and its thatched roof had seen better days. From the street it looked like a botanical display window, although the plants on the windowsills didn't seem like they would let much light in through the small panes of glass.

Louise was standing on the doorstep ringing the bell when she received a text from Sindal.

> 57,500 kroner rolled up and hidden in a cookie jar in the kitchen.

She had already rung the doorbell twice and now put her finger on the button again and held it down long enough for the sound to make it all the way upstairs, in case Eva Nørgaard was napping. She was about to text Sindal back to praise him when the door was finally opened by a young woman who couldn't be much older than her early twenties. Her hair was short and dark, a stripe of piercings ran all the way up her ear, and she looked pale and exhausted.

Louise identified herself and explained why she had come, and the woman hesitantly introduced herself as Lea.

"My mother's not home," she said a little brusquely, staring down at the floor. "She went shopping."

Louise waited to see if she would be invited in while they waited for Eva, but that didn't seem to be Lea's intention.

"I'll just wait for her out here," Louise said, pointing over at her car.

"My mother is completely devastated," Lea volunteered before Louise started walking back to the car. "She didn't go to bed at all last night. When I arrived this morning, she was still lying on the sofa. She can't take any more death."

Just then, a woman on a bicycle braked to a stop beside them. Louise took a step back as Lea stepped out of the doorway.

"Mother, it's the police. She's here to talk to you."

Eva Nørgaard loosened the scarf around her neck, regarding Louise.

Her hair was tied back and her eyes seemed teary, but perhaps that was just the wind from her bike ride.

"I'll be right there," she said dully. "I wasn't expecting you to come to talk to me. I already told the two officers who were here yesterday about my job at the inn."

Louise explained that she was in charge of the travel unit that had been brought in to assist the Funen Police with the investigation. "I've already read your witness statement," she said. "I'm here to talk to you about the child."

The housekeeper took a bag out of her bike basket and handed it to her daughter.

"Could you just set this in the kitchen?" she asked, also not seeming like she was going to invite Louise in. "The child?" she repeated, looking at Louise in confusion as she leaned her bike against the house.

"At the inn," Louise elaborated. "We found a child's bedroom up in Dorthe's apartment and toys in the private courtyard. As part of our investigation, we need to get in touch with the child's parents."

"There's no child," the housekeeper replied tersely. But after a moment, she added, "At least, I've never heard of there being a child's bedroom upstairs in the apartment. After Nils passed away, it was only Dorthe living up there."

She opened her coat, as if she were too hot from her bike ride.

"I can't comment on the sun-garden, because I never went there," she continued. "I've always respected that Dorthe didn't want her employees in the private portion of the inn. It's only reasonable that she should be allowed to separate her work life from her personal life. Otherwise she would never be able to get away."

Louise agreed with her on that.

"But has she looked after a child—?" she tried again.

"Not that I know of," the housekeeper interrupted. She was standing in the doorway now, and Louise realized that the rest of the conversation was going to take place here, outside.

"Do you know anyone from Dorthe's social circle?" she asked instead. "Any friends who socialized with Dorthe when she wasn't at work?"

Eva Nørgaard seemed to mull the question over for a moment, then she shook her head.

"I can't remember her having any visitors, if that's what you mean."

"But what did she do when she wasn't working?"

A car drove by on the road, and Eva waved hello.

"Well, she's pretty much always at work. She was keeping the whole place running on her own. So maybe she just relaxes when she's off? She usually goes upstairs to her place and takes a little morning nap after she's cleaned everything up after breakfast. There's a bell at the front desk, so if anyone rings it, she can hear the bell in her apartment and she comes down."

She looked at Louise as if to make sure she understood that you didn't really have much time you could call "free" when you owned and operated an inn.

Louise nodded.

"Then she comes downstairs again around two in the afternoon to check the reservation book and see if we need anything. Our agreement is that I leave a note if we're getting low on anything or if something needs to be done in the rooms. Mostly we just see each other before I ride my bike home. But I never go upstairs and bother her when she's resting. It's always been an unwritten rule that if you needed to reach Dorthe when she's in her private residence, you sent her a text and then she would come down."

"So you've never been up to her apartment?" Louise asked.

The housekeeper shook her head.

"She's never been to my place, either," she replied a little sharply.

Louise momentarily pondered whether she should bring up the fact that the child's bedroom had evidently been occupied until very recently, then decided that she probably wouldn't get much out of it.

Suddenly, Eva began to cry. She stepped back into her front hall, quickly wiping away her tears; her daughter had disappeared into the living room.

"You must forgive me," she said, clearly embarrassed as she rubbed at her eyes. "I lost my son six months ago. I'm not so strong when it comes to death."

"I'm sorry for your loss," Louise said compassionately.

"He was only nineteen," she continued. "He got sick."

They stood in silence for a bit.

"I don't know what to say about the child's room. I don't know anything about it," Eva continued slowly, as if she were making an effort to put the words together lest it sound as if she were back-stabbing her now-deceased boss. "We certainly didn't have what you would call a close relationship, but we get along fine and she's a good boss."

She paused and then apologized.

"She *was* a good boss," she amended, as if she had only just real-ized she was talking about Dorthe as if she were still alive. "I've been very happy working at the inn. And it never bothered me that she didn't share her personal life. I actually valued that. Our rela-tionship was based on work, but we were friendly. Although I can see now that maybe I didn't really know that much about her. I just never thought about it before."

"That's completely understandable," Louise said quickly. "No need to apologize. I'm just trying to find out who knew her so we can get some help filling in a fuller picture of the life she lived out-side the inn. We need to locate the child's parents."

"If she had a life outside the inn, I'm not aware of it. But talk to Jack Skovby. He's known them longer than I have. He and Dorthe got along well," Eva replied as she removed her coat inside the house.

"It's possible that we may need to speak to you again. I understand, of course, that this is a rough time. Everyone we talk to describes Dorthe as well liked, so it's no wonder this is a shock to you. But please let us know if you happen to think of anyone we should talk to. To be completely honest, we need to know more about her. And of course we're very interested in identifying the child."

Eva nodded slowly, but still didn't look up.

"It's a difficult time," she said at last, finally meeting Louise's gaze. "And incomprehensible. I wonder what will happen to the inn now."

Lange had asked the same thing that morning, and Sindal had replied that Dorthe was the sole owner since inheriting the property from her husband. It would probably be put up for sale if no one in the family decided to take over running it. And there was no indication of that, he had said.

"It's closed for the time being," Louise replied. "And it will probably take some time before the estate is settled and it can eventually be put up for sale."

She figured that Tåsinge probably wasn't exactly teeming with jobs, so she understood the housekeeper's concern.

"Some of my things are in the linen room," Eva remembered. "Just a bag with a change of clothes and some toiletries."

"You're welcome to come by. It's no trouble," Louise said. "I can also bring it to you if you tell me where to find it."

Eva shook her head.

"I'll come by myself," she said. "Or I'll get Lea to stop and take it with her when she drives back to Svendborg. She took over her brother's little car after . . ."

She didn't finish her sentence, nor was it necessary. Louise had noticed the black Fiat Punto parked next to the house.

"There will probably be someone at the inn for the next few days, although maybe not all the time. But obviously we'll make sure that it's locked so no one from outside can get in."

"There's no rush," Eva hurried to say. "It's not anything I need."

Louise pulled out a card and gave Eva her number.

"You can just call, and we'll figure out what works best for you."

Eva thanked her and they said goodbye, agreeing that Eva would call Louise if she needed to talk to her about anything.

CHAPTER 7

Louise walked up the stairs to the inn's upper floor while she waited for Dorthe Hyllested's doctor to return her call. She had tried several times to get through to Dorthe's GP, Søren Lindberg, but only reached the medical secretary, who explained that the doctor was seeing patients until three that afternoon.

She took a bite of the sandwich Sindal had brought her from a café in Svendborg. The others had already eaten theirs by the time she returned from visiting the housekeeper. They hadn't found anything else of interest tucked away in the inn. No more stashes of cash. Illicit money, Sindal had said, Borre smoothing it over by insisting that it was probably just tips. Rather a lot of money for tips, Lange had grumbled.

Sindal and Lange were working on locating guests who had spent time at the inn over the weekend. Both those who had only eaten in the restaurant as well as guests who had rented rooms.

Lindén had sent a summary of all the emails that were in Dorthe's personal inbox as well as the emails the woman herself had sent, and had also provided a rundown of all incoming and outgoing calls from Dorthe's cell phone. Borre was reviewing those at the police station in Svendborg.

Louise stood for a moment in Dorthe's living room and looked around. While the others went through the apartment, she had asked Sindal to look for photo albums among the folders he had searched. He'd found two albums with only family photos in them, he explained, along with pictures from when Dorthe and Nils first took over the inn. Then there were pictures of Dorthe and Nils that Louise suspected were from when they met. But for the last several years, no new pictures had been added to the album, and Lindén hadn't found anything noteworthy in Dorthe's cell phone, either. There were tons of atmospheric pictures, sunsets behind the inn, happy guests and family gatherings, but no children apart from Dorthe's sister's.

Louise walked into Dorthe's bedroom and opened the closet, which was just inside the door. The curtains looking out at the street were open, and the bed was unmade. Dorthe's alarm clock was set for six o'clock. Louise tried to visualize Dorthe's early morning. The breakfast buffet needed to be ready by seven-thirty a.m. with hard-boiled eggs and freshly baked bread. The bread was delivered by the local baker, and on Tuesday morning the baker had come to the inn at seven. Dorthe had been working in the kitchen then, as she usually did, and according to the baker, there was no indication that she was upset, afraid, or behaving differently than usual. The order was for thirty rolls, twenty pastries, three loaves of rye bread, and four loaves of graham bread.

Sindal had commented that it was a generous order given the number of guests, after which Borre had dryly remarked that there was still a portion of the population who did not deny the pleasures of good, freshly baked bread.

Louise pushed the hangers of shirts and pants to the side. Nothing was hidden behind the piles. Nor on the shelves of folded tops or in the woven baskets for the bras and underpants. There was nothing here that stood out significantly from the things she had in her own wardrobe.

The bedroom was reminiscent of the inn's guest bedrooms, lightly decorated in the slightly nineties romantic style with dried bouquets and Japanese landscapes in black lacquer frames. On the dresser there were two bottles of perfume and a magnifying mirror. The top drawer contained toiletries and makeup. But in the second and third drawers there were more toys, along with children's jeans, T-shirts with colorful pictures, sweatshirts, and knitwear. Nice and nicely maintained, but obviously used. She picked up a couple of sweaters and noted that they should fit a five-year-old according to the tag at the neckline. Louise folded them up and had just pushed the drawers closed again when her cell phone rang.

Dorthe's doctor introduced himself and apologized for not calling back until now.

"It's just so incomprehensible that something so awful could happen in our small community," he began. "Everyone loved Dorthe."

"That's certainly the impression we've gotten as well," Louise agreed. "At the moment we're having a hard time finding a motive for the killing. So I hope that you can help me by answering a couple of questions."

"Of course," he said obligingly.

She tried to picture what he looked like. His voice sounded a bit hoarse, and he didn't have a particularly strong Funen accent.

"We're trying to track down anyone Dorthe had close relationships with—people who knew Dorthe well—but I'm also interested in finding out something about a child who seems to have been staying with her at the inn. Did she ever mention a child that she was particularly attached to?"

It was quiet for a moment, but then the doctor cleared his throat.

"As far as close relationships," he began, "Nils was without a doubt her closest. On top of being married, the two of them also had a very tight friendship. I've always had the sense that they had a strong understanding of each other—a very special bond. I think that's the reason that you haven't found a large circle of acquaintances. They had each other and they stuck together. After Nils's death, I had a few long conversations with Dorthe because I was genuinely worried about whether she would get through that loss. Whether she could endure that grief on her own. But she was a strong woman, and she rallied with a strength I wish we all possessed. I got a clear sense that it was the inn and her will to keep it running that kept her on her feet."

There was a short pause before he continued in a serious voice.

"Naturally, I'm bound by my obligation to maintain a patient's confidentiality, but given this tragedy, perhaps it makes sense for you to be aware of this," he said. "Dorthe got pregnant almost four years ago. She lost the baby when she was in her fourth month. She was thirty-four and had wanted to become a mother for a long time. That's the only thing I know about a child. It was a tremendous source of grief for her, and it led to a breakdown. But that time, too, she rallied. And she's never mentioned becoming pregnant again."

"I assume that you would know if she had applied to adopt after she lost the baby," Louise said.

"There was never any mention of that," the doctor replied without hesitation. "Nor have I heard her express a desire to adopt."

"Could she have had a foster child living with her lately?" Louise suggested instead.

"Not that I'm aware of, and that would also have to go through the municipality, and the child would be registered to that address. If that was the case, she didn't select me as the child's doctor. I can't imagine that at all. I would have heard something about it. It's been a long time since she's talked about having children, and not at all since Nils passed away. I had the sense that she made peace with the fact that she would remain childless."

Louise thanked him and had only just hung up when her cell phone rang again. It was Lisa Lindén.

"Over the last two years Dorthe Hyllested has bought children's clothes from the Blue Pages and from a children's clothing shop in Svendborg called Oscar's. She may also have bought some from the Føtex grocery store in Svendborg, where she did a fair amount of shopping. But I haven't reviewed all the specific receipts yet. You'll get those later. I'll scan what I've found and send it to you."

"Thank you," Louise managed to say before Lindén had hung up. Annoyed, Louise called the investigator back. "I need you to look into the children's clothing right away," she said sharply, hoping that that would also signal that she was the one who decided when a conversation was over.

It was quiet for a moment, then Louise heard papers shuffling.

"Snowsuit, pajamas . . . It's honestly easier if you look at it. She's been consistently buying used clothes through ads. I've printed them out. She had a Blue Pages user account, and it wasn't especially hard to see what items she looked for. She set up her profile two years ago and wrote to a woman in Fåborg, who was selling boys' clothes for a two-year-old. And since then you can follow the season and age consistently. There's quite a clear pattern in the ads she was interested in. She bought used boys' clothes."

"And when did that start?" Louise asked.

"She contacted the woman in Fåborg in October 2017."

"And the most recent purchase?" Louise asked.

"It was this August, when she transferred money to a seller in Odense, who was selling boys' clothes for a four- or five-year-old. She also bought picture books and some toys. This summer she bought a swing set from a seller in Millinge, also here on Funen Island."

"So those purchases have been made consistently since October 2017?" Louise asked.

Lindén confirmed that.

"I had been planning to come out to your office so we could meet each other properly," she said. "But then I stumbled across this, and time got away from me. And now I need to go home to pick up my kid. But I'll keep searching tonight."

"That's totally fine," Louise replied without commenting on the part about the kid. "Well done, Lindén. Thank you."

"Thank you, too," the data researcher replied, not seeming to notice the praise. "But on the other hand, there's nothing in the text messages or emails that even hints at parenting a child," she continued.

"Has she resold any of the children's clothes?" Louise asked.

"No," Lindén replied quickly. "She's only bought. I haven't seen anything for sale on her end."

So maybe she didn't want people connecting her and the inn with a child, Louise thought, walking back into Dorthe's living room.

When they ended their call, she continued into the kitchen, then moved on to the small, hidden bedroom beyond. She stood in the doorway for a long time, studying the space before finally walking over to the bed and removing the pillowcase from the pillow. She carefully folded it and placed it into one of the evidence bags she kept in her jacket pocket. She was well aware that she probably wouldn't get away with forcing a DNA analysis of the pillowcase through as a rush request. But it needed to go to the Forensic Genetics Department so an investigation could be started.

Louise no longer had any doubt. This was not just a place for spending the occasional night. A boy had lived in this room, and she wanted to know who he was.

Back in the kitchen, she sat in a chair at the dining table and tried to collect her thoughts. Even though everything inside her trembled with reluctance, she was forced to contact the Missing Persons Department and ask if they had received a report of a missing little boy. In 2017, she herself had been in charge of the Missing Persons Department, and she didn't remember a report like that coming in. But there was no getting around it. She was going to have to contact Eik.

CHAPTER 8

There was silence over the phone for a long time.

"I didn't think you wanted to talk to me," Eik finally said.

"And I didn't," Louise replied tersely. "But this is about work. We need to talk."

"I see," he replied slowly.

"I'm working on a case where we have a missing boy," she explained, asking him if they had a missing person report for a boy around the age of four or five.

There was silence for a moment.

"Why don't you want to talk to me?" Eik asked in a voice that was very far from the one Louise knew so well. "Why don't you want to see me? Why can't we talk?"

She sat and stared at the trivet on Dorthe Hyllested's dining table.

"Can't we try to stick to my topic?" she returned dismissively, vaguely registering her own fear of confronting what had happened when they parted ways in Thailand. "As I said, the boy's about four or five years old. We don't know where he is and we don't know who he is, but something's wrong, and we want to find him."

"Why, Louise?" Eik persisted. "The two of us have always been able to talk to each other. That's been one of our strengths the whole time. It's one thing for you to break up with me and go home. But we need to be able to talk about what happened. I miss you, damn it!"

"I'm not ready," she defended herself. "I'm not ready to see you, and I don't actually want to talk about what happened."

"We need to," he exclaimed, frustrated. "We were together. We were a family. We were out on the adventure of our lives, and suddenly it was over. You went home, and now you don't want to talk about it. I have a right to understand what happened. You owe me an explanation."

"You don't have a right to anything at all," she snapped. He was the one who had failed her, and she instantly felt her heart contract in her chest.

There was silence again for a long time.

"We don't have anything about a boy that age in our active investigations," he said then, his voice back to normal. "The last one was Nabil, Moroccan father, Danish mother. The father took the child to Morocco, but the parents got back together again and live in Gladsaxe. And we're looking for a fourteen-year-old girl from Hadsten. She's been missing for two weeks. It seemed to be a row with her stepfather, and everything indicates that she's staying with a girlfriend. We just haven't had any luck figuring out which of her girlfriends. She sent some cryptic messages to her mother, so we know that she's still alive, at least."

"It's not her," Louise interrupted. "It's a boy in our case. I just wanted to know if you had a missing person alert out for a child that age."

"Do you have a description?" Eik asked. "Any characteristic features?"

"Nothing," Louise replied. "I have a boy's bedroom where one shouldn't exist. A bunch of clothes and toys, but no child. And nothing that ties a child to the inn."

"Oh, you're on the Tåsinge case," he said then. "Congratulations on the job. I heard you got the new travel unit. Are you stuck?"

She was about to tell him to shut up, but she stopped herself, instead telling him about the child's bedroom in the private apartment and about Dorthe, the childless innkeeper.

"We've been searching for friends from her social circle, but there don't seem to be any. And the employees there have never heard of a child staying in the apartment. We have no clue who the boy is, but I think he could be the key to what's happened. So, I need to find his parents."

"I'll do a detailed search so I can be sure there's not a missing person report out there that's just been digitally misplaced somewhere. Although it should come up when I search by age and gender."

There was silence between them again.

"Thank you," Louise said. "Call me if you find anything."

"Wait a bit before you go to the media," he said right before she hung up. "If the press hears the story about a mystery boy, they'll go crazy. They'll have a field day, then you can forget about finding out who killed the woman. Let's just try and see if we can track him down ourselves first."

Louise heard what he said, but the only thing that stuck was the little word "we."

She hesitated, then admitted that of course he was right. The minute she started searching for a child in connection with the murder, they would be inundated. It was one thing for Grube to have his hands full in his office on Hans Mules Gade in Odense, but a media frenzy in Tåsinge would put an end to their ability to get any work done in peace and quiet.

"I'll check all the registries," Eik promised, "including the international ones."

Louise thanked him, and suddenly there was something between them that reminded her of the before-times. Back when they were partners. Back when they were good together.

Finally, she ended the call, sitting in silence for a moment. Then she retrieved her bag to bring the missing boy's pillowcase to Odense.

CHAPTER 9

Camilla was standing in the frozen food aisle at Præstø Brugsen when Eik called. She was buying ingredients for a chicken stew she had promised her father when he'd started going on about potpies.

"Hi," she said in surprise.

"I need your help," Eik began. They'd talked a couple of times since he and Louise had broken up. This was something Camilla had not mentioned to her friend, but she was still hoping they would get back together once the dust had settled. "Can you watch Charlie for me?"

Camilla got in line at the checkout behind a couple of young guys who appeared to be buying up all the chips in the store.

"I'm in Præstø," she said. "So unfortunately . . ."

He knew she had a soft spot for his dog.

"When will you be back in town?"

"Friday or Saturday, probably." She started putting her groceries on the conveyor belt as the chips boys moved forward to pay.

"You could just bring him down there with you," Eik said, unfazed. "He's easy to look after, and you know him. But what the heck are you doing in Præstø?"

Camilla shook her head when asked if she needed a receipt.

"I'm playing Yahtzee with my dad and trying to have fun," she replied drily, picking up her shopping bag to head to her car.

"Walking Charlie would do you good. I'm sure it would do your dad good, too," he continued.

Camilla could just picture it: Eik's enormous German shepherd in her father's cramped, cigar-smoke-filled living room.

"It won't work," she apologized. "Another time. You know I love him, though, and I'm glad you asked."

Now his tone changed.

"Camilla, I need you to come pick him up."

"I can't do it, Eik. Another time."

"You need to," he repeated urgently. "I'm away. He's at home by himself. The key is at Ulla's, and there's no one but you who can go get him without him attacking them."

"What the hell, Eik!" she exclaimed so loudly that the boys with the bags of chips turned to look at her. "You can't do that! What if I'd been away on a trip?"

Suddenly she burst out laughing. This was a perfect example of the brash South Harbor approach to life that she tried to remind Louise of whenever her friend seemed to forget why she had fallen for Eik in the first place.

"I wouldn't have left if I'd known you were away on a trip," he defended himself. "I asked Markus. He said you were taking time off work."

"Couldn't your daughter just take care of him?"

"Stephanie flew to Bristol yesterday. She left school early when her mom died. Now she's been offered the chance to make up her exams. When that's done, I'll go over and help her get the last of her things packed so we can get it all home to Denmark."

"I can ask Markus," she offered.

"That won't work," Eik replied right away. "He'll be ripped to shreds the second he opens the door and tries to go in."

"So we ask Jonas. He's watched him before, and Charlie gets along great with Dina."

"Jonas has his hands full right now with Melvin's girlfriend being so sick," Eik replied.

Camilla hadn't heard anything about that.

"Well, all right, then," she said, giving in. She had already made it out of Præstø and was almost to the road that led to her father's country place. Instead, she headed toward Rønnede and the highway on-ramp.

Eik thanked her and she immediately sensed how distracted he sounded now that she had agreed to watch his dog.

"What's so important that it made you just drive off and leave your dog?" she asked before he had a chance to end the call.

"I'm on my way to Tåsinge," he replied. "I can't say how long I'll be gone. Apparently there's a missing boy no one seems to know about who may have been staying at the inn before the murder."

Camilla had largely gone off-grid and had no idea what boy he was talking about. "A missing boy?"

"That part about the boy cannot come out in the press," Eik continued emphatically. "Haven't you talked to Louise?"

"Yeah," she replied. "But she didn't mention anything about a boy. She just wanted to know what we'd written about the widow's murder."

"So they probably hadn't found the child's bedroom yet when you talked to her," he said. Camilla knew that Eik trusted her. What was said would stay between them. That's how he was. "Tell me," she said.

"All I know is that the deceased owner of the inn seems to have had a child living with her in her private apartment. A child that, according to Louise, shouldn't have been there. The couple that owned the inn didn't have any children."

She registered the familiar sinking feeling, momentarily regretting having agreed to watch the dog, then quickly coming around again.

"Let's just agree that I'm talking to you as a friend and not as a journalist. Plus, I'm on vacation. I'm not working at all this week," she added quickly. She couldn't help herself, though. "*But* if it turns out that there's a story about the boy, you have to promise to let me know. Fair is fair, since you've made me come all the way into the city to rescue your dog."

"I thought you were on vacation," Eik retorted.

But Camilla could tell from his voice that it was a deal.

He backpedaled all the same. "I'm not the one leading the investigation. You'd better take that up with Louise."

Just then, something else occurred to her. "Does Louise know that you're on your way out there?" she asked. "Have you talked to her?"

"We talked, but that was before I started driving," he replied, and Camilla instantly knew that her friend had no idea Eik was on his way. "Searching for a missing person is my specialty, and right now we need to figure out who the boy is. I have a feeling it will work out without having to launch an official search."

"And Louise is fine with your coming?"

"I'm sure she'll be totally fine with it," was all he said.

Camilla parked in front of Eik's preferred watering hole, a bar called Ulla's Place, right around the corner from his little South Harbor studio in the red apartment building.

When she walked in, several of the tables were already taken even though it was only four-thirty in the afternoon. The rank smell of cigarette smoke and stale beer hit her as she shut the door behind her.

She noticed the curious eyes that followed her as she walked over to the plump, middle-aged woman at the bar. Ulla was pouring drinks into low glasses while she chatted with the man sitting on the barstool across from her. He was wearing a sailor's hat, which was pulled low over his gray curls as he accepted one of the glasses Ulla pushed over to him and downed it in one go.

The carpet was sticky under Camilla's feet as she walked past tables with full ashtrays. Two people were playing pool but paused to watch her as she passed them on her way to the bar.

Ulla's hair was dyed a charcoal black and her eyebrows pulled up sharply. There was recognition in her eyes when she spotted Camilla, and the bartender stuck her hand into her pocket and pulled out Eik's keys before Camilla even made it to the bar. Camilla had never been sure if there had been something going on between Eik and Ulla before Eik met Louise, but the two were obviously very close friends.

Along with the keys to Eik's apartment, Ulla also handed Camilla a bag of dog treats.

"He usually likes these," she said.

For a second, Camilla considered suggesting that Ulla take care of the big German shepherd while Eik was away. Then a group of young guys interrupted the thought by tumbling loudly through the door, reminding Camilla that this was, in fact, a bar, and she simply cared too much about Charlie to do that to him. Instead, she took the keys and the bag and thanked Ulla.

Camilla made for the door, ignoring the eyes that had turned toward her in the little time warp of a dive bar that Ulla had created for her patrons.

She heard Charlie whining on the other side of the door as soon as she hit the landing of Eik's apartment.

"Hello, old thing," she said loudly enough to give the dog a chance to recognize her voice. She hoped Eik was right in his belief that Camilla would be able to unlock the door without the retired police dog lunging for her head. Getting one of Ulla's treats out, she put the key in the lock. Charlie was whining loudly now, but he wasn't growling, Camilla noted, reassured.

"Guess who gets to go for a ride," she babbled through the door as she turned the key and slowly opened the door to the apartment. She saw Charlie's pointy snout push through the crack, his tongue hanging out of his mouth as he eagerly shifted from foot to foot behind the door.

"Hi, old boy." She held out the treat as she pushed the door all the way open.

Camilla didn't have time to react before Charlie leapt forward and, tail wagging, tried to jump up, but the injury to his right rear leg kept him on the ground. Instead, he dragged his leg along behind him as he danced around her.

She squatted down and put her arms around him, letting herself be overwhelmed by his expression of loving joy at their reunion. Then she got back up and managed to wrangle him into the living room. No wonder he was happy to see her and nosed her to go for a walk, she thought, taking in the small apartment. She had briefly lived there herself with Frederik and Markus while they waited for their apartment in Frederiksberg to be renovated. But the apartment seemed even smaller now with the large dog bouncing around in it. During a police operation back in the day, a bullet had lacerated Charlie's thigh muscle, and he was enjoying his retirement with Eik, who had taken him in.

But it wasn't only Charlie filling up the place, she thought as she started collecting his things. The sleeper sofa was made up for Steph, and a mattress had been moved over by the window for Eik. There wasn't much floor space left.

Camilla looked around one last time. She had attached the leash to Charlie's collar and was about to go when she took pity and walked over to give a solitary green plant a little water before grabbing the trash bag from under the sink. She had been Louise's friend long enough to know that you could never predict how long a police case might take. Then she ushered Charlie out into the stairwell and locked the door behind her.

"What's the deal with the boy?" Camilla asked the instant Louise answered her cell phone.

She had only just sat down in her car, pulled on her big sweater, and rolled down the back window so Charlie could have some air during the drive back to Southern Zealand before she called her friend.

"What are you talking about?" Louise replied curtly.

"The boy who shouldn't be at the inn," Camilla said, honking in annoyance at a big beer truck that seemed to want to turn around in front of her. "What makes you think he's disappeared?"

There was silence between them.

"Who've you been talking to?" Louise demanded.

"Calm down. I talked to Eik, and I understand that there's information you're withholding from the public."

"I'm not fucking calm," her friend replied, annoyed. "What else did you manage to squeeze out of him?"

"I didn't squeeze anything out of him." Camilla quickly defended herself. "And of course none of it's going to come out. I'm just curious."

"And why did you talk to Eik?"

"Because he asked me to look after Charlie," she began, hesitating now that the conversation had gotten off on the wrong foot. She wondered whether she should mention that Eik was on his way to Tåsinge but decided to let them navigate that themselves, instead taking the easy way out. "He said that he was going to check on the boy."

She thought for a moment before she continued. "I just wanted to know why it was so important that I drop what I was doing to take care of his dog. That's why I asked."

"What about Steph? Couldn't she watch the dog?" Louise asked, still sounding skeptical.

"She just left for England. She'll be over there for a month to finish taking her exams and complete her degree."

She immediately sensed from the cavernous silence that Louise hadn't known about that. So Jonas must not have said anything. It grew awkward and she regretted having mentioned it, worried that she was going to end up hurting her friend.

"I thought you weren't working right now," Louise said, pointedly not pursuing the information about Steph. "Are you back in the city?"

"No, I was out grocery shopping when Eik called. I just picked up Charlie and now I'm on my way back to Præstø. You could have mentioned that there was more to the widow's murder. Why do you think the boy disappeared?"

Louise was obviously still cursing Eik, but Camilla ignored her irritation.

"Let's hear it," she prompted. "You asked me to look into what we'd written about the murder. I did that and I sent it to you."

"Yes, but I didn't get anything out of that," Louise said tersely.

Camilla could hear that Charlie had fallen asleep in the back seat. He was snoring loudly enough that she figured Louise could hear him, too.

"It's not really my fault that intern-Jakob isn't especially passionate about murdered widow stories," Camilla said. "So, let's hear it now. What's going on?"

"You sounded pretty disinterested the last time we talked." Before Camilla had time to defend herself, Louise continued. "How is your father doing? Is Frederik's safe room finished?"

"Come on," Camilla pleaded. "I just needed a little peace and quiet."

"We don't know anything yet," Louise said then. "That's how it is with police investigations. We turn over every stone. Right now we're just speculating, because it seems that there was a boy staying in the deceased's apartment. That's all it is."

"And why are you speculating?"

Again, silence.

"Because no one seems to know that Dorthe Hyllested was looking after a child for someone. She didn't have any children herself, and no one has seen her with a four- or five-year-old boy. That's it. There's probably a completely banal explanation for it. We just need to find it."

"And that's why you contacted Eik," Camilla said.

"That's why I contacted the Missing Persons Department," Louise corrected her. "To find out if there were any open investigations into a missing child of that age."

"Okay," Camilla said, trying to find a new angle of approach. "Does that mean that you suspect the widow kidnapped a child and was keeping it confined in her apartment at the inn?"

"Stop," Louise cut her off sharply. "I don't want to be pumped for information, and I don't want to hear you getting all worked up about the situation because you're suddenly bored down there in Southern Zealand. I have to go."

Camilla didn't have time to respond before her friend ended the call. Nor did she have time to prepare Louise for the fact that Eik would be arriving in Tåsinge very soon.

CHAPTER 10

"What are you doing here?" Louise demanded roughly when she stepped into the parking lot behind the inn. She had been looking out the window up in Dorthe's apartment when Eik's worn-out Jeep Cherokee pulled off the country road.

He closed his car door behind him and came over to meet her.

"Since you don't want to see me in a personal capacity," he said, "it's just my luck that our jobs are bringing us together."

"Our jobs are not bringing us together," Louise snapped. "I called and asked for information. I didn't request in-person assistance from the Missing Persons Department, or from you for that matter."

They had been working together when they started dating, and their boss, Rønholdt, had stepped right in and made it clear that one of them needed to leave the department. That was Louise. The special search service she had led, which dealt with missing persons cases that had potentially resulted from a crime, had been decommissioned, then Eik was back to his old job in the Missing Persons Department.

Now here he was standing in front of her, and she felt completely unprepared. Her heart pounded irritatingly hard, and she was forced to look away to avoid eye contact with him. She forcibly pulled herself together.

They hadn't seen each other since they parted ways during their long trip around the world, where Louise had ended up alone on a beach in Thailand four months in. She'd prepared several times to behave like a grown-up and suggest that they meet over a cup of coffee to talk through what had happened, but she hadn't gotten her act together yet. Even though she had known that there was a risk they would run into each other someday. And apparently that day was now.

"You didn't need to come all the way out here," she said as soon as he reached her.

He was about to give her a hug, but Louise quickly pulled away and he let his arms fall.

"If there is a little boy who has disappeared, we need to do everything we can to find him," he replied, and she noted how his gaze lingered on her face as if he wanted to ascertain whether everything was the way he remembered it. She felt uncomfortable having him study her so indiscreetly. The boundary and privacy that normally existed between colleagues no longer seemed to be there between them, and it was going to need to be rebuilt for her to be able to work with him again.

"There's nothing else apart from what I told you on the phone," she explained, but she still stepped aside so he could enter the inn's dark interior. They proceeded into the kitchen and through the swinging doors to the restaurant.

Sindal and Borre were still contacting the sellers from the Blue Pages who had been in touch with Dorthe when they sold their children's clothes. They hoped to come across someone who could say whether Dorthe had revealed anything about the child she was buying the clothes for when she made the purchase. Or if the child had been with her.

Lange had gone to the National Forensic Center in Fredericia to get an update on the forensic results for the material collected from the crime scene, while the canine units were making their way across the middle section of Tåsinge, still searching for the murder weapon.

"Do you want some coffee?" Louise asked.

Eik slipped off his leather jacket and tossed it on a chair, then brushed his longish dark hair back and pulled a package out of his back pocket.

Louise was about to protest that he would even consider smoking indoors, when instead he pressed a piece of chewing gum out of a small blister pack.

"I'm trying to quit," he explained, noting the look in her eyes. "You've been telling me to for a long time and I'm trying to do something about it now. Steph gave me a book about it."

Louise broke the eye contact, feeling slightly ashamed by the hurt she felt that his daughter's words had evidently gotten through to him where hers had failed.

"May I see the boy's bedroom?" Eik asked.

They made their way over to the stairs across from the front desk, Eik questioning Louise on whether the deceased's neighbors had seen the child. "A boy that age is usually quite a handful. You've got to run off that energy."

Louise explained about the toys in the courtyard.

"No one seems to have noticed that there was a boy living here," she added, opening the door into Dorthe's apartment. "We've talked to the neighbors, and the local officers have been over to the grocery store to find out if they knew anything about him. We've talked to all the nursery schools and day cares in Tåsinge. None of them know anything about the deceased taking care of a young child."

She showed him to the boy's room and then stepped back a bit. Something about his presence broke down all her defenses and made her feel insecure, unsure of herself and all the rage and love she had shoved down when they split up. As soon as she'd seen him get out of his car, she'd realized what a huge mistake it had been that they hadn't talked to each other the minute he came home from the trip. The distance that had arisen because of her silent rejection had erected an artificial barrier between them, or maybe just around her. Eik seemed relatively unaffected by the situation and genuinely happy to see her, which made Louise all the more unsure.

"We've talked to everyone around Dorthe," she said, "her family, the staff at the inn, and residents of the local community. She's never had any connection to a child. And that's the only reason I contacted you."

Eik stood with his hands in the front pockets of his black jeans. He chewed his gum vigorously but didn't touch anything in the room. He just looked at the boy's life laid out before them. Then he turned to the shelf and started pulling out the books one by one. He opened them and looked at the first few pages of each, while Louise stood by feeling foolish for not having thought to check if there was a name in the books. She watched him in silence as he pulled out a new book, looked inside it, then put it back again. Once he had made it through the entire collection, he turned to her.

"It's one thing to buy clothes for a child from the age of two.

Those could have been purchased for a couple of parents who were hard up. But they've been enjoying picture books and bedtime stories. There's also a little age progression in these books."

Eik had always been good with small children. Louise had no idea where he got that from because he'd never lived with one himself. Stephanie was sixteen when she came into his life, so his experience hadn't come from her. And Louise certainly didn't have that experience, either. Jonas was twelve when Louise became his foster mother, and it had always been difficult for her to relate to young children. She had no idea what to read to them when they were two, or which books were appropriate for a four- or five-year-old. She stepped into the room and saw that the earlier books were small and square with a mouse named Maisy: *Sweet Dreams, Maisy* and *Maisy's Day Out*.

She felt the heat from Eik's body as he walked past her in the cramped space. He leaned over the desk and studied the two drawings lying next to each other. One had "Mama" scrawled in fiery red, crooked letters above a stick figure standing under a large sun. The other drawing was something like a rocket heading into a blue sky.

"There's something wrong here," Louise repeated as Eik straightened back up.

They stood for a moment looking at each other while he nodded thoughtfully, and this time she maintained the eye contact.

"You're right," he admitted. "Something is very wrong."

Louise led the way back through the apartment and locked the door behind them.

"When did the husband die?" Eik asked as they descended the stairs.

"A good six months ago."

"So the child was born before his death."

Louise nodded thoughtfully before walking over to her computer to check for the emails Lindén had promised to send. Nothing had arrived, so she called her instead.

There were children's voices and noise in the background, and annoyance had already seeped into Louise's voice before Lisa Lindén had time to say her name.

"Do you remember the date when the deceased contacted the first advertiser about children's clothes?" Louise asked, prepared for the investigator to have to locate the information in her papers. But the answer came back promptly.

"October 21, 2017," Linden replied, shushing a nearby child.

"Thank you," Louise said, then apologized for having had to bother her when she was picking up her kid.

"Anytime," Lindén replied before hanging up.

"A year and a half before the husband's death," Louise confirmed, looking over at Eik, who was helping himself to some coffee from the machine. "He died just before Easter this year, so there's no doubt that they were together when the child was born."

Eik offered her a cup, but she shook her head. He picked his jacket up from the chair.

"I'm just going outside for a smoke. The gum's not good enough when I need to think."

She nodded and considered going with him but remained standing there in the kitchen instead. He had left the door to the parking lot open and after a moment she felt the fresh air coming in from the back hallway.

She closed her eyes for a second, realizing just how much she wanted her first investigation in this new unit to be a success. A solved case that she would be proud of and excited to talk about, something other people would notice. Something the police big-wigs would bear in mind. But the fact was that she didn't control shit, certainly not now that Eik was here. She cursed, tried to pull herself together, and was about to launch into a long mental tirade about how worthless she was when she heard Eik's voice outside, followed by his rapid footsteps on the gravel.

"You'd better just come," he called into the kitchen as if he sensed that she was standing in there hiding.

It was the tone of his voice that made her get to the back door in a single bound.

"What's going on?" she asked, realizing to her surprise how easy it was to shut down the voices that had just been berating her in her head.

"There's a girl here who'd like to speak to you," he replied, pointing her to the bench that stood along the wall of the hotel facing the road.

"Hi, Lea," Louise exclaimed in surprise, seeing the housekeeper's daughter sitting hunched over, practically disappearing into her dark blue quilted jacket as if it had been pulled up around her like a shield. "Have you come to pick up your mother's things? You can just go on in or explain to me where I should look."

"It's not that," the girl said in a low whisper once Louise had reached the bench.

Only then did Louise see the tears pouring down the young woman's cheeks.

Without saying anything, Louise sat down next to her. The sobs rose through Lea's body, making the girl shake. Louise sensed

Eik standing over by the door, but her attention was focused on Lea, who sat with her hands clenched, staring down into her lap as the sobs rolled silently through her.

Louise carefully reached out and put her hand on the girl's shoulder.

"What happened?" she asked, and Lea flinched slightly.

Again there was silence between them, then Lea sniffled and took a breath.

"I want to confess that I was the one who did it," she said. It came out meekly, but Louise heard every word. She waited, keeping her hand resting on Lea's shoulder the whole time.

But when Lea didn't say anything else, Louise cleared her throat to indicate to the girl that she was going to take over.

"Did what?" she asked, coaxing her to continue.

It didn't seem like Lea had heard her, so Louise let her be. They just sat together for a long time in the silence that waited expectantly between them.

"I didn't mean to," Lea continued suddenly. "I didn't want anyone to die. That wasn't my intention. I was just so angry."

Louise squeezed Lea's shoulder gently. If Eik was still standing in the doorway, she no longer noticed him.

"Murders often happen precisely because of anger," Louise explained in the same gentle tone. "Won't you tell me what happened? What led up to it? Why did you get so angry at Dorthe? Did it have something to do with your mother?"

The girl turned toward Louise in a sudden jerk, the autumn sun glinting off her ear piercings.

"No," she blurted out in a loud, shrill voice. "I wasn't angry at Dorthe. I hardly knew her at all. But I was the one who killed Nils."

CHAPTER 11

Louise put an arm around Lea as she led her into the inn. Lea walked with her head bowed and her eyes on the floor as she and Louise moved through the kitchen and over to the swinging doors, which Eik held open for them.

Eik pulled out a chair for Lea and asked if she needed a cup of coffee or a glass of water, but the girl only gave a weak shake of her head in response.

Louise sat down next to her and Eik took the seat across. Without their having discussed it, he was the one who pulled out his cell phone, set it to record, and placed it on the table.

She admired the calm way he reoriented. She hadn't fully understood what the girl's visit was about herself, but it seemed as if he had the situation fully under control, even without having heard about Nils and the accident on the ladder.

"He ruined our lives," Lea began tearfully once they had sat down. "It was his fault my brother died."

The words barely made it out before she leaned forward, sobbing, and hid her face behind her hands. Louise put her hand on Lea's shoulder again and felt the despair raging through her young body.

"It was an accident," Louise reminded her, but the housekeeper's daughter shook her head.

Louise felt Eik's gaze from across the table and hoped that he would remain quiet. She wanted to give Lea time to compose herself and find her own way to approach what she had come here to tell them. It was silent for a long time in the semidarkness around the window table while Lea struggled to stop crying. It seemed as if some powerlessness had been released within her, as if it had burst through a defense no longer strong enough to hold it back.

Louise gently squeezed Lea's shoulder again in an attempt to calm her down. She wanted to pull the young woman to her, but instead let her cry it out and recover on her own so they could maintain a professional distance between them. But Lea's grief was so overwhelming that Louise found it hard to remain unaffected.

"How did your brother and the innkeeper know each other?" Eik asked from across the table after some time had passed. Louise felt grateful that he'd spoken up as she tried to calm the girl. It seemed as if the question finally sank in when Lea sat up and wiped her face with her jacket sleeve.

"Nils was in love with my brother," she replied matter-of-factly. "He made Aske do things that weren't good for him. Things he didn't want to do."

Eik seemed unaffected by her claim and nodded to her as she spoke.

Louise had turned to the girl in surprise.

"He was the one who made Aske sick," Lea continued angrily. "He ruined my brother."

"Was your brother gay?" Eik asked.

"Yes!" she replied defensively. "And so what? Everyone was so outraged that Aske was different. But he wasn't into old men who wanted to sleep with him and pressured him to sleep with other people. My brother wasn't like that."

"Why are you coming to tell us this now?" Louise asked. She left her hand in place but pulled back a little so she could see the young woman. She was twenty-two and seemed frail, even though she wasn't especially slender. And she was brimming with grief and anger. Her voice was loaded with aggression when she turned to Louise to answer.

"Because," she began, taking a deep breath to get her temper under control, "I want you to know what was going on here at the inn. What kind of place the inn was when Dorthe's husband was alive. Nils ruined our lives."

"Could you elaborate on that, please?" Louise asked when Lea paused once again.

She had clenched both hands tightly and was staring intently at her white knuckles. She stayed like that as she began to explain.

"Aske once told me that Nils had said everyone was allowed to live out their lusts and pursue their attractions, that it was natural. And my brother agreed. He was only fifteen when he came out and he was definitely searching, too. Aske was never ashamed of who he was. But the adults took advantage of him. The whole thing was supposed to be a secret. You had to be discreet, and it had to become something you didn't talk about, just because they themselves didn't dare to be true to who they were. Because they weren't brave enough to tell their wives that they liked men. They wanted to feel secure at home and in that part of their lives they showed off with their wives and children, and so they came here to Tåsinge to live out their hidden desires and be who they really were."

Again, Lea hid her face in her hands.

"I hate them," she whispered furiously through her fingers. Then she quickly brushed her tears away and returned her gaze to Louise.

"Did those men force your brother to have sex, or did they pay him for it?" Louise asked.

Again she saw the girl's anger build almost into an explosion, but Lea shook her head.

"My brother wasn't a rent boy back then, if that's what you're implying," she exclaimed, pulling away from Louise.

"I'm not implying anything," Louise said, a little more firmly. "I'm trying to find out what it is you've come here to tell us."

Lea slumped again a bit.

"What happened here at the inn?" Louise tried again.

"It wasn't here at the actual inn. It was out at the forest cabin."

She pointed in the direction of the kitchen, the parking lot, and the woods.

"The cabin belongs to the inn," she said, "but it's completely isolated out there. It was supposed to be something exclusive, something fancy with a hot tub and champagne, but in reality it was just a male brothel."

She was quiet for a moment, as if she were thinking.

"A well-organized weekend fuck with room service and a breakfast buffet," she summarized. "No one paid Aske to go there. He wanted to. He contacted some of the guys online and then they reserved the forest cabin so they could be together without any risk of the other guests seeing them."

"But something changed?" Louise asked.

Lea nodded.

"Something happened and not long after that he moved in with me and stopped going out there. That was when I suspected that he started charging money for it. The whole thing changed. He changed. My mother was the one who discovered that he was starving himself. He got worse and worse, but he didn't want to talk about it."

She sat for a moment, staring straight ahead.

Louise and Eik gave her time to recover, but it only took a moment before she straightened up, ready to say more.

"About two weeks after Aske's death, I saw Nils standing up on that ladder. I was on my way down to get eggs. My mother wanted to make a roast lunch for us the next day, for just her and me, the way we used to do before Aske got sick. He waved at me as I drove by. I remember that I slammed on the brakes and turned in to the parking lot out back. As I got out of the car, I yelled to him that it was his fault my brother was dead. He yelled back that my brother had gotten sick, and that he was sorry about that. I got so angry that I ran over there and knocked the ladder over."

She closed her eyes and squeezed them shut, as if she were trying to push the memories away.

"I didn't mean to, not really," she began quietly. "It was as if my body reacted without my mind taking any active part, like it was something my body did on its own."

She shook her head slightly.

"I can still remember how heavy it was when I tried to pull the ladder away from the wall, much heavier than I had imagined. I got up onto the bottom rung and put all my weight into forcing it backward. I don't think he understood what I was doing. It wasn't until the ladder moved under him that he realized he was going to fall."

She looked quickly over at the swinging doors that led to the kitchen and the parking lot behind the inn.

"I saw him toppling backward as I ran back to my car, but I didn't see him hit the ground. I hurried into the car and pulled out of the parking lot without looking back. I didn't think it would kill him. I just wanted to show him that I wasn't going to silently accept what he had done. I was going to make him understand what he had taken from us when Aske died."

When she paused, the silence felt heavy.

Louise gave her a moment before clearing her throat.

"Did Nils hurt your brother?" she asked then.

It was as if the anger, the guilt, and the strength suddenly left Lea. She bent over the table as tears streamed down her cheeks.

Louise glanced quickly over at Eik, who remained silent, as the young woman fell apart before them.

"I'm going to be forced to ask you to repeat everything you just told us when you come to the police station," Louise finally said.

Lea nodded without looking up. She wrapped her arms tightly around her torso as if she were trying to hold herself together despite the despair that was tearing her to pieces.

"Before I call my colleague who will drive you to Svendborg, do you think you can explain to us where the forest cabin is located?"

Lea nodded, still without looking up. Her gaze reached down only to her folded arms, as if the world stopped there.

"Follow the gravel road into the woods," she said with quiet disgust in her voice, as if the cabin moved closer when she mentioned it.

Louise glanced at Eik again and she could see that he agreed. There was no reason to push the young woman. Her cries were deep and heartrending, and Louise wanted Borre to deal with her while they went into the woods to look for that cabin. With this information, a somewhat different picture of the married couple's relationship emerged, and she was surprised that no one in the family had mentioned Nils's sexuality.

They waited together until Lea Nørgaard was picked up and watched the squad car as it drove away with the young woman inside. If it turned out that the forest cabin was occupied, maybe the boy was in it.

CHAPTER 12

The narrow gravel road that led to the parking lot continued into the patch of woods behind the inn. Lea had explained that they should drive until they reached the fork in the road and then head right. That would take them straight to the cabin. It turned out that there was also a footpath that led to the cabin from the parking lot, the entrance nearly hidden by two enormous rhododendron bushes.

Louise and Eik decided to drive. As the fall forest closed in, Eik had to maneuver his car around the roots of a fallen tree. The big potholes in the road had clearly been left unaddressed. Even though Eik tried to avoid the worst of the bumps, the car bounced painfully along.

"Gross endangerment," Eik said. "If they accept that, she'll probably get off with just one year in jail."

Borre had obtained Nils Hyllested's medical records the same day Dorthe was found. He'd suffered a serious pelvic fracture from the fall but hadn't actually died until a week later, his death ruled the result of a complication in connection with his operation.

Louise knew that Lea was at risk of ending up with a much harsher punishment than the one Eik had outlined.

"The prosecutor's office might also think that this was aggravated assault resulting in death," she countered. "If Lea maintains that she deliberately knocked him off the ladder, then she's risking six to eight years in jail."

"But he didn't immediately die from the fall," Eik pointed out. "He died from the complications that ensued."

His profile and beard stubble seemed to tug at Louise's hand, and she had to forcefully restrain herself to keep from stroking his cheek. He was so familiar and yet so distant. The feeling of his skin. And hers. His body, which used to make her feel safe, still attracted her. But the pain from the betrayal was stronger. It had settled over her, and Louise didn't know how it could ever be erased between them.

The cabin came into view.

Black logs with white mullioned windows and a sod roof. Eik drove right up to the front door and when he stopped the car, Louise realized that her hopes had already been dashed even before they started looking around. From the moment she found out about the cabin, she'd been hopeful that maybe it would give them a natural explanation for the boy's bedroom in Dorthe's apartment. Maybe a girlfriend or an acquaintance lived in the cabin with the little boy, who occasionally spent the night at Dorthe's place. But there was no shadow of life here.

When they got out of the car, Louise stood for a second and looked around at the clearing where the house was located. A little woodland meadow ran alongside the cabin, but outside of it they were surrounded by tall, old trees. If you didn't know about this place, there was nothing to reveal that it was here.

Eik walked up to the house and pressed his forehead to the window-pane, leaning forward to look inside. Louise followed.

"There's no one here," he announced a little unnecessarily after peering into two more windows.

Through her window, Louise saw a large TV set on a rectangular console, and across from that was a deep sofa. Between the two windows, there was a small dining table with high-backed chairs.

Eik had disappeared around the house, but after a moment he was back again. He grabbed the door and, after confirming that it was locked, checked under the doormat with professional thoroughness. He looked under the big flowerpot, where only the remnants of a network of roots were left in the desiccated potting soil. Then he ran his fingers over the rafters jutting out below the roof, but he didn't find a key there, either. Before Louise had time to object, he smashed his leather-jacket-clad elbow through the pane of glass in the door. No alarm went off, just the silence of the woods and the clinking of broken glass as it landed on the floor inside.

He quickly reached through and unhooked the latch to get the door open. Louise watched as he stepped in and kicked the glass out of the way before handing her a pair of latex gloves and walking into the living room.

Louise stepped through the front door as she pulled on the gloves. It smelled stuffy and musty, and she immediately had the sense that it had been a while since the place had been aired out. The front hall was all coolness and shadows.

It was dark here. There was a row of brass coat hooks on the wall and a stand with two umbrellas in it next to the door. She noticed the dark red runner on the wooden floor and the rosette lamp on the ceiling before she followed Eik into the living room.

"No boy," she noted.

He shook his head.

"No one at all." He ran his fingers over the coffee table. "This place has been empty for a long time."

Behind the living room, there was a large bedroom with doors opening onto a wooden deck. Louise walked over and looked out. The deck was noticeably newer than the cabin itself. When she opened the door and stepped outside, she spotted the cover over a sunken hot tub. She squatted down and lifted it up, revealing dark and murky water. She didn't need to stick her hand in to know that it was cold, the pump turned off. It looked as if it had been sitting unused for some time.

Louise locked the door behind her and opened the two closets in the bedroom. Some thick chair cushions for the outdoor furniture were stacked in the bottom of one, but otherwise there were only hangers and a rod. It struck her that the style of the forest cabin was very different from the rest of the inn. It was more stylish, the furnishings more austere, no fans or Japanese pictures in black lacquer frames. The bed was wide, the headboard a tall square upholstered in dark gray fabric. There were black Bestlite bedside lamps and a thick lambskin rug on the floor on either side of the bed.

Louise pulled out one of the nightstand drawers and found herself staring straight down at a naked man's erect penis on its way into the mouth of another man. The stack of glossy, foreign gay magazines lay alongside a remote control and a transparent rectangular plastic box full of condoms. She picked up the top magazine from the pile and determined that it was from January 2018. She put it back and closed the drawer before walking around to the nightstand on the other side. More condoms and small tubes of lube with unbroken seals. *No obligatory hotel-drawer Bible here*, she thought, closing the drawer again.

When Louise returned to the living room, Eik had opened the doors of the rectangular TV console. She could see an old DVD player on the shelf as he turned to her with a stack of DVDs in his hand.

"Porn," he said. "All men."

"Yup." She nodded and told him about the nightstand drawers. There really wasn't any indication to suggest that straight couples ever visited the forest cabin. It seemed very specifically to have been designed for men, just as Lea had described.

Louise went into the kitchen. Neat and tidy, she noted. There was a Nespresso machine, a champagne cooler, and champagne glasses. A phone hung on the wall with an explanation that you needed to dial 9 for the front desk and 0 for the inn's kitchen. There was a minibar cabinet under the kitchen counter with a little key-hole in the top left corner.

"I suppose it's really just a sort of hotel suite," Eik said, coming to join her.

Louise nodded.

"There's nothing for us here," she remarked. "It's clear that the cabin has been like this since Nils died, but it is odd that Dorthe didn't use it again. I'm surprised that an inn in a relatively remote location chose not to use all its guest rooms, instead focusing this place on a specific group of guests. For that to make any sense at all, we have to assume that there was plenty of demand for this place."

She watched Eik expectantly. He just nodded.

"Otherwise they would have included the cabin in their selection of room types," she continued. "A suite is always more expensive than a standard room."

"Try to see how it's listed on their website," he suggested. "I have a feeling that the cabin was something the innkeeper might have run separately, as an independent part of the business. Maybe that's why his wife didn't keep the place going."

"But it's not that hard to throw away the porn magazines and the movies, either," Louise objected. "Dorthe could have easily opened this place up to all kinds of guests. She could get a higher price for it than the nine hundred kroner a standard double room costs."

"Maybe she didn't feel like she could manage it," Eik suggested. "Maybe she didn't think she had the time to run over here and serve food and drinks. Or clean, for that matter, once she was on her own at the inn."

Louise nodded and admitted that that could be the explanation. Dorthe and the housekeeper had surely had enough to do already with the inn's fourteen main rooms.

While she googled the inn to see if the forest cabin was listed on the website, Eik came out of the bedroom with a porn magazine in his hand. He walked over and propped it in front of the window he had broken and fetched a wine cooler from the kitchen, positioning it so the magazine was covering the hole he'd made.

"I'll call a glazier when we get back to the inn," he said in response to Louise's skeptical glance at his jerry-rigged fix.

"There's nothing on their website about this place. It's not listed at all and there're no pictures of the cabin," Louise said as they walked out to Eik's car.

Before they got in, she called Camilla.

"Could you do me a favor and find everything that's been writ-ten about gay men in Tåsinge?" she asked the instant her friend answered.

"Weren't you about to get a secretary for your new depart-ment?" Camilla asked, irritated.

"Just do it," Louise urged. "Thanks!"

She hurriedly ended the call before her friend could object or start asking too many questions about what was going on. And before Camilla began grilling her about how she felt seeing Eik again.

She sensed him looking at her as they bounced their way back out on the bumpy forest road. But before he had a chance to com-ment on her phone call, she dialed Lisa Lindén. She wanted to ask her to dig up everything she could find on the forest cabin. The investigator's phone went to voicemail, so Louise had to make do with leaving a message.

"Find out if there are reservations in the system that seem like they might fit with the cabin," she emphasized. "And please obtain the names of any guests who've stayed out there."

She still had her cell phone in her hand as they reached the park-ing lot at the inn.

"I'd better go talk to Lea's mother," she said. "I'm not sure she's been informed that her daughter was taken in for questioning."

Eik nodded and offered to drive her after he grabbed his bag with the computer in it from the inn.

"I have my own car," Louise replied, pointing to the unmarked police car.

Eik nodded again, and for a moment, Louise thought he looked disappointed.

"Then I'll drive to Troense and see if they have a vacant room."

Louise had expected him to drive back to Copenhagen, but in a way felt relieved at the prospect of him staying, relieved to have at least one member of the investigative team she knew and trusted. She was annoyed, too. She hadn't asked him to come, and now she felt like he was crowding her. But she didn't let herself say anything.

Louise didn't pay much attention to Eik opening the door into the inn's small connecting hallway. It wasn't until she heard loud voices from inside that she remembered she had locked the door behind them when they left to go to the cabin, and Eik didn't have the key. She ran to the door but stopped abruptly when she reached the kitchen.

Eik was straddling a blond man, who was lying on his stomach with his arms behind his back. The first thing Louise noticed was his red hoodie and frightened expression.

"Name?" Eik said from atop the man's back.

"Jon," he replied weakly, "Isaksen. I work here. I just came to pick up some of my things."

"He's the cook," Louise said from the doorway.

Eik released his grip and scrambled back to his feet, the cook lying still and watching him warily.

"Just get up," Eik said.

Jon Isaksen hesitantly got to his feet, backing away from Eik.

"I didn't realize I wasn't supposed to go inside," he apologized.

"But you are aware that your workplace has been closed down as a result of the murder that was committed here, I presume? And when there's crime scene tape up, that usually means not to go inside."

Louise could tell that Eik was angry. There was nothing apologetic or accommodating in the tone of his voice.

"I am aware of that," Jon Isaksen said. He was almost as tall as Eik, but stronger and with a beer belly. In his early thirties, Louise guessed, trying to remember what Borre and Sindal had said about Dorthe's cook.

"Can we talk to you for a moment?" she asked, pointing toward the dining room. He nodded quickly and followed Eik, still keeping a little distance.

He didn't look like a cook, Louise thought as they sat down at a table. His neatly groomed full beard and hair, which looked freshly cut, were one thing, but it was mostly his eyes that made her think that he was better suited to work in a bank or an accounting office. He didn't seem robust enough to stand covered in sweat in a busy restaurant kitchen. There was something cautious and hesitant in his demeanor, which, to be fair, could easily have been the aftermath of his trip to the floor with Eik. But it was also his movements, the way he was looking at them.

"How long have you worked here?" Louise asked.

"I've worked at Strammelse Inn for five years," he replied clearly, as if he were taking an oral exam.

"What do you know about the young boy who lives here at the inn with Dorthe?"

Jon Isaksen's mouth fell open.

"There's no young boy living here," he replied once he had recovered. It almost seemed as if he resented the question. As if the police were implying that he didn't know his employer very well.

Louise noted every twitch in his face, his roving eyes. She memorized every little reaction, then nodded briefly when Eik leaned over the table.

"Do you know about the forest cabin?" he asked, and Louise saw right away how the cook's face fell. His eyes went to his hands, his fingers fidgeting anxiously, and Louise had time to exchange a long look with Eik before Jon looked up again.

"Yes," he said, nodding. "But it's shut down. We don't use it for guests anymore."

There was something in his voice that seemed eager to explain, but even so, he stopped himself.

Neither Eik nor Louise said anything, waiting for Jon to begin again.

"While Nils was still alive," he explained, "guests stayed out there."

Louise wanted to yell that they knew that much. But she waited for him to keep going on his own.

He didn't, so Eik leaned forward again.

"The forest cabin doesn't seem to be included in the inn's reservation system. Do you know why that would be?"

The cook pursed his lips uncertainly.

"I don't have much to do with the reservations. But I made the food for the guests in the cabin. They had their meals delivered to them. That was the whole point. It was used for VIP guests who wanted discretion."

Louise raised one eyebrow, and she saw a rapid twitch on Eik's lips.

"They rarely came up here to the inn itself," he continued. "They were welcome to, of course, but breakfast was also served out there. And then they called over here to the kitchen when they needed something. It often happened, for example, that there were special orders for lobster, oysters, or fjord shrimp when they were in season. In other words, things we didn't have on the regular menu. But of course they could always order off the menu like our other guests, and that was true for the wine list, too. As long as the last order was placed before nine-thirty p.m. They could also order drinks as long as there was someone in the restaurant, then Nils handled the deliveries."

"Is it true that Nils was gay?" Louise asked.

The cook's eyes flitted as he turned his face toward her. But then he nodded.

"And the forest cabin was his domain?"

He didn't seem to understand what she meant, so she elaborated. "I assume it was mostly Nils who looked after the guests who stayed in the cabin."

"Yes, it was pretty much just him," Jon replied, nodding again. "When Nils was alive, Dorthe was mostly at the front desk and she oversaw the rooms. It was always Nils who looked after the guests, both here at the inn and over there in the forest."

"Was he also the one who made up the rooms after the guests left?" Louise asked.

"No," he replied. "That was Dorthe. She took care of all the rooms."

So she knew what was going on, Louise thought.

"But the forest cabin isn't in use anymore?" Eik asked.

"That stopped when Nils died," Jon confirmed.

"If it didn't go through the inn, how did he and the guests get in touch with each other?" Eik asked.

Jon Isaksen only shrugged apologetically, as if he were genuinely sorry that he couldn't help.

"I don't know," he replied, seeming calmer than he had before. "I would be notified a day or two in advance when guests were coming for the cabin so I could buy extra supplies. But I was never involved in the actual reservation."

"So you didn't get the names of the guests who stayed out there?" Louise tried.

Jon immediately shook his head, and Louise couldn't figure out if he reacted so quickly because he was lying or because he was afraid of becoming further involved in what was likely a business the innkeepers had not been paying taxes on since the cabin rental wasn't listed anywhere.

"I know that you've already talked to my colleagues from Svendborg, but it's possible that we may need to speak with you again," she said. "We already have your number, and I would also like to ask you to contact us if you feel there's anything more we should know."

He nodded quickly, and this time Louise had no doubt that it was relief she saw in his eyes.

She had just stood up to see him out when a high-pitched voice called: "Hello, is anyone here?"

Before they reached the kitchen, an energetic woman with voluminous curly hair came swooping in the door with a smile that was even bigger than her hair.

"Finally!" she exclaimed, extending her arms to hug Louise. The whole thing happened so fast that Louise didn't have time to see what became of Jon before she disappeared into the black-haired woman's embrace.

"Who do we have here?" Eik asked curiously from the table.

"Lisa Lindén," the woman replied, holding her hand out well before she reached him.

It wasn't that Louise hadn't thought about the team's digital forensic investigator. She had just imagined a quieter, more introverted, nerdy type. She was in no way prepared for this explosion of a woman with her big hair and nut-brown skin.

But instinctively, Louise liked her. And it was very clear that Eik felt the same way. His eyes lingered on Lisa's slender figure, and if it weren't for the fact that Louise had immediately felt a burning sting of jealousy, she would have laughed out loud when she saw how he quickly straightened his posture and smoothed his hair back. She was also fairly sure that he'd thrust his chest out slightly.

Lindén turned her attention to Louise again, growing serious.

"You have to explain what's up with the cabin, and what exactly you want me to find out. I didn't get anything from my search, so I need something more specific to go on. Can you give me some more detailed search terms?"

Eik had stood up, taken off his leather jacket, and pushed up the sleeves of his black sweater so that his pronounced forearms were on display. He busied himself by the coffee machine and offered Lisa Lindén a cup as Louise asked her to have a seat.

Even though it was only a brief instant, Louise noted how Eik and Lindén looked at each other when she accepted the coffee he offered her and asked for a little milk.

Louise brushed it off and focused.

"I don't know what there is to work with," she acknowledged, drawing a blank. "The inn has a log cabin back in the woods, which was apparently used by gay couples."

"Not necessarily couples," Eik corrected her, and she looked at him in annoyance. "They may not have been couples, but men who wanted to meet discreetly without drawing too much attention to the fact that they were with each other."

"Right." Louise nodded, agreeing with him. "The cabin was used by men who most likely met in secret: rendezvous, dates, hookups. I don't know what the hell you call it when it's something to be kept hidden. We heard from a witness that it might be mostly married, seemingly straight men who came out here for a bit of a fling."

Lindén put a big clip in her hair, then her fingers raced over her phone screen at the speed of lightning.

"I'm just taking notes," she informed them. "So . . . sex weekends, gay, fuck, cabin, Tåsinge."

It mostly sounded as if she were listing them to herself. Louise looked over at Eik, who wasn't even trying to hide his fascination with their new acquaintance.

"Right," Lindén said, straightening up. "I have something to start with now. Do you have the coordinates of the cabin's location?"

She looked at Louise as if that were an obvious thing to secure as one moved around the countryside.

"No," Louise replied. "But the cabin is in the woods right behind the inn, so you can quickly drive over there and get whatever you need. It might also be helpful for you to see the place yourself."

Lisa was on her feet again before Louise had time to finish.

"You'll hear from me," she said, and then she was gone just as suddenly as she had appeared.

"What the hell was that?" Eik asked with a delighted smile.

"She may be this investigation's best asset."

CHAPTER 13

Camilla bent down patiently to wipe up the mess. This was the second time Charlie's long tail had knocked her coffee cup off the low table. They had only just arrived home from her father's place in Præstø the first time the German shepherd had cleared the cup and candle off the coffee table with a single swish of his tail, looking like he'd scared himself as both rolled across the floor. Now he had done it again, but this time she probably should have seen it coming when she flopped down on the sofa and called him over so she could pet his big head.

She had cut her visit to her father short and had been in the car on her way back to Copenhagen when Louise called and ordered her to start performing new Infomedia searches in the newspaper's digital archives. Camilla had tried to get ahold of her friend several times to find out what had happened, since it was no longer the murdered widow that she was interested in. But Louise's phone went to voicemail every time. As soon as Camilla got the sense that Louise was rejecting her calls, she became even more persistent in her attempts to reach her.

When they'd spoken that first time, Camilla had been pretty irked, to put it mildly, that her friend kept pestering her the one time she was trying to take time off without constantly keeping an eye glued to the news. She'd decided to spend a week down at her dad's place in an attempt to reset from the stress that was creeping into her life from the constant juggle of people and projects. But Louise had insisted, hadn't given Camilla a chance to say no. Yet now that she had gotten started, her friend couldn't even be bothered to answer the phone.

Louise could just go to hell, Camilla thought as she sat searching for the articles Louise had asked for. Although now she was curious about what was going on out there, and the truth of it was that she wasn't entirely opposed to being put to work. She'd been getting tired of Yahtzee and a slice of cake in the afternoon. And she had the unsettling suspicion that her father felt the same way.

That morning he had dropped a discreet hint that there was a used Mercedes over in Fakse Ladeplads that he'd like to check out. And Camilla knew her old used car dealer of a father well enough to know that once he had a car on his radar that he might be able to make a little money on, he couldn't concentrate on anything else.

He had also started talking about his card group and a cake he wanted to try baking the next time they met, so she had seized that opening and excused herself, saying that some work had come up that she needed to drive back into the city to handle. Her father had gotten up out of his armchair immediately, ready to send her away. Although he had seemed a little sad that she was leaving so soon with Charlie. The two old men got along well together.

Camilla was returning to the kitchen with a rag as Frederik came out to join her. She turned toward him and shook her head.

"Then it's settled," she said, wringing out the cloth so a puddle of milk and coffee poured into the sink.

He raised a questioning eyebrow.

"What's settled?"

"We're not getting a dog," she said. "They need more space."

"We have three thousand square feet," Frederik reminded her. He was the one who had started talking about getting a dog now that he had moved home from the United States permanently, but Camilla was not on board. Mostly because she couldn't picture herself going for walks in Frederiksberg Gardens three times a day. "Eik and Steph are living in six hundred square feet, and it sounds like it's going great over there. Maybe we just shouldn't have so many knickknacks."

He pulled her in close.

"Or maybe we should get a tiny dog," he suggested.

"My coffee cup is not a knickknack," Camilla objected into his armpit. "And I'm not getting any of those tiny dogs."

She kissed him and pulled free from his embrace.

"Well, we're already one step closer," he said quickly, laughing. "Now we know we're looking for a medium-sized dog."

Camilla shook her head at him. He was such a zero to one hundred type. She knew that if she gave him even the slightest opening, he would have a dog purchased before the day was over.

"We're not looking for anything," Camilla said, trying to distract him by sounding extra sweet. "I'm sure that you can borrow Dina and walk her as much as you want."

Her husband actually had walked Jonas and Louise's Labrador several times, something he had arranged on his own, so she knew he was serious. And Markus was rooting for a dog with Frederik. It was mostly Camilla who didn't have the energy. Just then Charlie came padding over to them and sat down on the floor right in front of her, as if he expected her to have a treat ready for him if he gave her the same look that had worked each of the other times he'd sat down that way.

"The alarm company will be done today," Frederik said, sitting down to scratch the dog behind the ear. Camilla threw the dish-cloth into the sink and went over to get herself a fresh cup of coffee. "And they promise that the workmen will be out of here by four at the latest, so no more noise."

It had been so noisy and dusty that she had been beside herself since the workers had invaded the apartment to set up what they called a safe room but what in her view might as well have been called an air-raid shelter. Iron girders, concrete walls, and a specially secured door that reminded her of the door to a bank vault. A panic room, she had sneered when Frederik started talking about wanting to have one installed.

And now it was here. The room that would give them security because her husband was publicly known to be one of the wealthi-est people in the country. Not that you could tell as much from their furniture, which still consisted of a good mix of Ikea pieces and some of the old things they had both brought with them when they moved in together.

Just then, one of the workers walked into the kitchen with an electrical device in hand. He explained that he had just tested the communications system from inside the box.

"When you close the door from inside the box room, the lock is activated automatically," he explained. "The alarm company is no-tified immediately and a car will be sent over here right away."

Frederik nodded with interest and followed the man out to the safe room. Camilla felt claustrophobic just thinking about it, but she followed them anyway.

"When an intruder enters the apartment, you might not have your phone on you," the security guy continued. "A person is rarely prepared to be surprised by a burglar or hostage taker."

He opened and secured the iron door and pointed to a small white intercom that resembled the alarm panel by the front door.

Camilla could tell that he enjoyed seeing how uncomfortable she became when he mentioned kidnapping. She shook her head slightly at Frederik, who was almost as excited by the finer details of the security equipment as she herself had been when she'd picked up her new car. But they were different that way, she thought. Frederik wasn't into fancy material goods. The nerdy stuff was more him.

When she returned to the kitchen, a text came in from Louise, who was eager to hear if Camilla had found anything. She took it as an excuse to carry her coffee and a roll of cookies into her office while Frederik had fun with the security guy.

Nothing came up when she searched specifically for "gay" and "Tåsinge." Camilla expanded the search to "Svendborg," and then two articles came up about an assault on a gay man. The assault was so serious that the victim had been taken to the hospital. There was also a letter to the editor from the spokesman of an LGBTQIA+ group, strongly criticizing hate crimes.

The letter writer decried anyone who had something against people with a different sexual orientation than their own, pointing out that in a time when English Facebook users could choose between seventy-one different gender identities, Danes should be past the hatred of any identities outside the customary male/female understanding of gender.

Camilla kept searching, but nothing came up that pointed her toward a gay network in Tåsinge, nothing that tied Tåsinge to sex-themed weekend stays or brothels for men. No leads.

She logged out, then remembered an article she'd once read about a gay couple who had met each other on the dating website boyfriend.dk. They were among the first in the country to be approved for adoption, and they'd joyfully shown off their little daughter in the newspaper.

Camilla went to the dating site, which described itself as Denmark's undisputedly largest community for gay, lesbian, bisexual, and trans people. She didn't get very far, as a log-in was required to access and snoop through the profiles. Another wave of annoyance at Louise shot through her. The police's computer team must easily be able to get around the password requirements for these sites.

Camilla closed the page and instead picked up her phone and went onto Instagram. She searched for pictures there that were tagged with certain words. First she tried "#tåsinge," which brought up a lot, though they were mostly pictures of Valdemar's Castle. There was also an old oak tree with an enormous trunk. And then there were sailboats, aerial photos, and of course pictures of the cemetery where Elvira Madigan and Sixten Sparre were buried.

But nothing came up when she entered search terms like "tåsinge sex," "tåsinge gay," "tåsinge queer vacation." So she tried "#tåsingelover" and "#tåsingegay." Nothing. It wasn't until she tried "#tåsingeloveweekend" that four posts came up. In one, a big, smiling, lanky guy with his arms lovingly wrapped around a slightly heavier man looked up at the camera in a sunset selfie.

The three remaining pictures were from the woods. One where they were both sitting in an outdoor hot tub and toasting the camera lens with two glasses of champagne, the bottle sticking out of the wine cooler on the deck behind them. The next two were views of the trees taken through an old window comprising many smaller panes of glass. In one you could see a roe deer standing very close to the cabin. The last picture was just of the tops of the trees and the sunlight.

Charlie had lain down under the desk with his head on her feet, which were now so asleep they tingled all the way up into her calves.

She clicked on the Instagram profile that had posted the images. It was the skinny man's account. Under the profile picture, it read, *Thomas E, software developer.* There was a link to a website, which she clicked on.

Thomas Engstrøm was a freelance programmer who lived in Slagelse. From his profile, she could see that there were many pictures of him and the man from the cabin, some from Paris (#parisloveweekend) and Rome (#romeloveweekend). Nothing about their weekend trips seemed clandestine, she thought.

She screenshotted the profile and texted it to Louise.

> I think this guy might be familiar with the place. Check out the cabin in the woods and the two men. Sincerely, your now former secretary.

CHAPTER 14

Louise had only rung the doorbell once when the door of the thatched farmhouse opened.

Eva Nørgaard looked smaller and paler in the plaid shirtdress she was wearing. But she was composed as she invited Louise inside.

"Have you talked to your daughter?" Louise asked, noting that Eva had been watering her plants. The watering can sat on the floor next to a dishpan holding a wild heap of dead leaves and small, dry stems that had been snipped off.

Eva Nørgaard nodded and asked Louise to have a seat on the sofa.

"Lea had nothing to do with the accident," she said despondently, shaking her head. "Ever since Aske's death, my daughter has blamed herself that there wasn't more we could do for him. She's filled with such guilt at not having been able to help her brother. It's almost as much of a sorrow for me now to see how burdened she still is by the pain from his death."

She paused for a moment before looking urgently up at Louise.

"She wasn't to blame for Nils's death," she repeated. "The day it happened, Lea called me when she got home from work and said that she had yelled at him and chewed him out while he was standing up on the ladder. But it wasn't until that evening that we heard he had been admitted to the hospital after a fall."

"What does your daughter do?" Louise asked.

"She works in a frame shop in Svendborg," the mother explained. "But you have to understand that she's trying to take on the guilt to soothe her own pain. Did you notice her arms when you talked to her?"

Louise shook her head.

"Lea began cutting herself, even before Aske died," she explained. "Powerless, that's how she feels. It's very distressing for a mother, first to watch her son waste away. He faded away from us slowly. But it's just as unbearable to watch your daughter fall apart because she couldn't do anything to save him."

Eva bowed her head and went silent.

"What did your son die from?" Louise asked quietly.

"He stopped eating," Eva replied, still staring down at her hands, which lay motionless in her lap. "It took a while before I discovered how bad it was. During that phase, I saw him only every few weeks. Of course I noticed that he was losing weight. I just didn't realize how serious it was. He was staying at Lea's place, in her little apartment, and I thought that maybe they didn't care that much about putting a proper meal on the table. It was different when they both lived at home, and I was the one in the kitchen."

"What about their father?" Louise asked.

Eva glanced up quickly.

"Yes, what about him?" she replied sharply. "Frands lives in Vejle with his new family."

A heavy silence arose between them, but Louise let it hang there until Eva picked up where she had left off.

"Let me be honest. Frands struggled with Aske's sexual orientation. It was the reason we got divorced. He blamed me for not trying to 'talk sense' into our son. He thought I encouraged Aske to follow that path, and I did, no doubt. I've never had any problem with who he loved. But the moment I realized that he was gay, I knew it would cause problems for him. Especially when it came to his relationship with his own father. Frands was extremely conservative—not very tolerant when it came to this. And it didn't help that Aske would provoke him. He would leave his gay magazines out on the table." She pointed at the coffee table.

"And he brought his boyfriends home many times. My husband just couldn't stand that, even though he never had anything against Lea's boyfriends spending the night. I wasn't good at dealing with his aversion to his own son. That's why we got divorced."

"Did your children stay in touch with their father after the divorce?" Louise asked, mostly out of curiosity.

Eva shook her head. "But Frands did at least come to Aske's funeral."

Eva eyed Louise urgently once again.

"You have to believe me when I say that Lea is having a hard time. She started grief counseling but dropped out because she didn't feel like the other people in the group were having as hard a time as she was. And as I said, it's not just grief that she's carrying around. It's self-blame because she doesn't feel like she stepped up when Aske needed her to. But the truth is that he became very ill. He couldn't bear the life he had begun to lead, and there was nothing Lea could have done to cure him. He developed anorexia and, quite simply, starved himself to death. Our doctor did what he could to help and at one point Aske was hospitalized in the psych ward for eating disorders. They tried to save him, too. But Aske didn't want to be saved. He wanted to die."

Louise looked at Eva, but the other woman wasn't crying. There were no tears, just bottomless despair.

"I hope you understand that Lea is willing to take the blame for all sorts of crimes to soothe her own pain," she said after they had sat a moment in silence. "If she had pushed Nils off the ladder, that wouldn't be something she hid for six months. She would have broken down and confessed a long time ago so she had somewhere to put her guilt."

She paused again and this time the grief was so clear in her eyes that Louise nearly looked away.

"My daughter is grasping at the straws that might give her a chance to take accountability for her brother's death," Eva said quietly. "Lea knew that the police were at the inn, so it was easy for her to get your attention by confessing to something that in reality was a tragic and unfortunate accident. You need to make them understand this at the police station. My daughter needs help. She doesn't need to get away with punishing herself."

Louise nodded thoughtfully.

"I'll talk to them," she promised before asking the housekeeper to tell her about Dorthe and Nils. "Your daughter mentioned that Nils was in love with her brother, and she told us about the forest cabin. We would really like to contact the guests who stayed out there to understand how the rental process worked and who went there."

Now it was Eva who nodded thoughtfully.

"I only knew about the forest cabin through Aske," she said. "Actually, I took some comfort in knowing they met in a place like that rather than in more exposed places where they risked provoking people. At the time I didn't know that Nils owned the cabin. I also didn't realize that it was rented out specifically for the purpose of allowing men to be together undisturbed. I have to say that my understanding was that it wasn't something my son felt forced to do. He was very open and searching . . . But I don't know any of the people he met with."

Louise watched her as she got up and went into the kitchen. A moment later she returned with a cell phone that she held out to Louise.

"This is my son's old phone. The one he used before he moved into Lea's place," Eva explained. "Maybe you can find some of the guys he hooked up with by looking through it. The code is 7111. I don't know how they contacted each other, either. We didn't talk about that. I was just happy that he seemed happy, and I didn't realize that there was anything covert going on."

"It's not my impression that there *was* anything covert," Louise hurried to say after she had taken the cell phone and promised that Eva could pick it up at the police station the next day. "We just want to contact anyone who knew about the place and can tell us who used it."

She thought she saw clear understanding in the mother's eyes, which confirmed for her that Eva didn't condemn her son for who he was or the way he had lived his life. It made Louise wonder whether she would be as accepting if Jonas was as "searching" in his sex life.

She changed the subject then, bringing them back to the boy

who had been staying at the inn. The housekeeper still seemed just as baffled, and repeated that she had never seen Dorthe with a child.

"We feel very convinced that he was already staying there before Nils Hyllested died," Louise said. "We're still looking for him and are therefore very interested in gaining insight into the lives of the couple who owned the inn."

"I didn't know that much about Dorthe and Nils before I started working at the inn, and I've never heard Dorthe mention a child."

She shook her head to emphasize that she didn't know what else to say, and Louise believed her. Now that the housekeeper had laid everything else out on the table, there was no reason to doubt that she was telling the truth about this, Louise thought, finally standing up.

"But I knew about Nils," Eva added, following Louise to the front door. "It was something Aske told me. Not that I think he did anything to my son, but I'll admit that I did wonder how Dorthe felt about it. I mean, that her husband had this other side to him. From the outside, they seemed to have a good relationship and it obviously worked for them. In the time I've known her it was quite clear that she missed Nils. And it wasn't easy for her to run the whole business on her own, either."

Eva had opened the door, and as Louise put on her coat, she asked one last time that the police not blindly accept her daughter's confession.

"Maybe you can get a psychologist to talk to her, or someone else who can help."

"I'll call and tell them what you just said," Louise promised.

She found herself wanting to ask whether there was someone

who could come and look after Eva during this time, which couldn't be easy for her, either. But she brushed her concern aside to keep her focus on Nils and Dorthe Hyllested. She wanted to know everything about the two people who had run Strammelse Inn for the last eight years.

CHAPTER 15

Søren Hyllested lived in Hammerum outside Herning, not so far from the place where he'd grown up with Nils and their older brother, Hans.

Louise looked out the car window and nodded as Lange enthusiastically told her about the time Bjarne Riis had bicycled around this area when he was young. Even though bicycle racing had never interested her in the least, she found herself smiling at the excitement her older colleague displayed as he described the roadblocks and finish lines that he had helped set up when he'd been a police officer in Herning. It almost sounded as if Lange were taking a small part of the credit for the "Eagle from Herning" making it all the way to the yellow jersey and the Tour de France winners podium. Although he wrapped up his story before he got to the doping scandal and the abrupt fall from stardom.

"The brother works with sheet metal and has his own workshop on Silkeborgvej," Lange explained, finally back on task. "He knows we're on our way."

Louise nodded again. When she had returned to the police

station after her visit to Eva Nørgaard, she had asked the team to dig up everything they could about Nils's and Dorthe's pasts. Lisa Lindén had been freed up to concentrate on Aske's old cell phone, which needed to have all the relevant information and names emptied out of it. After that she would try to figure out if anything that had happened out at the cabin might be related to Dorthe's murder.

"Dorthe was in charge of the inn's reservations, so she was probably involved in it one way or another," Louise said, adding that, due to that fact, she was most interested in the missing reservations for the forest cabin. "They must have communicated somehow."

She had already forwarded Camilla's message about the computer programmer from Slagelse to Lindén, but when they spoke before Louise and Lange had left for Herning, Lisa had said that the programmer hadn't called back yet.

"Then you need to chase after him," Louise had retorted. And then they had left. Two hours in the car, and she had been on the phone for most of the ride while Lange had quietly driven them across Funen Island and up through Jutland as darkness fell.

"Dorthe Jensen was twenty-four years old when she was hired by the Munkebjerg Hotel," Lange continued his summary. "She began as a maid, then became the housekeeper, responsible for all the rooms. From there, she moved on to the front desk and ended up as the hotel's front desk manager. The couple had been married for eleven years. They got married three years after Dorthe was first hired as maid. They ran the inn in Tåsinge together for the last eight years, and the down payment for the inn was paid out of an inheritance Nils received when his father died. His father had owned a large farm in Hammerum, which the oldest brother kept running until the farm went into foreclosure seven years later. Nils's mother is still alive and lives in a nursing home in town."

Lange turned in to a parking lot next to a small warehouse that appeared to be the brother's workshop. A lit-up sign out by the road read "Sheet Metal Fabrication," and before they had time to get out of the car, a broad-shouldered man in a boiler suit came out a door in the gate.

"The police," he remarked before they reached him. Louise and Lange nodded in unison and followed him when he invited them into his private home, a single-family unit that was connected to the workshop and still smelled of supper.

"This is Tina," he said, pointing into the living room at a woman who was sitting in an armchair knitting, a crutch lying on the floor next to her chair.

"I just had my knee replaced," she explained from the living room, pointing down at the crutch, "so I'm not trying to be rude by not coming in there to say hello."

"That's quite all right," Louise said quickly as she took a seat next to Lange at the round kitchen table.

"Coffee?" Søren asked, pointing to a pot on the counter.

Lange nodded, while Louise declined, realizing that hunger was beginning to take its toll on her.

"Maybe they'd like something cold to drink," his wife called from the living room.

"No, thank you. I'm fine," Louise hurried to say. "We won't stay long."

She didn't mention that afterward they had to go to Vejle to talk to a cook who had previously worked with Nils in the kitchen at the Munkebjerg Hotel.

"It was quite a shock when we heard about Dorthe," Søren began. "You just don't imagine that something like that is a thing that could happen to someone you know. Certainly not to someone in your family. Have you gotten any closer to finding out who did it? I wouldn't be surprised if it's one of those outsiders, folks who've moved in from off island. You mark my words. That's what I told my wife, too."

Louise was already annoyed but didn't have a chance to stop him before he continued.

"It looks like there are refugee asylum centers in Svendborg and at Langeland," he went on. "I googled it when I heard what had happened. I suppose something was stolen, too?"

He didn't wait for a response, and while Lange listened calmly, Louise tried not to take the bait. That was easier said than done, although she didn't blame the man for clutching at potential explanations and possibilities. She certainly understood that the family was shocked at the brutal murder. She just didn't have the time to listen to his unfounded suspicions.

Even so, she let him continue for a little while longer before she interrupted him.

"Did you ever find that it caused problems between Nils and his wife that your brother was also interested in men?"

Clearly annoyed, Søren received her interruption with narrowed eyes, giving her a look she couldn't interpret.

"My brother wasn't gay," he said, emphasizing the word "gay" with a bit of scorn. "Where did you hear that from?"

"We heard that from people who knew him," Louise couldn't resist saying, regretting it right away when she felt Lange's disapproving look. "At any rate, people close to your sister-in-law believe he was active in the gay community."

"That's not true," the brother said firmly. "He was married to Dorthe, and before her, he was with a woman named Line, who he'd dated at school. What a bunch of dirty nonsense to come up with. If someone's trying to smear my brother's and sister-in-law's reputations now that neither of them is here anymore, then maybe they're the ones you ought to start looking into."

It was clear that Louise had stepped on his toes. A vein stood out in his temple and his jawline grew sharp. But she couldn't really assess whether he was angry on his own behalf or his brother's. To be fair, they still didn't have any proof that what Lea, Eva, and the cook had said was true, although they did have reason to believe it, she reminded herself as the man's angry glare cut into her. The forest cabin wasn't proof per se. She was well aware of that.

"Thank you so much for your time," Lange said a bit abruptly, and stood up. Louise reluctantly followed him and called goodbye into the living room, where the knitting lay quiet in the woman's lap. The sheet metal worker's wife was asleep.

"I know," Louise said once they were in the car. "I shouldn't have said that. I should have let him talk. I'm sorry."

She didn't look at Lange while she apologized.

"No, damn it," he exclaimed. "That was fine."

That was the first time she heard him swear.

"Now we know what kind of attitudes Nils faced from his own family. He didn't have an easy time of it. I was actually sitting in there thinking about where you might have gone back in the nineties, if you lived in Herning and you were gay. I'm guessing there probably weren't very many places, so I wonder if people went to Copenhagen."

Louise considered that for a moment before nodding. Then she pulled her cell phone out of her purse and called Sindal.

"I want you to look into whether Nils Hyllested was known in the gay community in Copenhagen. Find someone who was part of the old scene and knows people."

He accepted the order without commenting on the lateness of the hour.

"Lindén is in touch with two of the men she found on Aske Nørgaard's cell phone," he said. "She's talking to one of them now and it sounds like all the reservations for the forest cabin were entered into the reservations book under the name of Jens Jensen. Only the name was listed, no personal contact information. No room numbers were assigned for those reservations, either. According to Lindén, the reservations stopped about a year before Nils died. So, either they changed the procedure or the cabin hasn't been rented out since February 2018."

Louise couldn't make sense of that and left him hanging on the phone while she processed this new information.

"Try some of the gay bars and dance clubs," she finally said. "Right now we know that Nils was involved in the community, but we don't actually know for sure if he was interested in men himself. We need to figure that out. I also still want to know everything there is to know about Nils and Dorthe Hyllested as a married couple."

"Dorthe," Lange corrected her. "Dorthe and Nils Hyllested, the woman always comes first."

She smiled at him and followed the traffic as they came out

onto the highway and headed down toward Vejle and their appointment with Steffen Lundbo, the current chef at Gastronetten and former sous-chef at Munkebjerg Hotel, where he had worked with Nils.

They walked into the restaurant and found that only a couple of the tables were occupied. A dishwasher was alone in the kitchen.

"Try out back," he said when they asked for the chef.

Steffen Lundbo stood under an awning, a cigarette between his lips and his eyes on the cell phone in his hand. When he saw them, he quickly stuck his phone in his pocket and threw away the cigarette.

"I didn't think you were coming," he said, wiping his hands on his apron, as if he wanted to wipe away the smoke.

"Sorry, it got a little late," Lange said, holding the door open for the chef.

"Would you like anything?" Lundbo asked, turning toward the kitchen as if he were ready to serve them. But they both shook their heads and informed him that they just wanted to talk to him briefly about Nils Hyllested.

"We actually used to get together once a year," Lundbo said, "the old gang from Munkebjerg, I mean. But the last few years it didn't happen, and then of course, Nils died and Tobias moved to Kenya, so the whole thing fizzled out."

He offered them something to drink, and Louise took a Coke and scooped up a handful of the nuts Lundbo set on the table in front of them.

"Can you tell us if it's true that Nils Hyllested was gay?" Lange plunged right in.

The question seemed to surprise the chef, but after a second he nodded slightly to himself.

"Well, that wasn't something he ever addressed directly," he began. "And he was dating Dorthe from the front desk, so we didn't ask, either. But there was always something different about Nils. And I think we all thought that. It just wasn't something we talked about in that way. I guess we all felt like, just come out of the closet if that's what you want."

This was not a confirmation, just conjecture, Louise thought, once again.

"What was he like?" she asked as the door to the restaurant opened and a waiter greeted an elderly couple.

"He was a nice guy," Lundbo offered. "We always teased him that he was a little shit."

He held an arm out as if he wanted to show that Nils wasn't very tall. That hadn't occurred to Louise from the picture she had seen of Dorthe's husband. He had blond hair, a little thin on top, and narrow shoulders, but it was mostly the twinkle in his eye and the laugh line in his cheek when he smiled that had stuck with her. He looked a bit like a sixteen-year-old being confirmed in the Lutheran Church in that boyish way that some men have, even though they're not teenagers anymore.

"On the other hand, he was insanely fast," Steffen continued. "Nils worked his ass off compared to the rest of us when we threw parties, and he was good at organizing. So you were always glad to work the same shift as him. He was a good coworker and a real pal."

He put the emphasis on the word "pal" and looked thoughtful for a second before he shook his head slightly.

"It wouldn't have made any difference if he was gay," he said then. "He could have just told us. But there was Dorthe, so we didn't really think about it too much."

He started to stand up. The waiter had cleared another table and was on his way over to the elderly couple with two glasses of wine on a tray.

"When he died, we all went in together on a wreath, but I didn't attend his funeral. It was right around Easter, and I couldn't find anyone to fill in for me, so I had to stay here," he said, as if his absence required a special explanation.

He asked about Dorthe's funeral and Lange replied that a date hadn't been set yet. They thanked him for his time, the waiter cleared their table, and they left the restaurant and the chef behind.

McDonald's. It didn't happen that often, but tonight, Louise didn't have any objections. Two cheeseburgers, French fries, and a large soda for each of them.

She was so hungry that she doubted two burgers would be enough. She considered adding some chicken nuggets as well given that the kitchen would be long closed when they got back to the hotel in Troense. But she came to her senses and now that she was halfway through the second burger, it was probably just as well, she thought, crumpling up the wrapper and putting it back in the bag.

Lange sat humming along to the songs on the radio, and oddly enough it didn't annoy her. It was actually nice that he didn't expect them to talk the whole way back to Tåsinge.

They had just passed Odense when Louise's cell phone rang, and "Jonas" lit up on her screen.

"Hello," she said happily, noting the wave of warmth that

washed through her body. But once her son started talking, she had to ask him to repeat himself. At first she struggled to understand what he was saying, but when his words finally sank in, they clenched around her heart, right were the happiness had just been.

"When?" she asked, sensing Lange's eyes on her. The sadness in the boy's voice made Louise curl up involuntarily, as if her body were instinctively trying to encapsulate the pain and prevent it from spreading to all her cells. She listened, unable to stop her tears.

"How is Melvin taking it?"

"He was the one who found her," Jonas said, barely holding it together. "He had just seen her, but when he came back, she was dead."

He started crying again, and Louise quietly cried with him. She deeply regretted that she had promised him so confidently that this wouldn't happen. She glanced over at Lange, who asked in a whisper if he should pull over.

Louise quickly shook her head. Even though she couldn't possibly have foreseen that Grete Milling's death would happen right in the middle of her investigation, which was proving to be more complicated than she had anticipated, she needed to get back to the hotel as soon as possible to get her car and drive to Copenhagen. On the other hand, she knew that she needed to get back to Tåsinge so she could meet with the rest of the team at eight tomorrow morning.

There goes the night, she thought, a little ashamed that she was letting work fill her time when her downstairs neighbor's girlfriend had just died.

"Did she die at home or in the hospital?" she asked, trying to make her voice behave in hopes that she could convey a little comfort to her son.

"Here at home," he sobbed, struggling to get his tears under control before he continued. "We thought things were starting to look up."

The way he said "we" touched Louise. She and Melvin were the people closest to her foster son. Jonas belonged with their downstairs neighbor. The two of them had developed a friendship, which had long since grown so close that Louise thought of them like grandfather and grandson. When Melvin had had a heart attack and collapsed on the landing, Jonas was the one who had found him and administered CPR until the ambulance arrived. Over the years the two of them had built a relationship that Louise had never had with her own grandparents.

"Melvin talked to the doctor this afternoon," her son said. "Grete had been given some medicine that they said would help and she seemed to be doing a little better. I saw her today when I got home from school, and we were joking around. I said that if she hurried up and got healthy, she would have time to do some gardening in the community garden plot before they closed it down."

Louise no longer noticed the dark countryside streaking by, or the radio that Lange had turned down. Grete had inspired Melvin to join her plot in the communal gardens a few years ago. Since then, their houses had been the quintessence of sunshine and coziness—fresh strawberries and newly dug potatoes. Melvin and Grete had spent most of their time out there, maintaining the garden and drinking coffee together under the big trees. Louise almost couldn't bear it. What would happen now to the pretty little plot that Grete had tended for more than thirty years?

"The ambulance just picked her up," Jonas continued, and Louise thought she heard something being pushed across the floor.

He lowered his voice.

"Melvin was crying when they drove away with her, and I don't know what to say to him. What should I say?"

"You don't have to say anything," she replied. "I think it's enough for you to just be there. I'll hurry home so we can all talk about it. Right now it's completely normal for you both to feel shaken and sad."

"Melvin just went in to make her bed," Jonas reported.

After Grete had moved in downstairs, Melvin had furnished his bedroom with two single beds, each up against its own wall. It had been touching to follow the two elderly people as they found their way together, filling the loneliness in each other's lives. They had been good together. Now it was empty again down there.

"Melvin wants to talk to you," Jonas said, and Louise quickly wiped away her tears. She was embarrassed that Lange, whom she hardly knew, was sitting so close and witnessing her grief. It was a reaction she would normally have tried to hide, but in such close quarters it was impossible to pack away her despair and pretend the death didn't affect her.

"I'm so terribly sorry that Jonas had to go through this," was the first thing Melvin said when he got on the phone. "It's so unbeliev-ably hard to comprehend that today is the day she had to leave. Just when we were starting to think she was getting better."

His voice was low and somber in a way that made Louise think her neighbor was using all his strength to talk to her. She wished she were home so she could just walk downstairs to support him.

"I'm coming home now," she said before he had a chance to con-tinue. "I can leave Tåsinge in . . ." She glanced over at Lange.

Twenty minutes, he mouthed.

"Twenty minutes, so I can probably be there by eleven o'clock."

"There's no reason for you to drive all that way," Melvin exclaimed immediately. "There's nothing more we can do right now. I think we all need to get some rest and recover from what's happened."

"Exactly," Louise replied. "I'll come home and be with you."

"You'd better talk to Jonas again," he said and sounded almost apologetic when he continued, "I'm afraid I'll already have gone to bed before you get home."

Louise could hear her son say something in the background and again felt ashamed for thinking that the death couldn't have come at a more inconvenient time for the investigation. She knew she wouldn't be able to provide much support at home because she would be thinking about when she could get back to Tåsinge the whole time. But the three of them comprised their own little family, and Grete had become a part of that family.

"Don't drive home," Jonas decided when he got back on the phone. "I'll stay down here with Melvin tonight. And I can bring Dina down here," he said.

Louise could picture them: a seventy-nine-year-old, a seventeen-year-old, and a deaf Labrador retriever. The three who were the framework of her everyday life. Her security in the life she had cobbled together when she moved back into her apartment after her failed trip around the world.

CHAPTER 16

When they got back to the hotel in Troense, Lange asked if Louise wanted to grab a beer in the bar behind the restaurant. It surprised her a little that it was still open. And that there were people in there. She stood and thought it over for a moment before nodding. She felt like everything inside her had been peeled away, both the hard and the soft. The pain of Grete's death and her guilty conscious about not being with the people who meant the most to her kept bringing tears to her eyes. But then there was that nagging hint of irritation that Grete's death had happened *now*. She was torn, and terribly grateful that Jonas had decided for her that she should stay in Tåsinge.

"Just a draft beer," she replied when Lange asked what she wanted.

"How about a little chaser?" he offered, pointing to a row of bottles of Gammel Dansk, Jägermeister, and whatever other bitters were lined up behind the bar. Louise thought again and was about to shake her head when she heard her colleague order two shots of North Sea Oil, a licorice bitters, and thought that a little shot of alcohol might soothe her. So when he handed her the glass, she thanked him and downed the sticky brown bitters in one gulp, while Lange made do with sipping at his. And she didn't object when he asked the bartender to refill her glass.

They sat down on a couple of the high barstools at the end of the bar, and Louise glanced around. She recognized Jack Skovby's wavy brown hair and broad shoulders right away. He stood with his back to them, talking to two men around his age over by a booth in the rear of the bar. The two men had been shooting craps; the dice were strewn across the table, but the game seemed to have been interrupted when Jack showed up. He had his hands in the pockets of his fleece jacket and talked while the others listened.

A couple sat close together in another booth over by the window. They looked like they were in that stage right before wanting to suggest that they go get themselves a room. Louise felt the heat in her body as she downed her second North Sea Oil. A slow peace settled over her, and she felt a tiny bit dizzy. Not from the alcohol but from the whole day. It felt like a lifetime ago that Eik had turned up unannounced. When she and Lange had returned, she'd noticed Eik's old Jeep out in the parking lot, so she reasoned that he was still here. They hadn't talked since parting ways after he'd tackled the cook to the floor at the inn.

Eik also knew Melvin and Grete. He would understand her grief, but he would also understand her sense of obligation to stay. Eik was here to find the boy, but solving the murder was on her.

Lange still had a little beer left in his glass when he got up and announced that he was heading upstairs.

"I'll see you tomorrow at eight o'clock?" he asked and Louise nodded but remained seated. He eyed her with concern. "Are you okay?"

She nodded again.

"I'm just going to stay for a minute," she said, nodding at the rest of her beer.

"It's totally fine if you need to go to Copenhagen for a couple of days. Everyone will understand and we'll keep at it here while you're gone."

Louise quickly shook her head and thanked him for his concern.

"It's not necessary," she replied, trying to sound competent and even-keeled. "It's fine. Right now the investigation comes first."

She saw his raised eyebrow and heard how hollow her words sounded.

Louise would text Camilla and ask her to take care of Jonas and Melvin so they wouldn't be alone in their grief. Her friend had known her foster son even longer than she had. Jonas and Markus had been in the same class and had been each other's best friend. They still were.

Lange looked at her once more before he nodded and said good night. There was something disconcerting about having to be cheered up by a stranger. Once again her thoughts turned toward Eik, who was just upstairs, probably asleep already.

She nodded when the bartender asked if she wanted another beer. The drink put a pleasant filter over her feelings and made her drowsy. It was now almost ten-thirty. She would have been home soon if she'd set off when they got back.

But now with the alcohol deadening things, she felt even more convinced that it would have been the wrong move to drive home. She wouldn't have been any comfort. She had tried so many times before, tried to be there for someone else while she was in the middle of an investigation. It was never successful. Her mind would have remained entirely focused on Tåsinge. She knew that.

Louise was far away in her own thoughts when someone tapped her on the shoulder.

"Hi," Jack Skovby said.

She turned quickly toward him and discovered that his buddies had gone, only the dice left on the table. The couple in the booth was still there. He with his arm tightly around her and she with her hand dangerously close to his crotch. Louise looked away, embarrassed.

"Hi," she replied.

"Can I buy you another beer?" he asked.

She really wanted to refuse but ended up saying yes anyway.

"Just a small one."

He unzipped his fleece and sat down next to her. He was wearing a dark blue T-shirt that fit tightly across his chest. They sat in silence while the beers were poured.

"How's your investigation coming?" he asked, sounding as if he had copied the dialogue from a detective movie.

Louise watched him for a moment before she answered. When she'd first seen him standing in the bar, her initial impression was that he had just popped his head in to give the other two men a message. But now it seemed like he was ready to pump her for information. And he wouldn't succeed at it, she thought, turning the tables on him.

"You told me earlier today that you've known Dorthe and Nils since they took over Strammelse Inn. How was their relationship?" She was about to pull her arm back from the bar when he set his own right next to hers. Warmth radiated from his skin where it touched hers, and he was so close that she could clearly smell his scent of fresh air and sun-kissed skin. She left her arm where it was.

He started nodding, as if he wanted to confirm what he had said before. But before he said anything, he caught her gaze and made a toast. Louise looked him in the eye and felt her stomach lurch worryingly.

"They had been here several months, maybe half a year, when Nils contacted me. He wanted me to cut down some trees in front of the inn and asked if we could make a deal for me to come mow the grass. We got along well, and when there was something they needed done, they called me."

She wanted to ask what the married couple's relationship had been like but decided to let him talk. There was something urgent about the look in his green eyes. He looked at her as if they already knew each other. It embarrassed her a little, but it was also soothing. She felt less alone in the acute grief vibrating within her, reminding her that death had just taken something from her.

"They got along very well out there," he continued. "And that's not usually so easy for newcomers who move to Tåsinge from outside the area. Those of us who live here are used to a bunch of pottery types coming here and settling down for a while. But they usually move on once they discover that no one wants to buy their junk. So we just wait and see with new people before we accept them."

His arm grazed hers, and he leaned forward a little as he spoke. Louise smiled at the remark about the pottery types. Her own mother was a potter and made a living off the things she made out in her workshop in Lerbjerg. But she understood exactly what he meant.

"I think they were happy living here, and they did a lot to gather people at the inn. They created some traditions for us locals. Æbleskiver and Santa Claus for the kids on the first Sunday in Advent, followed by grilled sausages out back. Nils and the cook were responsible for that, then everyone paid for their own drinks. They always held a midsummer celebration at the inn, too. They arranged the bonfire in the field across from the inn, and we brought our own meat to barbecue. They were good at that sort of thing, so it felt like they really belonged."

Louise was glad she had stayed at the bar instead of heading upstairs with Lange. Jack's deep voice and local Funen dialect calmed her. But she wasn't drinking anymore, only sipping.

"What do you know about the forest cabin that Nils and Dorthe rented out?" she asked without getting into what she herself knew about it.

It was the hesitation behind his eyes before he replied that he didn't know anything about a cabin that convinced Louise that he did. She also figured that someone must have built the deck to have room for the hot tub. Although obviously it could have been someone other than him.

"Did they have a good marriage?" she asked instead, and again he hesitated in that evasive way, as if it unsure how to respond. But then he shrugged.

"I don't actually know," he said. "I didn't see them together very often. When Nils was alive, he was usually the one who called me when he needed my help with something other than mowing the lawn. I mostly only spent time with Dorthe at the inn, at events, or if I took my daughter there to eat."

That fit with the image of the busy innkeepers, which Louise had also heard from other people.

"I have a ten-year-old daughter, who lives with her mother in Copenhagen," he explained. "We separated when Isadora was four. Unfortunately I don't get to see her very often, but when she comes to visit, we have a good time."

He explained to Louise that it had not been a very amicable divorce. The mother had been granted custody and wasn't particularly generous when it came to Jack's desire to spend time with his daughter.

Louise didn't think Jack was whining, exactly, but she couldn't quite figure out if he was upset that he wasn't part of his daughter's life or if it was the mother he missed.

By the time the bartender announced that it was last call, Louise had laughed more than she had in a long time. Jack had a wry view of reality, and she recognized it from her own. She had accepted his attentions and enjoyed the care and interest he'd generously shared when she told him about Grete's death. She'd also learned that he had grown up on the farm he had since taken over from his parents, who were both dead, and he had a dog named Basse, a mix of some kind.

Louise hadn't noticed when the couple in the booth left, and she was thinking, *Maybe they've just slid down underneath the table,* when Jack asked if she wanted one last beer.

She shook her head and said that she should probably head upstairs instead.

Not once had he mentioned anything even hinting at the rumors about Nils or indicated in any way that not everyone in Tåsinge had been equally enthusiastic about the couple who ran the inn. Louise regretted that she might have put too much stock in the statements others had made. If there was no truth to their claim that Nils had been in love with Aske, then she had wasted an entire day looking in the wrong direction.

They didn't have anything on him right now other than the fact that the forest cabin was furnished like a guest room for gay men. There wasn't actually anything wrong with that, she thought, and regretted that she hadn't asked Jack Skovby a few more questions when she'd had the chance.

Jack paid and they both stood up, Louise suddenly feeling awkward that she'd told him about the grief that had landed in the middle of her life. But the tone between them had grown familiar, and she'd needed to sit in a bar and talk to another human being. She hadn't been out with anyone since Eik, and it felt good to be comforted. So when Jack had told her about his failed relationship and his pain at being without his daughter, it had felt natural to tell him about Jonas and their downstairs neighbor.

"Doesn't he have a father who's there at home with him?" he had fished.

But Louise hadn't answered that, and Jack had only smiled and left it at that.

She quickly collected her purse from the floor, then Jack gallantly held the door for her and let her exit the bar first. The restaurant was locked, so they had to go outside and walk around to the hotel's main entrance so she could get in. He walked the few yards over to the door with her.

"Do the police always wrap up their workday in a bar when you're out here in the countryside like this?" he asked as they stood on the sidewalk.

Louise shook her head.

"Today was something special," she replied, noticing her voice choke up as she thought about Grete, Melvin, and Jonas. "Thanks for the company. It was nice to get my mind off things for a while. Fortunately, it's not every day someone you care about dies."

"No, fortunately not," he repeated emphatically. "I still can't wrap my mind around the fact that someone murdered Dorthe. I was very fond of her."

He spread his arms out and pulled Louise into a long hug.

Louise let herself be embraced, inhaling the scent of grass, trees, and wood from his fleece jacket. She had just straightened up to take a step back when she made eye contact with Eik. He'd come around the corner from the end of the building and was now standing behind Jack, carrying a box under his arm.

The whole thing happened so quickly.

Jack let his arms fall, and Eik didn't bat an eye as he stared at her. Then he gave her a brief nod before disappearing into the lobby.

Louise pulled herself free from Jack's embrace and threw out a flustered goodbye.

"We may contact you again," she said awkwardly and far too formally, taking a couple of steps backward.

He held his arms up in a gesture of confusion and tried to make eye contact, but Louise looked down.

"Of course," he said finally. "Just call me if there's anything I can help with."

CHAPTER 17

Frederik and Markus were still asleep when Camilla and Charlie left the apartment in Frederiksberg. It had been tough selling the idea to her editor in chief, Terkel Høyer. She had pitched him her story about the inn in Tåsinge that had a hiding place out in the woods for gay men, but only managed to hook him once she explained that she needed to go out there anyway to return Charlie to Eik and would have direct access to information the police were withholding from the press.

She pulled on a warm sweater, tossed her heavy coat into the basket slung over her shoulder, then shut the lid of the insulated travel mug she had just filled with coffee. She called for Charlie while she searched for his leash.

The police information thing wasn't entirely true, of course, as there didn't seem to be any information about the cabin that was being withheld in the first place. It was the missing boy from the inn that she couldn't tell anyone about yet, but Terkel went for it anyway. Her boss had always had a soft spot when he sniffed an opportunity their media competitors didn't have access to. And she had also reassured him that the newspaper wouldn't have to reimburse her for the bridge toll or her mileage since she had to bring the dog to Tåsinge anyway.

Camilla tossed her basket into the car before taking Charlie for a walk along the sidewalk in Frederiksberg, her affluent Copenhagen neighborhood. Then she realized she had forgotten all about the poop bags. She looked around, but the only person she saw was a jogger across the street who was moving along at a pace that didn't leave time to focus on dog poop, she thought, feeling a little ashamed as the German shepherd pulled in close to the wall of the building and squatted down.

The night before, she had checked out Aske Nørgaard's Facebook and Instagram profiles, and in both places she had found flirtatious references to hookups in the woods, including mentions of the hot tub and champagne.

It wasn't so much the actual flirting on social media that had piqued Camilla's curiosity. It was a picture of Aske taken after he had obviously had the crap beaten out of him. The picture was on Instagram with a caption that read, *When it hurts to be who you are,* alongside a broken heart emoji.

When they made it back to the car, she got Charlie settled and set her GPS to Tåsinge. After seeing Aske's picture, she'd read an article about boys for rent, learning with no small amount of surprise about a thriving gay sugar daddy scene where the pairs often found each other through social media. The article said that while in the past young men mostly turned tricks to survive, nowadays it was more about money and gifts. And to be seen, Camilla had thought. The product was the same, but the packaging was nicer, as the journalist had put it.

She turned on the radio and thought about Aske Nørgaard and the forest cabin. Apparently one of the new things was for young men to sell pictures and videos of themselves in sexual situations either alone or with others. Payment was handled through the MobilePay app.

Camilla had tried to get in touch with Louise, but her friend had not gotten back to her. Instead, she'd caught Eik to ask if Louise was with him. She wasn't, but he said that Camilla should just bring Charlie along, because he was planning to stay in Tåsinge himself.

She had tried picking his brain about the boy and why the police were linking him to the murdered widow, but she didn't get anything out of him. She also didn't get anything out of him when she asked him to buy some poop bags.

"We're in the countryside," was all he said. "We don't use those out here."

She gave up and promised to call later.

The fall morning fog lay thick over the Great Belt Bridge as Camilla crept along behind the red taillights of the vehicle in front of her. The coffee was drunk, and Charlie was snoring in the back seat. She regretted not having eaten before they left and decided to pull into the first gas station after they got across the bridge. Then maybe she could also resolve the poop bag situation while she picked up more coffee and a couple of rolls, one for her and one for Charlie.

She had told Frederik that she had an assignment in Tåsinge, but she hadn't mentioned that she had packed a small bag just in case there was more to the story and she ended up spending the night there.

It hadn't been hard to find Aske's mother when she searched the Krak.dk site for "Nørgaard." She hoped that her call to the mother would kick off a series of articles she had wanted to write for a long time. It was spurred on by the fact that even though there were about thirty terms in Danish for various gender identities, people still weren't able to feel like they fit in, like there was room for them. They didn't feel included, and not enough was being done to make sure they felt welcome. There were already articles about how there weren't changing rooms at the swimming pool that worked for everyone. But to Camilla it was more about people who were in a minority population having a hard time finding their place in society. The ones who stood by themselves, even if that came with costs.

That was the part her editor had rejected point-blank. He didn't think *Morgenavisen*'s readers would be interested in that, and was of the belief that people simply had to decide for themselves whether they wanted to dress like one gender or the other. Or be called "they" instead of "he" or "she." And his reaction was precisely what had convinced Camilla that she should write these articles. Even if she had to do it in her free time. And the gentlest way to start was with a young gay man who had also been attractive without seeming too femme, something else that Terkel didn't care for.

Before Camilla got to Tåsinge, she called Eik to ask where she could meet him to return Charlie. He sounded apologetic when he asked her to hold on to the German shepherd a little longer. He was waiting for an important call that might result in a quick return to Copenhagen, but he would be coming back to Tåsinge after that.

Again he refused to give up any information, and Camilla agreed that they could meet after she had finished her interview.

She had already set up an appointment with Eva Nørgaard: At first Aske's mother had been completely dismissive, but when Camilla explained that she had read about the assault that happened to her son and wanted to write about standing up for who you are, Eva had given in.

Over the phone, the mother had explained that Aske wasn't the only one who had felt the homophobia and outright hatred that was directed at queer individuals. A number of other people in Svendborg, Odense, and Fåborg had also been subjected to that. Camilla already knew this. A quick internet search had unearthed several articles about hate crimes directed at those who stood out in one way or another.

Smoke rose out of the chimney of the little farmhouse as Camilla drove up. The morning fog had lifted, and a gray haze lay over the fields. Eva Nørgaard came to the door as Camilla parked beside the house. She seemed a little nervous, her hands in the pockets of an open cardigan, her eyes following Camilla as she rolled down the back window a little to give Charlie some fresh air while he waited in the car.

Camilla was greeted by the fragrant aroma of fresh coffee as she was led into the low-ceilinged living room where green plants took up most of the light, reminding her of a botanical garden. Between the windows overlooking the road, the dining table had been set. A sugar-dusted roulade cake that had been cut into thick slices waited on a porcelain serving plate.

"When you called, I thought it was to talk about what happened to her over at the inn," Eva said as they sat down across from each other. "I don't want to talk about that, but I do want to speak up for my son."

Camilla nodded and assured her that the interview wouldn't touch on the murder.

"My colleague is covering that case," she explained. "But I've heard about the forest cabin where your son went."

"How did you hear about that?" Eva asked, suddenly seeming a bit guarded.

Camilla considered her words carefully.

"To be completely honest," she began, "it just so happens that my friend Louise Rick is leading the murder investigation, and she asked me to find out if anything has been written about the cabin. To me that's the most interesting thing, because it seems to be an offering targeted at gay men." Camilla paused briefly and leaned back while she looked out the window between the stems of the green plants. Then she turned to Aske's mother again.

"This series of articles is probably geared mostly toward readers who think like I do," she admitted. "I didn't think people's sexual orientation and gender identity still caused problems. But now I see that that was a naïve, big-city view since it does still appear to be something that angers people and draws contempt. And that's just not fucking right."

She put her hands up apologetically, but her anger rose like a bolt of lightning.

"And what's crazy," she continued, "is that young people seem far more open-minded about their orientations when it comes to partners. You fall in love with a person and not with a gender."

Here Eva interrupted her.

"I don't know anything about that," she said. "But I can assure you that being open-minded about gender identity and sexual orientation is not the norm around here."

"No," Camilla conceded. "I see that now. And that's what I'd really like to help change. We shouldn't accept it leading to violence or disgust."

"How are you planning to prevent that?" Eva asked soberly.

"By educating people," Camilla replied, matching the other woman's gravity. "By telling your son's story and showing that there are victims behind hate crimes. And that those victims include young people who are brave enough to stand up and be true to themselves, brave enough not to be ashamed or hide."

Eva had tears in her eyes, and she had begun to nod as Camilla continued.

"I just never thought gay men were something to be looked down on. So many with strong personalities are role models after all. Even on Denmark's *Dancing with the Stars,* two men danced together. And won!"

"Aske never tried to change himself," his mother said. "And I'll be the first to admit that sometimes he pushed the boundaries when it came to showing who he was. I don't think he was any older than sixteen when he let himself be photographed as a model in a men's magazine. And that wasn't something he went behind our backs to do. He was completely open about it. He was curious, searching."

She paused for a moment before she continued. "And I also think he was driven by his own desires. He didn't feel there was anything wrong with it. It really pushed his father's buttons, but Aske didn't care. He defended himself by pointing out that his father would sit and drool over the page-nine girls in *Ekstra Bladet*. And he was definitely right about that."

She smiled slightly.

"He was good at defending himself and good at showing how what he felt and wanted was no different. But that was not how his father saw it."

"But you backed him up?" Camilla said, pulling out her phone once Eva had given her permission to record their conversation.

"Yes, whether it was him or a young woman allowing themselves to be photographed semi-naked, it didn't matter to me," she replied. "But for my son, I think it was mostly an attempt to make a stand for his cause. That's what I thought in the beginning anyway, but then he started to change."

"How so?" Camilla asked.

Eva sat for a moment, staring down at the table. Neither of them had touched the cake, but Camilla drank some of her coffee to give Eva time to collect herself.

"The assault," she finally replied. "I suppose that was really when it changed, even though I thought it came long after that."

Camilla nodded solemnly. "I saw the picture on Aske's Instagram."

Eva paused again and took a sip of coffee.

"He changed," she explained slowly. "By that point, my husband and I had gotten divorced and that gave us a little more peace here at home. Maybe this sounds wrong, but it was as if his father's disgust . . ."

She hesitated briefly, then corrected herself, saying that it was more denial than disgust.

"He wouldn't accept that his son was gay, and maybe we could have preserved the peace at home if Aske had shown more restraint. But I would never agree to that. I was proud that he stood up for himself, that he wasn't ashamed of anything. That's how I raised both my children. But at some point it seemed as if his joy vanished, as if everything that had shot off sparks and invigorated him was extinguished. It wasn't so obvious right after the attack. It took about a year before I realized that he was sick."

She paused again, and when she continued, her voice was choked up. "I blame myself for not paying more attention, for not seeing it."

She looked up at Camilla.

"But it came in several stages. First the assault, which was awful. When the hospital discharged him there was a long period when he seemed insecure and unsure of himself. Then once I started to believe that he was doing better, mentally and physically, it was as if he withdrew into himself even more."

Eva topped off their coffee, as if she needed a breather before she could continue. Her eyes were wet with tears.

"You don't understand what it's like to watch your child fall apart and fade away before your very eyes," she said, her gaze on the table. "I don't think he realized where he was headed himself."

"What happened?" Camilla asked.

"He was starving himself. He was in such terrible shape. And it was awful to witness because I couldn't do anything. He was searching for something in a way he couldn't handle, and I think he drove himself to a point where he couldn't stop."

"Was he selling himself?" Camilla asked, afraid the question was too direct, but Eva didn't seem shocked.

"We never talked about that," she replied. "But it was as if all the joy and desire he had, had vanished. He became more cynical, if that makes sense."

Camilla shook her head, not understanding.

"It hardened him," Eva tried to explain, "as if in some way he had started to loathe himself, too."

Now the mother cried outright, quickly wiping away her tears with the little napkin that sat next to the cake plate.

"That was what hurt the most," she whispered, "what I had the most trouble understanding."

Camilla had planned to talk to Eva about the men her son had seen. About the resistance he had encountered from the local community, and the strength he had shown to his own father by not being ashamed. But right now those questions faded in the grief that had settled over Aske's mother.

They sat for a while in the silence that had arisen, then Camilla stood up and thanked Eva for having taken the time to talk.

"I'm really glad that you want to contribute, and I'll send you a copy of the article once it's finished. It's also possible that a few more questions may come up, so I hope it's all right if I call you if that happens?"

Eva got up to see Camilla out.

"You're welcome to call, and you're also welcome to come by again. Although it's probably a bit of a long trip for you, of course."

Camilla smiled at her in response.

"We didn't even get to eat the cake," Eva said, as if it had just occurred to her that maybe she should have served it. "You could take a piece with you."

"Now you're tempting me," Camilla said, nearly stepping forward to give this woman she barely knew a hug. There was a strength in Eva's grief that Camilla liked. And she could easily imagine the disagreements between Eva and her husband when the woman was defending her son. "I'm just trying to get an overview of the article so I can see if I'm missing anything. And then you'll hear from me."

"It's a deal," Eva said, waving as Camilla walked to her car.

Charlie had stood up in the back of the car and had his nose against the window, tail wagging when Camilla got in.

CHAPTER 18

Louise went upstairs for more tea. She had kidnapped a large glass from the hotel kitchen, taken two tea bags to make the tea extra strong, and added sugar and milk in hopes that the liquid would soothe her hangover. She had slept fitfully, waking up several times with a tingling sensation in her body. At seven o'clock, she had talked to Jonas to hear how he and Melvin were doing.

Their downstairs neighbor was still asleep, and her son said that he would be done at school at noon. Once he got home, he and Melvin would find an undertaker.

"We also need to figure out where she'll be buried," he said.

Louise couldn't help wondering if it was too much for a seventeen-year-old to be involved in this sort of thing. But she also knew she wouldn't be able to talk him out of it. Melvin was his friend, and her son would do what he could to help him. Grete didn't have any other family since her adult daughter had died.

"Are you coming home for the funeral?" Jonas had asked.

She'd immediately exclaimed that of course she was, her guilt at not already being there hitting her like a punch to the chest. But her son seemed collected, and both he and Melvin had slept. That comforted her a little.

She took a Spandauer pastry from the basket that the server had left behind when cleaning up after breakfast. Louise hoped that with the right mixture of salt and sugar she could stabilize herself following all the beer and North Sea Oil chasers. First, she'd eaten scrambled eggs with extra bacon. Now for the sweet. She had just returned to the table, where Lange sat concentrating on his laptop, when Eik walked into the hotel restaurant.

Louise quickly turned away and watched a middle-aged woman who came bicycling along with a rolled-up towel on her bike rack, heading for the swimming dock at the marina.

"Hi," Eik said, making a point to be loud as he came over to their table.

She pulled herself together and reluctantly turned toward him, knowing she needed to shake off her embarrassment that he had caught her in another man's arms. She didn't owe him anything, and they both knew that.

When their eyes met, she knew instantly that something was wrong, something that was far more serious than the awkward situation they had found themselves in the night before.

Eik pulled out a chair and sat down next to Lange, who was working on his fourth or fifth cup of coffee. Lange had suggested that they use the hotel restaurant for their office this morning instead of driving to the police station in Svendborg.

Louise had been reading the reports Borre and Sindal had sent regarding Nils Hyllested's dealings with the gay community in Copenhagen, while Lange dove into the information that Lisa Lindén had brought in that morning.

A remarkable number of guests named Jens Jensen continued to show up in the Strammelse Inn reservation system, even though the forest cabin no longer seemed to be in use. Louise's head was far too tired to completely understand what that meant, but Lange had asked Lindén to move heaven and earth to find out who was hiding behind those anonymous reservations. Someone still didn't want to admit to staying at the inn.

Lange offered to get Eik a cup of coffee, but Eik shook his head. The look on his face made Louise scoot forward in her chair.

"The results are back from the DNA analysis from the child's bedroom," he announced. "I've just come from the police station in Odense."

Lange nodded and Louise realized that the two of them must have spoken earlier that morning. If Eik had managed to pressure the forensic genetics crew in Copenhagen to expedite evaluation of the pillowcase, that was because he had convinced them that as soon as he got the results, he had something to go on, something she didn't know about.

"Well done," she said, nodding appreciatively at them.

Eik pressed a piece of nicotine gum out of the package and stuffed it into his mouth before he took a deep breath and continued. "The DNA had a match," he said, then fell silent.

Louise and Lange watched him expectantly while he stared down at the table for a moment, chewing his gum so intently that his jaws bulged. Then he looked up, as if waiting for a reaction that wasn't coming.

Eik ran his hands through his straight dark hair and then propped his elbows on the table.

"There's a good reason that no one has asked about him or come forward." He fell silent again.

Louise knew him well enough to know that this was not a good sign.

"Out with it," she said, sounding more annoyed than she'd intended.

"The boy from the room is named Simon Funch and he's from North Zealand," he continued.

"North Zealand!" she repeated, shocked and cursing herself for not having brought a couple of headache pills downstairs with her. The ones she had taken when she woke up were already wearing off.

Eik looked at her and nodded.

"And," he continued somberly, "the boy is presumed to have died in a plane crash two years ago, when a small private jet crashed here, outside Tåsinge. Only one person survived: the boy's mother. His father and his two older siblings died in the crash and were later recovered from the water."

"But that can't be right," Lange exclaimed, and Eik shook his head again.

"No, it can't," he agreed. "But the boy's body was never found. After he disappeared in the water, a major search was launched, which we were involved in. And he was marked as missing in all the registries. The Missing Persons Department gathered everything on him at the time and since he was too young to have a dental profile, we got a court order that allowed us to obtain the boy's PKU card from the Statens Serum Institut."

Louise looked at him in surprise. The police rarely succeeded in gaining access to PKU cards, because the heel-prick blood tests that were done on newborns just after birth were carefully guarded. They were physically stored in a secure cabinet in a separate DNA database than the one the police normally had access to.

"Based on the PKU card, we were able to determine the boy's DNA profile. That way, it would be possible to identify the child if he turned up later on. Normally bodies wash ashore within a week or two. But it can also take longer and occasionally we do see Danish bodies wash ashore in Germany or Poland. That's why it was important to create a DNA profile at the time if we wanted to identify him later."

"But the boy in the room was there recently," Louise exclaimed. "The breakfast in the bowl was practically fresh."

Eik nodded slowly as the three of them digested the information.

"When you asked if we had a missing or wanted boy aged about four or five, I have to admit that I didn't have Simon Funch in my mind at all. We gave up hope of finding him alive a long time ago," Eik said apologetically as he looked at Louise.

"So, you think it could be him," Lange finally said. "There is some degree of uncertainty, though, when it comes to DNA."

"It's him," Eik said. "You're right that in principle there could be two or three people with the same profile, but in this case the age, location, and circumstances also play into it. So I can say with certainty that we have a match. That also fits with the fact that Simon Funch would be about four years old today."

"We need to get ahold of the mother," Lange said, already on his feet.

"No," Louise said firmly, noting with relief that the fog in her head was burning off. "We need to know more about the plane crash before we track down the mother. We need to confirm every-thing we can before we tell someone her son was here at the inn for the last two years while she's been walking around thinking he was dead."

Eik nodded.

"There has to be an explanation," Lange said, mostly to him-self. "How in the world would the boy, if it is him, have wound up with Dorthe?"

"I'm thinking more about what it must have been like for the mother, who has lived for two years with the grief of having lost three children. Plus her husband," Eik said. "I wasn't personally in-volved in the case back then. Olle handled it."

Louise quickly gathered her things.

"We leave for the police station in Svendborg in five min-utes," she said, already on her way up to her room to grab her purse and coat.

When Louise came back downstairs again, Eik was standing by the front desk waiting for her. Either Lange was already outside, or he wasn't ready yet.

"You seemed like you were having a good time last night," Eik said. Louise could tell he was trying to make it sound like a casual remark.

She was about to tell him that Grete had passed away the previ-ous evening, that she should have driven home to Jonas and Melvin but instead had chosen to stay, that she had sat in the bar and drunk beer while feeling ashamed that her work felt more important than an old friend's death. But she didn't say any of that.

"I was in good company," she responded instead.

"I just think you should know that your new beau did time for murder after he killed his father with an ax. Apparently he had only just turned seventeen at the time, and of course people can always change for the better."

And then he was out the door before Louise could react.

She was still standing there at the front desk when Lange came down the stairs waving a car key to indicate that he would be driving. She wondered fleetingly if he knew she had stayed in the bar and might still have a slight spike in her blood alcohol level, but she just nodded.

When they reached the parking lot, Eik was backing out.

"See you at the police station?" she called to his open side window, where cigarette smoke swirled out in a column.

He shook his head.

Louise watched his Jeep pull away from the hotel.

"I remember that plane crash quite well," Lange said once they were out on the road.

Louise had called the police station and asked Lene Borre to gather everything they had on the plane crash, the recovery work, and the search that followed when the body of the little boy wasn't found in the water. And the conversations they had had subsequently with the survivor.

Borre had seemed to be at a loss, but Louise promised to explain as soon as they arrived.

"At the time, I thought it was almost worse for the mother, who survived," Lange said. "Imagine being left behind when you've seen your whole family die, your husband and three children. It would be hard to move on."

Louise agreed.

"Unbearable," she said. "I wonder what's become of her."

He shrugged.

"I don't remember very much being written about the accident afterward. Sometimes the press has the decency to respect people's grief. And I suppose there wasn't that much to write about. It was a tragic accident."

"What happened?" Louise asked. They had reached Svendborg and were approaching the police station. He drove through the security gate into the inner lot where the police vehicles were, then parked around back.

Sindal was ready to receive them when they came in.

"Could it really be him?" the young investigator asked as they walked down a sad hallway to the office that had been cleared out for them.

"The DNA showed a match," Louise merely replied.

Borre looked pale when they stepped into the office.

"It's true that the body of the youngest was never found," she confirmed. "When the bodies of those who had died were recovered and brought ashore after the plane sank, he was gone. A major search was launched, and we worked on the theory that the boy had been caught in an undertow and carried out into the South Funen Archipelago. I was the one who was in touch with the Missing Persons Department at the time. We'd hoped that he would wash up onshore somewhere, so Helene could bury her youngest."

All four of them took their seats in the empty office.

Borre rubbed her face with her hands and shook her head.

"It can't be right," she said. "There must be a mistake. I just don't see how in the world he could have been living in Strammelse Inn. I mean, everyone was looking for him."

Lange nodded, while Sindal just stared at the stack of police reports. Most of it had been digitized, but there were pictures from the accident, pictures of the deceased from both before and after the small plane had crashed. They'd also printed out the witness statements so they could all read them.

Louise studied the stack of papers.

"Could you tell us what happened back then?" she asked, looking at Borre and thinking that they would probably get better information from her because she'd worked on the original case.

Borre nodded, visibly composing herself.

"As I said, I took part in the search," she began. "A major rescue and recovery operation was launched immediately after the accident. At first, of course, the focus was on getting Helene Funch to the hospital and recovering the others from the wreckage. The plane had sunk, but witnesses had seen where it crashed. When we arrived, Helene was unconscious. She was brought ashore out near Vornæs Woods, and she was still unconscious when the ambulance picked her up. Then they searched for more survivors. At that point we didn't know if there were any other passengers on the plane."

Lange took notes as his colleague spoke.

"The bodies of the father, a son, and a daughter were recovered. And, like I said, when they didn't find the youngest boy, an intense search was initiated. It lasted forty-eight hours. After that we contacted the Missing Persons Department, who took over—with our assistance, of course."

It was clear that she was moved by the accident, and she must have noticed her own loud and slightly hectic tone—she brought a hand up to her chest, as if trying to calm herself down.

"A search was underway onshore at the same time, in the hope that the boy had drifted ashore. But the wind and weather conditions instead indicated that he was carried away by the current.

"Everyone was very moved by the tragedy that struck the family. I feel it still. I was the one who looked after Helene Funch. She was hospitalized in Odense and suffered a complete breakdown when she realized that she was the only one who had survived the crash."

"When did this happen?" Louise asked.

"October 2017. It was the first Monday of the schools' fall break. I remember that because some of my coworkers had taken time off to go on vacation with their kids."

She pushed a clear plastic folder across the table, and Lange pulled out some pictures of the family, the parents and three children. A tall, dark-haired man with his shirtsleeves rolled up, a blond woman with a boy in her arms, and a boy and a girl all smiled at the photographer. Another picture showed only the youngest boy, dark-haired like his father, but otherwise resembling his mother with her same fine features, eyes squinting at the sun.

"He was two then," Borre confirmed.

There was also a picture of the parents alone: Helene and Kristian Funch. They had their arms around each other in front of a large house, and on the flagstones next to them sat a black Lab, looking regal, as if he owned the place.

Louise picked up the photograph and studied the woman. *Maybe thirty-seven*, she thought. The eldest child was probably in first or second grade. Helene Funch leaned her smiling head on her husband's shoulder. Her blond hair was twisted together and gathered at the nape of her neck, and she wore her sunglasses pushed up on top of her head.

"What happened to her?" she asked, looking at Borre.

Her colleague shook her head.

"I don't actually know. They were from North Zealand, but I think she was living on a farm out in Bjernemark after the accident. That's a few miles from Strammelse Inn. I was in touch with her some in the beginning, but it's been a long time now since we've spoken to each other."

Lange pointed to the boy the mother was holding in the family photo.

"So it's true that Simon Funch would be about four or five years old today," he established. Borre nodded. "Did you ever find out what caused the accident?"

"The weather conditions," she replied. "The plane was on its approach to land at the airport but crashed into the archipelago. The Accident Investigation Board was brought in immediately after it happened, but there was no indication of mechanical failure.

"The family took off from Grønholt Airport in North Zealand on Monday around noon, and we received the emergency call from a sailor in the area who had seen the plane crash."

She found the folder containing the Accident Investigation Board's report and witness statements and began to read out loud.

"The plane was owned by the Funch Alarm Systems Company. It was a Piper Cherokee Six PA-32-300, well maintained. The company plane could operate from smaller airports with grass airstrips, and it was used by the company's sales team and installation specialists when they traveled around the country presenting products, making bids, and installing the alarm systems. All of the smaller Danish islands have grass airstrips and the larger customers such as estates and manor houses often have serviceable grass fields where the plane could land."

The others listened quietly. Sindal had stepped out and now returned with an insulated carafe and cups. Lange nodded contentedly as the coffee was poured.

"The plane crash occurred on Monday, October 16, 2017, at one-ten p.m. There was a southerly wind, fog, and drizzle with low clouds at the time of the accident," she continued. "According to the Danish Meteorological Institute, the aviation forecast was for southerly winds, reduced visibility due to drizzle, and low clouds until after a front passed. Then they predicted the weather would clear up and there would be showers and westerly winds later in the afternoon."

She looked up from the piece of paper to see if they were following.

"At the time we interviewed a local pilot at the airport who had witnessed the accident. He explained that it wasn't exactly a day where you could follow the visual flight rules to land on a grassy field on South Funen. Funch must have planned the route to avoid flying over towns on the way and also made sure to keep a good distance from antennae and tall wind turbines. He thought that the mood on the plane would probably have been rather tense crossing the Great Belt since the required crossing altitude and glide ratio could not be achieved. But he also said that Kristian Funch was an experienced pilot and had done it before. He knew the route well and had flown over here many times before."

She glanced down at the report again.

"After they crossed the Great Belt, they followed the east coast of Funen and flew southwest toward Svendborg Sound."

Borre's eyes teared up, Louise noticed, but her voice remained steady.

"According to Helene Funch's own witness testimony to the Accident Investigation Board, just before the right turn toward Svendborg at Skårupøre there was a reduced ceiling, and the visibility was so bad it was essentially zero. Her husband was only able to see anything vertically downward. The passage south of Svendborg was too risky since the minimum altitude over urban areas couldn't be met. So therefore they followed the coast around Thurø and flew over Tåsinge Island after they passed Nørreskov on the right-hand side. When they reached Vornæs Woods and the coast, he began his descent with a long, gentle turn to the right out over the water."

She pulled one last piece of paper out of the folder.

"The summary version of the Accident Investigation Board's conclusion was that, 'during his approach to Tåsinge runway 11, the pilot did not recognize an unintended loss of altitude and increasing banking during the final portion of the approach, because all of his attention was probably directed toward the visual identification of the threshold to runway 11.'"

She paused and looked up to see if they understood.

"According to the witness at the airport, the right wingtip made contact with the surface of the water," she continued. "This slowed the plane's momentum, and it cartwheeled almost full circle and crashed just beyond the shallows. Three people died in the accident while Helene Funch and the littlest one remained alive. According to Helene Funch, water poured in the passenger door behind the pilot on the left side, but she managed to open the door lock at the top of the crew door on her side. She got herself and her son into life jackets before she—with Simon in her arms—slid out onto the wing and down into the water to get away from the fuselage before it sank. She lost consciousness in the water and rescue crews managed to bring her to shore, but they never found the boy."

"So the mother assumed he was dead?" Sindal concluded from over by the wall, where he had sat down on a low filing cabinet.

"That's what we all assumed," Borre replied, nodding to her younger colleague. "And to be honest, I still believe that. The police would have been informed if he'd been found. So many locals helped search for him. It was a big deal here in South Funen at the time."

Lange nodded.

"But you wouldn't know if someone kept him hidden after they found him," he said.

The room went quiet.

"No," Borre admitted, "we wouldn't."

CHAPTER 19

The air seemed stagnant, and the silence weighed heavily between them, everyone trying to make logical sense of information that none of them could make any sense of. Louise was the one to finally break the silence.

"If we imagine that Helene Funch discovered that Dorthe Hyllested had secretly taken in the son that Helene believed she had lost, you could easily expect a violent reaction," she said, feeling the goose bumps rise on both arms at the thought of the mother suddenly becoming aware that for two years her son had been so close by. You could hardly blame her if she murdered Dorthe after that, she thought.

"It would provide a motive for the murder at any rate," Lange conceded.

"But then where's the boy now?" Sindal asked and then answered himself. "With his mother?"

The others nodded and agreed that that was likely.

"But we need to be absolutely sure that it's her son who was staying in Dorthe's apartment before we go see Helene Funch," Lange said sensibly. "It would be cruel to awaken her hope and then snatch it away from her again."

Borre had fallen silent. She pulled out a chair and sat down.

"We can't be any more sure," Louise replied, her thoughts drifting to Eik. She wondered why he had just driven away, and then it hit her that he might have gone to see the boy's mother.

"Might I suggest that we talk to Jon Isaksen before we get in touch with Helene?" Sindal said, looking up at them. "He's worked at the inn for a long time, so he should be able to tell us what Dorthe's relationship with Helene was like."

"Did they know each other?" Lange asked, looking at Borre.

Borre shrugged.

"I don't know, but I agree with Sindal. Before we plunge in, we need to find out if there's a connection between Helene and Dorthe," she replied. "When you meet Helene, you'll find she doesn't exactly resemble the woman in the pictures. I mean, I didn't know her before the accident, but after it happened, she was listless and distracted. She seemed despondent, and even though I didn't know her, I could tell that she had changed."

"Is it possible that Helene made a deal with Dorthe to have her watch her son because she was clinically depressed? That might make sense," Lange suggested.

"But then Helene Funch would have been the first person to contact us after the murder," Sindal pointed out. "She would have come to see us right away to make sure that her son hadn't been injured."

Louise straightened up.

"Wait," she interrupted. "If they had found the boy, he wouldn't still be on the Missing Persons Department list, would he? We need to try to stay focused. What did Helene say at the time? Let's hear her whole witness statement."

She looked over at Borre and tried to concentrate.

Her colleague pulled up the witness statement Helene Funch had given while she was in the hospital in Odense. It appeared that she had been sitting in the front of the plane next to her husband and had had Simon strapped into a harness in her lap. The two bigger kids were sitting in back. The small, six-person private plane was, as previously described, owned by Kristian Funch's security company. He was an experienced pilot who had had his pilot's license for fifteen years and had often flown his family over to their vacation home in Tåsinge.

Borre began to read.

"We had had a bumpy ride coming over. My daughter got airsick and was throwing up, so I was holding a bag for her while I had Simon in my lap. Kristian seemed tense and was concentrating on looking for the runway. He descended lower and made one last turn before landing. I could see the white contours of the runway's threshold markings but was busy with my daughter and wanted to seal up the barf bag before the wheels touched down on the grass. I was sitting backward, facing her, and Simon started to cry in my lap. I didn't realize what was happening, but the plane suddenly banked violently to the right. Kristian tried to correct, but the plane practically fell out of the sky. There was a deafening noise when we hit the water."

Borre looked up. Her eyes were again filled with tears, and she didn't try to hide the fact that this was upsetting to her.

"It's like hitting concrete at that speed," she explained. "According to the search and rescue crew, the wreckage lay at a depth of eight feet not far from the coast. Helene went on to say that it was completely silent after that. She saw blood and the three lifeless bodies. The water poured in the crumpled passenger door on the left side by the two children in back. She described herself as heavily dazed and couldn't explain in any more detail what had happened. Everything had seemed normal, she said, until he lost control just before landing. It took a second before she realized that Simon was also alive and then she prioritized getting herself and her son into life jackets. She got the lock of the crew door open and made it out onto the wing before the plane sank."

"I agree with Sindal," Louise said. "Before we even consider arresting Helene Funch with the intent of charging her for the murder of Dorthe Hyllested, we need to know how well those two knew each other."

Borre let out an exclamation that clearly indicated that she thought they had it all wrong. But she merely shook her head exaggeratedly instead of objecting further.

Louise looked at Sindal.

"You and Lange drive to Bjernemark and keep an eye on the house, but don't go in," she said before turning to Borre. "The two of us will have a chat with Jon Isaksen. Once we've talked to him and know if there's a connection between Dorthe and Helene, we'll join Lange and Sindal. Once we're out there, it will be best if you take the lead when we talk to her since you two already know each other."

Borre didn't seem enthusiastic, but she nodded and stood up nonetheless.

They found the chef from Strammelse Inn out behind the apartment building where he lived, a few minutes' drive from the Svendborg police station. Jon Isaksen was working on his car, kneeling as he vacuumed the carpets. He obviously recognized Louise after the episode in the inn's kitchen, and quickly got to his feet and turned off the vacuum.

"Is there any news?" he asked as he came over to meet them.

Louise shook her head and said they had come to ask him a question.

He seemed uncomfortable but nodded willingly.

"Do you know Helene Funch from over in Bjernemark?" Borre asked.

She was about to explain, but he nodded before she had a chance to say anything more.

"Yes," he replied. "We deliver food to her. We've been doing that ever since the accident."

"Food?" Borre repeated.

"Dorthe usually drove it over there herself twice a week, but there were meals for all seven days of the week. When Dorthe couldn't bring it over, I did it. We also deliver to several of the elderly people in the area."

A shadow slipped over his face, and he slowly brought a hand up over his mouth as if something had just occurred to him.

"They haven't been notified," he said then. "I haven't informed them that the kitchen is closed. They would have received their meals today."

"Tell me about the arrangement Dorthe had with Helene Funch," Louise resumed.

"We make a weekly menu that just needs to be reheated. It might be meatballs in a curry sauce, chicken with asparagus, you know, prepared meals from the restaurant. That makes it easy for our customers. And in addition to that, we include sandwich fixings and bread, so they have food for lunches and such. The elderly folks who have a hard time grocery shopping are very happy about the service. It was something Nils came up with way back when. But for Helene Funch, I think it was more about her not wanting to leave the farm. I never see her anywhere. Before the accident, she and her husband used to come to the inn regularly. Especially when they were just here for the weekend and didn't feel like it was worth stocking up their fridge."

Louise nodded, thinking that an arrangement like that would be just the thing for Melvin. And, come to think of it, for her and Jonas, too.

"We prepare meals for eighteen people twice a week."

"So Dorthe went out to Helene Funch's place twice a week with food?" Louise asked to make sure she understood.

He nodded.

"Did they see each other apart from that? Socially, I mean."

He looked at her blankly, then shook his head.

"No! They weren't friends if that's what you mean. I don't think they knew each other aside from the business with the food. Our customers just make a regular bank transfer and then they get food for a whole month. You can also have breakfast delivered, but most of our customers don't opt for that. They're only interested in having a little lunch and then dinner."

Again, he appeared to be struck by the fact that the elderly customers hadn't been informed that the inn's kitchen had been shut down.

"Maybe I can still make it," he said. "Would it be okay with you if I serve the customers from my home instead? Just until someone figures out what will happen to the inn. If someone takes it over, maybe they'll decide to continue the prepared meal deliveries."

Louise nodded and said that she didn't see anything wrong with his making sure there was food for the people who had paid for it.

"But what you're saying," she continued, "is that the food deliveries were the only contact between Dorthe and Helene Funch?"

He nodded quickly, already seeming lost to considerations of what he would have time to cook and deliver.

"I've never seen them together. And when we deliver food to the farmhouse, Helene doesn't even always come to the door. Sometimes we just leave it out front. Other times she takes it, but it's not like you get invited in. At many of the other people's homes, they do ask us in even though there's not really time for it."

Louise and Borre quickly exchanged a glance before they thanked the chef for his time and returned to the car.

"It seems completely implausible that Dorthe would have kept Simon hidden from his mother while also keeping Helene alive by making sure she received food," Borre said, shooting Louise a look that displayed her disbelief in even sharper relief than her words had.

"Yeah," Louise agreed. "It seems pretty unlikely. And cruel."

CHAPTER 20

The rain poured down and the wipers chased back and forth across the windshield as they drove up the long driveway to the Bjerne-mark farm. On one side of the road leading to the gravel courtyard in front of the farm was a fir tree orchard; on the other side, an expanse of open fields. The main building was whitewashed and well maintained. The crowns of several tall trees rose behind the house, rustling in the fall wind.

Borre pulled in behind Lange and Sindal, who had stopped alongside a rustic wooden fence by the side of the road. They quickly ran over to the Volvo through the rain to fill their colleagues in on the information they had received from the chef.

"There can't have been any agreement between Helene and Dorthe," Louise said. "It doesn't sound like they had any contact at all aside from the business with the food, which was delivered twice a week."

"It makes no sense that Helene knew, or even suspected, that her son was still alive," Borre interrupted. "And it's absurd to imagine that she murdered Dorthe. The plane crash was two years ago and in all that time her world has been in ruins. If the boy had been found, that would have come out. She would have contacted the police if she suspected that her son was alive and living at the inn. Of course she would have."

She nearly snorted at the ridiculousness of any other possibility.

"Look, I'm not going in there with you," she finished. "If you want to go in and throw these accusations in her face, you'll have to do it without me."

"You don't need to come," Louise said quickly. "And I wouldn't dream of going in and throwing accusations in her face. But I'm sure you understand that we need to talk to her. If it is her son, we need to know where he is. And if he's not with his mother, we need to get out there and search for him."

Again, she thought about Eik and wondered if he was already several steps ahead of them. From where they had stopped, they could see the courtyard in front of the farmhouse, but she couldn't see any cars parked there. And certainly not an old, worn-out Jeep Cherokee.

Lange turned around to face them in the back seat.

"Louise and I will go in and talk to her," he decided, and Louise nodded. Her hangover from the morning had finally completely evaporated. Still, it was nice to have someone around who was a little faster at making decisions. She wasn't quite firing on all pistons yet.

"You two go back to the inn and go through the apartment one more time. Focus on finding more that can be tied to Simon Funch. Anything at all," Louise told Borre and Sindal. "See if his name appears anywhere, or if the deceased wrote anything about him.

Maybe she was especially interested in newspaper articles from when the plane crashed. She may have hidden them."

She pictured the dark-haired boy in the photo and wondered if there was anything else.

"Look for hairbrushes and toothbrushes," she added. "Be even more attentive this time. We have a lead now."

"If it's him, that is," Borre muttered, annoyed, but Louise ignored her.

Louise got out of the back seat to signal that it was time to get going.

"We'll text you as soon as we know how Helene Funch feels about the DNA analysis."

Borre had also gotten out of the car. She walked around to Louise now, so they were facing each other with rainwater pouring down their faces.

"You can't simply walk up to her and tell her that her son has been living at the inn," she said, now sounding seriously angry. "You don't seem to have the slightest idea how awful it must be to lose a child. To lose more than one. Imagine what it would be like years later, to have the prospect that the child might still be alive dangled in front of you only to then find out that we don't know where he is. Does she have to lose her youngest son all over again? You should think long and hard before you do this to her."

Louise let her rage. Sindal and Lange wisely remained in the car while Borre chewed her out.

"First of all," Louise began calmly, "I do not intend to go in and raise her hopes. But as the head of this murder investigation, it is my job to find out who killed Dorthe Hyllested, and now that it turns out that there's a child involved, I also intend to find out what has become of that child."

She paused for a moment. The silence echoed between them.

"I completely understand your concern," she continued then. "And it hasn't escaped my attention that the plane crash affected you. But you also need to understand that in an investigation like this one, situations will often arise in which one is forced to bring things out into the light, and it's not always possible to wear kid gloves and consider people's feelings. Because, as you know, it's people's feelings that often lead to murder."

Louise took a deep breath and wiped her face. She had had her say, but she wasn't entirely sure that it would clear the air between them. She walked over to the front door on the passenger side and opened it. Sindal quickly got out, and she got in.

"Let's drive over there," she told Lange, choosing not to comment on her disagreement with Borre.

The woman who opened the door was big, much bigger than in the pictures Louise had seen at the police station. It wasn't exclusively because Helene Funch had gained a fair amount of weight since the photos were taken. It seemed more as if her body had let go and flowed outward. There was something almost masculine about her figure and expression, very little left of the fine, delicate woman who had stood with her family smiling up at the sun.

"Yes?" she said measuredly, remaining in the doorway while she waited to receive an explanation for why they had come. She was wearing loose-fitting jeans with dirt around the knees and a thick sweater, which was unraveling around the armholes and had a big hole on one elbow.

Louise introduced herself and explained that they were investigating the murder of Dorthe Hyllested.

"May we come in?" she asked.

It was clear that Helene Funch wanted to say no, but she reluctantly stepped back a little and nodded. She pointed to the living room to the right of the front door and asked them to follow her.

Louise took in the grand, high-ceilinged entryway and the staircase that curved attractively up to the second floor, but the house still seemed lifeless and dark. She also noticed that Helene Funch was dragging her right leg as she walked, as if she had trouble getting it to keep up with her.

She knew from the police report that the mother had suffered a complex leg fracture in the plane crash, a broken collarbone, and a collapsed lung. There had been several operations on the leg, and she had been left permanently disabled.

"Have a seat," she said in a voice that didn't sound much louder than a whisper, pointing to two armchairs. Then, with a bit of difficulty, she sat down on the sofa across from them.

"I assume that you've heard about Dorthe Hyllested's murder," Louise began, and Helene Funch nodded. "We know from the chef at Strammelse Inn that they delivered food to you."

Again she nodded but didn't say anything.

"How well did you know Dorthe?"

Lange had remained silent, but there was something calm and confidence-inspiring about the way he sat, leaning back and following the conversation. He was the one Helene Funch spoke to when she answered.

"I didn't really know her other than that we said hello when she brought the food. Sometimes we exchanged a few words, and we also drank coffee together once or twice. And when the others were still alive, sometimes we ate down at the inn."

She spoke quietly and sadly. Her voice didn't change when she mentioned her family, Louise noted. She just spoke.

"It's incomprehensible that a murder could happen out here. It's so quiet and peaceful," Helene Funch continued. "As I said, it's been a long time since I've been to the inn in person. Not since the summer before the accident. So that would have been July or August 2017."

"And when did you last see Dorthe?" Lange asked.

She looked away while she thought it over, then she shrugged a little hesitantly.

"The days blend together, and I don't always notice when they come with the food. Often it's the chef who drops it off. Sometimes Jack brings it into the kitchen for me."

"Jack?" Lange asked, seizing on that.

Helene Funch looked up at him.

"He helps me," she explained. "He takes care of the farm and the land. He's the one who's in charge of maintaining the whole thing, both the house and the garden. And then he does the shopping for me and generally helps out."

She pointed first down at her leg and then at her shoulder.

"Result of the accident," she explained. "I don't have as much strength as I once did, so I'm limited in how much I can take care of myself. Jack handles the heavy lifting, and I put my energy toward the greenhouse and garden beds."

She nodded toward the back of the house.

There was something distant about her, Louise thought, something remote, as if she weren't fully present, not really participating in the life she still found herself in.

Helene cleared her throat and straightened up a bit in her chair.

"No," she said a little more clearly. "I can't say that I knew Dorthe. We were only in touch with each other about the meal plan she offered me. And I actually can't remember when I saw her last. Maybe last week, maybe the week before."

"So you haven't been to the inn recently?" Louise confirmed.

She shook her head right away.

"I haven't been to the inn since my husband and children were with me." She sounded slightly more irritable.

"Where were you Tuesday morning when Dorthe Hyllested was murdered?" Louise asked.

The confusion in Helene's eyes was so clear that for a second she didn't seem to understand the question. Then she pulled herself together and explained that she had been at home.

"Jack was here that morning," she said. "He went outside and fixed some of the panes of glass in the greenhouse. We're replacing them on the one side. From here he was going over to the inn to do some work there. He was the one who found her."

Louise nodded, then asked her to continue.

"Afterward, he called me to tell me what had happened. He was supposed to come back here so we could finish, but he postponed that and said he was going home. I was also very shocked. It's not pleasant living all alone when something so terrible happens so close by."

"I understand," Louise said and gave Lange a small nod. He leaned forward and folded his hands in his lap.

"I realize this isn't so easy to talk about, but I'd like to ask you a few questions about your youngest son," he began. Helene's body jerked. She didn't say anything, just turned toward him with a rigid stare. "I understand that his body was never found."

There was silence in the room as Lange focused on his own interwoven fingers, then straightened up.

"Have you seen your youngest son again since you lost contact with him in the water?" he asked, maintaining his eye contact with Helene.

Louise had thought she was the one designated to play "bad cop," and that Lange would be friendly, comforting, and understanding, but he was clearly taking on the unpleasant role here.

Everything about Helene's face seemed to contract. Her eyes became dark and dismissive, her lips pale and thin. It was clear that she was not okay with where he was going with this. But very slowly she began to shake her head.

Lange glanced quickly at Louise, and she sensed their silent agreement that Helene Funch would have reacted differently had she known that her son was alive. She would have practiced some reaction if she were the one who had murdered Dorthe for bringing Simon to her home.

Lange cleared his throat and Louise let herself sink back in the armchair to leave the scene to him while she studied Helene Funch and noted her reactions.

"Why are you here?" Helene asked coldly before Lange had time to ask his next question.

Again, he glanced quickly at Louise, and she hoped that he caught the faint nod she gave him.

"I'm asking about your youngest son," he began, "because I

would really like some clarification on whether he could have been at the inn with Dorthe. Recently."

"What are you saying?" hissed Helene Funch desperately. "What the hell are you imagining?"

He held up a hand to calm her down.

"What are you people playing at?" Her voice quivered with anger.

Lange let his hands drop back down into his lap.

"We found a child's bedroom in Dorthe's apartment," he said, jumping right into it. "The boy who was living in the room has been identified as your son."

The room was completely silent now, as those words hung heavily between them.

"I don't understand," Helene finally said, so quietly that they could barely hear her.

"We're operating under the assumption that your son is still alive," Louise clarified.

Helene shook her head so that her shoulder-length blond hair flipped back and forth.

"That can't be right," she whispered in dismay.

She clenched her hands as if she were trying to hold herself together.

"You must be mistaken." Her voice was tearful and distorted. "Why are you doing this to me? How can you allow yourselves to come here and say that Simon might be alive?" Tears began to pour down her cheeks in an unchecked flood.

They gave her time, and she sobbed heartrendingly and miserably. With clenched hands, she swept her tears away and wiped her nose on her frayed sweater sleeves.

"All my children are dead," she gasped hollowly. "My husband is dead. I wish I was dead, too. But I haven't had the courage to end it all yet. In the beginning I hoped that I could end my life by refusing to eat. I just wanted to lie in my bed until it was over. But then Jack came with Dorthe's food, and he also got me to get up and come downstairs. He built the greenhouse for me and coaxed me outside. If only I had had the strength to stay in my bed, then the whole thing would have been over and done with long ago."

Suddenly it was as if the significance of what they had said seriously registered.

"With Dorthe?" she said. "Why would my little Simon be with Dorthe?"

Tears were still streaming down her face, but her sobs had quieted.

Lange shook his head.

"I simply can't answer you yet," he replied.

"But how . . . ?" Her despair coupled with everything she didn't understand to silence her. She began to shake her head.

"It's no wonder that this comes as a shock," Louise said. "But the DNA evidence that was found in the room matches your son's, and we need to work on the theory that he survived and drifted ashore somewhere in the area."

"But why would he be with Dorthe?" Helene repeated, confused.

"Because it appears that she took in a child shortly after the accident," Lange said.

"So where is he now?" she exclaimed tearfully. "I want to see my baby."

"We're not sure," Louise said compassionately.

CHAPTER 21

Camilla parked behind the radio and TV store in Svendborg where Jon Isaksen now worked. Eva Nørgaard had told her that Jon had seen quite a bit of her son, and the woman had even speculated that the two might have dated, although Aske had never said so outright.

After handing Charlie off to Eik, Camilla had called Jon and arranged to meet. She'd learned that now that the inn was closed, he was helping his partner at the shop.

The first person she encountered when she walked in was a man in his fifties. His hair was cut short, and he was wearing a dark blue suit that seemed almost too stylish for the TV store's long rows of flat screens and Bose speakers. He introduced himself as Jon's partner.

"He's in back," he said, walking over to a door behind the cash register to shout into the storeroom that they had a visitor.

Jon came into view from behind a tall shelf of ring binders. The first thing Camilla noticed were the man's bushy hair and dimples, but as he came closer, she saw the uncertainty in his eyes and the quick glance he gave the door into the store.

"Shall we go somewhere else to talk?" she asked after they said hello.

He shook his head.

"No, it's fine," he replied. "Theo knew Aske, too, and he knows that we dated before I moved in with him."

There must have been about a twenty-year age difference between the couple, she guessed, but there had also been a large age difference between Jon and Aske. He offered her coffee or water, pointing over to the sink.

Camilla declined both, then took out her cell phone and asked if it was all right if she recorded their conversation.

Jon nodded, but still seemed uncertain.

"And you promise my name won't be mentioned?" he asked.

"Of course," she replied, pulling her blond hair into a thick hair band before she straightened her skirt and sat down. "The article is going to be about what it's like in general to come out as gay here in Svendborg. As you know, I've also spoken with Aske's mother, and she has agreed to let me write about her son."

He nodded now.

Camilla knew that he had talked to Eva after Camilla interviewed her. Eva herself had suggested that Camilla contact Jon, so he was aware that Eva didn't mind Camilla and Jon discussing her late son.

She looked at the floor for a moment, staring at the dust under the shelves as she thought that it must have been hard for Eva to work with her son's friend, to see him find a new boyfriend and create a new life.

"He was my first," Jon explained once they were seated across from each other at the high packing table. "I knew he was gay. I'd seen him out at the forest cabin when I brought the food out there. I suppose we'd known each other for a year before we started seeing each other in that way. But we never really dated, we just saw each other. I came to be quite fond of him and we got close."

"Was Aske paid by the men he met out at the cabin?" Camilla asked, noting how Jon again glanced over at the door to the shop before vigorously shaking his head.

"No, not at all," he replied then. "Aske wanted to do it. To him they were dates and the conditions at the cabin were a luxury that he couldn't afford himself."

"So there wasn't any pressure or coercion associated with those stays in the woods?" Camilla asked, and Jon shook his head again.

"But one night something happened out there," he continued. "Something got out of hand. Aske was violently assaulted by a man who wanted much more than he did. It got out of control. I saw him the next day, and he was really hurt. I said he should report it, and I think he wanted to. But I have this suspicion that he was talked out of it and given money to keep his mouth shut. He never said anything, but I had a sense that he was paid to forget what had happened. It was after that when he started to change, and I didn't see that much of him anymore. He deleted his online dating profiles and withdrew from his old life. It was as if he slowly became a shadow of his former self, but he wouldn't talk about it."

"Did he stop being involved with the gay community?" Camilla asked curiously. She'd noticed as Jon spoke that a series of small involuntary bodily reactions gave away how he was feeling. His eyes routinely flitted to the door into the shop, or became sad and filled with tears. His seriousness was clear from the tightness of his lips.

Jon had fallen silent and sat for a long time staring down at the table, before shrugging somewhat hesitantly, as if searching for a way to move on. But then he shook his head.

"I don't think so," he replied then. "But he changed. It probably took around three months before I saw him again, and by then I noticed he had money in his pockets. He showed me his new car and invited me out to a restaurant in the city afterward. He paid, but he didn't seem happy, and he hardly ate anything."

He paused again.

"I wondered," he admitted. "In such a short time he went from being exuberant and handsome to being completely withdrawn. I didn't understand it, but I felt like I wasn't good enough for him anymore. Like he didn't have a good time when he was with me anymore. But later on I realized that he wasn't having fun anywhere. I tried to talk to him, but he hardly ever had time to meet, and when it was finally possible, he seemed either tired or put upon and had to run off again right away. To be honest, I don't know what happened, and he was also downright hard to get along with during that phase. It wasn't until he got really sick that I started seeing him again. And then I regretted that I hadn't held on to him better, that I hadn't been a better friend."

"Was he prostituting himself?" Camilla asked, waiting until he hesitantly nodded and began to explain.

"There was this one night when we were in town, and we ended up down at the disco. A man came up to us that night. I'd never seen him before, but it was clear that Aske recognized him. The man pulled out two hundred kroner and said that Aske should go out back with him."

Jon seemed almost embarrassed as he spoke, Camilla thought, and she regretted that she hadn't accepted that coffee. It was cold in the back room and there was also something depressing about the pain in his voice. Maybe drinking a cup of coffee together would have helped.

"It was so uncomfortable and humiliating for Aske," he continued. "We left the place right after that, and that's when he told me that he sometimes did that sort of thing."

"You mean here in Svendborg? Or did that have something to do with the forest cabin, too?"

The chef shook his head.

"I don't know where it happened," he replied. "I was really hurt to find that out and I didn't want to hear about it."

Camilla's phone on the table between them rang. It was Terkel.

"Yes?" she answered, annoyed to be interrupted.

"Drop the gay angle," her boss said, sounding forced. "Concentrate instead on the plane crash that took place in Tåsinge two years ago. I just heard that the murder at the inn may have something to do with the plane crash."

"Stop," Camilla interrupted him, not bothering to hide her irritation. "You assigned intern-Jakob to cover that story, so just let him keep going."

"He's not an intern anymore and you know that perfectly well," Terkel corrected her. "Besides he's moved on to a drug case in Vestegnen. There didn't seem to be anything more to the widow murder."

Camilla was about to protest, but he continued.

"You're the one who wanted to go out there," he said. "Your sexual minority story isn't going anywhere, so you're changing course now and focusing on the plane crash. A woman survived. She was a mother of three and her husband was the one flying. Find out who he was. Where did the plane take off from? I want to know everything. And I especially want to know how the accident can be linked to the killing of the woman at the inn now, two years later."

Camilla quickly made up her mind and agreed. That meant she could stay in Tåsinge and keep working on the story about Aske. She was also curious to learn more about the boy at the inn whom Louise clearly didn't want to discuss.

After Camilla said goodbye to Jon Isaksen and politely nodded to his partner, she called the hotel in Troense to reserve a room. Then she started looking for a supermarket so she could stock up on all the things she already knew she was going to want as she spent the next several hours in front of her computer digging into the Funch family's private lives. And deaths.

She spotted a grocery store and pulled off to the side. Before she got out of the car, she sent first Frederik and then Markus a text to say that she was staying in Tåsinge until the next day. Then she went in to do some shopping. When she came back out again carrying a bag full of mineral water, Coke Zero, salted almonds, candy, and a sandwich she wasn't sure she would eat, she saw that her husband had called twice. She frantically tried to remember if there were any appointments at home that she had forgotten. A birthday she had overlooked or something she had promised to do.

"Hi, honey," Frederik exclaimed happily when she called him back. "Tåsinge sounds wonderful. I'll come join you."

"But I'm working," she replied, surprised that it had even occurred to him.

"I'll be quiet while you write. And I can also go for walks. But then we can spend the evening together, maybe find somewhere nice to eat."

"That won't work," Camilla said, not even open to negotiating. "I'll hurry and finish over here and then we can do something nice this weekend."

She could sense that he wasn't quite ready to give up. *He's bored,* she thought.

"Okay," he said reluctantly. "Maybe I can entice Markus into watching a movie."

She started laughing. Frederiksberg wasn't exactly Los Angeles. Camilla had predicted that he was going to be bored when he moved back home. But he had stubbornly reassured her that all he did in the United States was work, and that wasn't going to change, he said. But now he was struck by the fact that most people's everyday lives were not quite as flexible as his.

"I'll call you later," she promised and sent him a kiss through the phone.

The room Camilla let herself into had a view of the Troense marina. She tossed her small travel bag on the bed and was pleased with herself for having had the foresight to pack some extra clothing and toiletries before leaving home.

Even though rain was beating against the windowpane, she opened the window a bit and pulled the armchair in the corner out into the light before she took her computer out of her shoulder bag. She thought about the articles she had found about the crash. Camilla had read about how the Funch family had been forced to cancel a planned fall vacation trip to Disneyland in Paris because Kristian Funch had received a big assignment and needed to stay home. It had been a spontaneous idea to fly to Tåsinge, so Helene and the kids could spend their vacation at the farm with her husband joining them on the weekend, Helene Funch had told the journalist.

Camilla signed in to the hotel's Wi-Fi, broke open a large bag of colorful wine gummies, and sat down in the armchair in front of the window. She quickly read through the articles to brush up on the case, and also found a couple from *Hillerød Posten*, where it said that the family had lived out by Store Gribsø Lake, north of Copenhagen, and that they took off from Grønholt Airport in their small private plane.

By the time the bag of wine gummies was almost empty, she knew that Helene Funch owned the large farm in Bjernemark on the island of Tåsinge. She had bought it with the money she had inherited from her parents. She had been through a long course of rehab as a result of the plane crash. It didn't say what injuries she had sustained, just that she had resigned from her job as an international tax adviser with Deloitte in Hellerup, where she had worked since 2007.

Camilla wrote all her notes on a pad she had set on the chair's armrest. In several places it said that Helene was skilled and respected in her professional field. *Yawn*, Camilla thought, instead searching for something that described the more private side of the woman who had survived the plane crash. Helene Funch was born Helene Harlow. Her father had had a large law firm in Vimmelskaftet in Copenhagen. Helene was thirty-eight when the accident occurred. She had been married to Kristian for twelve years and was mother to Karl, eight, Sofie, six, and Simon, two.

Unfortunately there wasn't much there, Camilla thought, as she kept searching. But she didn't find anything else. She also went to Helene Funch's Facebook profile, but it wasn't accessible if you weren't friends with her.

When she unscrewed the lid off her mineral water to wash down the vast quantities of sugar, the water foamed over and spilled on her skirt. She ignored it as she began searching for Kristian Funch. It quickly became clear that a fair amount more had been written about *him*.

Kristian Funch, born 1981. Camilla noted that he was two years younger than his wife. Following a violent robbery at his parents' house in Allerød, he had decided to found the company Funch Alarm Systems. In an old birthday profile from the year he turned thirty it stated that he had been only twenty-six when he founded what would later become one of Denmark's largest alarm firms. His brother, Kenneth Funch, who was two years older than him, was a trained electrician and was subsequently hired as the company's first installer.

Camilla skimmed the rest. But it wasn't until she got to the company's website and recognized the logo that she realized that they were the ones Frederik had hired to set up the safe room in their apartment in Frederiksberg. On the website there was an impressive description of how the company had "expanded" in the years following Kristian's death and was now a big business with many prominent, wealthy Danes on their reference list. It also said on the website that Kenneth Funch had taken over the management following his brother's death. She wrote his name down along with the company's main number in hopes that he would offer up a few more private stories about his little brother and sister-in-law.

When she was put straight through to Kenneth Funch, she realized that the woman handling the phones at Funch Alarm Systems must have been instructed to put journalists through to the director.

The brother's voice was deep and welcoming as he asked what he could do for her.

Camilla introduced herself and began by saying that she hoped he didn't mind her calling to talk to him about his brother. She didn't say a word about the fact that it was actually more his brother's wife that she was interested in.

At first there was silence, then he cleared his throat and said that he didn't have any objection to discussing the founder of the company.

Camilla gave no indication that she had registered his making clear what he was prepared to talk about. She also let him repeat what she had already read almost verbatim on the alarm company's website. But when she tried to ask about the private plane, he clammed up.

And she quickly figured out that he wasn't interested in talking about his sister-in-law, either, but he did go so far as to say that the period after the accident had been a very difficult time for Helene.

He wasn't dismissive, Camilla concluded, but he also wasn't tremendously open when it came to furnishing her with new information. And she was seasoned enough to know that she wasn't going to get any further here. So she thanked him for his time.

He politely wished her a good day and hung up.

She sat for a long time staring out at the water and the small pleasure boats that looked like they had been prepared for the winter. A man was walking his dog and two boys came biking along the road. They were riding side by side in the middle of the road, yelling back and forth to each other. She packed away her maternal instincts, hoping that there wouldn't be any oncoming cars driving at too high a speed.

Not a single thing the brother had said could be used for the article Terkel had requested. Annoyed, Camilla shook her head and started searching again.

"Boring," she muttered to herself as she clicked through the web page's other information. She opened a new bag of candy, hesitated a second, and then also ripped the corner off the bag of salted almonds. She gave up on the company's website and switched over to searching the web for things that had been written about Funch Alarm Systems and its late founder.

An hour later, after she had emptied both bags and drunk the cola, she sat with equal parts anxiety and irritation in her body. There still wasn't a darned thing to go on when it came to the couple's personal lives. But it also wasn't their personal lives that had awakened her anxiety.

Underneath all the polished stuff, she had spotted the outline of a new story. It had come up while she was reading her way through the Trustpilot reviews of Funch Alarm Systems and comments from various internet forums where the security company had been mentioned. It appeared that the company had been on the verge of bankruptcy before Kristian Funch died. They did file for bankruptcy, but his brother got the company back on its feet. She had also found an inactive ad at the used aircraft sales site flysalg.dk, which showed that the little six-seat Piper Cherokee plane had been put up for sale before the accident.

The ad was placed two months before the plane crashed. But the anxiety that had begun to coalesce inside her didn't have much to do with the plane, either.

Camilla leaned over and picked her purse up off the floor to grab her cell phone.

"Hi," she said when Frederik answered.

She had found a photo online of Kenneth Funch, the older brother, who was now the director of the company. A broad-shouldered, heavyset man who stood in a work jacket with the company's logo across the chest. She had immediately realized that it wasn't the same guy who had been back home working in their apartment. This guy looked angry and not particularly accommodating.

"What do you know about Funch Alarm Systems?" she asked her husband. "Why did you decide to pick them?"

She could hear him hesitate on the other end.

"They were recommended to me," he replied before elaborating that one of his old friends who lived in a big home in Fredensborg had spoken highly of them. "He uses them for work, too."

Camilla nodded. She had met this friend only once and knew that he was a car importer.

"Plus, they have experience with safe rooms," Frederik continued. "Why do you ask?"

She figured he might be afraid that there was a new discussion looming about whether it had really been necessary to spend over two hundred thousand kroner on a safe room, so he mostly seemed relieved when she asked if he was aware that a number of customers had reported break-ins in their homes within a period of three months after having a Funch alarm system installed.

"What's striking is that the alarm didn't go off. It was primarily expensive designer furniture, music systems, and lamps that were taken."

"Someone always complains," he responded calmly.

"Yes, I understand that," Camilla said. "But the break-ins took place through windows where a sensor was installed, the kind that should trigger the alarm if the window is opened. And they didn't."

"Or the people who live in the house forgot to turn the alarm on," her husband pointed out.

"That could be," she conceded. "But it could also be that this specific sensor was defective, and that this specific installer knew it. And so it was easy to come back."

"Are you bored over there?" he asked.

"No, I'm not bored," she snapped, annoyed. "But it would be nice to know if the people responsible for our safety are on the up-and-up. And then it's interesting to hear how he managed to avoid bankruptcy proceedings while at the same time the company was hit by a storm of complaints."

"I thought you were interested in sexual minorities," her husband said. "I'm sure the Funch CEO will be thrilled to hear that you're accusing him of fraud."

She waited a second for him to protest and try to talk her out of it, but he didn't do that. He just wished her good luck with her work, and Camilla called Kenneth Funch again.

After that call, Frederik's comment felt a little unpropitious, because it was still echoing in her ear after Kenneth Funch had finished chewing her out and hung up on her.

CHAPTER 22

They were about to say goodbye to Helene Funch when Louise asked if she still used the house on Gribsøvej in Hillerød. She didn't. The house was just as she had left it almost two years ago. She didn't have the energy to put it up for sale, she said, and didn't feel ready yet. All the children's things, their whole lives were in that house.

Louise asked for permission to visit the house and without further ado was given the key and the code for the alarm, as if they didn't really have anything to do with Helene.

She seemed rambling and absent-minded but did manage to explain that a gardener was looking after the lawn there. No one had been in the house since the accident aside from the one time when she had gone home to pick up some personal items and a little more clothing before she settled down on Tåsinge Island. She prepared them for the fact that no one had cleaned or tidied the place since the day the family had left for their fall vacation.

Lange had suggested that they call Jack Skovby so he could come and stay with Helene during the hours it would take before her sister arrived from Frederikssund.

"What do you want from the house?" Lange asked when they were sitting in the car on their way back to the police station in Svendborg.

"I want to know more," Louise replied briefly, but then after a little pause added, "Let's assume that Dorthe Hyllested and her husband deliberately kept the boy hidden, knowing full well that he was Helene's son. At the same time, they brought her food every week after she came home from the hospital. That reflects an evil I've rarely experienced. And I simply don't believe that such a gruesome act just arises out of nowhere. If it turns out to be true, there obviously has to be something behind it. So we need to figure out if the two families knew each other or had some other connection that Helene Funch either is not aware of or is not telling us about."

In Louise's best judgment, Helene wasn't hiding anything from them. She had agreed right away that they could search the house. Nor had she objected when Louise asked for permission to go through her deceased husband's belongings. After he had considered this, it seemed that Lange agreed with her as well, that they needed to investigate whether there were any ties between Hyllested and Funch, something that could point them toward what could have gotten Nils and Dorthe to take Helene's youngest son from her.

"You're right," Lange told her. They had reached the bridge and left Tåsinge behind. "If there was a connection between the two families, maybe that can explain why the couple at the inn would have done this to her."

Louise's gaze drifted out over the water. She felt short of breath, as if the trembling restlessness racing through her body made her lungs tight. It was a familiar feeling of wasting time when she didn't have her nose directly on the trail. It wasn't constructive but felt like a giant kick in the butt and a reminder that she was behind, that she was staggering around in the dark unable to tell what direction the investigation she was responsible for should be going in.

"But where is the boy now?" she mumbled to herself as they drove into Svendborg.

"He's here somewhere and we'll find him," Lange replied with conviction. On the one hand, Louise thought he seemed like a foolhardy optimist who was trying to cheer her up. But on the other hand, there was something reassuring in that little "we."

She wasn't on her own in this, and she needed to pull herself together. Fucking stupid to get drunk in the middle of something so important, too. She thought about Jonas and Melvin. She ought to call them. Instead, she sent her son a text and a heart. She would call later, and if she ended up driving over to Helene's house herself, she could stop by Frederiksberg when they were done.

Eik stood just inside the door of the office Lene Borre had procured for them. Charlie lay on the floor by his feet and perked up, wagging, when Louise walked in.

She looked at the dog in confusion and asked where he had come from.

"Camilla was watching him. She brought him over this morning. I just picked him up."

Louise nodded slowly. So, her friend had arrived as well. She briefly wondered whether there was any point in giving Camilla the story of Simon and letting it leak out through her, but instead decided that it needed to be disseminated much more widely, even though she had promised Camilla that she would be the first to be tipped off. But the missing persons report needed to go out in all directions; therefore she was going to be forced to coordinate with Grube in Odense and call a press conference for later that day.

They would probably need to call in canine units from both Zealand and Jutland, she thought, not knowing how strong a search team Funen itself would be able to muster.

"There will be a press conference in half an hour," Eik announced, cutting her thoughts short. "And within the next hour, the first dogs will set out from the inn in four long chains. More will arrive this afternoon. We—"

"What the hell are you talking about?" Louise interrupted sharply, letting go of Charlie's ear, which she had been distractedly scratching while she thought.

"I'm talking about the fact that it's official now. A search has been launched to locate Simon Funch."

"You can't do that. This is my case!" she snapped angrily. "I just came from seeing his mother. How could you go to Grube behind my back?"

Charlie got up and slunk away.

Eik grew serious.

"I didn't go to Grube behind your back," he responded tersely. "Simon Funch was reported missing, and his case has been in the hands of the Missing Persons Department the whole time. I just took it over from Olle, who's on vacation. So now I'm in charge of it."

He paused to leave room for objections, but Louise just shook her head.

"I've called a press conference, and Grube is preparing for that at the police station while I've been sitting here and coordinating the search, which we're launching now. There's no reason to take it personally."

"I'm not taking it personally—" she began, but was interrupted when he continued steadily.

"There's a little boy out there somewhere. There's no telling what he's been through for the last two years, but now he needs to be found and brought home to his mother."

She opened her mouth to say something, but he beat her to it again.

"Besides," he added with a twinkle in his eye that annoyed her. "While I'm leading the search, you'll have time to concentrate on solving the widow murder."

She chewed on that for a minute, then nodded and gave in.

"I'm going to Zealand with Lange to go through the Funch family's house. We're working on a theory that there might have been some connection between the two families before the plane crash. Something that Helene either wasn't aware of or isn't telling us about. It might be something that made the couple who owned the inn take Simon from Helene. If that's the case, then maybe it will give us a motive for Dorthe's murder."

Eik made a little click with his tongue that caused Charlie to immediately stand up and come over to him.

"Let's go," he said, already on his way out of the room.

Louise watched him, confused.

"I said that *Lange and I* were leaving," she protested to Eik's back.

"We'll take my car," Eik said, ignoring her objection.

"Oh come on, for crying out loud!" Louise swore. She asked him to wait while she told Lange to go into Odense and assist at the press conference so they'd have some idea what Grube was going public with. Sindal and Borre were still in the apartment above the inn, and they answered right away when she called Borre to prepare her for the arrival of Eik's search teams.

"The first ones have already arrived," she replied, and Louise could hear the activity in the background. She filled her local colleague in on her conversation with Helene and explained that the sister was on her way and that Jack had promised to stay with Helene until she arrived.

"I also think a journalist has arrived," Borre announced, but Louise didn't ask about that. Instead, she told Borre about the press conference.

"You should prepare yourself for quite a few more journalists, but it'll probably be fine. Right now we can actually use them. You refer them to Eik Nordstrøm. He'll be the one to speak out when necessary." She felt Eik's eyes on her, but she was ignoring him right now.

After she wrapped up her phone call, she nodded and said she was ready.

They hadn't even reached Odense before Louise wondered if she could allow herself to take a nap so they wouldn't have to talk to each other during the trip to North Zealand. Two hours in a car. Together. There were many other things Louise wanted to do more. She and Eik hadn't seen each other since she broke off their long trip. That last night they spent together they had had sex on the little balcony outside their hotel room and things had basically gone straight downhill and to hell since then. They had fucked, fought, and broken up. That was how she thought about it. But that was mostly to wrap the breakup in a harsh note. The truth was that it had crushed her and torn her to pieces. She'd had an ache in her stomach and in her heart long after she had come home. Part of that, of course, had to do with her coming home to her brother's breakdown.

A breakdown that nearly cost him his life with two suicide attempts. Her brother's condition had suspended her own pain for a time, and all her focus had been on bringing him back to life. But by the time she had succeeded, her own misadventure had returned with renewed force. She wasn't worth loving. Louise had felt this her whole life, and now it was flaring back up with a vengeance.

A mere few days ago she'd still considered her heart torn like the emoji Camilla consistently sent her when she asked Louise how she was doing.

And that wouldn't do. It wouldn't do now, either, when she was sitting eight inches away from him. Everything about him entered her nervous system: his scent, his silhouette, his clothes. Eik only wore black. Not to strengthen his image, but because it was easiest to buy ten of the same black T-shirts and five of the same black jeans. Every morning he took a dip off the dock in South Harbor. Every day he drank at least ten cups of coffee. Every day he smoked unfiltered cigarettes, which were crammed into his jacket pocket.

She turned her face away. His smoking might be a thing of the past now if he could keep reducing the cravings with chewing gum. Neither of those things seemed to interest him at the moment. He sat silently behind the wheel and kept the old Jeep in the fast lane with a gentle pressure on the car ahead of them.

Neither of them said anything. Louise closed her eyes and leaned her head against the window. She needed to make this work, she thought. She could do it, too, if they stuck to their work rela-

tionship and left all the personal stuff out of it. Their old boss in the
Missing Persons Department had not been right, she realized, picturing Rønholt. He had insisted that either she or Eik would have
to leave the department because they were officially dating. But the
problem wasn't working together while they were having a romantic relationship; it was working together now that they were no
longer having that romantic relationship. She understood that now.
But Eik was damned good at his job. She was, too, and right now
the first priority was finding Simon and solving the murder.

The conversation flowed back and forth in her head as she sat
there with her eyes closed.

"It was wrong of you to just leave," he said suddenly, breaking
the silence in the car.

"Stop," she said without opening her eyes.

"You can't just run away because you think you hear something
that isn't being said. It's immature and childish."

Louise straightened up with a jerk and turned toward him.

"Do you want to hear what's immature and childish?" she
snarled.

He didn't answer, and she didn't want to start that conversation
when they still had an hour and a half of driving to do.

"We missed you," he said, and the blame was gone from his
voice.

They had crossed the Great Belt Bridge, and he slowed down
and pulled up to the tollbooth.

She didn't say anything at first, merely glanced over at him.

"Maybe you should have considered the consequences before
you broke up with me," she said then.

"You broke up with me," he returned. "You were the one who broke up with me and didn't want to keep traveling with us."

"Stop," she repeated, gritting her teeth. "You make it sound like it was my decision. Anyway, you made it rather clear that you didn't feel ready to commit to me, to become a family with Jonas and me. If that's not a breakup, how the hell would you have me interpret it?"

"You know I didn't mean to upset you or pull away from you."

She left him hanging without saying anything.

"Do we need to talk about this right now?" she finally said into the silence. "Let's try to focus on where we're going."

She stared stiffly out the windshield.

"Fine," he said. "You just need to know that I haven't withdrawn my marriage proposal. It is still in effect. The rest is up to you."

She shook her head at him.

"So it's still in effect until the next time you don't really feel like committing?"

Seeing her in Jack Skovby's arms must have really affected him after all.

"No," he replied as he sped up to pass someone. "It's always still in effect. I just need to practice wording it a little better before I say anything there's a risk you might misunderstand."

Again, there was silence, until Louise cleared her throat.

"Whatever."

She didn't look at him for the rest of the drive. The space in the large car felt far too cramped for everything that had been said. Charlie lay in the back snoring loudly and Louise wanted to climb back there and curl up next to the big German shepherd.

The Funch family's home was a heavy old redbrick house that sat right out on the road. Behind the house, Louise could see a yard extending all the way down to a big lake. She quickly hopped out of the car to escape from the claustrophobic silence that had settled during the last long stretch of the trip. She found the slip of paper with the four-digit security code in her purse and walked up to the front door.

Before she put the key in the dark oak door, she let her eyes slide across the front of the house. There were thick weeds all the way down the walkway and bird poop covering the pavers, which no one had bothered to wash. But because the grass on the narrow strips of lawn that ran alongside the house were mowed, it didn't look fully uninhabited. It just didn't look terribly well maintained. Bushes grew wild over the walkway in the yard and the shrubbery was dense between the trees in the fence.

She quickly entered 4813 into the alarm panel beside the door, and when the frantic beeping stopped, she looked around at the high-ceilinged entryway with curiosity. On a shoe shelf over by the row of coat hooks sat a variety of children's shoes, soccer cleats, and rain boots, all in different sizes.

Eik let her lead the way as they walked toward an open door that led into a living room. Louise thought there was something almost devout about the silence, but that fit with the shut-in feeling of stagnant air. Dusty and stale, a little like stepping into an empty church, though it wasn't cold in here in the same way. The light from the large windows looking out at the yard warmed the room up.

A blanket lay tossed untidily on the sofa, as if a person had just gotten up from an afternoon nap, and an open book sat on the neighboring table. It wasn't cluttered, that would be an exaggeration, but one clearly had a sense that the house had been left the way it would be if you knew you were coming back. They walked into the adjoining room, where a dining table and chairs took up almost the whole space. There was a glass vase with a dried bouquet in the middle of the table's shiny surface, and around that lay a crumbly dust of withered flower petals and small dead flies. The vase, which had once been transparent, had turned brown with calcium deposits from the rotten, now evaporated water. There were dusty, dead insects all over, and fly shit had left stains on the windowsills while spiderwebs hung down over the tall windowpanes.

From the dining room, they proceeded into the kitchen, which had been cleaned apart from a bag of oats left on the kitchen table. Mice had spread the oats across table and onto the floor, where they were now smeared together with the mice's excrement. But otherwise, nothing had been left behind that gave any insight into the family who had lived in the house.

They walked back through the living room toward the room on the other side of the large sectional sofa, which had a door to the yard. There was an enormous flat-screen TV mounted on the wall across from the three-piece living room set, and a basket of toys on the floor full of mostly dolls and plastic vegetables and fruits. There was also a play mat with a few stuffed animals, which must have been Simon's.

Louise had tried before to step into an everyday life that no longer existed with people who were no longer alive, to stand in the middle of the frame of what had been someone's life. She was being affected by it in the sense of feeling grief. Now she noticed other things. It wasn't what their life had been that captured her attention. It was the things that fell slightly outside of what their life had been that interested her.

Eik had remained in the living room, but now he followed her up the stairs to the second floor. The view from Helene and Kristian's bedroom was epic, as Jonas would have put it. They had a balcony that faced the yard and the lake. The fall golds of the treetops were like a carpet all the way down to Store Gribsø Lake. The bed was made. A folded nightgown lay on top of the bedspread, and there were a few articles of clothing on the floor by the laundry basket.

She had started opening the closets when Eik called to her from the other end of the hallway. He had continued down it to the farthest room. Names were marked in big, colorful wooden letters on the doors on the way to him. The three children's rooms were all in a row: Karl, Sofie, and Simon.

She was about to open the door into the first of the rooms when Eik called again. There was something in his tone of voice that made her speed up.

"Look at this," he said when she stepped into a large corner room with dark gray walls and a somber atmosphere.

Kristian Funch's office was as big as the couple's bedroom if you included the bathroom that went with the master bedroom.

Eik was standing by a large desk holding an envelope out to her.

The envelope read, "To whom it may concern," on the front.

He had put on thin latex gloves and now offered a similar pair to Louise. The writing on the letter had faded in the sunlight that hit the desk from the window.

The envelope was not sealed, so Louise eased it open and pulled out a folded piece of paper.

"A deliberate act," it declared on the top of the page. Louise looked up at Eik, who had come over to stand behind her so that he could read along.

"To avoid any doubt, I hereby assume full responsibility for my and my family's death. It was a deliberate act and my intention to crash the plane into the sea."

Eik was silent while Louise stood looking at those few sentences for a long time. It was signed Kristian Funch.

She turned the letter over, but it didn't say anything else. No explanations, nothing additional. Nothing. It had been printed out, the signature and date added by hand.

It was dated the same day that Kristian Funch flew his family to Tåsinge, October 16, 2017. Louise handed the letter back to Eik.

"See if you can find something else with his signature on it," she said, pulling her cell phone out of her pocket. Before he had time to respond, she turned her back to him and called Lisa Lindén.

"Kristian Funch," was the first thing she said. "Obtain a warrant and find everything you can on him: bank information, account statements, transfers, investments, correspondence, whatever. It's postmortem, so you'll need to go back and search. He died two years ago."

Lisa didn't ask any questions, saying that she would get started right away, and Louise was glad account statements were stored electronically for five years. Eik had pulled some papers out of a folder. She could see that he had started systematically searching for anything that would contain Kristian Funch's signature. They needed to confirm that he had written the letter.

Louise began opening the desk drawers. The desk and the drawers were unusually clean and orderly. And when she lifted her eyes and looked around, she noted that the office had been cleaned in a different way than the rest of the house. She quickly walked out into the hallway and over to Karl's bedroom. There was a soccer ball on the floor, some clothing, and a remote-control monster truck. The bed was made, but it was obvious that a child had lived here. She quickly checked the other two rooms and had the same sense. They were nice and tidy, but they hadn't been cleaned the way you would if you didn't expect to be back. Kristian Funch's office had.

When she returned, Eik handed her a purchase agreement. In 2016, Kristian Funch had bought a Land Rover from the British MotorGroup. His signature was identical to the one on the letter. Eik also found a gym membership with his signature on it.

"He didn't expect his wife to survive," Louise noted, nodding toward the letter on the desk. "But he clearly assumed that someone would come empty out the house and find the letter."

Eik nodded thoughtfully.

"But why?" he asked himself.

"Finances, the company, love, betrayal," she started listing.

"Were any of those going badly?" he asked, looking around at the big office. "Did his wife want a divorce?"

Louise shrugged. She had no idea. Helene hadn't given them that impression, at any rate.

"His brother took over the alarm company after Kristian Funch's death," she said.

Eik had squatted down and started pulling binders out of the cabinet across from the desk. Louise remained standing, watching as he flipped through them. There were various printed brochures from Funch Alarm Systems, some that had Post-it notes on them, and in other places there were little comments noted directly on the printed pages. Insurance papers, leasing contracts for the company cars. Employment contracts.

"Why didn't he keep all this in his company office?" Eik wondered, putting the folder back and pulling out a new one. It was for the plane, a Piper PA-32-300. The plane's logbook, airworthiness certificate, radio license, and insurance papers.

They continued searching in silence but didn't find anything that was personal in a way that helped them understand what was behind the action Kristian Funch had claimed responsibility for before the fatal accident occurred. No bank statements, no private documents that led them in any direction.

Louise's cell phone only had time to ring once before she answered it.

"A bankruptcy filing was received for Funch Alarm Systems," Lisa Lindén announced, "one week before the plane crashed. It seems to have been averted when his brother stepped in. But it looks like Kristian Funch had been draining his company for a long period of time. He withdrew large amounts of money during the year leading up to his death."

"Withdrew?" Louise asked. "What for?"

There was silence on the other end of the call.

"I can't say yet," Lindén finally responded. "But I'll find out once I get a warrant and can go in and pull his bank statements."

Louise had put the call on speakerphone so Eik could listen in. She thanked Lindén and said goodbye.

"She's good," Eik said. His eyes lit up in a way that made Louise smolder with jealousy.

They carried on searching in silence.

"He cleaned everything up before the accident," Eik confirmed once he finished with the last cabinet. "It's clear that everything that's left here is stuff that he doesn't mind other people seeing. It's pretty much only company related."

"Maybe he figured his brother would be the one to empty out the house. There's nothing here."

Louise could hear her own impatience, but there was nothing that tied the Funch family to Dorthe and Nils Hyllested.

"We're just staring straight at a family tragedy," she said in frustration, feeling like they should be spending their time going out and looking for Simon instead.

Only then did it occur to her why the office seemed so defunct. There was no computer, phone, or other electronics that she could have Lisa Lindén comb through. There was nothing here other than what Kristian had carefully selected to be found after his death.

She stood staring straight ahead for a long time even though Eik had left the office. Louise could hear him going back downstairs. She thought maybe he wanted to give Charlie a chance to pee before they headed back to Tåsinge. Without stopping to see Jonas and Melvin.

CHAPTER 23

"And you didn't notice the letter in your husband's office when you were upstairs packing your things?" Louise asked again.

Helene Funch shook her head once more. Shortly before this, Louise had been received by Iben, Helene's sister, a young woman with a long ponytail wearing tight workout leggings.

After Louise and Eik returned from Zealand, she had driven straight to Bjernemark while he had continued to Strammelse Inn to get an update on the search.

They still hadn't found Simon Funch. All they knew for sure was that the boy had been in the inn's parking lot, from where it was assumed that he had been driven away by car, as they had officially phrased it in the news Louise had heard as she was driving out to see Helene and her sister.

Helene had heard the same news. She explained that as she passively accepted the keys to the house back without asking any questions about it. The only thing she kept asking was who could have driven her son away from the inn. She was distraught and desperate and kept repeating that she couldn't understand how her little boy could be four years old.

Two birthdays she had missed. The words sounded like a painful monologue she was unable to stop.

Iben had seemed apologetic as she led Helene back to the living room and sat on the sofa with her arm around her older sister's shoulders. Like a soothing shield, Louise thought, studying the skinny younger sister for a moment. She looked like Helene the way she had looked before the plane crash, but didn't have much in common with the woman sitting next to her now.

Louise pulled the stationery out and set the envelope on the coffee table, feeling a twitch of tension in her face. She tried to relax, appear neutral, and not let herself influence what she was about to say. Still, she scooted forward in the armchair a bit and could tell right away that Helene was responding to her uncertainty.

The sister tightened her hold on Helene, and even though it was only her fingers that tensed, Louise noticed it.

"This letter is from your husband," she began. "It was on his desk, and this is going to be hard to talk about."

Helene sat bent forward. Her arms were squeezed together tightly over her chest, pulling her sweater up and revealing a little skin over the waistband of her pants.

Louise took a breath and eyed her sympathetically.

"It appears that your husband intentionally crashed the plane on the way over here," she said. "In this letter, he takes responsibility for his actions."

A clock ticked somewhere in the living room. The silence seemed deafening. Louise could see that Helene didn't understand what had just been said, and she couldn't blame her.

"Your husband wanted to take all of you with him in death the day the plane crashed."

Iben had begun to cry, but Helene still didn't react.

Louise passed the letter across the table and let her take it. She followed the woman's eyes as she read the brief lines. In silence, Helene set the letter back on the coffee table and stared blankly straight ahead.

Iben rested her head on Helene's shoulder. She was crying quietly, but there was still no reaction from Helene. Louise felt her cell phone vibrate in her pocket.

Helene was still staring into space when she finally began to speak.

"That can't be right," she whispered hoarsely.

The silence settled heavily over them once again.

Then Helene shook her head and looked urgently at Louise.

"I was the one who wanted to come over here. I was the one who made him fly us over. It wasn't his idea, so he couldn't have planned it," she said. "It's my fault."

There was an accusatory, angry light in her eyes now, as if Louise had done something she had no right to do, said something that she couldn't know.

"Tell me about that day you came over here," Louise asked. "I mean, before the flight."

Iben had stopped gripping Helene's shoulder and was now wiping her eyes as she stared at the letter in horror.

Helene seemed distant again. She sat shaking her head as if she were trying to collect her thoughts.

"That can't be right," she said again, still shaking her head.

"When did you decide to fly over here?" Louise tried.

"We did that on Sunday, the day before the accident. The children were sad and disappointed that the trip to Disneyland wasn't going to happen after all. Karl had shut himself in his room and wouldn't even talk to us. Simon didn't react, of course. He was too little and didn't know what he would be missing. But the two big kids had been looking forward to it. There was always something with Kristian's work. He was often away, but that's what it's like to be self-employed," she said, explaining that Funch Alarm Systems did jobs all over Denmark, so her husband traveled a lot. "But he had promised the children that this time nothing would get in the way of the trip."

Iben pursed her lips, as if she'd often had to listen to the details of her sister's family life.

"I was the one who wanted to come over here," Helene repeated. "The farm was our refuge, and I could be alone here with the kids when he had to work. We came every summer and for all our vacations and holidays. I love being over here. Or I did. Now I'm just here."

The phone in Louise's pocket vibrated again, but she let it ring and asked if the family always flew when they came to Tåsinge.

Helene shook her head.

"Only when the company wasn't using the plane," she explained. "But Kristian really loved to fly, and it's a beautiful trip. When we flew over here, we would get Jack to pick us up at the airport."

She pointed to the south.

"We keep a Land Rover over here, which Jack used when we were in Zealand. So the agreement was that he would pick us up and drive us out here."

Her voice began to sound strained, and she had a hard time getting the words out, as if she were pushing them out in bursts.

"Kristian didn't have anything to do with the accident," she said again. "I was the one who wanted to go."

She pulled away from her sister slightly, as if she suddenly felt claustrophobic sitting so close.

The phone rang again, and now Louise excused herself and stepped out to the front hall to answer the call. It was Lisa Lindén, who had accessed Kristian Funch's bank transfers.

"I've collected what's relevant into an email and sent it to you," she reported briefly, then hung up before Louise had time to react. Her annoyance returned and she decided to bring the young investigator in for a conversation when she was at the police station the next day. At the same time, she was somewhat impressed that Lindén had obtained a warrant and already trawled through Funch's bank info: one point to her. Maybe she should wait to educate her until the case was over.

From the living room she heard the two sisters whispering together, while she opened the email and started reading. It was laid out in bullet points. Brief information, date, name, amount. Transfers that had gone out of Kristian Funch's personal account, collected over a period of three years prior to his death. Not all of the transfers, but the ones Lisa Lindén had found relevant.

Louise leaned against the wall while she read. She ran her eyes over the numbers and letters on her phone's illuminated screen.

Amounts, large amounts. And names she recognized.

She stared straight ahead for a moment. In the living room, the whispering had quieted, and for a second she felt as if her hangover from that morning had returned with renewed vengeance, as if something were tightly wrapped around her skull, making her forehead throb. Simultaneously, though, something seemed to relax in Louise's consciousness, a sudden recognition of a connection between people who were no longer alive.

CHAPTER 24

Louise sat down again across from the two women. Both stared at her expectantly, but she took her time. Gathered her thoughts as she decided how she should begin.

"Just before he died, your husband filed for bankruptcy," she said. "It seems that he withdrew such large amounts for himself that it drained Funch Alarm Systems. Which is to say, the money was taken directly from the company's equity capital and not a share of the profits. I understand there had been several large investments in new systems in the years before that, so by subsequently withdrawing such large amounts, he forced his company to its knees. Do you know what he planned to use that money for?"

Perplexed, Helene looked at Louise.

"We've never had financial problems," she said, sounding annoyed.

"Could we try to focus on Simon," Iben interjected, putting her arm around Helene's shoulders. "You make it sound like my sister and brother-in-law didn't have things under control. You are aware that he owned a large, well-renowned company, aren't you? You're supposed to be finding my nephew and instead you're sitting here tossing out all sorts of accusations."

Helene put a hand on her sister's arm to stop her.

"I don't mind answering if there's any way this can help us find Simon," she said dully. "I'm not aware that my husband withdrew money from the company. We've never been short of money. I had a job that paid well before all of this, and Kristian's company was doing well."

Louise noticed that she didn't ask for explanations or object to the information she had just received. She just clearly didn't understand where Louise was going. She glanced down at her cell phone and the document Lindén had sent.

"Did you buy a house somewhere outside of Denmark? Or maybe a summer home?" Louise asked.

"My sister would know if her husband bought a house," Iben snarled angrily, and again Helene put a hand on her arm to quiet her.

"No," she replied quietly. "This is our refuge."

Louise nodded.

"In the thirteen months prior to his death, your husband withdrew about 2.2 million Danish kroner from the company. We've been able to locate some of that money via transfers, but we can't find the rest. I'm only asking because I'm trying to get an overview that I hope can help us understand what happened."

"To Simon?" Iben asked. "Is that what you mean? Does the money have something to do with Simon?"

Now Helene turned to her sister.

"Could you please go make us a pot of tea?" she asked. "I'd like to have this conversation alone."

The younger sister stood up reluctantly but nodded. Louise and Helene sat in silence and watched her leave the living room.

"A little more than a year before his death," Louise began once they were alone, "Kristian withdrew a hundred thousand kroner in cash. Do you know what he was planning to use the money for?"

Helene looked at her in confusion and shook her head.

"Two months later, your husband transferred seven hundred thousand kroner to Nils Hyllested at Strammelse Inn. How were the two of them connected?"

"To Nils?" Helene blurted out, not understanding. "We didn't know Nils. I mean, we went to the inn, but the two of them didn't have anything to do with each other. That can't be."

She spoke frantically, her body completely stiff. She looked out the window, her gaze disappearing into the October rain as her face slowly collapsed.

"Connection," she whispered softly. She had grown even paler when she turned to look at Louise again. "Did the two of them know each other?"

Louise let her sit for a bit with that question before she nodded.

"It seems so," she replied. "Some very large amounts were also transferred to Jack Skovby. Were you aware of that?"

She nodded and became present again now.

"Jack has worked for us for many years. There's nothing odd about that," she replied quickly.

"Your husband transferred a million kroner to Jack Skovby. The accompanying text indicated 'payment for agricultural machines.' Do you know which machines your husband was referring to?"

"Agricultural machines?" Helene exclaimed with her eyebrows raised and a sound that almost sounded like a crazy giggle. "Kristian wasn't interested in agriculture. That's why he hired Jack to take care of the land here. We've never had our own farm equipment."

Louise asked if Jack had been earning a fixed monthly salary when Helene's husband was alive.

Now it appeared that the conversation was beginning to tire Helene out.

She shook her head heavily.

"I paid Jack and that was something we arranged directly," she said, maintaining eye contact with Louise in a way that was almost provocative, as if the least of her worries right now was admitting that she skirted the tax authorities and paid him under the table.

"But," Louise said, "the same year your husband bought the agricultural equipment, he transferred thirty thousand kroner a month to Jack Skovby. His bank statements show that in just one year he deposited a total of 1.37 million kroner into Skovby's account."

Helene was about to protest but thought better of it.

"I was not aware of that," she said instead, her eyes filling with tears as she again clasped her arms in front of her chest. Her sister had come back to set the tea on the coffee table, but Helene sent her away again.

"Could the thirty thousand kroner be installment payments for a different purchase?" Louise suggested, but Helene dismissed that right away. "Could it be payment for repairs or other work done on the farm?"

Now Helene began to cry. Heavy sobs sent tremors through her body, and she rocked back and forth to soothe herself.

"My husband didn't have anything to do with Jack. Everything went through me."

"It seems that your husband invested a lot of money over here in

Tåsinge. How would you describe his relationship with the locals?" Louise asked, full of pity for the woman's complete confusion.

"I didn't know he had connections over here other than the ones we had in common."

"I'm sorry I have to put you through all of this. But it's important that we uncover your husband's connections."

"To find Simon," Helene said, nodding as she got her crying under control.

"Yes," Louise said, "to find Simon."

She could have added that it was also important to find out who murdered Dorthe Hyllested, but instead she said, "After seeing your husband's letter, we need to find out what made him make such a fateful decision."

Helene began to sob again.

"Did they take Simon as revenge for something Kristian did?" she asked through her tears.

Louise nodded slowly.

"That is a possibility," she replied. "What was your experience of that flight? Was anything different from previous trips? Think carefully."

Helene had clenched her hands and was pressing her knuckles against her mouth.

"I know that this is hard for you," Louise said compassionately. "But I want to ask you to remember if he said anything that you might not have thought was important at the time."

Once again Helene's gaze slipped over to the window, which was streaked with rain.

"I don't think he said anything. Other than that he loved me. It wasn't so often that he said that sort of thing anymore. But he seemed to be rushed as we were leaving. He always got distracted when he was in a hurry. I was the one who packed for the children, while he sat in the office and worked. We didn't usually bring very much with us when we came over here. We already had most things here."

She paused for a moment, her eyes lingering on the windowpane.

"I was getting ready to load everything into the car when Kristian said that we could fly. The weather wasn't optimal, but my daughter got carsick easily, so I thought it would be better for her to get the trip over with quickly. It was drizzling when we took off from Grønholt Airport, but the rain picked up. We didn't talk much during the trip. Kristian seemed very focused and tense as we crossed the Great Belt."

She stopped. Her face had stiffened as she thought back.

"At one point, the plane went into a nosedive," she said slowly. "At the time I thought it was a gust of wind. The children screamed in back, but they did that whenever they felt like they were on a roller coaster. Sometimes Kristian did it for fun, to make them laugh. But none of them were laughing. They were scared. It was different. Maybe that was an attempt to crash us into the sea and then he thought better of it."

She glanced at Louise, then away. Dismay made her eyes so dark that her pupils almost disappeared.

"Sofie started throwing up, and Karl started complaining because he had to sit next to her. Kristian told them to stop arguing. He seemed irritable, and it wasn't like him to scold the children. We barely spoke on the trip."

She paused again and looked directly at Louise, now with a vigilant eye.

"But I would have known if he had planned for us to die," she said. "We've flown that trip many times. I would have noticed if there had been something wrong. I knew him, and I knew the plane. He was focused. His palms left prints. I noticed several times that he dried them off on his pants. I knew the rest of the trip would be turbulent and regretted that we hadn't taken the car. At one point the visibility was so poor that we could only see what was directly below us. We were following the coast. I had to help Sofie by holding the bag while she threw up. Simon was crying."

She paused and became distant again, then something happened in her eyes and her body seemed to stiffen. Louise got goose bumps, seeing the fear that shone out of Helene's eyes, as if something had caught up to her after a considerable delay and with renewed force.

"We had descended, and he was getting ready to land. I could see the white outlines of the runway and noticed how the surface of the water was reflecting the clouds."

She tightened her hold on herself.

"Kristian screamed. I was scared and thought it was a wind gust that shook us. Just then he kicked at the right pedal and jerked the controls violently. We were losing elevation so quickly that I didn't have time to realize what was happening. I clutched Simon to me and closed my eyes."

Her voice was monotone now, as if she were recounting an event she had read about in a newspaper.

Louise realized she was holding her breath, experiencing the pain and feeling the plane break the surface of the sea.

"I don't know how long it took me to discover that I was alive. And that Simon was still alive. It must have happened quickly.

Parts of the plane were still above water. I saw my kids hanging limp in their harnesses in the back and I knew right away that they were dead. The same with Kristian, who was still sitting next to me. I don't know how I could be so sure, but I could see it. Right away. At that point my only thought was to get Simon out. I must have been in shock. I can remember how much my body hurt, but I didn't care. I was only concerned with getting the life jackets on and swimming ashore."

She paused, stared straight ahead for a long time, and then continued.

"I managed to get the door open. I had a hard time getting up out of the seat and reaching the lock. I can remember the feeling of the wing's smooth surface and the sensation of sliding down into the cold water. I held Simon right up against me. He was completely still, but I knew he was alive. They told me I lost consciousness in the water. And I lost him there, too."

She bent forward and cried heartrendingly. Iben had come back to the doorway, and Louise nodded to her as a signal that she could go over to her sister.

Louise was about to stand when Helene straightened up and asked her to stay.

"It can't be true that Kristian planned it," she said through her tears. "I was the one who pressured him."

She looked over at her little sister quickly before she turned her imploring eyes to Louise.

"It's my fault that they're all dead," she continued hoarsely. "My fault alone. I was the one who wanted to go away. Me, who wanted to go over to Jack."

She hid her face in her hands.

"Do you understand?" she said, sobbing into her hands. "I was the one who killed them."

Iben stared at her sister, shocked, and pulled away a little.

Louise stood up and walked over to the sofa, where she squatted down next to Helene and took her hands.

"You didn't kill your family," she said gently. "It was your husband who decided to take you with him in death. Did he know about your relationship with Jack?"

Helene clutched Louise's hands harder, as if she were clinging to her salvation.

She cast a hesitant glance at her sister before she shrugged.

"I don't think so, but maybe he suspected something. He often seemed absent himself when he was over here. Sometimes he drove to Langeland or other places. He put his fishing rods in the car and often came home late. I thought that maybe he knew and that was his way of reacting. Our relationship wasn't as passionate anymore and he was away from home a lot.

"I think the fishing was mostly about him needing a little time alone," she continued after a brief pause. "He never brought any fish home with him, so I thought it was probably mostly about the peace and quiet of standing around with his fishing rod that appealed to him."

"Are you and Jack still a couple?" Louise asked.

She shook her head.

"We still see each other, obviously, but not in that way. That ended when my family died. I can't accommodate those types of feelings anymore."

Iben sat paralyzed at the other end of the sofa, looking at her sister as if she no longer knew her.

Louise's phone rang and this time she got up right away to answer it. It was getting late, and darkness had settled over the living room. This time it was Eik. He was brief and specific when he delivered his message, and she didn't have a chance to ask any questions before he had hung up. They had found Simon.

CHAPTER 25

Camilla closed her eyes. She had shut the window, thrown the empty candy bags in the trash, and then fallen asleep in the armchair with the computer in her lap. Now she was startled awake by a firm and persistent knocking on the hotel room door.

Dazed and with her heart racing, she smoothed her hair and went to open it. Eik stood outside with Charlie at his side. He snappishly asked her to watch the dog, thrusting the leash into her hand at the same time. She took it reflexively. Then he turned around resolutely and was on his way.

"Hey!" she called after him. "Did you find the boy?"

But in a few long strides he had already reached the lobby downstairs and a second later she heard a car start in the parking lot. She looked down at Charlie, who had remained standing in front of her door, staring up at her with such an insistent look that she knew what it meant: *Go for a walk.*

Camilla glanced over at her computer, which sat in the armchair, and started resignedly putting on her coat.

Completely confused from just waking up and exhausted from her day, which had suddenly picked up speed, she locked the door behind her. It had begun raining again as she and Charlie walked over to the marina. She was hungry, and for a second she regretted not having accepted Frederik's offer to come out so they could have a nice time and eat together. Just now she felt like she had failed at both of the stories she had plunged into.

The instant she heard that the police had called a press conference in the Dorthe Hyllested murder case, she had rushed out to Strammelse Inn in hopes of finding Louise and getting her to confirm that there was a connection between the murder at the inn and the old plane crash. She had been met by two local officers, and it quickly became clear that she wasn't going to get anything out of them.

Then she had rushed to Odense to attend the press conference. There it was revealed that the police were currently searching for four-year-old Simon Funch. She had immediately sent everything she had collected on the Funch family to Terkel Høyer, thereby bringing Morgenavisen several horse lengths ahead of the other media outlets.

She had listened impatiently to a bunch of questions and answers, but nothing else had been stated that she could use. An older officer with a heavy Northern Jutland dialect and a calm demeanor had said that it appeared Dorthe Hyllested had taken the boy in. Several people asked if the boy had been held captive in a basement or attic. It also didn't appear that Helene Funch had received a ransom demand, so that suggested it hadn't been a kidnapping in the traditional sense. Finally, they requested that the press leave Helene Funch alone.

Camilla said hello to a couple of boys sitting at the end of the dock. She kept walking a little farther, then turned around and doubled back to ask if she could bum a smoke. They looked a bit surprised at her and Charlie, then one of them held out a pack and offered to light one for her.

She walked over to a bench and pulled her coat closed more tightly as she unaccustomedly let the smoke fill her mouth. Again she tried to call Louise and then Eik, but neither of them answered, and she felt the trembling unease she always had when something had happened. She had seen it in Eik's eyes and now she regretted that she hadn't grabbed her car keys right away and followed him.

After the press conference, she had gone straight back to the hotel in Troense to call Kristian Funch's unsympathetic brother. The other media foiks would no doubt ignore the police request and go after Helene, so she had immediately decided to take a side door.

"No," he had yelled when he answered her call. "I don't have any more to add to your insinuations and outrageous accusations." On the other hand he was prepared to inform Camilla that his lawyer had been briefed on the case, and if she wrote so much as a single line, the lawyer would start a fire neither she nor her editor in chief wanted to be anywhere near.

Camilla had almost been able to picture him as he raged, even though they had never met.

She had interrupted him to explain that she had called to talk about his nephew, and it quickly became clear that he had not been following the news. She had been prepared for a new angry outburst when she asked him to tell her what he remembered about the boy. But it didn't come.

Instead, it got quiet on the line, quiet in the way that only happens when there's still someone on the other end. Someone who is not making any noise.

"Simon," he had said. "I've always wished, for Helene, that they would find his body so she could have her little son buried with the others."

And then Camilla had explained that his nephew wasn't dead but had been staying with a married couple in Tåsinge since the plane crash.

"A married couple," Kenneth Funch had repeated, as if he could only pronounce a few words while his brain was working to understand. "Helene never told me that."

"She didn't know. She was only informed today. How do you remember your little nephew?" Camilla had asked.

It was quiet for a long time before the answer came.

"He was my godson," he said hesitantly, as if that was something he first had to go in and dig out from his memories. "A great little boy. Quieter and more cautious than his big brother. But he was clever and he was quick to learn how to walk."

Kenneth Funch's voice sounded choked up, completely different than when he was yelling.

"So he didn't die?" The sentence had almost seemed searching, as if it were an attempt to create a new reality.

"No," Camilla replied. "He didn't die."

"And where did you say he was?"

"With Dorthe Hyllested, who owned Strammelse Inn."

"Dorthe and Nils." He said the names slowly and thoughtfully, as if they also needed to be dug out of hidey-holes and remembered.

"Did you know them?" Camilla had asked, and he responded that he had been to the inn a few times when he was visiting his brother and Helene at their place in the country.

"How is Simon?" he asked.

"I don't know," Camilla had replied honestly, and explained that his nephew had disappeared.

Again there was a long, thoughtful silence, but then it came.

"Maybe Dorthe felt like Helene owed her a child."

Camilla had sat up immediately and asked what he meant by that, then he had explained that his sister-in-law had had an affair with their gardener.

"I never understood why my brother put up with it. But I figured maybe it soothed his own conscience about spending so little time with his family."

All the anger was gone from his voice.

"But what does that have to do with Dorthe?" Camilla had asked. "What do you mean that Helene owed her a child?"

Camilla stubbed the cigarette out with her heel and shivered. Then she got up from the bench and walked Charlie back to the hotel while she speculated about Kenneth Funch's response.

At first he had said that he hadn't really meant anything, but then he admitted that the gardener had gotten Dorthe pregnant before he started sleeping with Helene.

"Jack and Dorthe were going to have a child together, but by the time Dorthe lost the baby, he had already moved on with Helene. I know because Kristian was afraid he would get his wife pregnant, too."

After she had concluded her conversation with the brother, she had sent Louise a text, but hadn't gotten anything back. When Dorthe lost her baby, she also lost Jack to Helene Funch.

Camilla was drenched but decided to drive out and see Jack Skovby even though it was after eight.

CHAPTER 26

It was the dogs that had found Simon Funch. They had spread out in lines from the inn, heading toward Nørre Vornæs, after which the lines of some of the country's best tracking dogs and dog handlers had split up to search Vornæs Forest.

Louise spotted Eik's taillights on the side of the road a little way from the farm. She pulled over behind him and got into his car a moment later.

"The dogs alerted," he said, wiping the rain from his hair and pointing up at the light from the farm.

Just then the car's back doors opened and Lene Borre and Niklas Sindal got into the back seat. They had been following the search teams all day and contacted Eik immediately when the dogs picked up the boy's scent. Evidently Borre and Sindal had also insisted that no one should move in until Louise arrived.

"We know for sure that Simon has been in the yard and believe it's likely that he's in the house now," Borre reported.

Louise could hear from her voice that she was cold. Sindal explained that the dog handlers had just pulled back to let them go in.

"Who owns the farm?" Louise asked and turned around to the back seat.

"Jack Skovby," Borre replied.

She could feel Eik's eyes on her as she tried to gather her thoughts. She couldn't quite figure Jack out, but she didn't back down under Eik's persistent gaze. Instead she straightened up and started assigning roles.

"Borre and Sindal will go around the outside and we two will go in," she said and nodded to Eik. At the moment she didn't give a damn that this was his search. It was her murder, and the missing person case was part of her investigation. She considered showing them the texts from Camilla but decided she needed to first find out for herself what her friend meant when she wrote that Helene had owed Dorthe a child. And that had to wait.

She gave Sindal the keys to the car she had come in so that he and Borre could drive it.

Sindal and Borre had scarcely left Eik's car before he began.

"He was seventeen when he cornered his father in the workshop on the farm and bashed his skull in with an ax while his mother and little sister were in the house," he said. "After the murder he went into the kitchen and told his mother what he'd done."

"You've read up. I can tell," was all she said, but it stung all the same. Because of Grete Milling's death, her judgment might have been knocked a little off course when she drank with Jack at the inn. But dangerous? She hadn't had that impression from him.

The road curved in a gentle arc, and in the light from the car head-lights she saw a narrow strip of fenced pasture in front of the tradi-tional three-winged, thatched-roof, half-timbered farmhouse. The dog handler who had picked up the boy's trail had reported that the dog had led him across the field along Vornæs Skovvej and then continued toward the farm. Another handler had gone around be-hind Jack Skovby's property, but the tracking dog had reacted when they passed the driveway.

The handler didn't think there was anyone home at the prop-erty when the dog alerted. He had withdrawn and notified Borre, who had been behind him at the time. Somewhere on Søren Lolks-vej, he had explained.

Now Jack Skovby's Land Rover was parked in front of the house and there were lights on in most of the windows. As they pulled into the gravel-covered courtyard that was surrounded on three sides by the U-shaped farmhouse, a cascade of outdoor lights turned on and Louise noted that Jack Skovby must have recently renovated the large farm. The whitewashed brickwork still stood out crisply against the black-stained beams of the half-timbering. She won-dered how much of the money for the renovation had come from Helene's husband.

The rain stopped as Louise and Eik walked up to the house. She felt Eik's arm as he reached out to hold her back.

"Make it sound like this is purely routine," he said quietly, as if someone could hear them. "If he denies knowing the boy, we won't press him. We'll come back with a warrant instead so we can search the property."

Louise nodded and agreed. Her concentration sat like a gentle quivering under her skin, and she noticed Eik checked his service weapon before they continued to the front door.

They were still a few yards from the stone doorstep when the door opened and Jack Skovby stepped forward. He looked only at Louise as he moved to the side and invited them in, as if he had been expecting them. Eik stayed behind her as they walked into his front hall, where she saw Jack's fleece jacket hanging on a hook. He said that they didn't need to take their shoes off and asked them to come into the kitchen.

He seemed unsure. That attractive calm she had otherwise felt you could lean on was gone. Louise was about to introduce Eik when Jack spoke first.

"I was going to call you," he said, again addressing only Louise. He glanced toward the living room but didn't have time to say anything more before Louise stepped past him over to the doorway. The living room was long and wide with a large glass window facing out toward the yard, and she sensed Eik right behind her as she spotted the corner sofa and the TV, which was on.

Simon Funch sat wrapped in a comforter and seemed engrossed in a cartoon that silently cast sharp, flickering colors from the enormous flat screen. She recognized him right away from the old photos, with the delicate features and the dark eyebrows.

He looked over at them, but quickly turned his eyes back to the screen. His hair came down over his ears, but there was no sign of neglect in the face that had briefly turned toward them. No fear. In front of him on the coffee table sat a plate with what was left of a hamburger and French fries, and a couple of comic books had slid down onto the floor.

Jack stayed behind them as she watched Simon. The boy seemed calm and unaffected by their presence. He didn't seem eager to leave, either, she thought. She quickly contemplated whether she should ask Borre to come in and sit with him while she and Eik talked to Jack, but decided instead that the boy would be calmer if he got to enjoy his cartoon while they talked. It was eight-thirty, so he must be tired, and in a short while his life would yet again be turned upside down.

There was something about the boy's heavy bangs that reminded her of Jonas when he was younger. And even though she had only caught a glimpse of his eyes, she had the sense that he had learned long ago to withdraw into his own world and shut out the things around him. She felt sorry for him. And for Helene Funch. It wouldn't be easy for her to get her little boy back, either.

Louise walked to the kitchen and closed the door behind her.

"How long have you been aware that the boy was at the inn?" she asked once she had told Jack to take a seat at the wide, natural plank table.

There was something exaggerated and wrong about all the modern and newly renovated touches. A lifestyle that seemed too expensive and flashy for the old farmhouse. As if the house had been forced into another era. She thought again of the large amount of money Kristian Funch had transferred to Jack.

She sat down across from him and leaned so far forward that she could see the small brown patch in his green eyes. His scent settled in her nostrils, and she felt a pang of recognition.

"I didn't know that he lived there," he replied, shaking his head. "I'd never seen him before that day at the inn."

Eik came over and sat down next to her. She kept looking at Jack, trying to pick up on all the small vibrations and signals in his face as he spoke.

"Bullshit," Eik said a bit too loudly, and the two men stared at each other for a long time. Eik's shoulder-length hair and leather jacket did not go with the ostentatious designer kitchen. But then neither did Jack's appearance, Louise thought, noticing Jack look away and shake his head.

"I didn't know anything about the boy," he repeated. "Dorthe never mentioned him."

"And yet here he is," Eik said. "In your house, in your living room."

Jack's gaze drifted over to Louise, but she just watched him expectantly.

"I," he began and then looked down at his hands, which sat folded on the table. His cuticles were discolored by dirt and there were short scratches running up a couple of his fingers. "I was supposed to go over and mow the lawn at the inn. Before I left Bjernemark, I called Dorthe to ask if there was anything else that needed to be taken care of aside from the grass and the bushes she wanted cut back. There was also a tree that needed pruning and then she wanted to talk to me about some of the siding on the back of the inn. She suggested that I come in for a cup of coffee before I started on the grass. When I got there, there weren't any guests at the inn."

They had already heard all of that, Louise thought. Aside from his new tasks.

He still had his eyes fixed on his intertwined fingers.

"I entered through the kitchen. I always do that, mostly so I don't disturb any guests in the lobby. I called out to her and went into the restaurant, where I found her on the floor."

He gulped, and just as she had the first time they met each other, Louise thought he seemed pretty upset about the murder.

"I ran over and knelt down next to her. I realized right away that she had been attacked and that it was serious. I called emergency services and then I heard the revolving door behind me, and there was a boy standing there."

"Simon," Eik interrupted. "The boy's name is Simon."

Jack looked up at him now, before slowly nodding.

"Simon was standing there, right behind me, staring down at Dorthe."

Jack rubbed both eyes vigorously as if to distract from the fact that he had begun to cry.

"It was violent," he said hoarsely. "The dark blood had spread across the floor. Maybe I went into shock. I wanted to get the boy away from there. I was thinking only about getting him to safety. At the time, I thought the killer might still be at the inn. We ran out to the car and drove. Here, home."

"You knew that there weren't any more guests at the inn. And you knew that Dorthe didn't have children. Please explain what made you take the boy with you," Louise instructed, watching him attentively.

Lene Borre walked by outside the kitchen window. She signaled to Eik that he should come out and tell the others that the boy was in the house, and Eik got up and left the kitchen.

"I wanted to take care of him," Jack Skovby eventually responded, pleadingly leaning over the table toward Louise, so that they were suddenly much too close to each other. "I didn't want to do anything to him. The opposite—I was afraid something would happen to him."

"I'm with you so far," she said. "But I have a hard time understanding why you didn't tell the police about him."

He nodded. Eik returned to the room and sat down next to Louise. Jack stopped leaning in over the table.

"I thought it was a child Dorthe was babysitting. He was suddenly standing there as if he had appeared out of nowhere. I wanted to get him to safety. That's why I brought him home."

"But you didn't tell the police about him," Louise repeated.

He shook his head.

"I thought it was safer for him here than at the police station. I was sure his parents would turn up quickly."

She sensed the repugnance Eik was exuding and hoped that he would let her guide the conversation.

"I just wanted to help."

Jack Skovby propped his elbows on the table and rubbed his knuckles across his forehead hard, as if he were trying to clear his mind.

Louise could see that Eik was about to attack but shot him a look of warning.

"It wasn't until you started asking about the child's bedroom that I realized there was anything wrong," Jack Skovby continued, finally sounding stressed. "Like I said, I thought it was a kid Dorthe was babysitting. But when I realized he had been living at the inn with her, suddenly I didn't know what to do without being linked to the murder myself. I stalled for time and hoped that it would come out where the child belonged, so I could drop him off. Just deliver him, so I didn't need to be involved in it."

He paused for a moment before continuing.

"It wasn't until today when you asked me to come and be with Helene that I realized it was her son."

He didn't seem so confident in his explanation anymore, Louise thought. Not that he was clutching at straws. It was more like the seriousness of what he had done was only dawning on him now that he was being forced to put it into words.

"And it never occurred to you that you could have helped the police investigation if we could have talked to the boy?" Eik asked coldly.

Jack nodded slowly.

"But you wouldn't have gotten anything out of questioning him," he replied then.

Louise raised one eyebrow questioningly.

"The boy's deaf. He can't talk," Jack explained. "We communicated by pointing. When we ordered the food, I showed him the pictures and then he pointed. I've tried asking where he comes from and I really wanted to tell him that he didn't need to be afraid, but he didn't understand."

"How long were you together with Dorthe?" Eik asked, standing up. He slowly walked around to the other side of the table and stopped right next to Jack to look down at him. The question surprised Louise, and she backed off slightly to see where Eik was going with this.

It took a while before Jack finally responded.

"A little over a year," he finally said, clearly uncomfortable. "Almost two."

"You and Dorthe Hyllested were expecting a child together," Eik continued. "But you left her. Did that happen when you found out she was pregnant?"

Jack squirmed uneasily in the chair, now looking completely dejected.

"She wanted a child," he began and looked up at Eik. "I gave her that, and it was a tremendous source of grief for her when she lost it."

"But when Dorthe Hyllested miscarried, you had already moved on to the next woman, hadn't you?" Eik asked sharply. "You weren't there for her in her grief, were you?"

Louise looked at Eik. This was the first time she had ever found him to be so matter-of-fact.

"Because," Eik continued harshly, "by that time you had started a relationship with Helene Funch."

Jack Skovby nodded, and Louise took over.

"How did your relationship with Dorthe end?" she asked, cursing herself for not having called Camilla the second she received her text. Now here she sat, way behind compared to Eik.

"It ended reasonably peacefully," he replied in a way that clearly indicated that it might have been peaceful mostly for him.

"I fell in love with Helene, and it wasn't meant to hurt Dorthe. But these things happen."

He held out one hand apologetically. Eik nodded sarcastically and gave Louise a knowing look.

"Was Dorthe's husband aware that you were having an affair?" she continued, undeterred.

Jack nodded.

"Can you express that in a few words?" Eik asked impatiently.

"Nils and Dorthe weren't together anymore in that way," he said, as if that explained everything. "They got along well as a couple, but there was nothing intimate between them."

"So you mean Nils Hyllested was okay with it?" Eik asked.

Jack nodded again but caught himself and answered yes.

"It wasn't something we talked about, not like that, but since he couldn't give his wife a . . ."

He stopped, but they left him hanging and merely waited for him to continue.

"Right, well," he said, searching a little for the words. "Since he wouldn't give her a child himself, he was open to her seeing other people. He was willing to adopt the child and be a father to it. You could say that I was a donor for their child."

"Had you agreed that you would all have a child together or was the child an accident?" Eik asked. "Or maybe when Dorthe got pregnant, her husband stepped up to get you out of a tricky situation?"

Jack Skovby leaned forward in anger now.

"Dorthe masterminded the pregnancy thing, okay?" he said loudly. "She wanted to have a baby, but she didn't let me in on that or anything. I thought she was on birth control. That's what she told me."

"Did she only sleep with you to get pregnant?" Louise asked, pointing out that Nils could have gotten his wife pregnant.

"Nils couldn't," Jack replied with a provocative harshness, as if he had sacrificed himself through his actions. And maybe he had, too, Louise thought.

"He couldn't or he didn't want to?" Eik asked.

"He couldn't," Jack replied, a little more subdued. "Nils had had a vasectomy. He had that done even before he married Dorthe. It wasn't until several years after the wedding that he admitted it and by that point she had believed for a long time that she was the one there was something wrong with. She felt like he had tricked her. And he had, too. But Nils wasn't interested in women. Not in that way, but I'm sure you already know that."

"But they stayed together anyway?" Louise said.

He nodded.

"They loved each other," he replied. "They were good together, a good couple."

Louise thought that maybe Dorthe had found herself a new lover after Jack.

"Did she try to get pregnant again after that?" she asked.

He shrugged.

"I didn't see that much of her after we broke up. It wasn't until after Nils died that she got in touch with me and asked me to come help out at the inn again."

"Did you start up your relationship again?"

Jack shook his head.

"Not in that sense, if that's what you mean. I just worked and helped out."

It was quiet again until Louise stood up.

"You understand that we're going to have to bring you in to the police station, right?"

He nodded.

"We can get a warrant if you don't agree to let us search your house. We will also need to corroborate that you talked to Dorthe as you claim."

"So, you want to check my phone," he said.

Louise nodded.

"And your computer," she said. "We also need to ask you to explain why Helene's husband, Kristian Funch, transferred close to 1.4 million kroner into your bank account."

For the first time in their long conversation, he seemed to seriously lose his footing, but he quickly got back on his feet again.

"He didn't 'transfer' it," he exclaimed angrily, making air quotes with both hands. "He bought two big farming machines from me. Plus my labor."

"If so, they're machines that you never delivered," Eik said, moving toward him again. "Helene Funch doesn't know anything about the transaction, and I don't imagine that farming equipment in that price range would be easy to overlook."

Jack pulled away and folded his arms over his chest standoffishly.

"I'm not saying any more until I've talked to a lawyer," he spat out angrily.

"That's not necessary," Eik said and stood up.

Louise returned to Simon in the living room while Eik informed Jack Skovby of his legal rights, but she managed to see the color drain from Jack's cheeks when Eik said that he was being arrested, suspected of the murder of Dorthe Hyllested and the deprivation of Simon Funch's liberty.

Jack got to his feet so quickly that the chair tipped over behind him.

"I didn't fucking murder Dorthe," he yelled right in Eik's face, angrily lashing out at him.

"No, so you say," Eik replied calmly, and it happened so fast that Louise hardly had time to see the motion before Jack Skovby was lying pinned on the kitchen floor while Eik slowly secured plastic ties around his wrists.

In the living room, Simon had slid back into the sofa. He had pulled the comforter all the way up to his chin, and his eyes were slipping closed as he watched the TV screen.

There was something safe about the way he had curled up. Louise felt a deep compassion at the thought of what he was about to go through.

"Hi, Simon," she said from the doorway behind the sofa.

He didn't respond. She tried again, a little louder. He still didn't respond and when her cell phone rang, there was no reaction from the boy, either.

"I've just been informed that Simon Funch is safe and sound," Deputy Chief Superintendent Grube said and praised her for their efforts. "Great job, and so quickly after the press conference. The newspapers barely had time to get all worked up before you had him. Excellent work, Rick!"

She didn't say anything, not even that it was actually Eik's search and not hers.

"I contacted the duty desk to have them arrange for social services to send someone to the police station to assist during questioning."

She had been thinking that when questioning a child it was customary to have someone present the child knew well and felt safe with. That could be the parents, grandparents, or a teacher from the child's day care or school. But this boy didn't have anyone in the whole world.

"Simon Funch is deaf," she told Grube. "According to Jack Skovby he had to communicate with the boy by pointing."

She couldn't imagine how lonely it must have been for the boy not to be able to communicate. Especially after having been through such an intense experience.

"Are there any signs of abuse or neglect?" the deputy chief superintendent asked. "Does he need to visit the Forensic Medicine Department for a forensic examination?"

"I don't think there's any immediate sign that he's been through anything like that. He seems healthy and he's not malnourished," she said. "Although it's late, I would suggest that we get ahold of a child psychologist or an experienced social worker who can come out here and be with him until they decide where he should be placed."

"Placed?" Grube repeated. "He's probably going home to his mother. She must be desperate to be reunited with her son. Have you spoken with her? Does she know that he's been found safe and sound?"

"I haven't talked to her yet," Louise replied.

"She can come here to the police station, and I'll make sure that someone is ready to receive her."

"I wonder if we shouldn't leave it up to a professional to determine when he's ready to be reunited with his mother," Louise said. "I would suggest that he be placed in an observational home or with a foster family who understands his needs to begin with."

"But surely there's no one who understands those needs better than his own mother," Grube objected, starting to sound impatient.

There was a pause, but Louise didn't back down.

"He needs to be placed in a healthy environment with experienced people," she said then. "Initially the focus needs to be on taking care of him. Once he's ready, then he can be reunited with his mother."

Grube obviously completely disagreed, but she persisted. She had learned quite a bit about children and what they needed during her time in the Homicide Department, where they had worked with one of the country's most experienced crisis psychologists for years.

"You're forgetting," she continued, "that what a child can remember from their first two years of life is very limited. He can't remember his mother. Helene will be like yet another stranger to Simon."

Finally he seemed to relent.

"But you need to go out there and tell her that we've found him," he said.

"I'll do that first thing," she promised.

"No, first you drive him here, to Odense," Grube corrected, "and then you can go back and talk to the mother."

Louise was tired. She felt the irritation like small jolts in her chest and gave up on trying to wrap things up in a sweeter and friendlier tone.

"Simon Funch will stay here until a caregiver is found who can properly take care of him," she decided sharply. "Or, better yet, until we find a qualified foster care family with experience caring for deaf children. We don't know if he's learned sign language, but we need someone who can try to talk to him. Simon is not going to the police station. This will all be done in a private setting. You can contact Eik once you've found people who can take over from here."

The deputy chief superintendent was silent. Then he cleared his throat quietly.

"Of course I can't promise that social services will be able to provide people with those sorts of qualifications on such short notice tonight."

"No," Louise acknowledged. "But you can put pressure on the duty desk, and I'm sure they will move heaven and earth when you say that we've found the boy. Anyone who works in social services would gladly get out of bed to help give Simon a little bit of comfort after everything he's been through."

The anger moved Louise's voice down to a deeper register than usual. She had taken a couple of steps over to the sofa and saw that Simon had fallen asleep now, curled up into a little ball.

"He needs to be questioned," Grube persisted. "Right now he could be our most important witness in the murder case."

"That's not going to happen tonight," Louise replied. "He's staying here with Eik and me." She knew that Eik would be best suited to take care of Simon. He had a flair for being with small children that she didn't have.

"I understood otherwise from Eik Nordstrøm that Jack Skovby didn't know the boy before he removed him from the inn," he objected. "So it seems unlikely that Simon would feel safer at his place."

"That's true," Louise replied. "But right now, Simon is asleep on Jack's sofa. He's been here in this house since Dorthe was killed and at least he doesn't seem to feel unsafe here."

Louise was about to wrap up the conversation when Grube again cleared his throat as if that helped him think more clearly.

"According to Borre, the individual arrested resisted a search of his home. She wanted permission to search the home without a warrant, but I stopped her. We can't claim 'loss of purpose' and say that important clues could be lost if we have to take the time to go before a judge to obtain a warrant. We don't have anything on him. We're procuring a warrant right now and once we have it I'll send a team out there."

Louise was about to protest that he kept wading over her professional boundaries, since he himself had called in the travel unit. But she stopped herself when Eik stepped into the room.

He turned on the light farthest from the sofa and walked over to Simon. He stood looking at the boy for a long time before he picked up the remote control from the coffee table and turned off the TV.

"Who did you assign to question Jack Skovby?" Louise asked, thinking that Grube had probably also taken command of the questioning.

"Borre and Sindal," the deputy chief superintendent replied. "They're on their way in with him."

"Put Lange on that instead," Louise said. "He will be good at managing Skovby, and when you have a warrant, you can send Lene Borre and Niklas Sindal out here with a team of forensic technicians. We need to search the whole property."

She could hear Grube inhale, but he didn't say anything else.

CHAPTER 27

When Louise called from the car on her way to Bjernemark, Iben answered the phone. The sister told her that Helene had gone to bed, but immediately offered to bring the phone upstairs to her.

"Could you prepare her instead for the fact that I'm on my way over?"

"Have you found Simon?" Iben exclaimed. Louise sensed that she was on her way up the stairs. "Is he dead?"

Louise didn't respond. She heard knocking on a door, followed by voices.

"She's getting up now," Iben announced as Louise drove into the courtyard of Helene Funch's farm in Bjernemark. She turned off the engine and got out. For a moment, she tilted her head back and stared up into the heavy darkness while she tried to collect her thoughts.

The farm's main building was the only one lit up on the property. All the other buildings disappeared in the darkness. Even though Louise had grown up in Lerbjerg outside Hvalsø, the black-of-night silence in southern Funen unsettled her, and she shivered before she walked over to the house.

Helene Funch opened the door herself. Louise had trouble reading whether the look in her eyes was hope or fear. She stepped aside without a word so Louise could come in.

Simon's mother was wearing a soft gray velour outfit, which made her look even more vulnerable than she had in the well-worn gardening clothes. She tugged nervously at the cuff of the outfit's sleeves to make it stretch down over the backs of her hands.

"You found him," she concluded, shifting uneasily.

Louise nodded.

"Your son appears to be safe and sound," she said, then quickly stepped forward to grab Helene as she quietly began to collapse to the floor. Louise wrapped her arms tightly around the mother and held her up as Iben came over to help her sister into the living room.

"Where?" Helene asked so softly that it was nearly inaudible. She had started trembling, and Louise reached out and took her hands between her own. "Your son is at Jack Skovby's house," she said. "He appears to be doing well and doesn't seem to have been harmed. He's sleeping right now."

Helene immediately stood up.

"I want to see him!" she said.

Louise asked Helene to sit back down.

"You'll see Simon very soon," she said, "but first he needs to be questioned by the police. And he will also need a little time to process the things he's just been through."

"Does he speak?" Helene blurted out with hope in her voice.

Louise shook her head and explained that according to Jack, Simon didn't have any ability to communicate in Danish.

"We're in the process of locating a sign language interpreter so that we can find out if he's learned any way to communicate."

Helene sat for a long time digesting this new information about her son before she explained that the plan had been for Simon to have surgery to put in a cochlear implant.

"That's a kind of hearing device with an internal part and an external part, which provides a sort of artificial hearing," she explained. "But we didn't get to it."

"Why is my nephew at Jack Skovby's house?" Iben asked her from her chair. It seemed that only now did that information sink in for Helene.

"Did Jack find him?" she asked.

"Yes," Louise confirmed without going into detail. "He found him and brought him home, so that's where he is now."

"Oh, thank God," Helene mumbled.

Louise decided to wait to explain to Helene that Jack was at the police station, suspected of murdering Dorthe Hyllested. And that he had kept the boy hidden. But the sister ruined that plan.

"Where?" Iben asked. "Where did Jack find my nephew?"

Louise didn't have time to formulate an answer before the next question hit her.

"And when was he found?"

She could tell from looking at the sister that she had figured out that something was wrong, that Jack wasn't just a savior who had swooped in. Louise gave her a long look and hoped she understood that now was not the right time. That there was no reason to subject Helene to more, better to let her get used to the new reality, in which her son was alive and safe. But Iben persisted.

"Was he the one who murdered her?" she demanded to know. "Was he part of keeping Simon prisoner?"

Helene looked up at Louise.

"What does she mean?" she asked without looking at her sister.

Louise quickly decided that sugarcoating things wasn't going to help. Iben would keep at it until she understood precisely what had happened.

Louise leaned toward Helene.

"Jack brought your son home with him after he found Dorthe. He found him at the inn."

"Found him?" Iben said. "Was he looking for him? Does that mean that Simon has been with him since the murder at the inn?"

Helene didn't respond to her sister's questions. She concentrated on Louise, as if she were afraid of missing a single tiny detail about her son.

Louise took a breath.

"Yes," she replied. "Jack says that he's been taking care of him until the police identified the person who murdered Dorthe because he was afraid that something might happen to him."

Finally, something changed in Helene's face.

"At Jack's house?" she said. "Has my son been at Jack's house while you were searching for him?"

Louise nodded. She could tell from Iben's expression that she, too, was thinking about how inappropriate it was that Jack had been the one to sit with Helene while Iben herself had been on her way to Tåsinge. Although this time she was tactful enough not to say anything.

"When can I see him?" Helene asked, leaving the rest untouched as if it were too hard to deal with.

Louise reached out and took her hands between her own.

"It will be a few days at least, maybe a week," she replied.

"A week!" Iben repeated, aghast. "Why so long?"

Louise was about to say something, but Iben beat her to it.

"Helene has the right to see her son, the right to be with him. You need to bring Simon home."

She flung open her arms, as if embracing the whole house in one motion.

Louise seriously wanted to send the sister off to make more tea, but she thought better of it.

Helene had started crying, heavy tears dripping down onto her dark gray velour.

"Who is Simon with now?" she whispered.

"My colleague Eik Nordstrøm," Louise replied.

"And Jack?"

"No, it's just Eik watching him."

Iben was about to say something again when Louise turned to her.

"Could we have a moment alone?" she asked in a tone that made it clear that no response was expected. Reluctantly, the younger sister got up and went out into the kitchen.

Once she was gone, Helene looked up at Louise.

"Do you think Simon can recognize me?" she asked almost inaudibly. "Do you think he can remember me and know that I'm his mother?"

Louise thought about it and decided to be honest.

"Probably not," she replied. "But the body remembers, and it could be that your scent triggers his memory."

She paused.

"But?" Helene said, as if she knew there was more coming, something she wasn't going to like.

"But," Louise repeated and took a deep breath, "you need to prepare yourself for the fact that it's probably Dorthe he'll miss, Dorthe he'll grieve the loss of. Right now she's the one he has lost. Not you."

She noted a twitch in Helene's expression before she turned her face away, as if Louise had hit her.

"Which is why," Louise continued, "you could also use a little time to adjust to the reunion you two will go through. I certainly understand that it will be hard to come to terms with his not understanding right away that you're his mother. You will need to give him space and time, even though it obviously makes the most sense to you to have him come home right away."

Helene had started nodding but didn't say anything.

"I understand that this is a very sensitive situation and that you miss him," Louise continued. "You'll both need support as you find your way back to each other."

Helene pulled her hands back and wiped the tears from her face.

"But will he ever see me as his mother again?"

Louise should have restrained herself, but she nodded before she could censor the reaction.

"Yes, I think so," she said. "But I also think it's important that you give him time to process what he's been through. Dorthe's murder is a violent and traumatizing experience, and he'll need the help of skilled and experienced people to get him through that."

Helene nodded while she looked at Louise, still crying.

"Can I not see him at all?"

For a moment, Louise wished she weren't the one who had to come up with all the answers.

"I think you'll be able to see him soon," she ventured to say, even though she really didn't have any influence over that. "But in the beginning, I think you'll need to adjust to visiting him. It will probably take a little time before he's ready to move home to you."

Helene sat still, staring down at the table.

"But he's alive," she said quietly.

Louise nodded and had just gotten up to leave when Iben walked back in. She had opened a bottle of wine and now set glasses on the table.

"Wait," Helene yelled, running out into the front hall after Louise, who was about to put on her shoes. She walked over to the stairs and dragged her bad leg behind her as she climbed them. Louise heard a door open upstairs, and shortly afterward Helene came into view again with a brown teddy bear in her hand.

"Could you please give this to him?" she asked once she had come back down. She handed the bear to Louise with trembling hands.

CHAPTER 28

Camilla stuffed the two breakfast buns she had wheedled out of the young woman who was preparing the hotel breakfast into her bag. She had also succeeded in finagling a cup of coffee from the staff coffeepot, even though the restaurant wasn't open yet. She hurried back to her room for Charlie, and then she was off again.

She was tiring of Funen police officers by now, but she didn't give up. Yesterday evening she had driven out to Jack Skovby's place to talk to him about the child he had been expecting with Dorthe Hyllested. She had seen the police car in front of Jack's house from the road and also instantly recognized Eik's Jeep in front of the house. She had known right away that something was up and gotten out her press pass before walking up to the officers standing by the police car. They were the same ones who had turned her away from the inn and it didn't take them more than three seconds to ask her to leave the property.

She'd called both Louise and Eik from her car without any luck, although Eik had answered on her second attempt. She'd quickly filled him in on what Kristian Funch's brother had told her about Dorthe Hyllested and Jack, but Eik wouldn't budge when she asked him to tell her what was going on inside the house. All she had gotten out of him was that he would probably be late getting back to the hotel so it would be best if she held on to Charlie.

Now Camilla helped the big dog into the car, also stowing the comforter from the hotel room so she had a way to keep warm if she had to sit and wait for a long time. She'd remained in her car in the dark after her conversation with Eik the night before and nearly given up due to the cold when the door of Jack Skovby's house had opened.

She saw how Eik guided Jack Skovby out with both arms behind his back, very much in the position of a handcuffed man. The officers had been putting him into the back seat of the police car when Camilla had run up to the house, calling to Eik. She knew he had heard her, but he quickly vanished back into the house anyway and shut the front door again without turning around.

Then she had called the duty officer at the police station in Odense to hear if there was any news in the search for Simon Funch, hadn't gotten anything out of that, and had instead gone up to the house and put her hands on the kitchen window to look in. There had been no one there. She had walked back and forth along the nearly pitch-black country road with Charlie for fifteen minutes, waiting for something to happen, then she finally gave in to the cold and drove back to the hotel in Troense.

Her alarm clock had rung at six-thirty the next morning, and it was still dark as she and Charlie made their way back to Jack's farm.

She spotted Eik's car in the courtyard right away. Two police cars had also arrived. She left Charlie in the car and got out to walk up to the house.

Camilla had decided that she would stand there and keep knocking until Louise or Eik came out and told her what was going on. They fucking owed her that, she kept telling herself. She was about to knock on the door when she spotted Louise through the kitchen window. She was with a woman with short blond hair. Camilla quickly pulled away from the door, but not so far away that she couldn't still call to Louise.

She was standing by a white fence when Louise stepped out into the early morning light with the blond woman. They walked over to a small white car, which was parked behind the police cars, then the door opened again and Eik came out with his arm wrapped around the shoulders of a small dark-haired boy.

At first Camilla just stood and watched while the boy was led over to the police car in front, then she quickly got out her phone to take the very first pictures of Simon Funch. She zoomed in and saw him reach out to touch the police car, saw how Eik let him walk around the car before opening the back door for the little boy. Then she put her phone back in her purse again without having taken a single picture. She started walking back to her car.

"Wait," she suddenly heard Louise call.

"Hi," Louise said as she came over to Camilla's car. "Sorry I haven't called you back. All of a sudden things happened so fast."

"You found him," Camilla stated, glancing at the police car, which rolled past them just then.

Louise nodded.

"But we need more time before word gets out."

Louise looked like shit. They knew each other so well that she could tell right away that Louise hadn't slept at all. Her friend was on the edge, and it wouldn't take much to push her over.

She nodded and reluctantly promised to sit on the news.

"But then you need to give me something else," Camilla said. "You didn't even bother to respond when I wrote that you should investigate whether Dorthe had maybe felt that Helene owed her a child."

Louise nodded and apologized again for not responding.

"If there's any meat to that theory, I promise you'll be told," Louise said. "But not the boy. Just give us a chance to talk to him and have him examined before the press descends on us."

Camilla sensed that Louise was keeping her at arm's length and couldn't help but feel offended. She had kept her promise not to write anything when they found the child's bedroom at the inn, and now that she had found a connection between Dorthe Hylles-ted and Helene Funch, Louise was leaving her out.

"So, what do you have for me?" she asked coolly, walking over to the car to let Charlie out. The minute the big German shepherd saw Louise, he ran over to her and nearly knocked her into the fence in his excitement.

Louise looked at the dog in surprise and sat down to return his love. She really seemed worn-out, so Camilla retrieved her bag and handed her friend a breakfast bun.

"If you don't want to talk about the boy, then tell me about the Funch family and Dorthe Hyllested," she said as Louise stood back up and Charlie wandered over to pee on a fence post.

Louise accepted the bun and hesitated. She looked out at the fields for a moment, as if she were trying to divvy up what could be released publicly and what the police should keep to themselves.

"We know there was a connection between Nils Hyllested and Kristian Funch. Kristian transferred a very large amount of money to Nils, but we can't find any explanation for what the money was used for or where it went," she said.

Camilla was keenly aware that Louise was only giving her this tidbit because she wanted Camilla to start digging into what had happened to the money herself.

"Did that happen when Kristian Funch started draining his company?"

Louise nodded, revealing that Funch had also transferred very large sums to Jack Skovby.

"Does this have anything to do with the boy?" Camilla asked.

"We still don't know what transpired between Kristian Funch and the two men, or what their connection was. We're trying to clarify that. We have Jack in for questioning right now, so we're waiting to get an explanation from him that can hopefully shed some light on their interactions."

Camilla nodded slightly to herself and fished the second bun out of her bag to hand it to Louise, who had already eaten the first one.

"So, the money Kristian Funch withdrew from his company was transferred to Jack Skovby and Nils Hyllested," she stated as Louise took the bun.

Louise nodded, and even though she didn't say it out loud, Camilla knew that Louise meant it might be a good idea to take a closer look at what Kristian Funch had done in the period leading up to the plane crash.

Louise reached out and gave Camilla's arm a squeeze.

"I'm glad you understand that we need to care for the boy."

Camilla nodded and watched her friend disappear back inside the house.

CHAPTER 29

Eva Nørgaard appeared at the front door when Camilla parked in front of her farmhouse. She had called before leaving Jack Skovby's farm and asked if she could stop by even though it was only eight in the morning. Eva sounded like she'd already been awake for a long time and had immediately replied that if Camilla could pick up milk and some bread on the way over, she'd be very welcome. Her daughter had spent the night and had been about to head out by bike to pick up some bread for breakfast.

"Hi," Camilla said, handing Eva the bag with the bread, juice, and milk. Camilla was glad Lea was there, because Aske's sister no doubt knew more about her brother's private life than their mother did.

"I just heard that the police picked Jack up last night. Is that why you're here?" Eva asked, inviting her in. Camilla could already feel the heat from the living room in the short front hallway, where she took off her boots.

She shook her head.

"I'm here to talk with you a little more about Aske," she said before greeting Lea, who was lying on the sofa looking at her cell phone. The young woman pulled herself up to sit and nodded to Camilla. She was wearing a faded tracksuit with a heavy sweater over it, even though the fire in the tiled stove over by the wall was roaring.

"Are you okay?" Camilla asked the young woman. "I heard about the ladder, but I'm glad to see that the police didn't keep you."

"They don't believe I did it."

"I got a recommendation for a criminal defense lawyer," Eva said, as if that required any explanation. "The kids' father knew one, and he said right from the get-go that there was no evidence that Lea was to blame for the accident."

"But we don't need evidence," the daughter snarled, annoyed. "Because I said it was me."

Eva shot Camilla a quick glance, and Lea sank back into the sofa and concentrated on her cell phone again.

"It's terrible about the little Funch son," Eva said as she put the kettle on and got a jar of Nescafé out of a cupboard. "The police were here again yesterday, but I couldn't help them. I really hope they find him. I can't believe he could have been living with Dorthe at the inn all this time, if what the newspapers say is true."

She turned to Camilla with a watchful look.

"Is it true?"

"It seems to be," she replied. "That's the police theory at any rate."

Eva called to her daughter to see if she wanted a cup of coffee, too.

"Just juice," Lea replied from the sofa.

"There's obviously a lot I didn't know about Dorthe, even though I thought I knew her."

Eva handed Camilla the milk. The rolls had been placed in a basket and Eva got out three plates and knives. Then she opened the fridge and took out butter and homemade jam.

"We'll sit in the living room," she said as she carried the tray in.

Lea had sat down at the dining table. She looked pale and unhappy, and Camilla was overwhelmed with compassion for the young girl who had clearly fallen apart after her brother's death.

They got comfortable before Camilla began with what she hadn't felt she could ask over the phone. She turned to Eva now, who sat with her coffee mug between her hands.

"Did you get a probate court certificate after your son's death, so that you could administer his estate yourself?"

Lea didn't react to the question, but Eva nodded.

"Not because there was that much to administer," she replied. "But Aske had a little money and then there was the car he had bought a year before he died."

She paused, and Camilla nodded encouragingly for her to continue.

"My ex-husband said right away that he didn't want anything from Aske. So I figured I could manage the estate myself. I wanted Lea to get everything her brother had left behind."

Lea didn't look at them while her mother spoke, but she glanced up from her plate when Camilla asked how much money had been in Aske's account when he died.

"I know it's a very personal question," she hurried to add.

Eva and Lea quickly exchanged a glance.

"Around eighty thousand kroner," the sister replied. "And we had to pay the inheritance tax."

"That car that he bought, did he pay cash for it?" Camilla asked then.

They exchanged glances again, before they both nodded.

"We discussed it ourselves, where the money might have come from," Eva admitted. "He had only just finished high school when he got sick, you know."

There was silence again in the living room and she noticed that Lea had stopped chewing the bite she had just put into her mouth.

"Obviously this is extremely confidential information and I'll of course respect your decision if you feel I'm overstepping," she continued. "But I wanted to ask if you had any objections to looking at Aske's old account statements with me."

"We don't have his NemID code," Lea said right away, as if she had already tried.

Camilla nodded, then said that there was another way they could access it. She looked at Eva.

"If you were issued a probate certificate for your son's estate, we can access e-Boks. You upload the certificate on their home page and then we can get in that way to pull his account statements." She could tell that this had aroused some interest in Lea's eyes.

Lea rummaged through a little weekend bag that was sitting on the floor next to the sofa and pulled out a computer while asking her mother to find the certificate as if they were under some kind of time crunch.

Eva walked over to a dresser next to the tiled oven and pulled a folder out of the drawer. Shortly thereafter, she handed the certificate to her daughter, who had already opened her computer and was busily typing away. She was so fast, it almost looked like her fingers were hovering above the keys.

Camilla moved over to the sofa next to her. They sat together for a while, studying the home page.

"It's probably your mother who needs to log in to her e-Boks account," Camilla said, moving so Eva could come sit between them.

Eva set her cell phone in her lap once she had entered her NemID, then swiped the code on her phone's NemID app. She didn't quite seem to understand what they were doing, so Lea grabbed her mom's cell phone, took a picture of the probate certificate, and transferred the photo to the computer.

Camilla pulled away a little so she wasn't staring straight down at Eva Nørgaard's private e-Boks documents.

"Then what do we do?" Lea asked, looking over at Camilla.

"Try typing 'probate certificate,'" she suggested without being able to see what was on the screen.

The tip of Lea's tongue peeked out of the corner of her mouth in concentration as she typed.

"There's a form Mom needs to fill out and it says it can take up to ten days to process," she announced disappointedly, already uploading the certificate.

Damn.

Camilla suggested that they fill out the form. Then they just had to wait.

"I think I already filled that one out when I was dealing with the estate," Eva exclaimed, pointing at the screen, where a notification had appeared saying that the certificate was uploaded and being processed.

Camilla was about to butter a roll from the bread basket when Lea exclaimed that it had been approved, after which she started searching for her deceased younger brother's bank statements.

"When did the assault at the cabin happen?" Camilla asked, breaking the focused silence.

"August 2016," came Eva's prompt reply.

"Try going all the way back to that fall," Camilla requested. "Look and see if an amount of a hundred thousand kroner was transferred in at some point after that."

They both looked at Camilla, a little surprised, but then Lea nodded and clicked her way through the last two and a half years of account activity.

"Yes," she exclaimed. "One hundred thousand kroner were transferred into Aske's account on August 30, 2016."

Her eyes welled up with tears.

She passed the computer to Camilla, quickly wiping away her tears.

Camilla took a picture of the funds transfer and of Aske's account number.

Finally the connection dawned on Eva.

"Does that mean that someone paid my son not to report the assault to the police?"

Camilla nodded.

"There's no name associated with the transfer, just an account number," Lea said, while Camilla sent Louise a text.

> Kristian Funch transferred 100k to Aske Nørgaard, the housekeeper's son. Call me.

This time it barely took ten seconds before Louise called back. Camilla went into the kitchen, where she selected the picture of the account statement. She gave Louise Aske's account number and read her the number of the account the money had been transferred from.

"The transfer happened exactly ten days after Aske was violently assaulted by the man he was with at the inn's forest cabin. Find out if Helene's husband reserved the cabin that weekend," Camilla suggested.

"There are no names on those reservations," Louise replied. "They're all entered into the system under the name Jens Jensen."

Camilla heard Louise typing on a computer as they spoke.

"Where are you?" Louise asked.

"At Eva and Lea's. We've just been going through Aske's bank statements. After you told me about the large amount of money, I thought that maybe there was some connection."

"It's him," Louise mumbled into the phone. "The money to Aske Nørgaard was transferred from the same account that also transferred money to Jack Skovby and Nils Hyllested."

Camilla realized that Lea had come out into the kitchen with her.

"I'll talk to Helene and find out what she knows about the forest cabin," Louise said. "Right now we're also trying to find out what happened to the seven hundred thousand kroner that Kristian Funch transferred to Nils. It seems like the money was withdrawn systematically in smaller sums of less than ten thousand, so it didn't attract the bank's attention. Tell Eva Nørgaard that we'd like to talk to her again. Either I can send an officer out there or she can come to the police station in Svendborg. Unfortunately I won't be able to talk to her myself since we need to start questioning Simon Funch."

"I'll give her the message," Camilla promised, and was about to wrap up the call when Louise asked if she was driving back to Copenhagen.

"No," she replied. "I'm staying out here until tomorrow. I want to try to interview Helene Funch."

"You can't," Louise replied sharply. "We've advised her not to talk to the press."

Her voice softened a little when she suggested that they eat dinner together at the hotel. Camilla knew that was her friend's way of saying thank you and apologizing. She also knew that it was very unlikely it would happen now that the police needed to get to the bottom of how much Kristian Funch had had to do with Strammelse Inn before his death. And how much the couple who owned the inn had had to do with him.

In the living room, Lea had slumped into the sofa, face pale, tears seeping out from under her closed eyelids. She was a person falling apart. Eva showed Camilla a few pictures of Kristian Funch they had googled while Camilla talked with Louise. An iPhone sat on the table. Eva explained that it was her son's. She had gotten it back the previous evening after the police had finished going through it.

"Look," she said, passing it across the table. Camilla recognized Kristian Funch right away. He stood in profile in front of the hot tub behind the cabin. He was wearing only a towel around his waist and opening a bottle of champagne. He probably didn't realize Aske had taken the picture, she thought. Eva's son had also taken a couple of selfies, one with him raising his champagne glass to the lens and one with him puckering up and glancing at a naked back—Kristian Funch's.

The next pictures on the cell phone had been taken at the hospital. He was so bruised on one side of his face that his eye wasn't visible through all the swelling and discoloration. Camilla sat and stared at the little screen for a long time.

"That's what happened on the night that destroyed him," Eva said quietly. "All the visible traces of the violence went away with time, but he never healed on the inside. He became self-destructive and everything beautiful in him disappeared."

Lea opened her eyes. She sat staring straight ahead without wiping away the tears that were still trickling down her cheeks.

"I don't want that car," she said suddenly. "I don't want anything he bought with the money he got from that monster."

Eva reached out and put a hand on her daughter.

Camilla felt the same anger herself. An adult man, a wealthy one, had simply paid his way out of a police report. She knew that this sort of thing had undoubtedly happened before and would happen again. Aske Nørgaard hadn't done anything wrong. He had gone to the forest cabin because he had really wanted to be with Kristian Funch. And then he had been assaulted and paid to keep his mouth shut. He had lost everything in a relationship with an unequal power dynamic.

There weren't any more pictures on the phone. It was as if Aske's young life ended after what happened, even though he didn't die until a couple years later. There wasn't anything more to be documented in photos, no more joy to be shared or remembered.

"Did you know Kristian Funch?" Camilla asked.

They both shook their heads.

"I knew who he was, of course, and obviously everyone heard about the accident," Eva said then. "I also knew that they lived in that big farm out in Bjernemark. But I don't think I've ever met him."

No one had touched any more of the breakfast, and Lea got up and exited the room. Shortly after, Camilla heard the shower turn on.

"I don't think she'll ever get over it," her mother said quietly. "For my part, I'll never forgive that a young person's life meant so little to others."

"That's completely understandable," Camilla said, putting a comforting hand on Eva's arm. "It's twisted when someone thinks they can pay their way out of being held accountable for their actions. Especially when it's an adult behaving that way toward a child."

"Aske was no child. He knew what he was doing," Eva said thoughtfully. "But it just took away all his joy at being alive."

"How well did your son actually know Nils Hyllested?" It had occurred to Camilla that it could have been the innkeeper who had extorted Kristian after what happened at the cabin. Seven hundred thousand was an incredibly large amount of money. So much that it didn't just change hands. Or vanish into thin air.

"They knew each other," Eva replied. "But I don't think they were seeing each other in that sense. That's what you mean, isn't it?"

The water was still running in the bathroom in the back of the house, but otherwise the place was quiet.

"More specifically, I mean, was Nils on Aske's side? Maybe Nils went after Kristian Funch because he wanted to defend your son."

A vaguely sad look came over Eva's face. Not a smile, just a fleeting change in her expression as she shook her head.

"No one was on Aske's side," she said quietly, her voice filled with sadness. "I'm afraid that what happened was more the opposite. It made Aske go over to their side. So he became indifferent, too. About other people."

Camilla sat for a bit considering the woman before her, then she made a decision. She was going to have to disregard what Louise had told her. She wanted to talk to Helene Funch. Not about the child, but about her husband, a man who seemed to have lived rather a different life than it appeared.

CHAPTER 30

Louise looked around at the light, airy living room of the family's home. The windowsills were decorated and a large basket next to the sofa was full of yarn and a cheerfully colored knitting project.

Tine and Henrik Sommer had been foster parents for more than twenty years. Louise knew from the information she had printed out at the police station that they were in their mid-fifties. The couple lived in Tullebølle on Langeland Island, and Tine herself had been born with severe hearing loss and had therefore mastered sign language. In addition to that, they had mainly cared for foster children who were deaf or hard of hearing. Henrik was a social worker employed by the municipality of Langeland's Children's Welfare Board, where he worked with at-risk and vulnerable children.

She had to hand it to Deputy Chief Superintendent Grube: He had done well here. Not only had he had pressured the duty desk in Odense and child protective services until they had a foster family ready to receive Simon Funch early the next morning, but the family they'd found was experienced, was well liked, and seemed willing to clear their schedule at short notice to create a calm, safe environment for the little boy.

Tine smiled as she walked into the living room with coffee and juice. There was a basket of rolls on the table along with jam and sandwich chocolate, like that was something you always had on hand in case a little boy in need of some spoiling should suddenly come over.

The foster mother spoke slowly and in a low voice, as if the words clumped together in her mouth before they escaped, but Louise understood that she was taking pains to make sure her lips could be read.

"He slept well last night," Louise said. "But when he woke up, he cried. At first we thought it was because he was hungry or thirsty since he kept reaching out with his arms. Not to us, but straight ahead of himself, as if there was someone standing there we couldn't see. Someone who didn't come to pick him up. Eik tried to calm him down."

Louise had brought along the teddy bear that Helene had given her.

"I didn't dare give it to him, because I didn't know if that would trigger an even greater feeling of loss," she said as Henrik returned from the bathroom with Simon.

"We've already discussed the fact that we'd like to invite his mother to come over later today," Henrik said. "Just an hour to begin with, so they can meet each other. People talk about prelinguistic feelings that can awaken certain moods. In other words, from the time before the child has verbal language. So my hope is that her presence and her scent might elicit some emotions in him. Her presence may even have a soothing effect on him, even though he doesn't overtly remember her, because it helps him reconnect with some good memories. And in that way maybe he will experience a form of recognition."

Simon shyly glanced over at Tine and at the breakfast on the table while Henrik spoke. Louise thought that it must be overwhelming for him with so many strangers' faces. He had taken it well that morning once he'd calmed down. But anyone would react as he had if they woke up and two strangers were sitting with them. Simon had crawled back into the sofa and sat with the comforter clasped in front of him as he'd silently followed the team of police officers Grube had sent out to search Jack's house. But shortly after the team arrived, they were informed that the foster family was ready to take Simon. Louise had insisted that she and Eik question the boy themselves with Tine and Henrik's help. And it was agreed that they could do it without an observer present for Simon since Henrik was a professional himself.

Tine pointed to a chair at the dining table and smiled encouragingly to Simon, while she pulled out another chair and sat in it herself.

Louise and Eik sat down at the end of the table and let Tine and Henrik take charge.

Tine pointed to herself and said: "Tine." Then Henrik introduced himself with the same gesture. Then they pointed to him and said: "Simon."

The boy attentively followed the motions of the mouths and hands of the two adults who were talking to him.

Louise choked up.

Tine reached for the basket of breakfast rolls, and Simon hesitantly accepted one without taking his eyes off her face. She cut the roll for him, then pointed to the butter and looked at him expectantly.

Simon nodded and followed her hands as she buttered the bread. Then he pointed to the box of sandwich chocolate. Tine placed a sheet of the chocolate onto one half of the roll. Then she did something with her hands and again looked expectantly at him, but Simon didn't react.

"Thirsty?" asked Henrik on the other side of the boy. He raised his left hand and stuck his thumb into his mouth.

Simon nodded and looked over at the carton of chocolate milk.

Then the boy brought his right hand up to his mouth, letting his fingertips point to his lip.

"Hungry?" Henrik asked and lifted the plate up off the table to give it to Simon.

The boy smiled and nodded.

Louise blinked quickly and looked away for a second. She sensed that Eik was practically holding his breath while the foster parents and the boy searchingly tried to connect with one another.

They both remained silent as hands and fingers spoke. Every now and then, Simon looked down at the table. He had eaten half of the roll with the chocolate, but shook his head when Tine offered him the other half.

The boy looked up at Henrik now and moved his little index finger across his forehead. He put his hand over his heart before clenching both hands and rubbing his eyes with them.

Louise noticed how the couple exchanged an almost imperceptible glance before Henrik nodded to the boy and put his hand over his own heart.

Then Simon turned to Tine. Again he brought his finger across his forehead, put the palms of his hands together, and then put them against his cheek and closed his eyes.

"Mother is sleeping," Tine said out loud.

The boy again put his hands up in front of his face, turned his fingers toward his face and wiggled them a little.

Tine waited to see if there would be more before she nodded.

Tears welled up in the boy's eyes. He raised his small hand again and this time moved his finger across his throat and again clenched both fists, which he pressed against his eyes.

Louise was so moved by the boy that she decided that they shouldn't push him for any more than what he volunteered himself. Without ever having experienced sign language, she felt she understood every word that was being said between them. It was so emotional to see how he was finally able to expel everything that must have been bottled up inside of him ever since he came downstairs at the inn.

"Ask if he saw anyone downstairs at the inn when they found Dorthe," Eik instructed.

Louise was afraid that they would interrupt this nice moment that had just arisen between the three of them, who very clearly had a language together.

Tine leaned forward toward Simon, her eyes serious as her hands asked Eik's question. But this time, the boy didn't respond. He sat with wide eyes and followed her motions but shook his head slightly and looked down at the table.

Then he slowly brought up his hands and looked urgently at Tine as he beat his chest, cradled his arms, and then drew two circles in the air in front of him.

A thoughtful wrinkle appeared between the foster mother's

eyes and then she hesitantly shook her head. Simon repeated himself while looking at her urgently, but she still didn't understand. Her hands formed a question, which he didn't react to.

Tine turned to look at Louise and Eik, and Simon stared down at the table again.

"It's quite clear that Dorthe used some sign-supported speech with him, but I think they mostly developed their own language," she said. "I can't understand anywhere near all his signs, and it sometimes feels like we're talking at cross-purposes, as if some of the signs I'm using mean something else to him."

"We're probably just going to need to spend a little time with him, so we can learn to communicate better with each other," Henrik said. "Some things are easy to understand, but what Tine's saying is right. He also has some signs and a diction that they must have come up with on their own."

"So far, he's said that he came downstairs and thought his mother was sleeping. But she was dead. I tried to ask if he had seen anyone hurt his mother. But he didn't understand me. And I would really like to have permission to talk to him a little more about ordinary things. I think it would be good if we took a walk together or played a bit before I ask more about whether he saw Dorthe being attacked."

"That sounds like a good idea," Eik quickly agreed. He reached out and stopped his cell phone from taking video, removing it from the low stand he'd set up on the table to capture the conversation. They agreed that Tine and Henrik should first and foremost try to help the boy feel at home and safe in his new surroundings.

"But obviously," Louise interjected, "we are very interested in hearing what he saw downstairs at the inn. We are particularly interested in whether he saw anyone other than the man who took him away from the inn."

Tine nodded.

"We'll ask about it all, but it's also likely that he'll bring it up himself, as he did just a moment ago. If he hasn't had anyone to communicate with, it's only natural that he needs to get these gruesome things he's been through off his chest."

"And of course we'll make sure that all the conversations with him that involve the things he went through at the inn are videotaped," Henrik concluded.

"Thank you," Louise said and looked out at the yard, where there was a swing set, a playhouse, and other fun things.

It must be a big change, she thought. For two years, he had had a world constrained to Dorthe's apartment and the little walled-in patio behind the inn. Now his world had suddenly opened up, but he was all alone in it. She thought about Helene as well, who wouldn't be able to talk to her little boy when they were reunited later that day.

CHAPTER 31

Once they were in the car, Louise sent Borre a message to tell her they were on their way back to the police station to attend Jack Skovby's questioning. She had asked Eik to drive her to Svendborg before he went to pick up Charlie from Camilla.

Jack had spent the night in custody but had been brought back to the interrogation room at eight o'clock, where Lange had gotten to work.

Skovby maintained that the money that had been transferred to him by Kristian Funch had covered payment for two agricultural machines, which Helene's husband had bought from him in the spring of 2017. Lange had sent a text that read, "Combine Harvester, John Deere S690 (2012). Tractor, John Deere 6400 with front lift (2007)." Skovby had also been able to produce an email from Kristian Funch that said that he would make a bank transfer for the amount.

But during the search of Skovby's property, two farming machines identical to the ones he had allegedly sold were sitting in the barn behind his house and both were still registered in Jack Skovby's name.

Eik had been quiet since they left the single-family home after saying goodbye to Simon and his foster parents. He occasionally glanced around at the countryside, the water and the fields, but he didn't say anything. He didn't need to, either, Louise thought. It was obvious that he was preoccupied with the little boy.

She didn't have time to think before her hand reached out and came to rest on his arm. She gave him a squeeze and left her hand there. Since their first case together, she had noticed how Eik had a special frequency when it came to kids. Maybe because he hadn't always had anyone to be there for, she thought. Steph had been sixteen when she came into his life. Maybe it was another reminder of all the years he himself had missed, sitting across from Simon and seeing how much Helene had already missed of her son's childhood.

"Do you miss her?" Louise asked, still not pulling her hand away, even though he let go of the wheel with his left hand and put it on top of hers. They hadn't talked about Steph going back to England to finish school. It struck her that he was probably afraid she would decide to stay over there instead of coming back and living with him.

He nodded.

"I think what I miss most is all the things I didn't get to experience with her," he said. "Her childhood. All the things that are irrevocably over and that I can never be a part of. Sitting in there I realized how horrific it would be for Helene to discover that the person Simon misses is Dorthe. I don't think we can even imagine how hard that's going to be for her. First, the tremendous joy that he's alive, and then the grief of realizing that he has no idea who she is. How do you think she'll handle it?"

"I've tried to prepare her," Louise replied. "And it sounded like she understood that it would take time."

"He's clearly grieving losing Dorthe. He thinks of her as his mother. We should probably offer Helene some conversations with a crisis psychologist. We do that sometimes with family members in missing persons cases, if they don't have anyone they can talk to."

"She has her sister," Louise said, but then conceded that Iben didn't seem like the right person to help. "You're right. There's a risk she'll break down when she realizes that he doesn't love her back right away."

Their hands were still together. Eik occasionally absent-mindedly ran his thumb over the back of her hand, and she enjoyed the brief movements.

"But before we do that, I need to run Helene through the mill about her husband's relationship to Aske Nørgaard," she said, then relayed her conversation with Camilla. "Something happened between Aske, Kristian Funch, and Nils Hyllested. Now all three of them are dead. We need to find out if Dorthe's murder is somehow connected to them."

"And it doesn't have anything to do with Simon," he said.

She nodded and could see that Eik was thinking. He had withdrawn his hand, and she let her own fall back into her lap.

"There's something extremely savage and vicious about the way Dorthe behaved toward Helene," he said then. "Something that could only have come from an intense jealousy, grief, or anger that knocked her sense of justice completely out of whack. Such strong feelings often give rise to more of the same. They can function like catalysts and trigger a series of other circumstances. We've seen that often enough before."

Louise nodded.

"You're confident that it was Jack who killed her, then?" she asked. "You think he discovered she was hiding Simon and acted on Helene's behalf?"

Eik didn't respond, but Louise had her own doubts.

"Or that he and Helene did it together?" he offered after a pause.

Louise shook her head.

"I'm completely sure that Helene Funch didn't know her son was alive when I went to see her," she said. "If Jack found out about Simon and that led to a confrontation with Dorthe, then he did that on his own."

She let her gaze follow a wreath of golden treetops standing on the hill facing the country road.

"That could be the connection," she admitted after they had driven awhile in silence. "But it still doesn't explain the tie between Helene's husband and Nils Hyllested."

They had crossed Tåsinge Island and were nearing the Svend-borg Sound Bridge.

"Honestly, I'm more interested in figuring out how Nils and Dorthe found Simon and managed to bring him back to the inn unseen," Eik said, signaling that he would be taking the exit into Svendborg. "These men seem like a group of unsympathetic assholes, and it looks like your date was pulling the strings."

"They blackmailed Kristian Funch," Louise admitted, ignoring the part about her date. "But I don't think you're right that they're a group. I think it was Nils Hyllested and Jack against Helene's husband."

He pondered that for a bit, then nodded.

"You really have a lot at stake if you liquidate your company and allow yourself to be blackmailed to the tune of two million kroner," Eik interjected as he pressed a piece of nicotine gum out of the package with his hands still on the wheel.

"Two point two million kroner," Louise specified.

"And, like I said, everyone is dead now. Aside from your flame."

"Knock it off," she said. "He's not my flame."

"You seemed pretty comfortable in his arms," Eik said, not looking at her as he parked the car.

"He's not the one I went to the bar with," she replied, annoyed. "I had a drink with Lange. And when he left, Jack came over to talk to me. I don't know him, and I don't want to hear any more about it."

Louise angrily got out of the car and quickly strode into the police station without waiting to see if Eik was coming with her or leaving to pick up Charlie. After the door closed behind her, she stood for a moment trying to force her pulse to settle down. She knew it was ridiculous to let Eik's accusation hurt her, but it had meant so much when he had reached out and let his hand rest on hers. And now it felt as if he had pissed a big, disrespectful stream all over her attempt to renew a little of the love they had felt for each other.

CHAPTER 32

Louise had three cups of coffee with her when she knocked and walked into the room where Jack Skovby was sitting for questioning. She had been told that he didn't want a lawyer after all, even though he had been informed of his rights as the accused. He had also voluntarily agreed to let the police search his property without a warrant, because he didn't have anything to hide, as he put it.

His thick, wavy hair fell across his forehead as he sat hunched over with his arms resting heavily on the table. He didn't look over at the door when she came in but glanced up quickly when she set the disposable coffee cup in front of him. She didn't say anything, just pulled out a chair and sat down next to Lange.

Jack stared down at the scratched beechwood tabletop.

"He was a bully," he said as if he were picking up the conversation where it had been interrupted when Louise came in.

"Just try telling the last part from the beginning," Lange urged, taking a long drink of the steaming coffee. Louise watched him, fascinated that his throat could handle that.

Jack glanced quickly over at Louise and then nodded.

"I was seventeen when I killed my father," he said in a mono-tone. It sounded like an unsentimental fact. He didn't try to pre-tend that he regretted it. "He beat my mother. He beat my little sister. And he beat me. And it had been like that for as long as I can remember."

He looked up again now and folded his hands together on the table in front of him.

"I mean, it wasn't like he just walked around and hit you if you had talked back or if my mother happened to say something that set him off. He hit when he wanted us to do what he said. Instead of taking the time to ask for something or explain how he wanted it, he would hit. It saved him time."

He didn't bat an eyelid as he spoke.

"My parents were summoned to the school once because my sister's teacher reported that she had come to school with bruises. She wouldn't normally say anything, but that morning he had brought her out to the stable because he wanted her to sweep the feed and bedding out of the stable aisle before she went to school. She did that every morning after he had fed the horses. But that morning he hit her because she had gotten off to a late start and was trying to hurry so she wouldn't be late to school, too. He hit her so hard her eyebrow split in two. And it always enraged him when we started bleeding after he hit us. My mom wanted my sis-ter to stay home from school, but he wouldn't hear of it. So, the teacher officially reported him because people at the school knew that was how things were at our house. During that talk, my mother promised that it wouldn't happen again."

He paused for a moment before looking up at Lange.

"Everyone knew it wouldn't last. My father knew it, too. He

didn't even try to make excuses or apologize. He just sat there without saying anything because he thought it was his right to break his own children like you would break a horse. My sister was there for the talk. She told me about it when they got home. That afternoon I went out into the stable and killed him with the ax."

Jack slumped down now and hid his face in his hands.

It was quiet. Only Lange moved. He sat there rotating his coffee cup. Then he said, "And could you please repeat the description of how you killed your father with the ax."

Jack lowered his hands and stared straight ahead without looking at either of them.

"I hit him several times on the back of the head with the butt of the ax," he said, glancing at Lange. He didn't look at Louise. He only stared ahead, gazed down at the table, or shot fleeting looks at Lange.

"I served my time, and I don't regret what I did. No one understands what it's like to live with constant fear. None of us were ever ourselves, because we were always afraid of him, afraid of seeing him. Afraid of his mood and of the blows that came out of nowhere."

He now looked almost eagerly at Lange and Louise in turn.

"It's not that I'm trying to sound like a saint. I don't actually care what people think about what I did back then. I did it to give my mother and my sister a life, a life where they weren't scared all the time, and wearing obvious marks from his beatings. I don't regret it," he repeated. "My mother stayed on the farm until she went into a nursing home. That's where she lives now, and I visit her once a week. If my father were still alive, she'd be the one who was dead. My sister got married. Her husband's from Tåsinge, too, but they live up in Frederikshavn now."

He let his arms drop down alongside his body and gazed up at them with candor, a look Louise recognized: *Let's do this. I don't have anything to hide. I stand by my actions.*

Very noble, she thought, irritated.

Lange had pushed aside his empty cup and looked down at his paperwork now.

"You have a daughter with Christina Hald," he continued.

Jack immediately crossed his arms in front of his chest but nodded.

"Isadora is ten now."

He nodded again, and Louise immediately noted the hard glint in his eye.

"You've been trying to gain custody of your daughter for several years," Lange read from the report.

Jack kept nodding.

"She lives with her mother in Copenhagen."

"Yes," he replied. "Her mother is beyond any hope of reform. She's mentally ill and has turned my daughter against me. She had no right to move so far away with a kid who's both of ours."

"It says here," Lange continued, "that she reported you to the police for several violent assaults and that she has been hospitalized after you beat her."

"None of that is true," Jack interrupted. "She has systematically tried to portray me as a psychopath because she found a guy in Copenhagen. I wouldn't agree to Isa moving so far away and then suddenly all this came up. I've never touched her."

"Christina Hald has a restraining order preventing you from visiting her address in Copenhagen," Lange continued. His jovial Northern Jutland friendliness had vanished now, like dew in the sunlight. He looked straight at Jack and waited.

"She's overreacting," Jack replied. "I have a right to see Isa, and if Christina doesn't honor our agreements, then I have to go pick up my daughter myself."

"Have to force your way into her apartment and take your daughter away from her mother against both of their wishes."

Jack lunged forward in the chair.

"I haven't done anything to my daughter," he exclaimed angrily. "I have a right to see her. She's my child, too. Don't sit there and make it sound like I've done something that any father wouldn't have done. Which is to be with my child."

"But there's a reason you lost your right to see Isadora," Lange said calmly.

Jack pressed his lips together and for a moment he seemed to regret that he'd turned down having his lawyer with him.

They sat in silence before Louise leaned forward.

"I'd really like to talk to you about Kristian Funch," she said, changing the topic. "What do you know about his stays at the inn's forest cabin?"

Jack's eyes suddenly looked wary. It took a moment before he answered.

"I didn't know very much about Kristian Funch," he finally said. "As you already know, I was more interested in his wife."

There was a hard glint in his eyes.

Louise ignored his provocation. They sat for a bit, staring at each other.

Then he continued, "I did know that he went out there."

"Did you also know that he assaulted Aske Nørgaard and then paid the young man a hundred thousand kroner not to go to the police?"

Louise didn't know this for sure, but she was assuming that was how it fit together.

Jack stared down at the table again, but he slowly began to nod.

"I didn't know that he paid him to keep quiet. But I definitely knew something had happened out there that no one would talk about. I heard that from Nils."

"Did Helene know that?" Louise asked.

"There wasn't anything between Helene and Kristian anymore, not sexually. There really hadn't been since their youngest was born—that's what she told me at least. I think she knew that he was getting his needs met elsewhere. That was my sense anyway."

"Did she know that he was also interested in men?" Louise asked.

"That I don't know," he replied. "I knew because I'd heard it from Nils. He told me one night that Funch sometimes rented the cabin. Probably when his wife thought he was out installing alarms in Jutland."

He said that last part mockingly.

"I felt sorry for her," he said. "It can't feel very fucking good when your husband wants young boys more than the wife who's given him three children."

Yeah, right, Louise thought. He felt sorry for her.

"We actually talked about it a bit one time," he continued. "When I was trying to get her to leave him. I had fallen in love. We were crazy about each other at that point. But she didn't want to.

She said that she desired me and thought about me all the time. But she loved her husband, and she didn't want to leave her family."

Louise realized that what he had just said was a fairly accurate description of most of the people involved in the investigation. Dorthe and Nils Hyllested had apparently also loved each other and had chosen to stay together even though they desired other people, same as Helene and Kristian. Love and desire were two different drives. The one was deep, the other hard to control.

She thought about how young Aske Nørgaard had paid attention to and followed his desires, but had never managed to find love. The others had tried to forge a path for both. Nils had seen men the whole time but had established a cover story in his relationship with Dorthe, because he couldn't cope with standing out as different in Central Jutland, she thought.

Dorthe had gotten pregnant by Jack after she had discovered and accepted that her husband couldn't get her pregnant.

"Kristian Funch wasn't gay," Jack said. "It just turned him on. That's what Nils said anyway. But I mean, either you're gay or you're not, right?"

He glanced at Lange with his eyebrows raised.

With his Northern Jutland calm, Lange remained unflappable. He just let Jack talk and sat there ready to strike if anything should come out that they could use.

"So you don't think it's plausible that Kristian Funch and Nils Hyllested had actually started seeing each other and were planning to leave their wives and start a life together? A life without Helene, the kids, or the company that Kristian had built?" Louise asked.

She could sense there was something he wasn't telling them,

but it didn't actually seem like he was lying. More like he was paddling around to avoid getting into certain areas or corners.

"Like, as a couple?" he asked with a mixture of disgust and admiration in his voice.

Louise nodded.

"I'm thinking about the large sum of money Kristian Funch transferred to Nils." It occurred to her too late that Jack might not have known about that, that it might have been a mistake on her part to bring it up.

She noticed Lange's look, but Jack's only reaction was to shake his head.

"I can't imagine that," he said and sounded more composed again.

Louise decided to keep going.

"What do you imagine made Kristian transfer seven hundred thousand kroner to Nils not long after the incident with Aske at the forest cabin?"

Jack clammed up now. He shrugged but averted his gaze.

He knew, she thought. And she already knew that she wasn't going to be able to get him to tell them. Not until they had put him through the wringer, at least.

Louise got up, telling Lange that she was going to drive out and talk to Helene Funch before she was reunited with Simon up at Langeland later that afternoon.

She kept her eye on Jack to see if he was concerned that she was going straight to Helene with the information he had just given them. But he didn't react at all.

CHAPTER 33

There was something depressing about the heavy rain that beat against the car's windshield as Louise drove toward Tåsinge that afternoon. Jack Skovby had been returned to his cell and Deputy Chief Superintendent Grube had summoned her and Eik to what he called a debriefing, which actually amounted to his having made the trip from Odense to South Funen to inform them that now that Simon Funch had been found, Grube no longer required the assistance of the travel unit or the National Investigation Department. He had thanked them profusely for their contribution, then he had made it clear that his own staff of Funen investigators would take over and wrap up the case.

Louise had barely had time to fathom what that meant before Eik had leaned in over the desk so close to Grube's face that the deputy chief superintendent instinctively pulled away a little in his blue desk chair.

"You can forget about that," Eik had stated, vigorously chewing his nicotine gum. "You called for our assistance, and you accepted the special unit's time and resources. That obligates you, too." His rant had ended with him telling Grube about some rules that applied where he came from.

"In South Harbor we say: When you go out together, you also go home together. And those are the guidelines we're following." Then he'd signaled to Louise that they were leaving.

Without a word, she had stood up to follow him, not because she was afraid to defend her own position or stand up for P13, whose very first case was going to vanish into the sand if she pulled out now, but because she was so astonished at Eik, who otherwise rarely raised his voice. He had called Funen's deputy chief superintendent both small and incompetent before he got to the bit about South Harbor. But most of all she was speechless because he had gotten so mad on her behalf.

For his part he could cross Simon Funch off the missing persons list. He had succeeded in identifying the child who had lived with Dorthe Hyllested, and then later found the boy safe and sound. She was the one who still had an unsolved murder case, one that, to put it mildly, just wouldn't budge.

"We won't be going home together on this one," Grube had chirped feebly. "I've already spoken to Søren Velin and I'm stepping in as lead investigator for the final round of the case."

So you can grab the spotlight on a case that ended up getting a lot more media attention than you anticipated, Louise thought angrily as she followed Eik. But then she turned around anyway, went back, and flung open the door to Grube's office.

"I'll be the one who takes Helene to Langeland when she is reunited with her son," she had said and then slammed the door shut again before he had a chance to respond. A burning rage flared up inside Louise at the thought that she could have been at home with

Jonas and Melvin, supporting them in their grief, but instead had been here while Grube, that mooch, ordered her around.

Her son had messaged that morning that they had ordered flowers for the church. They had also ordered a bouquet for Grete's casket, and Melvin had chosen the outfit she would be buried in. That death felt so distant because it had occurred while Louise had been away, even with her daily calls to Jonas. She had called him again before setting out for Tåsinge, and he had insisted that he and Melvin could easily plan the funeral without her coming home.

He had moved downstairs and was sleeping on the sofa at Melvin's. They were having a good time, he had said more than once, and Louise was glad. He and the old man both deserved that. The two of them got along well. They did when she was there, too, but it was different when it was just the two of them. She could tell. Or maybe that was just something she told herself to help her make peace with the fact that she hadn't gone home.

Helene Funch had thrown on a long down jacket and stood waiting under an umbrella outside the main door as Louise drove into the courtyard. On the front step next to her sat a large brown weekend bag, which she picked up when she spotted the car.

Before Louise had driven out to Bjernemark, she had stopped by the hotel in Troense to pick up her things and pay for her room. She had also left a message for Camilla that the case was being handed over to the Funen Police and that she would be driving back to Copenhagen later in the day. Camilla had called her right away, but Louise didn't pick up, so Camilla sent a text.

"Do tell," Camilla wrote.

"Later," Louise had replied.

And then she had been overcome by emptiness. Eik was already on his way back to Copenhagen. Before she left Svendborg, she'd seen him walking Charlie in the parking lot behind the police station. She had wanted to embrace him, disappear into his arms and his leather jacket that smelled like smoke. But when Eik had spread his arms out for a hug, she had pulled away instead, and it had been an awkward farewell. It stung that Grube had kicked her off the case, and she knew there was a risk that her emotions would get the better of her. So she had made do with giving him a quick nod as he slowly lowered his arms again.

She could feel his eyes on her as he stood there watching her get in her car. But he hadn't said anything. And she had sat there long enough to hear him call Charlie to him and see him back his battered Jeep out and leave the parking lot.

"How did he look like he was doing?" was the first thing Helene asked when she opened the passenger-side door to get in. "Has he grown a lot?"

Louise didn't have time to answer before Helene proceeded.

"I've brought these things." She pointed down at the bag. "Of course he's grown out of them, but maybe they can help him remember."

On the phone that morning, Helene had repeatedly asked if her little boy had been molested or abused, if he had said anything, and if it was possible to talk to him.

"When do you think he can move home with me?" she had also asked, but Louise had refrained from guessing.

Now that she was sitting in the car and they were on their way,

Helene was quiet. She seemed troubled in her big down coat. And nervous. They had made it all the way across Tåsinge Island before she turned to Louise.

"Do you think we'll ever find out what happened?" she asked. "How they found Simon and got him back to the inn?"

Louise thought carefully before she shook her head.

"No," she replied. "I don't think so. We can imagine how they found him, but we'll never know for sure."

Louise briefly considered the theory that Dorthe had felt that Helene owed her a child, but she kept it to herself.

"But don't you think they knew that it was our son?"

"They probably did," Louise merely replied. She thought about the life jacket the boy had been wearing when he floated away from his mother in the water. Of course the couple from the inn had known that he had been on board the plane that crashed. And of course they had known who the boy's parents were.

"We'll also never know where he drifted ashore or how long he was lying there before someone found him. Do you think he was conscious?"

Her voice sounded frail, and Louise understood her. While the emergency response team had been struggling to rescue her and bring her ashore, her son had drifted ashore somewhere else. Louise assumed that Nils or Dorthe had found Simon immediately after he had washed up onshore. But now Grube could scramble on his own to locate witnesses who had seen the couple from the inn in the area while the rescue work was going on. Or in Vornæs Woods, where Simon had probably washed ashore. They must have found him before the first search teams arrived. And if they had been in a car, no one would necessarily have noticed that they had a toddler with them as they drove back home.

Maybe only one of them had found him, Louise thought, noting that she was having a hard time letting go of her preconceptions of what had happened. Maybe it had initially been intended as an attempt to help the little boy, but then it had turned into an opportunity. A child who had come to them. A boy who was presumed to have died in the crash. Drowned.

"It's probably not healthy to think about it too much," Louise said as they drove over the bridge onto Langeland Island. "The most important thing is that your son is alive, and you'll get to have him home again."

"But you will follow up on what happened back then, won't you?" Helene insisted, and Louise felt a certain satisfaction in saying that she thought Helene should contact Deputy Chief Superintendent Grube and ask him to explain that part.

"You need to push for that," she said. Helene Funch didn't seem to care in the slightest whether there were any developments in solving Dorthe's murder. For her, it was all about the injustice that had been committed against her family, and Louise couldn't blame her for that at all. But she couldn't help but feel as if Dorthe Hyllested's death was slipping through everyone's fingers now that Simon had been found safe and sound.

They had ended up behind a wide, slow-moving farm vehicle on the narrow road to Tullebølle, where the foster family lived, and Louise could sense Helene's nervousness increasing. She clutched the handle of her weekend bag and sank into her coat and down in the seat.

The heavy vehicle ahead of them kept launching little clods of dirt at their windshield. Louise's cell phone had vibrated a couple of times, but that would have to wait. The first call was from Grube. Now it was Lange. She assumed that by now Lange—along with Borre, Lindén, and Sindal—had been informed that she had been taken off the case and that they now reported directly to the deputy chief superintendent. But then it occurred to her that of course Lange would be affected the same way she was. He would be sent back to North Jutland without having wrapped up the case and without knowing if he was part of the new travel unit or if it had been a onetime thing. She hardly knew herself. But she intended to fight for the group's legitimacy once she got back to Copenhagen. After all, it hadn't been her idea. Other knowledgeable decision-makers had been behind it. Although those same decision-makers had been conspicuous by their absence when it came to insisting that she was in charge of this murder case.

She could see the house now. There was a white station wagon parked by the entrance to Tine and Henrik Sommer's driveway. She slowed down and before they got all the way to the house, she pulled over to the side of the road and turned to Helene.

"If the press tracks you down at any point, obviously I can't forbid you from sharing your story with them," she said, glancing at the white car. "But I want to prepare you for the fact that it can be surprisingly difficult to see yourself splashed all over the front pages. And it's easy to say things that you might later feel were too personal."

Helene didn't really seem to be listening. She had leaned forward toward the windshield and was staring stiffly up at the yellow house. But at least she had warned her, Louise thought. Frankly it was surprising that the press hadn't already pounced on the boy's mother.

She drove past the white car and pulled into the driveway, turning off the engine. The front door opened and Henrik came out to greet them, but Helene sat frozen, staring straight ahead. Louise put a hand on her arm and gave it a squeeze.

"It'll be fine," she said. "You don't need to do or say anything. You just need to be there. Give him time, talk to him. Talk to the foster parents and remember that Simon only arrived at their house today. It's all new to him. It's been a turbulent week full of unfamiliar faces."

"I will never forgive Jack for not bringing my son to me," she said darkly. "He of all people knows how much I'm suffering. He knows how my world fell apart. I don't understand how he could do this to me. We loved each other once."

She was talking mostly to herself, Louise thought. Still, it hit home, the involvement of the man she had trusted, the one she paid to make everything run smoothly, the lover she had been so eager to see that she had been willing to fly even though the weather conditions were bad. No wonder she felt like he'd let her down.

"I can't help wondering," Helene continued, "if Jack did this with Dorthe; were they in on this together?"

"Jack maintains that he didn't know anything about Simon. That he didn't know there was a child living at the inn," Louise said, trying to comfort her.

"Of course he knew," Helene replied, her voice trembling. "Why else would my son have calmly gone off to stay with him?"

She turned to face Louise, as if she were accusing her.

Because that's a calm, trusting boy you've got, Louise thought, and because he didn't view his time with Dorthe Hyllested as something he needed to be rescued from. That's also why he was trusting when Jack took him away from the place where he had seen his mother lying dead on the floor.

Louise didn't say anything but instead gave Helene's arm another squeeze, just as Henrik Sommer opened the passenger-side door to help the nervous woman out of the car.

"My wife and Simon went down to the stream with a fishing net."

It was still pouring rain.

"The stream is right here behind the yard." He pointed down alongside the house. "We had rain gear and rubber boots that were only slightly too big, and he seemed very curious to see what they could catch."

"That sounds nice," Louise said, but Helene stared in near terror down at the line of low trees that must be the edge of the stream.

"Come in," the foster father said, gently taking hold of Helene's elbow to lead her in out of the rain. "They promised to be back by three."

Louise turned to look at the white station wagon. There was no one inside it, but Henrik Sommer followed her gaze.

"My brother-in-law," he said. "Morten has his own psychology practice in Odense. He came by to pick up some table decorations Tine made. Their parents are celebrating their golden wedding anniversary next weekend. But I asked him to stick around because I thought . . ."

They had come in the door, and he turned toward Helene.

"That it might be nice for you to talk to someone. About everything. And about how you should relate to Simon. We're very aware that this will also be a difficult process for you. You're going to need someone to lean on as you and Simon slowly find each other again."

Louise looked at Helene Funch. Helene looked confused at first, but then she nodded. Her gaze lingered on the foster father, as if he had just become a lifeline she could cling to. Someone who understood what it was that she had lost.

The brother-in-law sat in a chair in the kitchen, but when they came in from the front hall, he got up right away and impulsively gave Helene a hug. He was tall and bony but had a big head of curly hair that softened his look.

"Are you nervous?" he asked as he let go of her.

She nodded, not seeming particularly surprised by the long hug from a strange man. Instead she seemed more like she finally felt seen, Louise thought, recognizing that she could have done better herself in that regard. She should have thought of bringing in a professional who could prepare Helene for this meeting, someone who understood what she was facing, like Eik had suggested.

Louise remained over by the door as they pulled out a chair for Simon's mother.

"There's no reason to be nervous," the psychologist continued. "We don't know how much he remembers. But when they come in, we'll be sitting here talking. You'll greet him, of course, and then we'll wait and see if he comes over to you on his own. But," he said, reaching out for Helene's hand, "you need to be the grown-up here. You need to rein in your emotions so that this doesn't become too overwhelming for him. And I know that must feel pretty unreasonable. But the thing is, you risk scaring him if he discovers how unhappy you are and how overwhelming it is for you to see him again."

Helene nodded.

"I completely understand that you feel a need to shower him with all your love, but he won't be able to grasp that. So this meeting will be the hardest for you, without a doubt. It will take some artistry to balance it, but I promise you that it will come back to him if you just give him time."

The psychologist was a little too physically demonstrative for Louise's taste, but his words worked. Helene Funch nodded as he spoke, and her eyes grew calmer, as if she were handing over some of the responsibility to him. She asked if he could stay for the whole visit.

Morten nodded, and it occurred to Louise that there probably weren't any golden wedding anniversary table decorations in the house in the first place.

"He has to come to you," the brother-in-law continued, "but it's not like we're going to sit and pretend we're not here. Or try to hide the fact that we're happy to see him. It just needs to happen at Simon's pace."

Helene nodded and described the things she had brought from Simon's bedroom.

"Can I give them to him?" she asked, looking toward her weekend bag in the front hall.

"I recommend that we just be sitting here in the kitchen when they come back, to see if he wants to be with us or if he withdraws a little. Remember that he only just met Tine and Henrik today."

She nodded again.

"But if he seems interested, we can sit down in the living room with them and then you can show him what you brought."

He reached out and took her hand again.

"You mustn't take it as a rejection if he pulls away. He might be tired or shy. It's all new to him, and he's carrying around a lot of grief. So, it's not a rejection of you as a person if he prefers not to hang out with us today. And that will change once he gets used to you coming to visit him."

Tears began flowing down Helene's cheeks, but then they saw Tine walk past the kitchen window, a fishing net bobbing along right behind her.

Helene straightened up and quickly dried her cheeks. Louise stepped back into the front hall and was standing by the coat hooks as the door opened and Simon came in, followed by his foster mother.

Louise smiled to him and raised her hand in greeting.

He held a small red bucket out to her. She couldn't really see whether he had caught tadpoles or insects with the net, but he seemed as proud as if he had a magnificent salmon.

She gave him a thumbs-up to show that she was impressed. Simon set the fishnet on the floor, got out of the wet raincoat and the slightly too big rubber boots, and was on his way into the kitchen with his bucket when he suddenly stopped.

He looked hesitantly at his mother and Morten. He seemed unsure whether it was okay to go in. But Henrik Sommer immediately waved him in, and Louise tried to make out the signs they exchanged. Tine had also come inside. She walked over and gave Helene a hug and said in her slightly slow way that it was wonderful that she had come.

"This is a great kid you've got here," she said. Even though Louise remained out in the front hall, she could see Helene's eyes fill with tears, but she quickly got them under control and smiled at her son.

Simon looked back and forth between Helene and Morten. It was clear that the foster parents were making a big deal about how much they liked Helene, going out of their way to show that she belonged here.

Simon's mother's eyes lingered on him, studying every inch. She took in his hair, his height, and every detail of his facial features. Louise could tell that Helene was struggling to seem natural, trying to force herself to look away, but she kept glancing back at the little boy as if she could touch him with her eyes. Two years had passed since she had lost consciousness in the water and he had drifted away from her. It wasn't hard to understand that she couldn't get enough of him.

The psychologist pointed to the red bucket and asked if he could see it. Simon walked over to him right away and held the bucket out with both hands. Helene leaned forward so she could see, too. He stepped a little closer to her and smiled as something happened down in the bucket.

It was so intense that Louise almost felt like she could see Helene's senses soaking up her son. But Helene didn't move. She sat motionless and let Simon show them what he'd caught. The boy's eyes went back to Tine, who had taken a jam jar out of a cupboard.

Simon walked over to the counter and together they poured the murky water from the stream into the jar and held it up to the light. There was obviously something swimming around in it, because the boy pointed with his finger, following it across the jar, but Louise was focused on how Helene was sitting, clasping her hands together in her lap. Every now and then Morten reached out and gave her arm a squeeze. A comforting little gesture that showed that he was there for her, that they were in this together.

Tine and Simon said something to each other in sign language. They were standing with their backs to Louise, so she couldn't follow along. Tine got out a glass and asked if anyone else was thirsty.

"Or maybe coffee instead," Henrik replied as his wife got a pitcher of juice out of the fridge.

"That sounds wonderful," Morten said, as if he were answering for both himself and Helene. "Why don't we go into the living room?"

The foster father glanced at Simon, who was drinking a glass of juice, before he nodded.

"Just bring your bag in with you," Morten told Helene, but she didn't move. She simply sat there staring at the boy even though the psychologist had stood up. For a second the kitchen got quiet, and it was clear that Simon noticed that something was going on over by the table. He turned toward them and looked uncertainly at Helene.

Henrik Sommer jumped in to try to save the situation. He pointed into the living room and with signs he suddenly got Simon to laugh and run over to the sofa.

Helene had started to cry. The tears flowed in perfect silence until she leaned forward and sobbed into her hands. Morten was getting cups out of the cupboard, so Louise brought the weekend bag into the kitchen before walking over to put her arms around Helene.

"It's going to be all right," she whispered into Helene's blond hair.

"I can't," she moaned so softly that Louise could barely hear her. "I can't bear that he doesn't know who I am. I remember him so clearly. I could instantly recognize his scent, the way he holds things with such concentration."

A deep sob forced its way up through her. Tine had quietly shut the door so they couldn't be seen from the living room.

Louise squatted for a long time, holding Helene in her arms.

"I can drive you home and then you can come back tomorrow," she offered.

Helene was about to protest. She dried her eyes and looked over at the closed door to the living room, but then she nodded quietly.

"Only if I can come back tomorrow," she whispered.

"You can come back tomorrow morning and on all the days to come until he's ready to move home to you," Tine said, eyeing Helene earnestly, as if she wanted to emphasize that she was always welcome and that they were in no way trying to separate her from her son.

"But I would like to say goodbye," she said then and opened her bag. "May I give him this?"

She held out a worn old stuffed dog to the foster mother.

"He inherited it from his two older siblings, and Simon loved it when he was little. It was always with him. He wouldn't sleep without it."

"Just go right in. You're welcome to give it to him," Tine said, smiling at Helene.

Helene got up uncertainly with the stuffed dog in her hand.

Over on the sofa, Henrik had pulled out a memory card-matching game, which Morten was setting up on the coffee table. Simon was sitting on the same side of the coffee table as his foster father and watching with curiosity as the square cardboard pieces were laid out.

Helene hesitantly walked over to them clutching the dog. Her son was preoccupied with the game and the colorful drawings he would need to remember the locations of. She walked over to sit down next to the psychologist, but Henrik quickly got up and said she could sit in his spot.

Simon turned over a picture of a green watering can and sat with his hand hovering over the cards while he contemplated where he would have the most luck finding one that matched it.

He threw his arm up in victory shortly thereafter when he found a pair.

"This is for you," Helene said slowly and clearly. She handed him the stuffed dog and he sat with it in his hands for a moment before he set it on the sofa and redirected all his attention to the game.

Louise could sense the disappointment pouring out of Helene. Her back was completely stiff, and she sat frozen until everyone at the table had taken their turns and it was Simon's again. There were eight pieces left to be turned over and remembered.

Helene leaned on the sofa's armrest for support as she stood up with difficulty. She looked at Simon, who had just matched a pair of melons, and then began to walk back to the kitchen. She had almost reached Louise when Henrik called her back. She turned around, her eyes welling with tears.

Simon had stood up and was looking at her, his hands signing a question.

"He's asking what happened to your leg," the foster father explained.

Helene looked down at the carpet.

"I was in a serious accident," she replied, looking at Simon as she spoke. The boy had turned to Henrik, who interpreted her answer.

Simon turned to Helene again and stroked his cheek as he pointed to her. Helene reacted instinctively and took a long step toward him, but Henrik managed to react before she reached Simon.

"Another round," he said, pointing to the cards on the table. Morten had stood up and gone over to Helene. He put an arm around her, and they walked into the kitchen together. Louise stood for a second trying to get her own emotions under control, then followed the others and offered to drive Helene home.

"Tomorrow is fine," Tine said as Helene cried quietly. "You can come for lunch, so we can eat some sandwiches together and go for a walk. It lightens the mood if we're doing something. Then the interaction becomes more normal, and we get to experience something together."

Helene couldn't say anything, but she nodded, and Morten wrote his number down for her.

"Call me," he said. "I can also come by your place once you're home so we can talk. It's perfectly natural if you have a heap of questions, and right now it's important that you don't start feeling rejected, because that's certainly not what I saw in there. Quite the opposite."

"But he didn't care about the stuffed dog," she said, sounding choked up and hollow. "He didn't even recognize it."

"Give him time," he said. "He's dealing with a lot, and things have got to be incredibly overwhelming right now. Consider that he probably hasn't seen anyone other than the married couple who took him in."

"Stole him," came a low hiss from Helene.

"It'll take time, but I believe you will find your way to each other. You're his mother and he can easily adjust again. He just needs to get to know you."

Louise was grateful that the foster parents had invited the brother-in-law over so there was also someone there to look after and understand Helene. His authority clearly imparted some strength to her. She had an unquestioning confidence that he was right when he said it would work out.

He had his arm around her as they made their way to the door together. In the entryway he helped her into her long down coat. Once they were out of earshot, Louise saw her opportunity to ask Tine if Simon had said anything about Dorthe's murder. The foster mother followed her lips attentively, but then shook her head.

"Although of course I can't understand everything he says," Tine began. "But he hasn't said anything about the actual murder. He says that he came downstairs even though he wasn't allowed to go down there alone. But his mother didn't come back upstairs even though she had said that she just wanted to get her cell phone, which she had forgotten down there."

Louise glanced over at the front hall to make sure the others weren't listening in.

"He had had cornflakes that morning, and then Dorthe had gone down to the restaurant to look after the guests just like she normally did. She had promised that they would go outside and play on the swings, but then she didn't come back upstairs. After he had waited for a long time, he went downstairs. As I understand it, Dorthe usually locked the door so he couldn't just go from the apartment into the inn. At any rate it seems like he didn't usually go downstairs into the inn's restaurant. He wasn't allowed to, he says. But because she was just going to grab her phone, the door wasn't locked. And he got scared because she hadn't come back so he went down there."

Out in the front hall, Helene had her coat on. She stood talking quietly to the psychologist, who had opened the front door, letting in the cold fall wind.

"I'm returning to Copenhagen later today," Louise said. "So a team from Svendborg will be in charge of the investigation from now on. But if Simon says anything more, you should call Deputy Chief Superintendent Grube. He's in Odense, and he's your contact going forward."

Louise walked over to the door and peered into the living room. Simon was once again preoccupied with the game. It was just him and Henrik playing now, turning cards over for each other. The boy had set the stuffed dog in his lap, so it was sitting between his skinny arms as he rested his chin on the dog's head. She considered getting Helene so she could see that but decided not to. There was no reason to push her emotions, which were already in such turmoil, around any further.

Louise waved to Simon. Feeling sad and pent-up, she said goodbye. She would have liked to talk to him herself about that morning in the inn's restaurant, but she needed to accept that Grube was taking over now. And she had to trust that the boy would be allowed to stay out here with Tine and Henrik, where they were obviously able to handle his needs. Fortunately, she was confident that the foster parents wouldn't allow him to be pressured into anything he wasn't ready for, and that comforted her.

She said goodbye to Tine and thanked Morten before she went out to the car to drive Helene home.

CHAPTER 34

It turned out that a full deluge of North Jutland anger had struck the Odense police station late that afternoon, with a force that had made the walls tremble all the way to the police offices in Copenhagen. Lange was not merely angry that he and Louise had been taken off the case. He was so indignant and furious that Grube wouldn't let them see the investigation through to its end after they had come so far, he had staked his job on it.

Grube had called several times, but Louise didn't answer. He could go fuck himself. He would just have to try to talk the Northern Jutlander down himself, she thought, while she drove home across Zealand. Grube was the one who had brought Lange into the investigation in the first place, so he could also take the punches now that Lange was angry about having been treated unfairly. She was just outside Køge when Søren Velin called her, and she sensed right away that he was annoyed at the series of messages she had left him since departing Tåsinge.

"The thing is," he began, "our funding for P13 is so limited that when a police district believes you've accomplished what you set out to do and doesn't need you anymore, then I need to bring you back home."

"But we haven't accomplished what we set out to do," Louise corrected him. "We arrested Jack Skovby when we found the boy at his house, but we don't have anything to tie him to the murder. We had hoped we would get that. But that's going to be fucking hard to do now that the investigation has been halted."

"Grube thinks you got the right guy."

"Grube doesn't know shit. He wants to go out and gloat, but it's going to come back to bite him," she said. "And if this case ends up in the stack of unsolved cases, then I will personally see to it that the name of whoever decided to halt this investigation comes out."

"Leave him alone," Søren Velin said calmly. "It's better that we dedicate your resources to another investigation."

"But this will look like a failed effort," Louise continued angrily. "We need to show strong results if we're going to justify P13 being granted a budget that will enable us to bring together a handful of the country's best homicide detectives in the future. With a start like this, no one in any position of power is going to take us seriously and then we'll never be on the budget."

She intentionally ignored the fact that Søren Velin was actually one of the police people in a position of power.

"Nothing has failed so far," he said tensely. "You arrested someone, and that person has been charged with the murder."

"We don't have shit," Louise snarled. "But do you know what? That's not my problem anymore. It's Grube's. But this is ridiculous, and it's fucking unbecoming of you not to stand up for me. And for the travel unit. This is your unit. And it's your responsibility to make sure we don't end up looking like a fiasco. I don't want my name held up as the flag bearer for something nobody takes seriously. We had a deal. You made me an offer, which I accepted on the condition that every ounce of energy would be put into establishing a strong, one-of-a-kind investigation unit."

She had to rein herself in several times so her anger didn't get the better of her.

"On the bright side, you'll avoid all the boring paper pushing when it's time to wrap up the case," Velin said, possibly trying to lighten the mood in a sad attempt to be funny.

Louise hung up.

She was tired. Tired and hungry. Jonas had asked her to call when she was a half hour from Frederiksberg. He and Melvin were going to make meatballs for her, he had messaged, with gravy and potatoes.

She had happened to say once that nothing was as good for the psyche as a proper grandmotherly meal, and her son had never forgotten. But honestly, right now she could use an ice-cold beer more than a hot meal. Or a big glass of red wine or maybe a strong gin and tonic with extra lemon slices. Louise finished her lukewarm Coke Zero and slowed down as she came to the traffic light in Folehaven.

Dina met her out in the stairwell. The yellow Lab jumped up on her when she reached the fourth floor with her weekend bag over her shoulder. The scent of security wafted from the kitchen, and she was struck by the joy of knowing someone was there waiting for her.

"Hi," Jonas called through the open front door. As she stepped into her apartment, Melvin came out of the kitchen with an apron around his waist. Louise gave her downstairs neighbor a long hug and asked him if he was okay.

"As okay as you can be," he said, but smiled to smooth over his grief a little.

Jonas appeared from the living room with his cell phone in his hand.

"Camilla just called. You should call her. I think she wants to lure you out to Café Svejk for a beer."

"Oh, I'm not up to that," Louise said immediately, promising that she would call her friend back eventually. "But not until after we've eaten."

Suddenly she couldn't remember the last time she'd eaten anything more substantial than a breakfast bun. The night before she had been so preoccupied with Simon, who had just been found, that she hadn't even thought about food. But now the scent of the meatballs from the pan in the kitchen made her almost dizzy with hunger.

"I'll text Camilla," Jonas promised, and she thanked him as she opened the fridge and then asked if Melvin wanted a beer, too.

"Well, since you asked," he said, moving to get out beer glasses. Louise flopped down in a chair at the dining table in the kitchen.

"Will there be many people at the funeral tomorrow?" she asked, nodding when Jonas asked if it was okay if he had a beer, too. That reminded her of the time just after he had moved in with her. How uncertain he had been about whether he belonged. He was the one who had asked if he could live with her after his father's murder. It had been a temporary arrangement to begin with. She had been moved at the time because he didn't have anyone else, no one he was close to. Now, many years later, she couldn't imagine him not being there. He and Melvin were her family, and Eik had been on the verge of joining them.

She needed to have a proper talk with Eik at some point, she thought. Things were too unresolved and difficult. And somewhere in her heart it had also become pretty clear that she wasn't ready to give him up.

"Maybe ten," Melvin replied. "Twenty max. Grete didn't have much family. Her sister's coming down from Sakskøbing, and the rest are friends from the community garden. That's what growing old is like. There aren't so many people left."

Louise nodded.

"It will be nice," she said.

"And Eik is coming," Jonas informed her.

She looked at him in surprise and noticed he was watching her to see how she took the news. She nodded and said that that was sweet of him.

"Camilla's coming, too, along with Frederik and Markus," Jonas continued.

"But they hardly knew her," Louise said, looking over at Melvin to see what he said to that.

"They're coming to support us," Jonas explained.

Louise smiled, thinking it was probably also because he hadn't been completely sure if she would be home.

"Then there will probably be more than twenty of us," Melvin said.

"Will that be a problem for the reception afterward?" Louise asked.

"No, not at all. We'll go down to Beli's Bar. We reserved the room in back," Melvin replied. "It'll be good if we can just make it a nice, pleasant farewell."

They had planned the funeral service at the church where Jonas's father had been pastor. Melvin's wife, Nancy, was buried there, too. Louise accepted the plate her downstairs neighbor had dished up for her. The gravy was steaming, and she asked Melvin and Jonas if they wanted another beer. But they had only sipped theirs, whereas she had finished hers completely.

It was eight-thirty when Lene Borre called. Louise had just cleared the table and loaded the dishwasher. Melvin had gone downstairs after a little dessert and coffee, and Jonas had retreated into the living room.

"We just released Jack Skovby," the inspector informed her. Louise got out a corkscrew and squeezed the phone between her ear and her shoulder while she cut the foil off a bottle of red wine and got a glass out of the cupboard.

"The Crown Prosecution Service didn't think we had enough to keep him in pretrial custody," she continued. "We talked to Helene Funch again and even though she doesn't owe him her loyalty anymore, she still confirms that Jack was with her in the time leading up to the murder. Also, Lindén found his car on a surveillance camera at the OK Gas Station on Skovballevej. After that his cell phone can be traced to Strammelse Gade, where he made a call. Shortly thereafter he transferred money by MobilePay to the friend he had just talked to. The whole thing is recorded in the cell tower data and corroborated by the friend. In other words, he wasn't at Strammelse Inn when the murder took place."

"Has Grube officially announced that you had to drop the charges and release him again?" she asked, thinking about Jack. Even though he was a jerk, there was also a part of him that she had found attractive and charming. Grube had thrown him to the lions based on nothing. Exactly as she had predicted. She felt sorry for Jack Skovby, even though she was the one who had brought him in for questioning. But she wasn't the one who had gone public, singling him out as the murderer.

"Nothing has been announced yet," Borre replied. "But they're writing a press release. It'll be sent out in the next half hour. I just thought you should hear it from me before it was released."

Louise thanked her and wished them all luck with the investigation.

"There's also something else," Borre continued.

Louise took a sip of her wine, knowing instinctively that she wasn't going to like whatever was coming.

"Yes," she said when her colleague remained silent.

"Helene Funch gave an interview to the *Funen County News* tonight. It's up in their web edition right now, but it'll be in the printed paper tomorrow."

Louise put her cell phone on speaker and searched for the paper.

"Thank you," she said, ending the call as she found the article and poured herself another glass of wine while she read.

There were pictures of Tine and Henrik Sommer, an archive photo the newspaper must have had from a previous article about the foster parents. There was also a picture of the house in Tullebølle along with several large portraits of Helene. One really zoomed in, where every single grief-laden wrinkle in her face was visible and emphasized. Probably not exactly a picture Simon's mother herself would have chosen, Louise thought. She looked like what she was: a woman falling apart.

But the article was good, she determined after having read it all the way through. It was a touching description of what it felt like to find out after two years of intense grief that the little boy you thought you had lost was still alive. She also talked a bit about her first meeting with Simon earlier in the day. How he had tried to comfort her when he discovered the injury she had suffered in the plane crash.

"No, we still haven't discussed what happened back then," she answered the journalist. Helene Funch didn't say anything about how she and her son weren't even able to communicate in the usual sense.

Helene had shown restraint, Louise thought and wondered briefly if she should text her, then decided against it. It wasn't her case anymore, and if she didn't want her anger to flare up again, she was going to have to let it go. And suddenly after two beers, half a bottle of wine, and with Melvin and Jonas so close by, that felt easier to do.

Instead, she sent Jack a text. She wrote a brief message telling him that she was back in Copenhagen and was no longer working on the case. And that she was sorry that Grube had been an ass to him. "Hope you're OK."

It took only a second before he wrote back.

I'd rather have you and the big city cop than that incompetent asshole. Everyone fucking thinks I did it!!!

She didn't respond, but then another text arrived.

> Life goes on, but one peep from him and I'll fucking press charges.

Louise typed out a response and clicked send.

> Do it.

She set down her cell phone before it turned into a regular conversation. She wanted to write more, but she controlled herself and went to join her son in the living room instead.

CHAPTER 35

It turned out to be far from just friends from the community garden plot in Dragør and their own close-knit circle who attended Grete Milling's funeral. The church was almost half-full, and a woman Grete's age came up to Louise and said that she and Grete had worked together at KTAS, the old phone company on Nørregade. They had both started out as switchboard operators and while Jytte had stayed there as a bookkeeper, Grete had moved across the street shortly thereafter to Daells, the department store, where she had first worked in their mail order department and then later gotten a job in their women's clothing department.

"She was there for many years," Jytte explained. Louise had had no idea about this. She hadn't gotten to know Grete until she investigated a case down in Roskilde.

Melvin had prepared the pastor well, she thought, as his heartwarming words brought tears to her eyes several times during the service. She stole a glance at Jonas, who was sitting next to her in the front pew, between her and Melvin. Tears poured down his own cheeks, and he made no attempt to stop them.

Maybe it was also bringing to the surface how much he missed his father. Jonas had said goodbye to him in this same church, after all. She put a hand on her son's arm.

On the opposite side of the church aisle, Eik sat with Camilla, Frederik, and Markus. She had offered Jonas the chance to have Markus sit with them so the boys would have each other, but Jonas didn't want that. He wanted to sit with Louise and Melvin. Their downstairs neighbor seemed calm even though he was no doubt the one who would miss Grete the most. One evening when they had been sitting in the living room doing their best to finish off a tin of Quality Street chocolates, he'd called Grete his companion for the last part of life's journey.

Louise felt a pang in her chest as they neared the end of the last hymn and the notes from the organ began to ebb away. She quickly dried her eyes and looked over at the pews across the aisle. Eik nodded briefly to her, and she stood up. Along with Camilla and her family, they were ready to serve as the pallbearers.

Louise pulled her cell phone out to take one last picture of the white coffin covered in flowers in front of the altar. Just then it rang silently and as she went to reject the call, she realized there was a whole string of missed calls and message notifications that had arrived while they had been sitting in the church. Jonas shot her a scolding look, which made her quickly stuff her phone back into her pocket and walk up to the coffin with the others.

Jonas and Markus walked in front, then came Louise and Eik, while Camilla and Frederik lifted the handles in the back. Slowly and in time, they began to walk out of the church.

Melvin had stood up and now bowed his head as they walked

past him. Louise almost reached out and asked him to walk with her, but instead she focused on stepping calmly forward to the door, past the faces of all the people Grete had known before she entered their lives, friends and acquaintances, memories and experiences.

The hearse had backed up to the front of the church and two female undertakers stood on either side of the open rear door. Louise felt the pang in her chest again as she saw how Jonas bowed his head, pressing his chin to his chest to keep from crying, which made his shoulders stiff.

The coffin was slowly pushed into the hearse. The church bells rang, and it started drizzling again. The rain had otherwise stopped that morning, but now a few drops hit Louise's face. She stepped back and went to stand next to Melvin, putting her arm around him and leaning her head against his.

She had received more calls, she discovered when she pulled out her phone to film the hearse as it drove away. She was about to click on the camera app when yet another text arrived, its contents legible in the notification across the top of her screen.

The sender was identified underneath: Lene Borre, Svendborg Police.

Jack's dead. Murdered. Please call back.

CHAPTER 36

Melvin held a plate out to her with a piece of kringle on it, but Louise turned the pastry down and smiled at him. There was something touching about the way he embraced the mourners, walking around among Grete's acquaintances he had never met before and trying to make everyone feel comfortable so that it was a pleasant and heartwarming farewell.

He and Grete had not gotten to spend that many years together, but it had been enough time for him to have grown very fond of her. My friend, he had called her. Not girlfriend or companion, but friend.

Louise knew that it hadn't escaped Melvin's attention that she kept glancing down at the cell phone in her hand. He didn't comment on it, but she also noticed the looks Jonas shot her from time to time. She tried to be present and to appreciate the lovely reception they had arranged.

Eik had withdrawn into a corner in the back of the room with the vaulted ceiling, where he stood now talking to Frederik, but every so often she caught him looking at her. They had parted poorly back in that parking lot, and she knew it was up to her to repair that.

Melvin leaned over to her.

"Just go," he whispered. "I'll wrap things up here."

When they had arrived at the reception, Louise had immediately gone to the bathroom and read her messages. They were all from Lene Borre. The first four were pictures from the courtyard in front of Jack's house. He had been shot in the head.

Borre had not skimped on the details. As if she were trying to get Louise's attention with the violent images.

There was a close-up of the entry wound in the back of his head, but other pictures were of his face. There was a big hole where his left eye had been. His ear on that same side was missing, and there was a single picture of the hunting bullet that had pierced his cranium.

Borre asked her to return to Tåsinge and resume the investigation with them. She wrote that Grube had been trying to get in touch with her all afternoon. He wanted her to send more details from the questioning session she had conducted with Jack Skovby. In other words, he wanted Louise to feed him information so he had something to go on now that his prime suspect had ended up as a victim and been definitively ruled off his list.

Her first instinct was to act pissed and hurt. She felt like Grube could go fuck himself. But those pictures Borre had sent from Jack Skovby's courtyard made her put away her anger and instead call Søren Velin.

"I'm going back to Svendborg," she said, her voice too loud in the empty bathroom.

"So Grube asked you to come back without going through me?"

he ascertained, annoyed. "I'll have a chat with him. It's no good that he keeps making up his own rules for how he handles the travel unit's assistance."

"He hasn't called me," Louise interrupted. "I've put myself back on the case. Jack Skovby was shot and killed in front of his house around noon today. I'm leaving for Tåsinge in the next hour. You need to get the paperwork in place and agree on the practical details with Grube. I'm going to see this investigation to the door, and that's how it needs to be."

She hung up before he had time to object, but she kept the phone in her hand as she returned to the reception so that she could keep an eye on the effects of her announcement. But nothing else came.

She kept picturing the images of Jack's face. He had been wearing a fleece jacket and was lying in a contorted position, as if he had been about to turn toward the culprit.

"Out with it," Camilla said straightaway. Without Louise quite noticing, her friend had succeeded in getting her alone in an out-of-the-way corner, so the chatty older people couldn't hear them.

Louise denied that anything had happened and was saved just then by her cell phone ringing in her hand. She excused herself and quickly walked out of the room. It was Grube again—not as cocky this time—wanting to know if she had encountered anything in her investigation that could serve as the basis for such a violent killing. If Velin had had time to contact him, the deputy chief superintendent was flat-out ignoring it.

"I'm coming to you," Louise said. "I'll leave Copenhagen within the hour."

"You don't need to do that," he replied quickly. "But if you could help us over the phone to get a little closer to a motive for the killing, that would be good."

"I'm coming," she repeated. She expected him to protest again, but he didn't.

"Would you prefer that we wait to remove the body from the courtyard until you've seen him?" he asked instead, and she realized that the distant tone he had used when he sent her away was gone.

Determined to solve the two murders in Tåsinge, she decided to put away her anger as well.

"If the technicians are done out there and you've secured everything we need on and around the body, it's fine with me if you move him. But make sure that we have photographic coverage of the body from every angle of the courtyard."

"The forensics team is still working out there. It was a neighbor who found him. She saw him lying in the gravel and thought he might have taken ill. When she ran over to him, she saw the blood."

"Have you started bringing in witnesses?" she asked.

"There isn't anyone," he replied. "We've been to the surrounding houses, and I have people out on the country roads to stop drivers who may have been driving in the area when the murder took place. Lindén is pulling the information from his cell phone to see who he talked to and where he was up until the murder."

Louise sensed that he was holding something back. There was silence between them for a moment.

"And?" she said.

"And I just sent Borre and Sindal out to bring Helene Funch in for questioning."

Of course, she thought. That could hardly be avoided. But Helene had far too much to lose now that she had just been reunited with her son. She had a motive, and probably a strong desire, but she also had too much at stake to be sent away for murder.

"Of course she needs to be questioned," Louise conceded quickly. "But based on the impression of Jack Skovby I've managed to form, the motive for the murder could also lie in a lot of other places. He was such a hustler. I have the sense that he was a master at doing things for his own gain. He openly blackmailed Kristian Funch—that whole silly story about the sale of the agricultural machinery wasn't something we would have found if we hadn't had cause to dig into Funch's old bank transfers. Jack managed to land that money without arousing anyone's curiosity. He was a reseller and a swindler, and a lot of people could have had reason to be mad at him," she said.

She could sense that Camilla had come outside and was standing behind her. Louise started walking down Smallegade to get away from her.

"I'll be there in two and a half hours," she said, turning to walk back to the restaurant. "Talk to Helene about how much she knew about the things Jack was involved in. We also need to find out what the connection was between Nils Hyllested and Jack. And have Lindén take a thorough look at the account that was used when Kristian Funch transferred money to Nils Hyllested. We need to know what the money was used for and if Nils and Jack were up to something together."

Just off the cuff, Louise bet that Jack had spent his part of the money fixing up his farmhouse. But it was hard to see those sorts of newer improvements at Strammelse Inn, nor did Dorthe seem like someone who had been awash in money, she thought, catching sight of Jonas just then as he emerged from the restaurant. She hurried back toward him as she wrapped up her conversation with Grube.

Her son had brought her coat and bag with him and held them out to her.

"Just go," he said. "It was good that you came home and joined us. It really meant a lot to Melvin, too. But Markus just showed me that there's breaking news about a new murder in Tåsinge."

Louise smiled a little sadly at him, when it suddenly hit her that she hadn't fully realized that he had turned into such a mature, responsible young man.

"Thank you," she said, taking her things. "I'm going to go home and pack a small bag, and then I'll go."

She realized then that Camilla had disappeared. As they walked back to the restaurant, Jonas said that Eik had left, too, but only to walk Charlie in Frederiksberg Gardens.

CHAPTER 37

Helene Funch had put her hair up and was wearing a long, dark blue wool dress. Her cheeks and eyes had received a bit of makeup, but it was mostly the look in her eyes that Louise noticed when she stepped into the office at the Svendborg police station. The woman's eyes had come alive, as if the world around her had once again begun to interest her.

Simon's mother was sitting by herself at a table in interrogation room 1 when Lange walked in with Louise. The North Jutland native had greeted her, and Louise was pleased to see that he, too, had put away his anger and decided not to quit his job. He'd seemed energetic as he gave her a quick update on the questioning so far.

First and foremost, it was clear that Helene Funch didn't have a shadow of an alibi for the period of time around the shooting. But she did have an obvious motive, which she was in no way trying to downplay, Lange had explained.

She had been alone at home. Her sister hadn't come back until around two p.m. The two siblings had had a big argument after breakfast, which had resulted in Iben leaving the house in running clothes at around ten a.m. Iben had explained that her sister had been angry and hurt after their argument. Helene blamed Iben for not being there for her in the period after the plane crash and for not doing anything to help her find Simon.

Niklas Sindal had been the one who spoke to Iben, and his opinion was that Helene had essentially blamed her little sister for not having discovered that Simon was being kept hidden in Dorthe Hyllested's rooms. It was clear from his voice that his sympathy did not lie with Helene Funch, Louise thought.

It sounded like Simon's mother had had a minor meltdown in which she had also blamed her little sister for begrudging her the great happiness she felt at the prospect of getting Simon back home again. Borre's understanding was that Helene's anger had been triggered by a relatively innocent comment about how the boy first needed to feel ready for Helene to become his mother again. And then Helene had unleashed a real tirade, which had left Iben so flummoxed that she'd asked how it felt to have slept with the man who had kept Simon hidden. After that, she had slammed the door and left.

Sindal had said that Iben had subsequently gone for about a four-hour-long walk while she cooled down. According to him it sounded as if there was something more between the two sisters. At any rate, she had walked all the way out to Vemmenæs Point and back. He showed on a map that that was way over on the far side of Tåsinge Island. Iben had walked down Vornæsvej and gone past Strammelse Inn, but had not been near Vornæs Skovvej, she said. And she hadn't been seen anywhere near Jack's house, either.

Several witnesses had seen her walking along the side of the road, but they were still working on confirming that she had made it all the way out to where she claimed she had.

Helene had no witnesses. No one could confirm that she had been in her home all morning, preparing to drive to Langeland to spend the afternoon with Simon. But she didn't get to do that, because the police had brought her in.

Even though Jack had more or less taken over the Funch family's large Land Rover, Helene had now demanded it back. It was parked in her courtyard when Lene Borre and Niklas Sindal arrived at her place. She had also demanded that Jack return a riding mower and several smaller machines, which had been purchased at her expense, and then she had fired him, saying that he should never show up at the farm in Bjernemark again.

Lindén had confirmed that the call was registered in the call list. Two other calls between Helene and Jack were also listed. They had taken place that same morning after the argument with Iben. But Helene couldn't really account for those calls. First she didn't remember that they had occurred. Later, she thought that the calls must have been about the things she had asked Jack to return. At no point during the questioning so far had Helene seemed affected by Jack's death, Lange had said.

Louise was struck by the fact that none of her colleagues really seemed to react to her being back in Tåsinge and part of the investigation again. No one had commented, either, about her having been sent home. To the contrary, they seemed happy to see her and accepted her leading their investigative team again as if that were completely natural.

———

"I keep thinking that Jack was in on this with Dorthe," was the first thing Helene said when Louise sat down across from her. "There was something between them before I fell in love with him. I also know that she was expecting a child with him, which she lost. Maybe they imagined that they could raise my son together. Maybe he went back to her when he saw how I looked after the accident. He knew Simon was alive. Even so, he kept me from seeing my son. That was something they did to me together."

She leaned in over the table and it was clear to Louise that the woman across from her was not in the least concerned that she might very well end up being taken into custody and charged with the murder of Jack Skovby before the day was over. Completely unrepentantly and very directly, Helene said that she would never forgive Jack for taking Simon home with him instead of bringing him to her.

There was nothing in her statement or her tone that seemed placating, or like it shouldn't be taken literally. In a way, it seemed like it really hadn't dawned on her that she was the police's obvious lead suspect in Jack Skovby's murder case.

Louise contemplated Helene for a moment as she considered her words.

"There's no indication that Jack knew that your son was alive," she repeated, just as she had told her before.

"He lied," Helene blurted out. "Of course he knew it. He did this to hurt me, so he could milk me for even more money. Only now I can see how well it suited him to see me suffer, so he could be sure that I kept needing him."

She leaned over the table a little farther, holding Louise's gaze.

"I don't even know how much money I've paid him in the last two years, but it's a lot. And you told me yourself about the amounts he got Kristian to transfer. He took advantage of the fact that I trusted him. He convinced me that he was there for me, that he wanted to help me. Do you have any idea how that feels? Do you understand how much this hurts?"

She looked urgently at Louise, her eyes sparkling.

"That man can rot in hell without my feeling the least bit sorry for him. I can't believe I didn't figure out what he was made of."

She thought for a moment.

"My sister was right. It's my own fault, too. I should have realized that he was deceiving me. I should have noticed that he was using me. But I just wanted to be left alone. I felt a sense of security having him take control, so I didn't need to make decisions about anything. I wanted to die, or at least not have to deal with anything other than my own misery. But I should have realized that something was wrong."

Helene leaned back now and crossed her arms.

"Have you thought about this? About how Jack was sleeping with me while apparently also doing business with my husband, without my knowing that they were talking to each other? Do you have any idea how humiliating and hurtful that is?"

Louise nodded to concede that she did understand.

"Jack deserved to die," Helene said harshly. This wasn't the first time Louise had experienced that sort of massive outburst from someone who had actually killed another human being. They usually came as a form of justification for the terrible act. But in general killers tried to conceal their own violent emotions during questioning. Well, that wasn't the case with Helene Funch. She made it clear, at full volume, that it suited her just fine that Jack Skovby was no longer among the living.

Louise sat in silence, watching the woman across from her. Something about her very forthright appearance gave Louise the feeling that Helene Funch was in shock. That far too much had happened to her, and she was quite understandably unable to process or cope with it all.

Louise got up and announced that she would be back in a moment. Helene just nodded. Out in the hallway, Louise walked quickly down to Borre's office to ask her colleague to print out the pictures she had taken of Jack as he lay in the courtyard with half of his face blown off, as Sindal had so poetically put it.

"Preferably a couple of them, where you can see his face close up," she requested.

"What's left of his face, you mean," Borre said, and Louise nodded.

They were revolting. Louise hadn't known him that well, and even so, she felt incredibly uncomfortable looking at the pictures. The vacant look in his remaining eye, the blood, the empty lifelessness of his fit body.

She returned to Helene and set the pictures on the table in front of her.

"This is how he was found," she said, pushing the pictures toward her a little. "Did you shoot him?"

Helene Funch barely looked at the pictures, then she began to shake her head no.

"No," she replied. "I didn't do that."

"Do you have a rifle in the house? Any other gun?"

Helene looked right at Louise. There were no anxious hands, clasping and unclasping each other. She wasn't worriedly stroking her arms. She sat completely still and denied that she had been behind the killing.

"But you won't get me to say that I'm sorry it happened," she added defensively. "Because I'm not. He deserved it. And I'm not going to mourn him."

"Where were you between eleven a.m. and one p.m.?" Louise asked.

She didn't blink before answering that she had been at home alone.

"And you can't think of anyone who can confirm that?" she asked.

"No," Helene replied.

"Did you watch anything on TV or talk to anyone on the phone?"

She thought the cell towers might help.

"No," Helene replied. "I didn't talk to anyone."

"You talked to Jack," Louise reminded her.

"When can I be allowed to go?" Helene didn't seem interested in this conversation. "I have to go out to Simon's. They're waiting for me."

"Why did you call Jack?" Louise asked to get Helene to describe the course of events again.

Helene Funch shook her head.

"I haven't talked to him."

"The first call, which was made from your cell phone to his, lasted for a good four minutes. It took place at 10:17. He answered your next call at 10:47, and this time the call lasted almost ten minutes. Nine minutes and forty-six seconds to be precise. What did you talk about?"

Helene began to seem impatient. She looked down at her watch.

"I need to be out there in fifteen minutes," she said. "I have to leave now. I'm already going to be late."

"What did you talk about?" Louise asked again.

Helene pushed her chair back a little and was about to stand up.

Louise repeated her question one more time, still with no response from Helene. Louise asked Helene to remain seated, looked at her watch, and then informed the woman that she was under arrest.

Simon's mother didn't bat an eye as Louise informed her of her rights.

"Do you have a lawyer, or would you like to use the appointed one you will be assigned?" Louise asked.

"I need to see Simon," she said instead of answering.

"Would you like to contact a defense attorney yourself or should we arrange one for you?"

They sat in silence for a long time. Helene's eyes were like bottomless pits, but Louise understood that was a response to the fact that her meeting with Simon wasn't going to take place.

"Could you please call my sister?" she finally requested.

CHAPTER 38

When Camilla was awakened by her cell phone vibrating, the room was completely dark and she had no idea where she was. Her body was sore, and her head felt woozy. When she had heard about Jack Skovby's murder at Grete Milling's funeral, she had driven straight to the newsroom, but her editor had not been prepared to send her back to Tåsinge. It wasn't until she had gotten ahold of Louise late that evening and found out that they had arrested Helene Funch and charged her for the murder that Terkel Høyer had given her the green light.

She was so weary of the fact that journalism had reached the point where the need to pay the bridge toll was what decided if you were allowed to properly cover a story or had to make do with sitting in the newsroom and following the police's press conferences online.

Louise had also seemed weary when they had drunk a late-night beer together at the hotel in Troense. Camilla had waited for her in hopes that she could learn a little more than the scant information that had been released so far about the shooting. But her friend hadn't said much beyond the fact that Jack had been gunned down from behind, not from in front, as Camilla had heard. And then they had just sat there in each other's company. They were both so tired. It had been fun to just speak about Grete's funeral and not say much about the fact that they were both going back to Tåsinge.

Her cell phone vibrated again. Camilla sat up in the narrow bed before she answered.

"Can we meet?"

Eva Nørgaard didn't sound the least bit tired, and Camilla realized that it was nine-thirty in the morning. In a daze, she got out of bed.

"I know you went home. But there's something I need to show you. Can you come out here right away?"

"Yes," Camilla said quickly. "I'm actually in Tåsinge and can be at your place in about half an hour. Does that work?"

"Yes," Eva replied. "But you need to meet me in Lundby. That's not very far from here."

Camilla wrote down the address, took a quick shower, and got dressed. Before she left her hotel room, she checked the newspaper websites to make sure there hadn't been any updated press releases about the murder that she needed to deal with.

Two murders on Tåsinge Island within one week was the big news, and of course everyone was trying to dig into the connection between Dorthe Hyllested and Jack Skovby. Camilla was the only one who had the scoop that the two had had a sexual relationship, which led to Dorthe becoming pregnant but then losing the baby. The other media outlets had quickly stolen the story.

Before she and Louise had parted ways the previous night, Camilla had promised not to write about Helene Funch out of consideration for Simon and the foster family. In return, she would be the first to know if the police thought they had enough to detain her for twenty-four hours for a constitutional interrogation with an eye to remanding her into custody. They were allowed to hold Helene for twenty-four hours before she had to appear before a judge. And the prosecution service would probably request closed doors because the police were still investigating the two murders, Camilla thought as she sent Terkel a text saying she was staying in Tåsinge to keep an eye on developments in the case.

She didn't write anything about going out to meet with Aske Nørgaard's mother, because her editor in chief still wasn't thrilled with the gay angle. Camilla slowed down as she drove through Lundby. She reached the school and yielded to a large truck before turning right onto Tangvejen. Up ahead she spotted Eva Nørgaard, who was standing behind her daughter's black Fiat Punto by a sign that pointed down an avenue-like gravel road lined by tall trees on both sides. The sign read, "Unique Health and Well-Being," and was decorated with leafy ferns and holistic symbols.

Camilla pulled over to the side and parked behind the Punto, but before she had time to open her car door, Eva had her face right up against the driver's side window.

"We're going down there," she said, not bothering to greet Camilla. She seemed hectic and pointed hurriedly down the gravel road. Without waiting for a response, she got into the Punto and drove off, leading the way.

The countryside was flat and seemed lush, even now that the fall colors had settled over the dirt-brown fields with their rich, shiny soil and golden treetops. The fields were separated by small berms and stone walls covered with dry, wild-growing grasses. Camilla slowly followed Eva. The gravel road was well maintained and smooth. It curved gently and tucked in behind a dense copse of trees; a large redbrick house suddenly came into view.

It seemed not just uninhabited but abandoned. Camilla felt an instinctive hesitation in her body when she saw Eva get out of the Punto and wave for her to follow, but she shook herself and got out of the car anyway. She walked over to Eva, who was standing at the foot of the steps leading up to the front door of the house, waiting for her. Two large stone lions guarded either side of the main door. They seemed out of place, far too pompous given the isolated surrounding countryside, even if the building they were guarding was large, with an addition that adjoined the main house and extended the original structure. It looked like an old, converted dairy, Camilla thought.

"There's no one here," Eva reassured her, leading the way up the front steps to the door.

Camilla leaned her head back, peering up at the house's dark windows. The windowsills were bare, and several of the windows looked as if they were boarded up.

"This is where my son prostituted himself," Eva said soberly. She stood with her back to the door, looking down at Camilla. "This place ruined him. It killed him. After what happened out at the forest cabin, my son started coming here."

"What kind of a place is this?" Camilla asked, feeling a tingle run down her spine.

"I've heard it called the Cave of Sin or the Amusement Park. To me it's more like Hell's Front Porch. It's a bathhouse, a gay brothel that Nils Hyllested and Kristian Funch started after Aske had the crap beaten out of him out at the forest cabin. You didn't pay for sex at the cabin, but here at Hell's Front Porch everyone understood the premise and knew what they were getting into, so problems didn't arise afterward if things got out of hand, not the way they had for Aske that time. I assume Nils and Kristian probably figured that when you were paid to make your body available, you couldn't come back and complain later if something hurt a little. Which was smart thinking."

There was no anger in her voice—only an icy-cold bitterness that swept toward Camilla, who stood as if nailed to the ground, listening.

"Can we just go in?" Camilla asked uncomfortably, casting another glance at the dark windows.

Eva nodded, turned around, and pushed down on the door handle.

"I was here yesterday. The place isn't locked," she said.

Camilla slowly walked up the stairs after her.

They entered right into a living room with lavender-colored walls. At either end of the room there were two low sofa sets upholstered in shiny dark brown leather, like the waiting room of a 1990s beauty clinic. There were magazines on the tables featuring muscular men with glistening naked torsos. Over by the wall there was a sideboard with glasses and an ice bucket along with several liquor bottles. It was all neatly presented in straight rows.

Camilla hesitantly walked over to a counter at the back of the room. There was a cylindrical red vase full of condoms next to a Mac screen. On the counter's glossy surface, tourist brochures for

Tåsinge had been spread out in an inviting fan, just like at the inn. The whole thing looked as if someone had just finished preparing the place for a new day.

Camilla looked questioningly at Eva.

"Someone has gotten the place ready to open," she observed.

Eva didn't respond to that. She had walked over to the sofa and was leaning on its upholstered back, as if she needed something to hold her up.

"I have always stood behind my son and taught him not to be afraid of his desires. But now I know that what he subjected himself to out here didn't have anything to do with desire. He was trapped in something that destroyed him. He lost his soul and everything that was beautiful and special about him."

She blushed a little.

"Jack Skovby owns the place, but he only used the fields around the house, so the property had fallen into disrepair until Nils rented it from him and got Kristian Funch to finance its renovation."

Camilla thought about the money Helene's husband had transferred to Nils Hyllested.

"Imagine what it must have been like for my son to align himself with the people who had hurt him. I don't understand how he could do it. Imagine also how it would have looked if it had come out that Kristian Funch, who was known throughout the whole country for ensuring other people's safety and security with his alarm systems and his well-regarded company, was also behind a place where men who were far too young made money by selling their bodies."

Her voice trembled a little, as if for a moment she had become frail, then turned neutral again as she walked over to a door next to the counter and asked Camilla to follow her.

They must have gutted the place when they renovated it, Camilla thought. There was nothing inside that resembled an ordinary family home.

All the doors were painted different colors, like in a day care so the little ones knew where they belonged.

Eva opened the door into the first room. The yellow living room was dark aside from the play of colors from a knee-high lava lamp that cast its lazy colorful blobs around on the walls. Camilla stood for a second before she realized that the dark shadow at the back of the room was a large cage. She turned on the light. Hanging from hooks on the wall there were whips and something that looked like black rubber suits.

"I'm waiting here," Eva said, returning to the lobby as Camilla proceeded to the next door. She opened it to a large hot tub in the middle of the floor. Behind that was a built-in cubicle, which Camilla guessed was a sauna. She was so preoccupied with the massive hot tub that it wasn't until she went to close the door again that she noticed the cupboard on the wall behind it. Enormous dildos of various shapes and colors hung there in rows. They were so big that in any other situation she would have assumed they were a joke. But there was no humor here.

When she had closed the door of the last room, she returned to Eva, who was once again leaning against the back of the sofa in the lobby. Camilla felt empty and could sense Eva's eyes on her back as she walked over to a sink next to the counter and washed her hands, as if she could wash off everything she had just seen. She needed to get out of there and was on her way to the door when Eva asked her to wait.

"I thought this nightmare ended when Nils died," she said, gesturing toward where Camilla had just come from. "I only recently realized that the place kept running without Nils."

She stared at Camilla for a long time with a dead look in her eyes.

"I've been so stupid," she said with heartbreaking despair. "I didn't see it. I was blinded by grief. I didn't notice anything at all."

She inhaled unevenly and heavily, as if she were preparing for something.

"I found out that Dorthe kept this place going after her husband's death. She made reservations for the men at the inn as if they had booked a regular stay. They arrived in the afternoon, got coffee and pastries, just like our other guests do. And then they were driven out here, or some of them drove themselves, of course. The next morning, Dorthe served them breakfast and then they went home again. I didn't think Dorthe would try to run a place like this after Nils. I still don't understand it."

She seemed far away for a moment.

"I think Jon knew," she added flatly. "I've had the sense several times that he wanted to talk to me about something important, but I assumed it was about Aske and I couldn't bear that. I had no idea until Dorthe gave herself away."

She had started talking faster, as if she had somewhere to be. But then she abruptly stopped and walked over to the front door and exited the house. Camilla hurried after her, slightly confused.

"I went shopping that morning," Eva continued indifferently, making her way down the front steps. "I wanted to stop by the inn on my way home to pick up a bag I had left there the day before."

She walked impatiently back to the black Punto as she spoke, directing the words into the air rather than to Camilla.

"I could already hear her voice when I came into the kitchen. Dorthe was standing in the restaurant, talking on the phone, and I was about to go in there when she started listing the facilities Hell's Front Porch here had to offer. Then she explained where it was located and mentioned a range of services I wouldn't have the imagination to come up with, words I didn't even know existed. She described the place in a completely blasé way, as if she were talking about an everyday thing."

Eva shook her head.

"At first I thought she was talking about the forest cabin. But then she mentioned the address and informed the customer of the price difference between a onetime visit out here compared to a stay at the inn, which also included unlimited access to the house here."

Eva had reached the Punto and leaned against it, again as if she needed support.

"I felt like I couldn't breathe," she continued, her voice firm. "At that point I was standing right by the swinging door in the kitchen. Dorthe was standing just on the other side. When she finished her call with the customer, she immediately made another call where she announced that a customer would be arriving later in the day. 'Get the yellow room ready and get hold of one of the young men,' she said to the person she was talking to. I opened the swinging door and saw that she had started folding the napkins while she talked. From the conversation, I understood that the room would be ready starting at six p.m., but the customer wouldn't arrive at the bathhouse until around eight, because he had booked a table at the inn's restaurant first."

She hid her face in her hands for a moment, but then quickly looked up again, as if she had just shaken something off.

"She made it sound so easy," she said then. "I think it was the routineness of it that affected me the most. I felt like the anger of the whole world was rising up inside me. And I don't really know what came over me. I mean, I don't do anything like that."

Camilla realized that she was holding her breath. Eva resolutely turned around to open the rear hatch of the car.

"I enjoyed every blow," she admitted calmly as she stepped to the side so Camilla could come closer. "And even though the anger has left me again and I have only the grief left, I can't even say that I regret what I did. I don't. It still feels right," she said and pointed down into her trunk by way of explanation.

Camilla slowly walked over to the car and hesitantly looked where Eva was pointing. In the trunk there was a hefty cutting board and a rifle.

"I'd like you to call the police and ask them to come," Eva said calmly.

Camilla stood mutely for a moment, looking at the serene woman in front of her. She felt a touch of uncertainty at knowing that Eva was able to kill a human being, but at the same time, a strong, sorrowful pain radiated from Aske's mother, which made Camilla step forward and put her arms around her comfortingly. They just stood for a long time, rocking each other back and forth.

Then Camilla pulled away a little.

"Have you talked to Lea?" she whispered. "Does she know?"

Eva nodded.

"She's at home," she answered. "I'd rather have the police come here so she doesn't need to see it when they come pick me up."

"Tell me about Jack," Camilla asked, her eyes on the rifle.

"I went to see him when I heard that he had been released. And then I shot him," she said, explaining that her husband had left the rifle behind in the house when he moved out. "He said that if Aske changed his mind and wanted to act like a man, he could use that to hunt with. It's been lying up in the attic ever since."

CHAPTER 39

"What are you doing?" Louise snarled after she had dragged Camilla into an empty office with her. At first Louise had refused to come out when she was notified that she had a visitor. But the woman at the police station's information desk was insistent and said that it had to with a woman who had come to make a confession.

And then Camilla had been standing there. With Eva Nørgaard.

"Do you understand that I've just come back from a constitutional interrogation? Helene Funch has been remanded into custody for four weeks on reasonable suspicion of killing Jack Skovby. And while Helene is having a breakdown because she can't see her son, you've been out for a drive with the killer? What the hell were you thinking?"

Louise was so angry that she was gasping for breath to keep from choking on her own rage.

"Now, you listen here," Camilla tried. "I had no way of knowing what she wanted when she asked if we could meet. But to be honest, I'm glad that I went out there and saw that place. I don't think you get what this is all about. Do you even understand what it does to a mother to watch her son fall apart?"

"If Eva Nørgaard has murdered two people, then she's murdered two people. And so I really don't care if you get all in a huff about there being bathhouses for gay men. Helene Funch has been hauled over the coals in interrogations, and instead of having the murderer arrested right away, you drove her back to her house to drop a car off for her daughter?"

"You need to go out and see that place," Camilla said, indifferent to the scolding. "It's important that you understand what Nils Hyllested and Kristian Funch started."

Lene Borre and Niklas Sindal had already been dispatched to the address in Lundby. Both murder weapons had been retrieved from Camilla's car, and Lange was preparing the interrogation, even though Eva had made a full confession the moment she sat down in the chair.

"You have to see what Dorthe and Jack were up to," Camilla insisted. "Out of pure greed. Dorthe made reservations for men for fucking sex vacations as if they had ordered some luxury stay at Falsled Inn. I want you to understand what those two did to searching young people like Aske. Of course Eva needs to be punished for what she's done, but you need to understand what drove her to that point."

Louise looked at her friend for a moment.

"This isn't about your personal sense of justice," Louise replied angrily. "This is about you wanting to see your story to the finish line. You've latched onto the story of Aske Nørgaard and in your fervor to bring that home you don't give a damn about our work. I wish you had fucking stayed in Præstø playing Yahtzee with your dad."

Now it was Camilla who lost her temper, no longer caring about sugarcoating her words or keeping her voice down.

"At no point did you, or your colleagues, for that matter, take any serious interest in Eva Nørgaard and what her son went through. If you had bothered to investigate what became of the money Kristian Funch transferred to Nils Hyllested, then it's actually pretty likely that Jack Skovby would still be alive. Is it because Aske was gay that he doesn't count? Or is it because you feel that he somehow deserved it? That if he could have just stopped in time, then he wouldn't have ended up unhappy and sick? Is that . . ."

Louise shook her head at her, turned around, and left. Then she walked into the interrogation room where Eva Nørgaard had just sat down for questioning. She could feel Camilla's eyes on her back the whole time and was well aware that her friend had a point. Not because Aske was gay, she thought. More because Nils Hyllested had not seemed particularly important to this case. That was her mistake.

Eva Nørgaard sat with a glass of water in front of her and didn't look up when Louise came into the room. Lange had already explained that the interrogation was to support the confession she had just made.

Once Louise was seated, he began. First, he stated the date and location of the interrogation, then Eva's name and personal identification number, and that she had confessed to the murders of Dorthe Hyllested and Jack Skovby.

"Is that correct?" he asked, looking at Eva.

She nodded and answered with a clear "yes."

Louise already knew that Eva had overheard the phone call at the inn and thus discovered that Dorthe had continued to run her husband's bathhouse. And that that had led to a violent altercation, in which Dorthe had yelled at Eva, claiming that no one had forced Aske to work for Nils and that Eva's son had been a prostitute who had always pursued adult men. According to Eva, Dorthe also claimed that Nils had always treated Aske well and had recommended him when good customers came to the inn. He had loved Aske.

"Yeah, really loved him," Eva repeated sarcastically, in a voice distorted with scorn. "She didn't even seem ashamed to have been caught. The opposite, really. She chewed me out for eavesdropping on her phone calls and sticking my nose into her business. I didn't do that. I just went there to pick up my bag. But once I understood what was going on, I had to confront her. And all she said was that I was free to go find another job if I didn't like what she was doing. And that was when she said the stuff about how Aske had just been a prostitute like all the other young male prostitutes."

Her voice broke now, but she didn't look away.

"I was so filled with grief and rage," she continued. "And I just couldn't understand how she could be so inconsiderate. Disrespectful. That's how it felt. She knew that Aske had gotten sick. She even sent a wreath to his funeral. But she brushed his death aside by disparaging him. And by continuing to expose insecure young people to transgressive situations like the ones that destroyed my Aske. I just took the cutting board and let her have it. Several times."

She blinked away her tears.

"And you didn't do anything to stop the bleeding when you realized how seriously those blows injured her?" Lange asked.

She sat for a bit, staring right at Lange, but then shook her head. She cleared her throat slightly.

"No," she replied. "I didn't."

She cleared her throat again.

"I'm not trying to apologize for anything," she said quickly. "But I've worked for Dorthe since her husband died. During that period, I felt like we had become close, that we were keeping the inn running together. I devoted my time and my energy to helping her make it a success. I was fond of her. I shared my pain and grief with her, and I thought we were friends. I really wanted the best for her. In all that time, she didn't tell me anything about that rotten place, which was still exploiting young boys. She knew about my unhappiness and my unfathomable grief, and she let me believe that we were close and that she wanted to help me. She also let me believe that she understood me and she agreed that it wasn't okay to exploit young, insecure people. It wasn't until I happened to overhear that phone call that I understood what she really was: a thoughtless, cynical person."

Eva bowed her head.

First Helene, and then Eva, Louise thought. Dorthe Hyllested had brought food out to Helene while little Simon, whom Helene was missing tremendously, was living with her and Nils at the inn. And she had drawn Eva into a closer relationship while she continued running the bathhouse that had destroyed Aske.

Louise sensed Lange's eyes on her but couldn't quite interpret what he wanted to convey.

"According to our pathology report, Dorthe Hyllested died as the result of a four-inch-long curved gash on the back of her head," Lange continued. "It is presumed that it took about fifteen minutes for her to bleed to death. Let me just ask one more time, Eva, if our understanding is correct that at no point did you consider going back into the inn's restaurant to help her or to summon help?"

Louise hoped Eva understood that Lange was trying to help her with his question, to lead her to say that she went back to help, or at least made an attempt. That would reduce her sentence.

"Yes, your understanding is correct," Eva Nørgaard replied, loudly and clearly. "I left her, knowing full well that maybe I could have saved her life. I felt a sense of peace when I saw her lying there."

Lange looked down at the table. Louise shifted uncomfortably.

"At that time, I was not aware that Dorthe was running the place with Jack," Eva continued on her own. "I was shocked when I heard that he had been arrested. I didn't know anything about the child or about him and Dorthe having had a relationship. I decided right away that I would drive up and turn myself in, so he wouldn't be charged with the murder that I had committed. But I had to talk to my daughter first; I owed it to her to tell her the truth face-to-face. She came to see me last night. We ate dinner together and I told her that I had killed Dorthe and that I was going to turn myself in the following day and accept my punishment. Don't get me wrong. It wasn't because I was looking for forgiveness. I just wanted her to understand that I didn't have any regrets. The next morning I heard that Jack had been released. I decided that I would talk to him before I came here to turn myself in."

She paused and looked out the window almost dreamily.

"I needed him to tell me what he knew, how much he knew

about that place. And I was also ready to tell him that I was the one who had killed Dorthe and apologize for his having been arrested. When I got to his place in Vornæs Woods, I saw him pulling out of his courtyard. I drove after him because I didn't feel like I could wait to talk to him. After all, I had already told Lea that I was going to the police station. It was awful saying goodbye to her, so I needed to get things over and done with."

She didn't make eye contact with either of them as she spoke. There was a distant look on her face, but Louise thought she seemed calm and in her right mind.

"I realized that Jack was on his way to the address in Lundby, and I followed him. I parked up by the road and then walked down there. He had opened a few windows, and I could see him moving around inside. He clearly felt right at home. He walked around tidying things up and putting out clean glasses. He swapped out the candles and got everything ready, like when we prepped the restaurant after breakfast. He was in there for an hour before he came out and drove back to his place again."

She looked directly at them now. First at Louise and then Lange, as if she wanted to be sure they understood that she stood by every word she said.

"I drove home to get the rifle I had up in the attic. Frands, my kids' father, had left it there. I put it in the car and then I drove back over to Jack's place. He had just gotten home when I arrived. He was still standing there in the courtyard. I stopped in the driveway and got out."

She pressed her lips together and clenched her hands.

"He admitted right away that he and Dorthe had taken over the place after her husband died. He explained how Nils had rented the house from him and that Kristian Funch had invested to get the place up and running. He made it sound like it was some little farm stand that they had inherited. He thought I was overreacting and said that there weren't any minors associated with the place. He also said that if *he* didn't run the place, someone else would just come in and do it. He simply didn't think there was anything wrong with what they were doing."

She paused for a moment to think, as if it were important to her to recount the words they had exchanged completely accurately.

"Places like that exist, he said, and then got aggressive. He said that if I wanted to report him, I was welcome to, but that it wouldn't be pleasant for me afterward. He didn't seem to care about me one way or the other. He turned his back to me, ignoring my attempts to get him to talk. I don't know what came over me, but it was like the anger of the whole world was rising up inside me again. I felt this overpowering urge to compensate for the feeling of injustice that had hounded me since Aske died, so I opened up the back of my car and took out the rifle. He didn't notice, probably just thought I was a confused, grieving woman. At no point did he even turn around to face me. I came up behind him until I was so close that I figured I was sure to hit him. I've never tried shooting before," she said.

She spoke slowly and clearly, and Louise did not find any obvious trace of regret. Both murders were cold-blooded but driven by grief and the desire for a form of justice. She had seen that before, yet she was struck by the serene calm of Eva Nørgaard's confession.

"I contemplated driving straight here. Instead I drove back to Lea, who was still at my house. But when I saw her, suddenly I couldn't tell her about Jack, which is what I had intended to do. I'm going to miss her so much. It was as if the seriousness and the consequences of what I had done didn't hit me until then. I needed a little time to say a proper goodbye to her. When I got home, I told her that Helene had been arrested, which was awful. I mean, I knew it was my fault, but at the same time it was important to me to try to make people understand what Dorthe and Jack had done, and Nils and Kristian before them. I wanted everyone to see what they did to other people, how they cynically exploited and are still exploiting young people's insecurity and fumbling, even after having witnessed up close how badly things went for my Aske. That's why I contacted Camilla Lind."

There was a loud knock on the door, although Louise had put up the red sign indicating that they were in the middle of an interrogation. Irritated, Louise waited for it to stop, but then Lene Borre stuck her head in with a serious expression and waved for Louise to come out.

Lange nodded briefly to her, and she got up.

"Simon is gone," Borre said once Louise had closed the door. "Someone took him."

CHAPTER 40

The October rain beat against the windshield as Louise, Lene Borre, and Niklas Sindal raced across the bridge connecting Tåsinge and Langeland. They drove with their lights and sirens on and the few drivers who were on the road were squeezed to the side.

Simon Funch was wearing dark blue rain pants and a green windbreaker according to the APB that had been distributed to every law enforcement agency in the country shortly before they left Svendborg. Two patrols had already been dispatched, and assistance had just now been requested from a canine team.

Maybe they had jumped the gun, Louise thought anxiously, but she had immediately called in the big guns. She didn't dare hesitate or procrastinate.

The boy had last been seen in the foster family's playhouse, which was next to their driveway out by the road. No neighbors had seen him leave the playhouse or yard in Tullebølle.

Shortly before Tine discovered that Simon was gone, one neighbor had heard a car accelerate out on the road. The neighbor hadn't seen the car.

"Where's Helene?" Louise had asked as she got in next to Sindal, who was driving.

"At the foster parents' house on Langeland."

He said that after Helene was released, her sister picked her up and drove her home to the farm in Bjernemark first, where she had taken a shower, and then they drove out to Tullebølle, where Iben had dropped her off and driven away.

"And where's Iben now?"

"We haven't managed to get ahold of her yet," Sindal replied. "She's not answering her phone."

Louise turned to Borre, who was sitting in the back seat with a computer in her lap and her phone to her ear.

"Have Lindén track the sister's cell phone," she instructed.

Borre nodded and signaled that it was Lindén she was talking to.

"And her credit cards," Louise added, assuming that she probably didn't need to explicitly state that they should move without waiting for a warrant. Sometimes you might operate in a bit of a gray area, but in this case there was no doubt that they were facing exigent circumstances and that important clues might be lost if they waited to go before a judge and obtain a warrant. They risked losing Simon. This way they had twenty-four hours to submit the violation to a judge and by then they would hopefully have found the boy.

"Check what cell phones have been out at the farm in Bjernemark," Louise said after thinking it over. "And who has been near the foster parents' address in Tullebølle."

She turned to Niklas Sindal.

"How did Helene Funch seem when you drove her home after she was released?"

"Why, what are you thinking?" he asked. They had hit the small back roads and he had slowed down and turned off the siren.

"I'm wondering if she said anything about being with Simon. Did she seem impatient that it was going to take time before she was allowed to bring him home?"

Borre leaned forward between the seats.

"Yes," she answered on behalf of her colleague. "She felt it was unfair that the foster parents were being allowed to build a relationship with him while she had to be the stranger who came to visit as a guest."

Louise nodded.

"And I have to say, I can fully understand that," Borre continued from the back seat. "Helene Funch has done nothing to bring this situation upon herself. She suffered a horrific tragedy and has accepted her fate and lived with her grief. Now that she has the chance to be reunited with her youngest son, I think it's totally unreasonable to exclude her like this. And now, on top of all that, she's been accused of two murders. If she ever gets over this, she should get a medal. And," she continued, "I wouldn't be surprised if we ended up with another case to deal with. I get where she's coming from."

Louise quickly turned around to face her.

"Get where she's coming from in what sense, exactly?" she asked.

Borre looked a little tired as she answered.

"I get where she's coming from in that she's pissed at us, so maybe she isn't planning to follow the instructions that were laid out for the reunion. She wants him home. And, like she said, why not have a psychologist move into her house if people don't think she can do it well enough?"

"Did she say that?"

Louise noticed Sindal was moving his hands anxiously on the steering wheel.

"And that's something you both knew about?" Louise asked, but neither of them answered.

Borre's cell phone rang. In the rearview mirror, Louise saw her nod several times.

"After Helene was released, there were several calls registered on her phone," she said after she had concluded the call. "They were between Helene and her brother-in-law, Kenneth Funch, the brother who took over her husband's alarm company."

Louise nodded and said that she knew who he was.

They had reached the house in Tullebølle. She had already seen several police cars on the road and there was one parked right in front of the foster parents' house, too. Before they got out, Louise called Grube and asked him to send a patrol out to Helene Funch's farm in Bjernemark. She wanted the sister and Helene's brother-in-law tracked to determine if they were with Simon right now. If it was Helene's family bringing the boy home, then they needed to be stopped before they managed to get too far away with him.

She turned to her two colleagues.

"I hope," she said, "that you understand that this isn't about what's fair for Helene. This is about a little four-year-old boy. I know that Helene doesn't see it that way, but he just lost the only person he knows. The woman he has considered his mother for as long as he can remember. Our efforts here are about helping *him* through this. Helene is the adult. He's the child."

What she wanted most of all was to call Eik. The search would get everyone's full attention, and suddenly she felt like she was in over her head. But Eik beat her to it. They were on their way up the driveway to the house when he called.

"I just saw the APB," he stated briefly. "I'm coming to you."

"No." Louise quickly fended him off and repeated what Borre had just said. And then she added that of course there was an extensive search underway, but right now they were doing everything they could to find out if the family was helping Helene get her son away from Tullebølle.

"We've put out an APB on Iben's metallic-red Mazda 3. But I need someone to keep an eye on Helene's address on Zealand until we know whether this is Helene's doing."

Eik seemed to agree with how she was handling the situation, which reassured her. Then he promised to make sure a patrol was sent to Hillerød.

She and the others had decided that she would go inside and talk to Helene Funch while Lene Borre and Niklas Sindal remained outside and waited for the canine unit. So, Louise went alone to the house and was greeted at the door by the pale face of Henrik Sommer.

Louise hadn't had time to reflect on what to expect when she saw Helene Funch. Since the report of the missing boy had been received, an efficient response had been put in motion. She had concentrated on launching a widespread search, had thought through a variety of scenarios, and had acted on the most obvious ones.

The whole time, she had had a clear sense that they were not dealing with a stranger abducting the boy out of the blue from the playhouse in the front yard. And on closer reflection she was also inclined to accept the possibility that Helene herself might have set this in motion in a desperate attempt to start building a new life with her son as soon as possible. But at no point had she had time to think about how Helene would be dealing with what had happened. How she was handling Simon's disappearance when she herself had been only a few yards away from him. That hit her now.

She took a deep breath and was about to walk into the kitchen when her cell phone rang.

"Kenneth Funch is staying at Krengerup Manor right now," Lindén announced, "where he's servicing the manor's alarm systems. He has been at that location since nine o'clock this morning and doesn't think he'll be done reviewing the new installations until sometime this afternoon. He says that shortly after he arrived at the manor, he called his sister-in-law to invite himself out to Bjernemark for coffee when he was done. He had read about her arrest and wanted to show that he was there for her. And of course that he didn't believe she had anything to do with the murders. They agreed that he would come over when he was done with his work once she was back from Langeland."

Okay, Louise thought, so that ruled him out.

"The second time her brother-in-law called, it was to suggest that they eat together at Falsled Inn, but Helene didn't want to be seen in public now, given that she's adorning the front pages of the country's newspapers. And he understood that, of course."

"Do you have anything on her sister?" Louise had withdrawn to the front hall but could see Tine sitting on a chair at the kitchen table. Her face was hidden behind her hands as she cried.

"Nothing on her yet," Lisa Lindén replied. "I tasked a colleague with procuring the surveillance video from the tollbooths on the Great Belt Bridge. But we can't wait for that, of course."

Louise grew more and more enthusiastic about Lisa Lindén, who—despite her bad habit of hanging up prematurely after she'd said what she had to say—thought for herself and took preemptive action.

"I'll find the sister," the young detective said with conviction, then hung up.

For a second, Louise stood alone in the front hall to compose herself. When she went into the kitchen, Tine Sommer glanced up miserably.

"I only went inside to get a plate," she said, crying. "I was gone for five minutes, max, and Simon was playing so well. He had made some figures out of clay and I wanted to bring them inside so they could dry and he could paint them later. His mother had just arrived, and I wanted to clean him up a little before he went in to spend time with her."

It was hard to understand her words because she was crying. Louise put a hand on her shoulder.

"It's my fault," she sobbed. "He was my responsibility, in our custody."

"Did you notice any cars out on the road?" Louise asked, but the foster mother shook her head.

"There wasn't anyone, no people or cars," she replied before hesitating slightly. "Or maybe I just didn't notice them. I really wanted to bring him inside now that Helene was here, but he wanted to stay out there and make more figures. There's a table and a chair in the playhouse and he was sitting there with the plastic molds he was using."

She shook her head in despair.

"I had given him some clay and he picked some of the tall grass out by the playhouse to use for hair. When I came out with the plate, he was gone. The chair was tipped over, but the clay figures were still there on the little table."

Louise managed to stop herself before she asked if she had also heard a car accelerate. Neither Simon nor the foster mother would have been able to hear that.

Helene Funch was sitting on the sofa wearing a cashmere turtleneck sweater and a pair of camel-colored wool slacks. She had dressed up, just like when they had arrested her. It struck something deep down in Louise to see how nicely Helene had dressed to spend time with her son. She had her hair up and was wearing a light lipstick. But she was extremely pale, and her face seemed as if it had turned to stone.

Henrik Sommer was sitting next to her. There was enough space between them that his closeness didn't seem intimidating even though there was something protective about his presence.

Louise said hello from the doorway and walked over to them, but Helene didn't react.

"I called Tine's brother," the foster father said, referring to the psychologist who had been there during Helene's first meeting with Simon.

She nodded, thinking that was wise. Right now she doubted whether Helene was mentally present at all. It was possible that Simon's mother had found it unreasonable that she wasn't allowed to bring Simon home right away, but it was clear to Louise that the woman sitting apathetically on the sofa was not in the process of kidnapping her own child.

CHAPTER 41

Camilla knocked for a long time on the door of the apartment where Eva's daughter lived. She had driven out to the house to see if Lea was still there, but the car was gone and now Camilla was beginning to worry. The situation had been very emotionally charged when they went to the house to park the Punto there and transfer the cutting board and rifle into Camilla's car.

The grief that lingered between the mother and daughter as they said their goodbyes was so overwhelming, and Camilla had realized the full horror of how much the young woman had lost. It wasn't Lea's choice that her mother had acted in the ways she had. She had already lost her brother, and now she was losing her mother, too. Crying, Lea had said that there wasn't anything more to live for, and her mother had tried to comfort her by saying that Lea was strong and that she would get through this.

"I'm still here, after all, and I love you," Eva had said.

Camilla had also tried to comfort her by saying that as soon as her mother had been sentenced, Lea would be able to visit her often.

Eva was the one who had asked Camilla to drive back over and spend some time with Lea after they parted at the police station. Camilla had explained that she needed to write her articles and send them to the newspaper first, but she promised to check on Lea afterward.

Camilla knocked again now and tried calling as well. She thought she heard the cell phone inside the apartment but wasn't sure. She quickly ran down the stairs and started walking down the street to see if the Punto was parked anywhere nearby. Then she ran back to search the side street and around behind the building. She also went into several of the neighboring yards adjoining Lea's address, then over to the bank parking lot, but the car wasn't there.

Camilla went back to the apartment, sat down on the stairs, and looked up Lea's father on Google. Frands Nørgaard. Apparently he lived in Vejle. There was a cell number, and he answered right away, but sounded very disengaged when he realized a woman he didn't know was asking about his eldest daughter.

"I haven't seen her," he said curtly, "and I don't know where she is."

"I'm worried about her," Camilla said urgently.

"That doesn't have anything to do with me," he replied before hanging up.

She sat for a moment staring at her phone, then she called Lea again. Her phone wasn't turned off but it didn't go to voicemail, either. Camilla wondered if she should bypass Louise and call Grube directly. But in the middle of the nationwide search that was underway to find Simon Funch, it probably wasn't particularly likely that the deputy chief superintendent would be all that interested in a young woman who wasn't answering her phone.

She sat for a bit with her cell phone in her hand and then decided to call Louise anyway, even though she knew that Louise had her hands full. Louise didn't answer, and Camilla let it ring several times and realized that her phone must be on silent.

She typed out a text instead.

Life and death.

That was their code, which meant that it was a life-and-death emergency and the other person needed to call back. The last time that message had been sent was when Louise was in Thailand, right after Eik had traveled onward with the two teenagers. It had woken Camilla in the middle of the night, and she had immediately gotten up and called back. But after the way she and Louise had parted, she wasn't sure that the code would still work. Then her cell phone rang.

"Yes?" Louise said. She sounded worried, Camilla thought.

"I'm afraid that something has happened to Lea," she said, quickly explaining that she couldn't reach Eva's daughter. "I've been out to Eva's house and now I'm here outside Lea's apartment. I know that you've already got a big search underway. Have you found the boy?"

"No," Louise replied, saying that she had just returned to the police station in Odense, where the search was being coordinated. "We managed to locate Helene's sister. We had suspected that she might have had something to do with Simon's disappearance, but she didn't. We have nothing. We have no idea where he is."

She heard the frustration in Louise's voice and regretted having disturbed her even for a minute.

"Right now, two men are reviewing the surveillance footage from five different locations here in Langeland. We have a roadblock on the Great Belt Bridge and canine units throughout the region."

"I'm sorry to bother you," Camilla said quickly. "But I'm afraid that Lea might be thinking of hurting herself. Could you put out an APB for her car?"

Louise asked when Camilla had last seen Lea.

"When she and her mother said goodbye at her mother's house," she replied and explained that she had been to all the places to see if the Punto was parked nearby. "I don't know the license plate number, but it must be registered under her name or possibly Eva's. It was Aske's when he was alive."

CHAPTER 42

Next door to the radio communications office, Louise sat in a small office that had been set up as an emergency command center with fewer staff than they had next door, where they were monitoring Funen's police patrols. A large map of all of Funen hung on the wall behind Louise, and next to that, maps of Tåsinge and Langeland Islands, where they were marking off areas that had already been searched for traces of Simon Funch.

A team of Funen officers she didn't know and had never seen sat with her, but everyone was focusing and taking calls and entering information so that she and Grube had an overview as they coordinated the search efforts.

They had wasted far too much time searching for Helene's sister with nothing to show for their efforts. Finally, a patrol happened to spot the red Mazda in a parking lot in Svendborg. Iben explained right away that the reason she had been in such a hurry to leave after dropping her sister off at Simon's foster family's house was that she had to get back to Svendborg in time for her massage appointment. After that they hadn't had any other obvious leads to pursue.

Louise stood up and joined the people next door in the communications office. She had looked up Lea Nørgaard's license plate number in the motor vehicle registry and handed that off with a message that the black Punto was now being sought as well.

"Will you send out an alert?" she asked, thinking primarily of the patrol cars and motorcycles that were driving around on southern Funen, Tåsinge, and Langeland. She had also written a brief description of Lea Nørgaard.

They took it, nodded, and were already issuing the alert before she went back to call Lange to find out if he was still at the police station in Svendborg. He was, and Louise could immediately tell from his voice that he needed a bucket of coffee right about now. He sounded worn-out and run-down.

When word of Simon's disappearance came in, Lange had stayed at the station and finished the interrogation. Once Eva Nørgaard was officially arrested, he had started typing up her confession and witness statement. And he wasn't quite done, he said when Louise got him on the phone.

"I want to ask you to talk to Eva," she said. "It's about her daughter. We're trying to find her right now and I'd like to know if there are any friends or family members she might be with. We're worried about her. Even though it's probably most likely that she went to see someone, we're afraid that she might be alone and suicidal." She covered for Camilla with her vague use of "we."

"Do we have any reason to believe she's a suicide risk?" Lange asked calmly, but she sensed that he had stood up.

"Yes," Louise replied. "The first time I talked to Eva, she said that her daughter had been engaging in self-harm. It had started after her brother's death. So, I believe we do have reason to be concerned. At any rate, we need to find her and make sure that she's not alone."

Just then the door to the command center opened and a red-headed officer who had been brought in to assist with the search stepped forward.

"We found the Punto," he said so loudly that the investigators who were concentrating on the big screens jumped in alarm. "It was seen in Landet and is now parked in front of the church."

Louise had no idea where Landet was and gave him a puzzled look.

"It's a town in the middle of Tåsinge Island," he explained in a way that sounded something like he was calling her out for not being from around these parts.

"And Lea Nørgaard?" she asked.

He shook his head.

"The car is deserted, but I have a motorcycle officer on his way out there."

"Have him report in as soon as he knows if she's in or around the church."

It would make sense if she was seeking comfort in the church, Louise thought. She took out her phone and called Camilla to tell her that they had located the car.

CHAPTER 43

Fourteen minutes, the GPS said as Camilla left Svendborg, driving far too fast back to Tåsinge. She felt deeply unsettled, the worry contracting inside her chest like a reflexive throbbing. She shouldn't have left Lea out at the house.

Camilla felt cold, even though the heat in the car was cranked up to full blast. She crossed the Svendborg Sound Bridge at high speed and passed the exit to Troense. The countryside raced by as she drove past campgrounds and nurseries. She had made it through Bregninge when her GPS told her to turn right.

Camilla slowed down and turned onto Skovballevej. Not long after that, she spotted the church. Her wheels sent gravel flying as she parked and then jumped out of the car. It was dead quiet. All the commotion was inside her. Her heart was hammering, the mixed feelings of failure, worry, and anxiety pushing her pulse rate up so her temples pounded. There was a police motorcycle and an ambulance in front of the church. She ran toward them in a panic.

"What happened?" she yelled as she spotted the leather-clad motorcycle officer standing in the church doorway. He stopped her and took a step forward, but Camilla shoved him and tried to squeeze past him into the church. "I need to know what happened. Is Lea in there? Is she all right?"

He gave her a blank look and asked her to clear the area.

"I know the girl who's in there," she said, trying to explain when he once again asked her to leave the church area. "You have to let me in. I'm the one who had the APB put out for her."

She had already discerned from the look in his eyes that he wasn't going to let her in. Camilla pictured Eva's unhappy daughter and reached out breathlessly to brace herself against the church's whitewashed wall as she slowly sank to the ground, letting her body slip down alongside the church wall with her face hidden in her hands.

More sirens approached and she felt the officer's firm grip on her shoulder as he pulled her up off the ground.

"I need to request that you leave the area," he said gruffly.

Camilla again began to explain, then gave up and gave in as he pushed her away once more. She retreated to the cobblestone circle where Elvira Madigan and Sixten Sparre were buried. An ambulance with its lights flashing came into view between the trees out by the road. She started running back toward the entrance to the church and pleaded with the officer once more to find out what had happened.

"Is she alive?" She gasped, noticing how short of breath she was from that brief run.

Another police patrol arrived now. It drove up and parked next to the ambulance, which had backed up all the way to the heavy church door. Would they have called in a full emergency response if she was already dead? She felt a flicker of hope before the middle-aged officer grabbed her arm and started leading her away.

A gurney was pulled out of the ambulance, and the officer shook Camilla off and quickly walked up to the two paramedics and accompanied them inside.

All three of the officers had disappeared into the church. Camilla paced back and forth anxiously, turning around hurriedly when one of the paramedics came running out and hopped into the ambulance. A moment later he raced back into the church with more equipment and something that looked like an oxygen tube.

There's hope, she thought and realized that she was pacing and repeating that short sentence to herself. She gradually grew completely soaked from the rain, belatedly realizing how cold she was. Her voice was stuttering and her teeth chattering as she spoke to herself.

She had just turned around to go back to the car to warm up when the oak door to the church opened and the two paramedics very carefully carried the gurney down the four steps at the front of the church. Camilla heard more sirens approaching in the distance.

Ignoring the paramedics' disapproving glances, she stepped forward and looked, petrified, at the dark hair of the little boy who lay on the gurney.

CHAPTER 44

The ambulance carrying Simon had already left by the time Louise reached the church. A new ambulance had arrived, but there was no activity around it. Its back door was closed, and the two paramedics stayed in the cab, keeping dry and awaiting instructions.

Louise joined Lene Borre and Niklas Sindal and was quickly briefed on how Simon had been found on the floor of the church. The crime scene technicians had entered the building and told the pastor, who had also just arrived, to leave the church. Camilla sat in her car in the parking lot, waiting for Louise.

Before Louise left Odense, Camilla had sent her a text. Very briefly, she wrote that she had seen them drive away with Simon. That was all she wrote, and she didn't ask any questions, either. She'd only said that she would stay there and wait.

Slowly, Louise opened the heavy church door. She already knew what awaited her inside, so she didn't want to enter the quiet interior of the church. The musty cold and darkness hit her as she walked past the coat hooks and the hymnals. To the right she immediately spotted the two ropes. One had been cut down. The other loop had come loose from the railing a few yards above, causing Simon Funch to fall about seven feet onto the floor before the noose had had time to strangle him.

She stopped inside the door and waited for the emergency doctor, who came over to her.

"It looks like a mooring line," he said, turning to the small landing in front of the choir box, where Lea had secured the two ropes. An old staircase with wide steps led up to the loft, which had a low railing made of dark and golden oak. It sat like a little plateau up in front of the church choir.

"She tied a noose and pulled the rope through. Then she secured the ropes to the railing. After that, she put the noose around Simon's neck and pushed him off. And then I'm assuming that she let herself slip over the edge. When she jumped, it presumably made the railing jerk under her weight, causing the knot in Simon's rope to come undone."

He pointed up at the place where the knot that had held Lea's rope was still secured to the railing. The ropes didn't look heavy, but they did seem strong.

"He had a reddish ligature mark high on his throat, but there was nothing to see on the back of his neck, meaning the noose wasn't pulled tight around his whole neck. That's what saved him when he fell."

"How long was he hanging there before Lea jumped and his knot came loose?"

The doctor shrugged.

"I can't say yet, but he could hang in the noose for about a minute without anything happening. When we cut the girl down we started CPR, but we were unable to resuscitate her and she was declared dead just before they drove away with the boy. Unfortunately, we arrived too late."

Eva's daughter lay under a white sheet on the floor of the church now. Even though she was covered, Louise recognized the contours of the young woman's body. And she didn't need to climb the stairs to the landing in front of the choir, where Lea had secured the two ropes, to understand how it had happened. It was up to the technicians and the pathologist to work out the details. There was so much helplessness and grief in what the young woman had done, Louise felt only compassion for Lea, even though her actions had been horrific.

Louise looked over at the white cloth on the floor one last time before leaving the church, reflecting that this was the first time she had experienced such a twisted, revenge-fueled case. She had no doubt that the reason Lea wanted to take Simon with her when she died was to punish the people who had taken everything from her, to get back at Dorthe Hyllested and Kristian Funch in a type of delayed revenge for what they had done to her brother, her mother, and her. But the only person she had hurt was Helene—a woman she had never met.

Louise heard the doctor talking to the technicians outside the church. There would be a forensic autopsy before Lea was removed.

She made room so the others could approach.

Camilla was sitting behind the steering wheel of her car staring straight ahead when Louise got there.

"Is she dead?" her friend whispered as Louise sat down in the passenger seat.

"Yes," Louise replied. "But Simon's alive."

"It might not even have been hard for her to get the little boy to go with her," Camilla continued. "Lea seems nice, after all, and there have been so many new people in Simon's life lately."

Louise almost couldn't recognize her friend's voice, but she nodded. She had had the same thought herself.

"He's a small, trusting boy," Louise replied. "And you're right: so much has happened, so many new faces. He didn't have a chance to figure out who belonged and who he should avoid. It must have been the same when Jack took him away from the inn after he saw Dorthe on the floor. And it wasn't unpleasant for him to be at Jack's house, so he didn't have any reason to think it would be unpleasant to go with Lea."

Camilla was crying.

"Is he going to be okay?"

Louise nodded.

"He's been taken to the hospital in Odense with a police escort. Helene is on her way there now with her sister and her brother-in-law. We've also called the foster parents, so there'll be someone there who can communicate with him as he's being examined. I'm heading in there later myself."

Louise shared her friend's grief and was ready to admit that her actions had let Lea down. She should have made sure that the young woman was not alone once her world had come seriously crashing down. She also thought briefly about Jack Skovby's daughter in Copenhagen, who had lost her father. So many losses because Nils Hyllested had tried to navigate a life of privation and shame. He had wanted to create a place of refuge, where people could be who they were, and instead he had created a place where only some—those with money and power—were free to be themselves. He had forgotten to consider that the young people who sold their bodies weren't mature enough to know how high a personal price they would end up paying. The fact that he was the most likely person to have found Simon after the plane crash and given him to Dorthe, as if the little boy were an object, might also have been an attempt to correct the imbalance in his life created by his inability to be who he truly was. He hadn't had the courage to admit that he had had a vasectomy and would never be able to get Dorthe pregnant and make her biggest wish come true, which was perhaps why he had plunged in way over his head when the opportunity to give his wife a child presented itself.

And Dorthe had taken what she could get after finding out that her husband was someone other than the man she thought she'd married. Then, instead of trying to be good and do the right thing when Nils died, she became the silent widow, continuing the unresolved and secretive life her deceased husband had set in motion.

"Poor Lea," Camilla whispered to herself. "Who's going to tell Eva what happened?"

"We will," Louise replied. "Together."

Louise smiled at Simon's eager expression. The boy's eyes lingered on Helene's hand, and he stood taut as a bow waiting for his mother to start the music so the balloon-popping dance could begin.

It had been three months since Helene's son had received his cochlear implants, but this was Louise's first time back in Tåsinge since they'd closed the case, and there was something unbelievably touching about getting to witness the world that had opened up to the little boy.

She knew from his mother that Simon had had a hard time adjusting to the small hearing aids and the new sounds that they let into his universe, and that he had spent a long time learning to interpret and understand them, but the joy on his face was so clear now.

The big, shiny silver balloons hanging from the ceiling said he was five, but when the music started, his focus was solely on the smaller, colorful balloons the children wore tied around their ankles.

Helene had missed two of his birthdays during the years her son had lived in hiding with Dorthe Hyllested. Two years, during which the grief and despair had eaten away at her and cast a shadow over her entire life. Louise could understand her desire to make up for those lost celebrations now.

The house had been decorated, the big flag had been raised in the yard, and classmates from the special education preschool Simon attended had been invited to his party. Louise hadn't had much contact with Helene since they had wrapped up the case, and when she received the birthday party invitation, her first instinct had been to decline with some made-up excuse for why she couldn't attend. It wasn't her way to stay in touch with people who had been involved in her cases.

And yet here she sat, smiling at the children as they struggled to pop the balloons tied to their friends' legs as soon as the music began. Louise had justified the decision by telling herself that Tåsinge wasn't very far out of her way—she needed to go to Odense that same day to attend Grube's twenty-fifth anniversary reception at the police station, after all—but the truth was that she hadn't driven to Funen for either Simon's or Grube's sake.

Louise had driven over the bridge for herself.

Because some cases got so deeply under her skin that they were hard to let go of. And if the case on Tåsinge Island wasn't going to become a nagging source of grief for her, she needed to see that Helene and her little son had moved on, that they had found their way into each other's lives again, that they had left their period of separation behind them.

And sitting here now, there could be no doubt about any of that.

Louise walked over to set her coffee cup on the table before giving Helene a hug and waving at Simon, with his balloon still around his leg.

Then she snuck out to drive to the police station in Odense.

ACKNOWLEDGMENTS

In *A Mother's Love* I was highly inspired by the scenery on beautiful Tåsinge Island, but Strammelse Inn and the forest cabin bear no connection to Tåsinge's other accommodations, and all the individuals in the story are purely imaginary. I have also taken the liberty of situating homes and farms so that they fit into my story. Hotel Troense exists and is a lovely place, however without the bar, which I added.

Again, many people helped me with the research for this book. And I would like to thank you all for welcoming me so openly and helping me get the details and the facts lined up so that my fictional reality is credible.

A big thank-you to former travel unit detective Tom Christensen and his wife, Lone Worm, who is also a seasoned policewoman. Not only were they both a tremendous help this time, as before with their insight into how investigations work, they also live on Tåsinge Island and helped me pick up nuances and local flavor for what Tom likes to call my tall tales.

Another big help when it comes to police work is Deputy Chief Superintendent Bjørke Kierkegaard from the Central and West Zealand Police. Thank you so much for repeatedly taking the time to explain the ins and outs of real detective work. And thank you for helping me create a new fictional Police District 13—you will now and forevermore be godfather to Louise Rick's travel unit, P13.

I also owe a big thank-you to "Captain" Michael Buch Andersen for creating the flight from Grønholt to Tåsinge. Thank you so much for your patient explanations and descriptions from your many years of experience as a pilot. They allowed me to put the pieces of the fatal plane trip together. Also, a big thank-you to psychologist Kuno Sørensen at Save the Children for your tremendous insight and help. Your assistance meant the world to me in writing the story of Simon Funch. Thank you!

I also owe my gratitude to Chief Prosecutor Ulla Greibe with the Funen Police in Odense. Ulla, you have helped me many times before, and you've done it again now. Thank you so much for taking the time to read through and explain how it would play out in reality.

As with all my books, I owe my heartfelt thanks to Chief Physician Steen Holger Hansen at the University of Copenhagen's Department of Forensic Medicine. You have been and continue to be an invaluable help to me, and once again I want to thank you for your time and your patience.

This story began with a thought that I was tossing around with my wonderful editor, Stinne Lender. Shortly thereafter, we went to Tåsinge for a few days to let the whole thing get under our skin. Thank you for understanding so quickly where I want to go with my stories. And for throwing yourself into them so wholeheartedly. Thank you for being you.

And a huge thank-you to the rest of my team at Politikens Forlag and Kenneth Schultz, who is the creative mastermind behind my beautiful covers. It's a tremendous gift to get to work with you all. And I can say the same for Nordin Agency. Thank you so much for getting my stories out to the world and for always wanting the very best for me.

I've dedicated this book to my very close friends Lars and Andreas. Our friendship means the world to me. Thank you for always being there for me.

And someone else who means so infinitely much to me is my son, Adam. Thank you for always getting me back on an even keel when I inevitably get a little off-kilter during a writing phase. You're my very best.